My Mad SCIENTIST

Kyli Brown

ISBN: 979-8-89324-978-1

Published by Franklin Publishers

Printed in the United States of America

For permissions, inquiries, or additional copies, contact:

Franklin Publishers

www.franklinpublishers.com

Table of Contents

Chpter 01

A Wayward June.

June 12th 1884 ~ In June's jubilant golden dawn, when sunbeams frolicked and pirouetted upon the emerald earth and across the sky. The air was alive with the sugary whispers of summer's sweetness distilled in every breath. The world unfolded like a delicate pastry, filled with fluttering petals and leaves. The heady aroma of freshly baked waffles wafted through the air, mingling with the giggly promise of summer's endless shine. Summer's warmth unwrapped like a rainbow-colored blanket, snuggling all in its cozy embrace. The sky with hues of azure, and the air was alive with the whimsical stirrings of summer's magic.

Sorry, wrong book…

Alice's emerald eyes fluttered open, blinking against the dim light filtering through the barred window of her asylum cell. The chill of the cold stone seeped through her thin hospital gown, causing her to shiver involuntarily. With a groggy effort, she propped herself up, rubbing the sleep from her eyes. Her hair, a tangled mess of wavy curls, framed her face, accentuating the weariness etched there. As her gaze wandered across the stark, sparse room, a familiar sense of hopelessness settled in, a heavy blanket made of despair. Another day trapped within these walls.

With a loud sigh, she swung her legs over the edge of her uncomfortable cot. Her feet met the frigid stone floor, a harsh shock to her bare soles that underscored her monotonous routine. A pang of anxiety twisted within her as she recalled the looming procedure that awaited her: the lobotomy. Clenching the rough fabric of her gown, she attempted to steady her racing heart, reminding herself that she needed to find a way to escape this nightmare. The sterile smell of antiseptic was suffocating, and as dread coiled tighter in her chest, her ears pricked at the sound of footsteps echoing down the hollow hallway. Each thud reverberated like a clock counting down to an inexorable fate. With every approaching footstep, her heartbeat quickened, thrumming like a caged bird desperate for freedom. Alice held her breath, her eyes darting toward the door as it creaked open.

Martin, one of the asylum attendants, appeared in the entrance, his imposing silhouette blocking the dim light from the corridor. He stepped inside, and a flicker of empathy flashed in his expression before he quickly masked it with his usual stoic demeanor. "Time to go," he said tersely, extending a rough hand toward her.

Alice hesitated; her feet rooted to the cold stone. The oppressive walls of her cell felt as if they were closing in, intensifying her sense of entrapment. But she knew she had no choice. With a resigned inhalation, she stepped forward, her movements tense as she approached Martin, who gestured for her to exit the cell.

As they walked down the sterile hallway, the chill from the stone floor crept through her thin stockings, sending shivers up her spine. The echoes of their footsteps served as a haunting accompaniment to her mounting anxiety. Approaching the surgical room, she braced herself against the overwhelming atmosphere, the metallic tang of medical instruments hitting her like a wall.

Martin led her to the table, where a doctor covered from head to toe in white flicked the sedative. Martin sat her down, and the doctor rolled up her strong dress, a bland, dark gray, heavy cotton dress, lined and quilted with black stitching. The sight of the syringe glinting in his hand ignited a fierce instinct to survive deep within her. In one quick motion, she grabbed the syringe, driving it into the back of the doctor's leg. He howled in pain and surprise, stumbling back, momentarily disoriented.

Seizing the opportunity, Alice snatched the keys from his pocket and bolted for the door. Martin lunged for her, gripping her long brown hair in a desperate attempt to pull her back. With a fierce shriek, Alice shoved him into a shelf lined with jars that held the remnants of tortured souls, a macabre display that sent a chill down her spine. The glass jars clattered as Martin lost his balance, giving her the precious seconds she needed.

With newfound determination coursing through her veins, Alice unlocked the door and dashed away, the sounds of his furious curses trailing behind her like a sinister echo. Adrenaline fueled her flight down the stark corridor, doors behind her slamming open as attendants unleashed chaos in their pursuit. She sprinted towards the staircase, each step of the three floors feeling like a marathon as panic pushed her forward. The dimly lit stairwell descended into darkness, light flickering above her head and casting elongated shadows across the stone walls. She dared not look back for fear of what loomed behind her, focusing instead on the distant hope of freedom. As she reached the bottom, breathless and trembling, her eyes scanned the corridor until they fixed on a door at the far end, weathered and worn, marked with faded letters that read 'Landry Room.' Desperation surged as she propelled herself toward it. Grasping the knob, she flung the door open. The Laundry Room was almost surreal, dimly lit and filled with forgotten furniture that seemed to whisper of its past. Dust particles danced in the beam of light from a grimy window, suspended in an eerie display as she stepped inside. But Alice's attention was drawn immediately to the window; it felt like her singular chance for escape. Closing the door behind her, Alice rushed to the window and yanked it open, the cold air biting at her exposed skin. The view below was disheartening patches of uneven ground, chains of scattered trees, and the imposing stone wall that enclosed the asylum. It was a long drop, and a knot of fear tightened in her stomach. But she had no choice. Freedom awaited just beyond. With one last deep breath, Alice climbed out of the window. The rain stung against her cuts, like tiny daggers pricking her skin, but the noise of her pursuers was fading. She could hear attendants and doctors furious shouts, and without turning back, she jumped, landing with a thud on the damp ground below. When she steadied herself getting up, her heart raced as adrenaline propelled her into the embrace of the stormy night, the cold rain washing away the horror of the asylum behind her. This time, she wouldn't let fear bind her; she would run until her legs could no longer carry her, escaping toward a world of uncertainty, but also a world filled with possibility. Freedom lay just ahead, and she was determined to grasp it. Alice's heart sank as the sound of the bloodhounds pierced the air, their deep, baying growls growing louder and more menacing by the second.. With a shaky exhale, she steeled herself and focused her remaining energy on the imposing iron gate separating her from whatever lay beyond. She grasped the cold, unforgiving metal, every muscle in her body screaming in protest. With a monumental effort, she pulled herself over, each second feeling like an eternity as the ominous howls grew ever closer. She landed in the mud on the other side, and whipped the mud away from her eyes, looking up at the old plaque, worn and rusted, that read 'Bedlam Asylum ~ founded in 1247'. With no time to lose, she sprinted into the surrounding trees, her hair whipping wildly behind her as the relentless rain pelted her skin like a thousand tiny needles. Each gasping breath felt labored, and every step was a struggle against the mud that threatened to swallow her whole. The trees loomed above, their twisted branches barely offering solace from the downpour. She stumbled through the unfamiliar terrain, the moonlight playing tricks on her mind, casting fluid shadows that danced malevolently in the darkness. Exhaustion clawed at her weak resolve, the cold seeping into her bones while her thick clothing provided little comfort against the merciless weather. The relentless pounding of the rain and the chaotic rustle of the wind echoed ominously around her, a haunting symphony of nature that matched the frantic rhythm of her heartbeat. She plunged deeper into the woods, the dense foliage became both her ally and enemy. Branches clawed at her hair and clothes, each snag pulling her back. But she fought through them, tearing herself away with a fierce determination fueled by sheer desperation. The sound of the bloodhounds began to fade, lost amidst the cacophony of rain and the whisper of leaves. Her muscles ached; her feet blistered from the oppressive mud. It wasn't before she had time to stop or slow down, she had tumbled down a slippery slope, her body rolling through the cold, wet underbrush. As she finally came to a stop at the bottom, breathless and disoriented, she lay there for a moment, feeling the cool road under her. Her ragged breathing filled her ears as she lay there, exhausted and vulnerable. As she attempted to push herself up off the ground, her strength faltered, and she collapsed back, her head swimming from exhaustion. The cold night air seemed to bite at her, making her shiver.

In the distance, faint lights pierced the darkness, a glimmer of hope against the imposing night. The faint sounds of activity accompanied those lights, and Alice's heart quickened, the spark of a chance for safety igniting within her. Weak, but driven, she summoned the last vestiges of her strength to prop herself up once more. With a shaky intake of breath, she took a moment to gather her bearings before she cautiously rose, her legs trembling with fatigue. As the sounds and lights grew clearer, the distinct outline of a horse-drawn road wagon became apparent. The rain had slowed it down, making it the perfect opportunity for Alice to seize her chance. The road wagon rumbled towards her through the stormy night. Her mind raced, her heart pounded. This was the opening she needed. The buggy drew nearer, its headlights illuminating the muddy road and her surroundings. Just as the buggy was about to pass by, she made her move. With a burst of adrenaline, she leapt towards the back of the wagon and hopped onto the back. The impact of her landing jostled the wagon, but the sound was lost amidst the rain. She clung onto the side, her hands grasping desperately at the wet wood. The cold and the dampness sent chills down her spine, but she didn't dare let go. She held her breath, hoping that her presence would go unnoticed as the buggy continued its journey through the storm. As the buggy continued, Alice used the bags of grain, rice, and potatoes to create a makeshift mound, hiding behind it as best she could. The bags helped to conceal her presence, their shape and bulk masking her form from the potential gaze of the driver. With her heart pounding, she held her breath, hoping that her makeshift hiding place would be enough to keep her undetected in the event the driver looked back. The road was rough and rocky, forcing the buggy to move at a slower pace. Each bump and jolt made her grip the bags of grain and rice tighter, her heart racing at every turn. Finally, after what seemed like an agonizingly long hour, the buggy came to a halt at Leicester Square. Alice's muscles ached, and her body was drenched in cold sweat.

Just as Alice began to relax, her heart raced in fear as she spotted a peeler -one of the city's blue-coated constables- turned at the driver's shout nearby. Realizing it was risky to stay, she decided her best chance was to make a quick escape. Without a second thought, she carefully emerged from her hiding spot, using the bags of grain and rice as cover. The peeler was distracted, providing her with a precious window of opportunity. Taking a deep breath to steady her trembling nerves, she started to carefully make her way away from the buggy.

"OI! SHE'S STOLEN FROM MY WAGON!"

The peeler, alerted by the driver's cry, spun around, his gaze fixed onto Alice. The tense moment hung in the air, the rain beating relentlessly around them. She had no choice but to act fast.

Alice bolted away, her feet slipping in the wet mud. The peeler yelled after her, but she didn't look back. She ran blindly through the storm, the rain whipping at her face, her body screaming in protest. She weaved through the old cobblestone streets of London, the rain pelting against the worn stones with a rhythmic patter. The street lamps provided fleeting glimpses of her surroundings in the storm-soaked night. The rain pelted down, turning the cobbled ground into treacherous terrain. She ran, her breath ragged, her feet slipping on the wet cobbles. Every muscle screamed in protest, but the adrenaline coursed through her veins, dulling the pain and fear. London's old, grimy parts surrounded her, its narrow alleys and decaying buildings providing a labyrinthine terrain for her escape. Each turn she took sent her deeper into the city's underbelly. Alice's legs burned with exhaustion, but she forced herself to keep pushing forward. She darted into a dark alleyway, its dimness swallowing her. The rain continued to pour around her, but at least the alley provided a momentary respite from the peeler's view. The alley was in between two townhouses, both clearly from middle-class families. Alice sighed in a mixture of relief and fatigue as the peeler rushed past the dark alleyway. She leaned back against the window, taking a moment to catch her breath, only to misjudge the window as being closed rather than cracked open.

Without warning, she tumbled backward, crashing through the apparently open window. "Shoot!" she gasped, instinctively trying to steady herself, but her flailing arms only succeeded in knocking over a small table. The vase that had perched there teetered precariously before plummeting to the ground with a shattering crash, the sound echoing against the walls like an alarm bell. The room was dimly lit and eerily quiet, but Alice barely registered any of it. All she could think about was finding a place to hide. With shaking hands, Alice scrambled under a nearby table, the tablecloth providing a thin veil of protection as her back pressed against the side of the sofa, wrapping her arms around her knees in a desperate attempt to hold herself together. The sounds of the storm raged outside, but here, it was quiet and soft. For a moment, at least, Alice had found somewhere dry. But as she huddled in the darkness, she knew that safety was just an illusion – and he would stop at nothing to capture her once again.

A Remarkable Incident.

Henry was a refined young man of 20, with a lean, fit physique. He had wavy brown hair with copper highlights, often styled with a forelock that occasionally fell over one side of his face, subtly hiding his right eye. His lips were parted slightly in sleep, the covers pulled up to his chin, and one of his arms was slung across his stomach, the other tucked underneath his pillow. His chest rises and falls with each breath. The room was filled with a soft, warm glow, the light seeping through the partially drawn curtains, giving the room a cozy, relaxed atmosphere. As the rain continued to splatter against the windowpane, Henry began to stir from his sleep as he turned over onto his side, burying his face in the pillow. Henry's sleep was abruptly broken by the sound of a crash downstairs. His body tensed, his mind immediately shifting from groggy slumber to sharp alertness. He reached for his glasses, quickly pushing them onto his face as he sat up in bed, listening intently for any further sounds. "What on earth…?" he mumbled to himself, flinging the covers off and slipping off the bed. He flicked on the lamp sitting on his bedside table, casting a soft, warm glow on the room as he grabbed a dressing gown, slipping it on over his nightclothes. Whatever caused the noise downstairs was undoubtedly an intruder in his home.

As Henry stepped out of his room, he padded softly down the wooden staircase, the polished steps creaking beneath his weight. He reached the parlor room, a lavishly adorned space filled with rich mahogany furniture, plush velvet sofas, and an elegant piano, was a place of warmth and comfort. Yet, at that moment, it felt strangely heavy, as if the very air had thickened, laden with something sinister. The glow of the fireplace flickered, casting dancing shadows upon the wall, revealing an array of trinkets and books perched upon the mantel. His mind raced as he crossed the threshold into the room. The sight before him halted him in his tracks: shards of glass littered the carpet, mingling with the droplets of rain that had encroached upon the intimate space. His eyes darted toward the open window, rainwater dripping onto the floor, confirming his suspicion that an inadvertent draft had caused the disturbance. "Must have been the wind," he murmured under his breath, moving hastily to close the window. The rain fell in a gentle pattern against the glass, but the atmosphere remained thick with unease. As bent over and picked the pieces up, and placed them on the table, when he heard a muffled sound emanating from beneath the table with the tablecloth next to the sofa—a faint stifle that sent a shiver down his spine.

Henry's heart quickened as he realized something, or someone, was hiding beneath the table. A mixture of fear and adrenaline flooded his system as he carefully approached the table. As he crouched down, he could feel his hands trembling slightly as his fingers reached for the edge of the cloth, his eyes darting from side to side as he steeled himself. The muffled sounds, while barely discernible, added to the suspense and the mystery that hung heavy in the room. Despite his fear, Henry's curiosity overpowered him, compelling him to uncover the secret tucked away beneath the table... with a deep breath, he quickly lifted the fabric, the faint light of the fireplace illuminated a 18-year-old girl, soaking wet and trembling, her long, unkempt brown hair clinging to her pale cheeks. Dark green eyes stared back at his hazel eyes, wide with fear. She wore a gray quilted dress that hung off her malnourished frame, the fabric soddened and tattered, and her legs were adorned with torn stockings.

They both moved backward slightly, their eyes locked in a moment of shocked stillness. Henry sat on the floor, leaned back on his palms. For several long moments, neither of them spoke, the only sound being the relentless rain outside and their own shallow breathing. He swallowed hard, his mind racing. Who was she? How did she end up here, soaking wet and terrified, in his parlor room?

Henry's mind raced as he looked at the young girl in front of him. He couldn't believe what he was seeing. A stranger, hiding beneath his table in the middle of the night, soaked to the bone and clearly terrified. His heart thumped loudly in his chest as adrenaline coursed through his veins. "Who are you?"

Alice cowered back from him, her breath coming out in ragged gasps. She was clearly frightened, her slender body shaking with fear. "Please, d-don't hurt me," she whimpered, her voice trembling with each word as her hands clutching at the torn fabric of her sodden dress.

Henry's features softened as he noticed the girl's genuine fear and pleading. Despite the circumstances, he found himself unable to look at her with any malice. This was not a simple burglar or thief, but a scared and desperate girl. "Hey, hey... it's okay," Henry swallowed, still taken aback by the situation. His mind was racing with questions, but he forced himself to slow down, to try and make himself seem more reassuring. Henry swallowed nervously as he prepared to introduce himself. "My, uh, my name is Henry... Henry Jekyll," he said, stammering slightly. "May I enquire what your name is, miss?"

Alice's trembling lessened marginally. "A-Alice," she managed to stutter, her voice quiet and barely above a whisper. She was still wary of him, her body tensed as if ready to bolt at any moment. "I'm sorry...I-I didn't mean to...I just... I was..." She cut herself off, her words trailing off into another heavy silence as she dropped her gaze towards the ground.

Henry noticed the way she kept flinching and stuttering, and he knew he had to handle this situation carefully. "It's alright, Alice," he said gently, his voice still soft and soothing. "You're safe here. We don't need to rush into anything. But you're soaking wet and clearly cold. Let's get you into some warm clothes and something to eat, alright?" He offered her a reassuring smile, hoping it would help to put her at ease. "Come, follow me," he said softly, as he began to slowly stand up, holding out his hand to help her.

Alice hesitated for a moment, her eyes flickering between his hand and his face, unsure of what to do. She was still scared, and the instincts to run away and hide were strong. But there was something about Henry's calm demeanor and gentle soothing words that seemed to calm her panicked mind, and she reached out cautiously, placing her pale, trembling hand in his.

He gently clasped her hand in his, his touch light and reassuring. "There we go," he said softly, guiding her out from her hiding place. "Let's get you out of these wet clothes." He carefully led her to get out from under the table, keeping his pace slow and steady, not wanting to alarm her.

Suddenly, Mr. Poole burst through the door, clad in wool, his usual calm composure replaced by a frenzied, sleep-deprived fervor. He brandished a cricket bat, his eyes darting around the room. His hair, usually neatly combed, stood up in chaotic tufts across his head, and his voice, ragged from sleep, cut through the night like a jagged edge. "Oi! Who's there!? I'll give you such a what-for that you'll think twice before trying to pilfer my prized collection of ceramic gnomes!" he shouted, his grip on the bat tightening.

Henry was startled by the sudden appearance of Mr. Poole, the cricket bat hanging over his shoulder, dressed in a woolen jumper. The usually composed butler looked uncharacteristically disheveled and tense. "Mr. Poole! Put the bat down, it's just me," Henry called out, putting himself in between the girl and the butler, blocking her from view. He held up his hands in a peaceful gesture. "It's alright, there's no thief, no one trying to steal your gnomes. Just…just put the bat down, please."

Mr. Poole's frantic frenzy halted in his tracks, his eyes widening as he took in the scene before him. Mr. Poole's mind is immediately abuzz with the sight and implications of what he is seeing. His eyes darted between Henry and the strange girl, his brain working overtime trying to make sense of the scene. This was quite the unusual situation. Henry had never brought a lady over to his residence, at least not that Poole could recall. The sight of them, both in their nightclothes and the girl drenched to the bone, created a rather peculiar picture. Poole lowered the cricket bat, his grip loosening its hold. "Ah, Master Henry, I didn't expect to find yeh here with a…" He paused, his gaze lingering on the girl, noticing her ragged appearance. "…A. fine young miss at this hour."

"Mr. Poole, I can explain," Henry began, his voice steady yet tinged with a hint of embarrassment. He knew that the circumstances likely appeared scandalous to the butler, "It's not what you think. This girl,

Alice, she…she needed help. Could you kindly fetch some warm clothes and a towel for Miss Alice?" Henry's voice was calm but firm as he requested. He knew that the first step was to get the girl warm and dry; the explanations and questions could wait.

Poole nodded in acknowledgment, his gaze flickering between Henry and the shivering girl, before he bowed his head. "Of course, Master Henry," he replied briskly.

Henry's attention quickly shifted back to the girl. He gently placed his hand on her trembling shoulder, his touch light and reassuring. "Don't mind Mr. Poole, he's harmless as a fly. Just a touch, um, excitable at times," he said, offering her a small smile before continuing. "Let me lead you to the bathroom; we need to get you warmed up and out of those wet clothes." He led her in and shut the door behind them. The dim light of a single Gaslamp cast the room in a warm, yellow glow, and a single bathtub sat in the center of the room. Henry moved to the bathtub and began filling it with water, making sure it was warm. He glanced over his shoulder at her, observing her for a moment. His eyes swept over her, noting the way her gown hung limp and cold on her slight frame. He couldn't help but wonder just what she'd endured. Henry continued to fill the tub with hot water, watching as it began to steam gently. He turned to look at Alice once more, "That should do it."

Alice nodded, her heart racing as she hesitantly made her way over to the tub. She stood there for a few moments, staring down at the steaming water. The thought of finally getting warm overwhelmed the doubts swirling in her mind. With trembling fingers, she reached for the hem of her damp, heavy dress, her hands shaking from the cold and pain as she started to pull it over her head.

Henry, seeing her hesitation and noticing the trembling in her fingers, quickly averted his gaze. His cheeks heated up, realizing he had not expected her to change in front of him. He knew he had to give her some privacy. He awkwardly cleared his throat and kept his focus anywhere but her. "Um, I'll just… take the gown once you're done," he said, a slight discomfort evident in his voice.

She looked back at him for a moment and nodded, "Thank you, sir." She moved quickly and stepped into the warm water in the tub, a sigh of relief escaping her lips at the feeling. Her skin was sensitive to the touch, and she could feel the heat spreading, chasing away the cold that had settled into her bones. The water was warm, just shy of burning, but she welcomed the sensation, and she slowly sank down, the water rising almost to her shoulders. She began to relax, letting out a deep sigh, the tension in her muscles beginning to ease. The fear and panic that had consumed her began to recede, leaving her feeling exhausted.

As Henry picked up the wet dress, he found it curiously heavy. The fabric was damp and clung to his hands, leaving an imprint on his skin. But, most disturbingly, he noticed a small insignia embroidered on the front of the dress. As he held it out to inspect it, his heart stopped in his chest. It was the symbol of Bethlem Royal Hospital. He stumbled back, a mixture of shock, confusion, and an odd sense of realization overwhelming him. The realization struck him like a cold shower. 'Was she an escapee from the institution? Was she mad?' Henry stood frozen for a moment, the implications of the dress's insignia sinking in. The thought of someone escaping from a mental asylum was horrifying, and the idea that she was potentially unstable or even dangerous sent a shiver down his spine. But another thought quickly followed - the girl in the bathroom, the one he had just helped into the bath, was someone who had been locked away, subjected to God knew what within those dreaded walls.   Henry clenched his jaw, trying to calm the whirlwind of thoughts racing through his mind. He needed to remain calm and composed, for her sake and his own. With a deep breath, Henry took a moment to compose himself. He carefully draped the wet dress over a chair before making his way back into the parlor, where Poole was waiting. "Mr. Poole," Henry began, his voice strained but composed. "I need to speak with you for a moment." He gestured toward a nearby chair, silently asking the butler to take a seat.

Poole lowered himself into the chair with a mix of curiosity and concern etched on his face. His eyes remained fixed on Henry, silently waiting for him to begin. "Aye, Master Henry?" he responded, arching an eyebrow questioningly.

Henry took a deep breath, organizing his thoughts before speaking. He knew he had to tread carefully. "Mr. Poole, that girl in the bathroom, she currently in the bathtub, warming up and drying off. But I need you to keep this matter between us for now, at least until I've had a chance to understand the situation better."

Poole nodded, understanding the need for discretion in this situation. "Aye, Master Henry. Your trust is my trust. I won't breathe a word to anyone, not even a squeak," he replied, his tone low and serious. But a subtle smirk still lingered at the corner of his mouth, unable to resist teasing his master a bit. "Though, I must say, Master Henry, I didn't expect to find you in your nightclothes with a young miss in such circumstances," he added, a hint of humor in his voice.

Henry's cheeks tinted pink at Poole's teasing. A mixture of embarrassment, he let out a small sigh, running a hand over his face. "Can you please prepare some tea and something for her to eat?"

Poole nodded again, his smirk growing slightly as he saw Henry's embarrassment. "Certainly, Master Henry," he replied, standing up from his chair. "I'll have that in a jiffy." With that, he left the room, heading to the kitchen to prepare the requested tea and food. Poole couldn't help but ponder the situation in his mind, chuckling to himself at the unusual circumstances.

Meanwhile, the room was filled only with Alice's steady breathing and the soft splashing of the water. Her muscles, which were used to the cold, hard bed of the asylum, relaxed in the comfort of the warm water, and she carefully began to wash herself, her movements slow and deliberate. As Alice finished washing herself, she carefully stood up from the tub and wrapped a towel around herself. She glanced at the mirror, the steam from the bath still lingering in the air and caught sight of her reflection. Her hair, long and unruly, hung damply down her back, the tangled locks a mess from her time in the asylum. She took the scissors and with each snip, her hair fell to the floor in messy chunks. The act of cutting her hair felt liberating, and she couldn't help but feel a sense of control and power over herself, something she hadn't felt in a long time. Once her hair was cut, she looked at her reflection again. The curly, choppy bob gave her an almost feral look, but she smiled, nonetheless. She felt lighter, free. She looked down at the messy scene of her discarded hair on the floor. It was a physical representation of everything she had left behind - the asylum, the pain, the memories that haunted her. Carefully, Alice scooped up the hair and threw it into the trash, then dressed herself in the soft, dry nightgown that Poole had left for her and slowly opened the bathroom door, ready to face whatever came next.

Henry glanced up as the bathroom door opened, his eyes widening at the sight of her. Her hair was shorter, much shorter than the traditional Victorian fashion. For a moment, he was speechless, his eyes tracing the jagged edges of her new haircut. Henry's heart skipped a beat as his eyes met hers. With her hair cut shorter, he could now see her face more clearly, and her eyes, the color of lush, verdant forests, were even more striking than before. Her gaze was filled with a mixture of vulnerability and strength, a testament to the trials she had endured. He had the urge to comment, to say something about her haircut, but he held his tongue, not wanting to make her feel self-conscious. Instead, he smiled warmly at her as he motioned for her to follow him. "Come on," he said softly, gesturing towards the dining room. "Let's get you something to eat."

As they entered the kitchen, Alice's gaze was immediately drawn to the room, which was a cozy but elegantly furnished space. The walls were painted a warm, brassy yellow, reflecting the soft glow of a gas lamp that hung from the ceiling. A long wooden table and chairs occupied the center of the room, a lace ablecloth adorning it. Along one wall was a large sideboard that held an array of fine China and polished silverware. An iron stove, warm and radiant, stood in one corner, the source of heat that warmed the room. The air held the subtle scent of baking bread and spices.

"Please, have a seat," he said softly, guiding her to one of the chairs. "I'll get you something warm to eat."

Henry made his way over to the counter, where a pot of broth was gently simmering. He ladled some of the hot broth into a bowl and grabbed a slice of bread, laying it delicately on the side of the bowl. He returned to the table and set the bowl of broth and bread in front of her. "It's just some broth," he said as he gently pushed the food towards her. "I hope it's alright."

Alice's eyes widened at the sight of the food, and her stomach growled loudly in response. She hadn't eaten a proper meal in what felt like an eternity. She practically pounced on the bowl, the aroma of the broth making her mouth water. Without hesitation, she dunked the bread into the broth and popped it into her mouth, nearly devouring it in one go.

Henry couldn't help but chuckle softly as he watched her scarf down the food with such fervor. But his moment of lightheartedness was cut short when he noticed Poole's disapproving gaze. Henry turned his attention back to Alice as she continued to eat her food at a fast pace. It was obvious that she hadn't been well fed in quite some time. He waited a moment, letting her eat for a few minutes before speaking. "Alice." His voice was soft and gentle, trying to not startle her. "Do you have somewhere to go?"

Henry noticed her embarrassment as she slowly slowed her eating, her cheeks reddening with a mixture of shame and hunger. As she shook her head, admitting that she had nowhere else to go, his heart sank. But he had more questions, and he needed answers. He took a deep breath before asking. "How long have you been in the asylum, Alice?" His voice was gentle but firm.

Alice's eyes widened, and her face paled visibly. She wasn't expecting him to know about her time there, and the question caught her off guard. "I-I….uh…" she stammered, her words catching in her throat. "How…how did you…" She couldn't bring herself to finish the question. She looked down at her half-empty bowl of soup, avoiding his gaze. She was reluctant to reveal the truth, but there was something about Henry's gentle firmness and the concern evident in his eyes that made it hard to lie to him. "9 years." She responded.

Henry's eyes widened at her answer. "Nine years?" he repeated, disbelief clear in his voice. It was unfathomable that someone could spend so long in such a place. His heart ached at the thought of what she must have endured. "That…that's far too long. How… I mean…how did you end up there in the first place?" He knew he was treading into sensitive territory, but he needed to know.

Alice's expression crumpled, and her eyes welled up with tears as the memories came flooding back. Her voice quivered as she spoke, "I…I…" A tear slipped down her cheek, and she looked away from him, her shoulders shaking slightly. "I was sent there for female hysteria…" she finally managed to utter the foolish words.

Henry's brow furrowed with concern as Alice managed to utter the words 'female hysteria'. His mind raced, trying to make sense of the information. He knew what 'female hysteria' was, but the thought of someone being institutionalized for such a lengthy period of time…it just felt wrong. Women were rarely sent away for hysteria for life, even if it was involuntarily, a few years at best if taken out by a family member, and for Alice to have been 9 or 10, somebody should have gotten her out. This felt wrong, all wrong. "But…but nine years? For female hysteria?

That seems excessive, doesn't it?" As Henry leaned forward in his chair, concern lacing his features, he noticed something that made his gut twist in discomfort. There, at the base of her neck, just above the collar of her nightshirt, was a thin, long and ragged scar. The sight of it sent a shiver down his spine. How had he missed it before? "Alice, what's that scar? How long have you had it, and how did you get it?"

"This…?" Her hand moved to her neck, touching the scar gently. She seemed uncomfortable and averted her eyes away from him. She was hesitant to answer, but she knew he was looking at her with so much concern. "I… I got it a day ago… From a kye"

Henry's eyebrows shot up at her response, shocked by the fact that she had just gotten it a couple days ago. "Just a day!" he repeated, his voice almost a whisper. "Why wasn't it stitched or treated?" Henry immediately stood up from his chair, the concern etched on his face deepening. "You need some antiseptic, pronto." He quickly moved to the medicine cupboard and rummaged through it, his hands moving deftly as he fished out the necessities and came back to her. "Take the shirt off your shoulder, please. I need to treat that wound."

Alice gulped, her eyes widening, her heart pounding. She hesitated, but she knew he was only trying to help. Her trembling hands rose to the collar of the nightgown and pulled it down just enough to expose her narrow shoulders, revealing the long, thin, jagged scar on her pale skin.

He set down a spool of black thread, a sterilized needle, and some cotton balls soaked in the antiseptic he used earlier. He knelt in front of her again. "Try to keep still and breathe normally," he said quietly, his voice filled with a calm composure. "I'll make this as painless as I can."

She nodded, her lips pressed together tightly as she tried to keep herself calm. Her hands gripped the edge of the chair tightly as she felt the cool sting of the antiseptic against her tender skin. She closed her eyes shut, her entire body trembling with nervousness. The pain of the needle puncturing her skin was barely noticeable compared to all the years she's experienced.

Henry worked swiftly and skillfully, the needle passing through her skin with a smooth, practiced motion. He took great care to keep the stitches even and neat, the sharp needle puncturing her skin with a slight pinch. He could sense her nervousness and tension, and he spoke softly to try to soothe her. "Almost done, just a few more stitches. You're doing fine." His focus was undivided as he stitched up the wound, his steady hand precise and careful. The tension in the room was thick, and he could feel her every breath. As he finished the last stitch, he tied the thread off with a neat knot before taking a moment to inspect his work. Satisfied with the result, he wiped away any excess blood with the cotton ball, his touch gentle. "All done." Henry paused. His eyes scanned her body, noticing for the first time the multitude of smaller cuts and scars that littered her skin. Concern and alarm washed over him, and he couldn't help but feel a pang of guilt for not noticing them earlier.

She exhaled slowly, her whole body still shaking as her eyes fluttered open. She tentatively reached up to touch the stitches with her fingers, wincing slightly at the tender soreness, "Thank you," she murmured softly.

As Henry rose to put away the equipment, he paused when his gaze fell onto her shoulder blade, just above the collarbone. There, amongst the constellation of scars, was a distinct bite mark. It looked like a human's teeth had sunk deep into her skin, more than once, like the branding on a cow. Henry's heart clenched at the sight of it,.

In the background, Poole called to him, his voice carrying a note of urgency. "Master Henry," he said. "I need a word with you. Urgently."

Henry's gaze lingered on the bite mark for a moment longer before tearing his gaze away. He shot a quick glance over his shoulder at Poole, the worry evident in his expression. He knew the butler meant business, and the matter must be important. Reluctantly, he tore himself away from Alice and walked over to join Poole. "What is it?" he asked, his voice tight with impatience.

Poole's demeanor was tense as he spoke, his usually stoic composure replaced with a sense of unease. He leaned in close, making sure that Alice didn't hear their conversation. "Shall I whistle for the Peelers, master Jekyll?"

Henry's eyebrows furrowed at the suggestion. "Send her back to Bedlam?" he replied. "Are you serious, Poole? It's obvious that she's been through enough. We can't just send her back there."

His voice was firm, his tone betraying a hint of annoyance at the butler's suggestion.

"With all due respect, sir," he said quietly, "the lass is a runaway from an asylum. She belongs there, sir. For her own sake and the sake of others. I know you have a heart of gold, and I admire your compassion, but do you truly understand the potential risks of this situation? What if she is a danger to us? When they come looking for her, what will they do to us? The last thing you need to do is make a name for yourself as the man who harbors lunatics."

Henry's frown deepened as he listened to Poole's words. He knew the butler was right, to some extent. It was true that harboring a runaway patient from Bedlam was risky and could lead to serious consequences for him. But still, he couldn't shake the sense of sympathy he felt for her. He ran a hand through his hair, frustration evident on his face. "You think I haven't thought about those things?" he sighed. "Of course, I have. But can you look at her and tell me she belongs back there? Please, Poole," he said, his voice taking on a pleading tone. "I can handle this. I can handle her. Just give me a chance. She needs help, not to be thrown back into that hellhole."

Poole's features turned into reluctance and disappointment. "Very well, sir," he said eventually, his voice laced with resignation. "But be warned, sir, this could end badly. She's a lunatic, after all, and who knows what she's capable of."

Henry nodded, his determination hardening. "I'm aware of the risks, Poole," he replied firmly. "But I can't just turn my back on her. She's lost and scared, and she needs someone to help her, not condemn her. You'll see" He turned to leave the room, his mind already racing with thoughts of what needed to be done. Firstly, he knew that the girl was severely malnourished and would need a specific diet to help her regain her strength. He made a mental note to devise a meal plan for her. He also thought about the matter of her living arrangements. He could have her sleep on the sofa, but she couldn't sleep on the sofa forever, it was not suitable. He would need to arrange a room for her, but that would have to wait until tomorrow. For now, the sofa near the fireplace would have to suffice. He was a doctor, after all, and he'd seen it all before. But this was different. She was more than just another patient. He walked back into the room and smiled gently at her. "You must be tired," he said softly. "You can sleep on the sofa tonight, near the fireplace. It'll keep you warm. But tomorrow, I'll make sure you have a proper bed and a room of your own."

Her eyes widened in shock, her head snapping up as she processed his words. "Wait, what?" she breathed, disbelief etched on her face. "I... I can stay here? With you?" She looked around, taking in the room and her surroundings with a mixture of surprise and hope.

Henry chuckled lightly, noticing the look of surprise on her face. "Of course," he replied gently. "You can stay here, at my home. I can't in good conscience leave you to fend for yourself in your current state." He paused, his gaze softening as he looked at her. "You'll be safe here, I assure you. And tomorrow, I'll make sure you have proper accommodations. You need a good night's rest after everything you've been through. You'll need a blanket, of course. One moment, let yourself get situated, you can leave the dishes there." Henry turned away from her, walking over to a nearby closet where he kept extra blankets and pillows. He rummaged through the cupboard for a moment before pulling out a soft, warm woolen blanket. He returned to her, gently tucking the blanket around her body, ensuring that she was as comfortable as possible on the sofa.

Alice sat there on the sofa, wrapped snugly in the soft woolen blanket She watched as he fussed around, trying to make sure she was comfortable, and she felt a mixture of confusion and gratitude. Why was he being so kind? Why was he willing to let her stay in his home, a complete stranger? But tiredness washed over her, her eyes struggling to stay open. The adrenaline from earlier had drained away, leaving her utterly exhausted. She slowly settled down onto the sofa, her head coming to rest on the warm pillow Henry had provided. Her mind was swirling with questions, but fatigue was winning the battle. The crackle of the fire nearby and the comforting presence of Henry nearby lulled her into a much-needed sleep. "Thank you, Dr Jekyll."

Henry looked up as she thanked him. He smiled warmly, his expression filled with kindness. "There's no need for 'Dr Jekyll,'" he replied softly. "Just call me Henry." With a soft sigh, Henry stood and watched over her for a few moments, making sure she was truly asleep. He couldn't help but notice how fragile and vulnerable she looked as she slept, her frail body practically enveloped by the blanket. The fire crackled and danced in the background, casting a warm, flickering light on the room. Satisfied that she was asleep, Henry quietly made his way to the stairs. With one last glance over his shoulder at the sleeping girl, he made his way back to his one bed.

Chapter 03

The Light In The Dark.

As weeks passed, Henry's kindness and patience enveloped Alice, making her feel at ease in her new surroundings. He moved with deliberate slowness, speaking softly and avoiding sudden movements that might startle her. With every step, he checked in to ensure she was comfortable and safe, respecting her boundaries and giving her the space to adjust at her own pace. As they went about their days, Alice would catch glimpses of the Loon Hunt's exploits in the London papers, and Jekyll and Poole worked tirelessly to keep her hidden from prying eyes, risking their own freedom in the process. As Alice settled into her new life, Jekyll grew increasingly cautious about sharing his secret with anyone he didn't trust implicitly. His parents, in particular, were off-limits - he wouldn't dream of revealing the truth about the mysterious girl living under his roof. If they knew, they would rather bury themselves alive than live with the scandal. Meanwhile, Poole took on a mentorship role, teaching Alice etiquette, household chores, and practical skills to keep her engaged and active. They introduced her to healthier options beyond bread and porridge, ensuring she received proper nourishment. As Alice became more at home, she began to form a peculiar yet profound bond with Henry. In the asylum, she had forged connections with fellow patients, but this relationship was different, like some old familiar warmth.

***

September 21~ Alice opened her eyes when soft morning light streamed through the curtains, casting a warm glow on the surroundings. It was still early, and the house was unusually quiet. She slowly rose from the comfortable bed, with a stretch and a slight yawn, and got dressed in her comfortable day clothes. After freshening up, she made her way downstairs to the kitchen, where she found Poole humming to himself while cooking, the aroma of sizzling bacon and eggs filled the air.

Poole stood over the stove, expertly flipping over the bacon as the eggs were gently folded. He had a content smile on his face, clearly enjoying his task. Poole turned his head as he noticed Alice walking into the kitchen. He smiled warmly at her, his eyes twinkling in the soft morning light. "Ah, Miss Alice". He looked back over the sizzling pan before continuing, "Would you be a dear and go fetch Master Henry?

"Of course, Poole," she replied softly, her voice still carrying a hint of sleepiness. "I'll go and find him right away." She turned and padded softly out of the kitchen, her footsteps quiet against the wooden floorboards. Her mind wandered for a moment as she wondered where Henry could be.

Alice walked through the foyer of the home, her bare feet softly padding against the tiled floor. The walls, painted in a soft shade of reddish maroon, caught her attention. It was a color that she had come to associate with Henry, as it seemed to be a favorite of his, always finding its way onto some part of his attire. Alice made her way through the parlor room, her gaze settling on the familiar surroundings. The room, adorned with padauk wood, gave off a warm and cozy atmosphere. The large sofa, positioned in front of the fireplace, and just in front of the fireplace, a spot she likes to read. On one side of the sofa stood the armchair, while on the other stood the table beneath which Henry had found her. The long windows, clothed in luxurious, long crimson velvet curtains, allowed a gentle stream of sunlight to filter into the room.

With no sign of Henry in the parlor room, Alice decided to check the study, which was located to the left of the foyer that connected back to the kitchen and Poole's room. However, much to her surprise, Henry was nowhere to be found in this room either. Alice knew that Henry wasn't in his room, so she realized that the only other place he could possibly be was the side building. She had never been to that part of the house before, and she was both curious and a bit anxious at the thought of exploring this new territory.

Alice went to the laundry room and stepped out into the yard, a space that once thrummed with life and color, now marred by an air of neglect. The remnants of a garden lay before her; the remnants of once beautiful flowers and greenery were barely visible under the weight of unkempt weeds and grass that had overgrown the area. Once she corset the yard, her gaze fixed on the building that stood before her. She felt a strange sense of curiosity stepping inside. The room was dimly lit by what little light found its way in from the windows, if they were windows. She stepped carefully over the packing straw and crates that littered the floor, her gaze falling on the tables laden with chemical apparatus. As she approached the far end, she noticed a small flight of stairs leading to a banister and a door covered in red paint. Alice took her time exploring the dimly lit room, taking in the strange and unfamiliar surroundings. Strangely, she couldn't quite put her finger on it, but this room didn't quite feel like Henry. However, there was a sense that this might be a part of him in a way she didn't yet understand.

Henry had been in his cabinet room, jotting down observations in a notebook on the new ingredients he'd gotten from the apothecary, when he heard the delicate clinking of glass from his lab downstairs. Curiosity piqued, he pushed away from his desk and walked over to the door, listening intently. He could make out soft footsteps and the rustle of papers coming from below. A small smile tugged at his lips as he realized who it must be. With a quick glance at his pocket watch with a blue whale etched on the outside, he opened the door and looked over the banister. He found Alice exploring the room, gazing at the array of equipment and beakers, "Ah, you're up early," he called, a warm smile on his face. "And I see you've paid me a visit."

Alice jumped slightly at the sound of Henry's voice. She spun around to find him at the top of the banister, his expression warm and inviting. "Sorry, Poole asked me to look for you," she blurted out, embarrassment flooding her cheeks at being caught snooping.

Henry chuckled, waving away her apology. "No need to apologize, I figured it was Poole that sent you," he said, his tone light and carefree. He began to descend the stairs, the sound of his footsteps echoing softly in the lab, as he rolled up his sleeves. As Henry reached the bottom of the stairs, he approached her, his gaze flickering to the array of supplies scattered around the room. "I must admit, I'm surprised to find you in here," he remarked, his eyes filled with a mixture of intrigue and amusement. "It's not often I have visitors in my laboratory." He leaned against one of the tables, his arms crossed over his chest as he looked at her.

She shifted awkwardly, her gaze darting around the room as if trying to gauge his reaction. "I was curious," she admitted, her voice a bit quieter in the confined space. She approached one of the tables, her fingers trailing delicately over the surface, tracing patterns through the dust. "I've never seen something like this before," she confessed, her gaze flicking up to meet his.

"After I moved out of my parents' house," Henry began, a hint of excitement in his voice, "I was fortunate enough to buy this place from the heirs of Dr. John Hunter. He was a surgeon, and this was once a medical theatre for students. I keep to the beakers preferably. I find being a physician much more stomachable than being a surgeon, though Lanyon has certainly made a life for himself in such a profession." he said, a little too quickly. He chuckled awkwardly, scratching the back of his head. "Anyway, So, I've made a few modifications here and there." He gestured around the room, a hint of embarrassment creeping into his tone as he continued. "It's a bit of a work in progress, really. I mean, I've tried to make it functional and… er, inviting in a way? Although I'm not entirely sure I've succeeded there," he added, trailing off slightly, realizing he had been rambling.

Alice laughed softly at his rambling. "I think it's charming, in a peculiar kind of way," she admitted, a smile tugging at the corner of her lips. "It suits you, in a way." She leaned against the table in front of her on her stomach, looking closely at an assortment of vials and beakers before her.

Henry felt a twinge of embarrassment, his cheeks tinged with the slightest hint of pink. He scratched the back of his head once more, looking around the room. "Well, thank you," he said with a small, awkward smile. "I appreciate that. Most people find it…eccentric, to say the least. But I suppose it's a reflection of myself in a way-"

"Have you always lived in London?" She pushed herself off the table, her gaze fixed on him.

The question caught him off guard; he wasn't expecting her to ask about his past. He shifted nervously, pushing his glasses further up on the bridge of his nose as he tried to collect his thoughts. Alice noticed the slight shift in his demeanor, as if he was uneasy about her question. "Um, no, I haven't always lived in London," he finally said, his voice a bit quieter than before. "I was born in Glasgow, actually. My parents lived there. When I was 10 years old, my grandfather passed away. My parents thought it would be best to move us away, to start anew. We came to London, and I've been here ever since." Henry tried to keep his voice steady, but there was a hint of pain in his eyes as he spoke.

Alice's expression turned sympathetic. She could sense that this topic was difficult for him, and she hated to bring up anything that might make him uncomfortable. But she was also genuinely curious about his past, and she couldn't help but wonder more about the young man standing across from her. "What was he like?"

Henry's gaze flicked up to the shelf behind her, where a framed photograph of his family sat on display. He walked around the table and picked it up. "My grandfather?" he asked, turning his attention back to her, a bittersweet smile on his face. "He was a fascinating man. A brilliant astronomer and lighthouse keeper, with a mind that seemed to know no bounds." He paused, taking a deep breath as memories flooded his mind. "He was the one who introduced me to science, you see, he wanted to be an alchemist when he was a boy and tried to get my father to have an open mind to it. My parents were always quite traditional in their thinking, but my grandfather… he saw the world differently. And when we found that common ground, we were thick as thieves." He displayed the picture for her view. "This is my family, taken several years ago." In the picture, Henry could remember every little detail. His mother, Catherine Hyde, when she still played piano, that is, sat in an armchair, with her vibrant copper hair in a deep hue. Her hair, long and wavy, framed her face beautifully, complemented her hazel eyes. Catherine was dressed elegantly in a lavender dress. His father, George Jekyll, standing behind her, was a solid figure. His hair was peppered with only a hint of gray. He had a well-defined jawline and deep-set blue eyes that held a watchful, imposing quality. With a penchant for tailored suits that gave him an air of professionalism. And then there was little Henry in between his mother and grandfather. Standing side by side, he bore a resemblance to his mother in his hair, eyes, and smile, but he had his father's nose. He stood tall and confident, with a mischievous glint in his eyes that was emphasized by his round glasses. And in front of him, his grandfather's dog, a black border collie, named Regulus. "And to the left of my mother is my uncle Edoardo and my aunt Gretel." He pointed to the couple, "He was always fascinated by the morbid and grotesque. He had a collection of all sorts of taxidermy pieces and strange curios, and Gretel was a hatter; that's how they met, actually." Henry's gaze drifted back to the photograph. He pointed it for her to see. "Do you see that little lighthouse in the background?" he asked, his voice tinged with bittersweet nostalgia. "That was my grandfather's lighthouse. He was the keeper there until the day he died," he said softly, a hint of sadness in his eyes.

When she reached the image of little Henry, she couldn't help but smile at the sight of the young boy in the photograph. He looked so different from the person standing before her now, yet there were still remnants of that same boy. She nodded in response to his question about the lighthouse, her gaze lingering on his face.

Henry noticed her smile, his own expression brightening in response. He placed the photo back on the shelf and turned to face her, curiosity lacing his voice. "What about you, Alice? You mentioned you've been in an asylum since you were ten. Do you have any family? Parents, siblings, anyone?" he leaned back on the table, putting his hands in his pockets.

Alice's cheerful expression disappeared, and a hint of pain flickered across her eyes. She fidgeted with the hem of her dress, hesitant to divulge her past. But after what he had just shared with her, it seemed only fair to open up a little. "Just my parents, Emmeline and Reginald, " she said quietly. "They were the ones who sent me to the asylum," She traced a pattern in the grain of the wood with her fingertip, avoiding his gaze. "I was supposed to be part of an arranged marriage with a boy from a family my parents were involved with. And you could imagine how I was when I found out. I didn't particularly get along with my parents. I'd escape them whenever possible, but after that, they tried to tie me back down to earth to ensure I'd make a good wife... I suppose they were worried I'd end up unwedded forever. I didn't have a lot of friends, like my mother's sister, my aunt Casey. But I didn't want what they wanted for me, Markis was so... Stoick, bland, for lack of a better word, clearly unimpressed. I didn't want my life to end before it started, and one thing led to another, and I... Might have bit him." As she mentioned biting the kid, a small smile flickered across Henry's face. He tried to suppress it, but couldn't help but be slightly amused at the image in his head. "After that, I suppose they didn't know what else to do with me." Her eyes flickered toward the photo of his family, a pang of longing and. "As much as I hated the asylum, it wasn't all bad… A bunch of outcasts in one home, and I had made a close family in the process. I'd do anything for them, I owe it to them for everything."

"Your parents sound… difficult," he said gently, "And the notion of an arranged marriage seems absurd. I mean, the idea of being forced into a union without any input from the actual individuals involved in the arrangement… It's like signing a contract without even reading the fine print." He shook his head, a hint of disbelief in his voice. "It's no wonder you didn't get along with them," he added, "If I'm being honest, my own parents can be quite overbearing and strict at times, but I doubt they'd ever risk the scandal against their name by sending me there."

"I suppose they thought they were doing what was best for me - at least in their own twisted way." Her gaze returned to the photo of his family. "Your parents must be proud of you, though."

He shifted slightly, a hint of unease creeping into his expression. "Oh, well you know, parents are… complicated," he said, his voice taking on a slightly forced tone.

"I suppose you're right," she said, her voice gentle, "parents can be quite complicated." She looked at him intently, sensing that his own relationship with his parents was not as picture-perfect as the image the small photograph on the shelf would suggest.

Their conversation was abruptly interrupted by the sound of Poole bursting into the room. He looked around, a perplexed look upon his features. "Excuse me, sir," Poole said, his gaze flicking over to Alice, "But your breakfast is ready, and Miss Alice was meant to fetch you this morning."

She bit her lip, silently scolding herself for losing track of time and forgetting her task.

Henry turned his head to face the interruption, his expression shifting from contemplative to slightly flustered. He hadn't expected to be disturbed in the midst of their conversation.

"It's alright. Thank you, Poole," he said, nodding politely at the butler. "I'll be there in a moment." He turned back to Alice, a slightly sheepish expression on his face. "I suppose we should head to the dining room before my eggs get cold, eh?"

She couldn't help but grin at his sheepish demeanor. She pushed herself off the table. She fell in step beside him as they made their way out of the lab and toward the dining room.

***

October 28th~ Jekyll, Mr. Poole, and Alice had just finished a nice warm breakfast. The smell of syrup still lingered in the air, a smell that tickled Alice's nose with delight, as she laid on the carpet on her stomach, reading a book. Henry was engrossed in a journal of his, adjusting his glasses back on the bridge of his nose, and every so often, biting the joint of his index finger feebly. Meanwhile, Poole's face was mostly shielded by the newspaper in his hands. Poole personally loved reading about detectives solving the impossible, but lately nothing had peeked his interest. Still, he enjoyed the latest gossip of London. The room was quiet and peaceful, with only the sound of rustling pages and the occasional sip of tea breaking the tranquility. Sunlight streamed through the tall windows, casting warm patterns on the carpet, illuminating Alice's book as she flipped a page.

Henry paused, lost in thought, as he considered the implications of the latest findings in his journal. He glanced over at Alice, a smile warming his lips as he observed the way her eyes danced with excitement over the words on the page.

Poole took a small sip of tea, lowering the paper slightly to observe the scene before him, noticing Henry's attention shifting to Alice, watched his boss' little smile with keen eyes. Poole quietly watched the interaction between his employer and Miss Lumsley, a slight smile forming on his face. He tried to hide his reaction by ducking his head deeper into the newspaper, pretending to read it more intently.

A soft knock on the door shattered the tranquility of the morning, interrupting the peaceful atmosphere of the room. Henry looked up from his journal, his expression shifting from contemplation to annoyance.

"Now who could that be?" he muttered, closing the journal in his lap with a frustrated sigh. Poole lowered the paper he had been skimming over, the sound of the knock catching his attention as well.

Poole placed his newspaper on the table, his demeanor professional but tinged with curiosity. "I shall go and see who it is, sir," he said, standing from his chair and approaching the front door.

As Poole made his way to the front door and began to open it, Henry and Alice exchanged a glance. They could sense that something was amiss, their instincts prickling in the air. Henry sat motionless, his journal forgotten on the table, as he strained to hear the conversation taking place at the door.

Inspector Thomas Hargreaves stood on the doorstep, his tall frame and crisp police uniform imposing. He looked through the crack of the slowly opening door, his face betraying a mix of concern and authority. The sunlight behind him cast a harsh glare, making it hard to see details of his expression. The atmosphere grew heavy with anticipation. "Good morning. Apologies for the intrusion, but I have a matter of urgency to discuss with the head of the house. We are on a city-wide LoonHunt, and this search is mandatory," he stated, his voice firm and direct.

Poole glanced back at his master, a silent warning in his eyes, as if his mind was racing through the options they had. He then turned back to the constable. "I'm sorry, but Dr. Jekyll is not available at the moment," he said firmly. "He is in a meeting and cannot be disturbed. Is there anything I can assist you with?"

Thomas Hargreaves gritted his teeth, annoyed at the response. He narrowed his eyes, his gaze hardening on Poole. "I understand the inconvenience, but this is a matter of utmost urgency. I'm sorry to inform you that we believe the individual we are searching for is here, possibly hiding in this residence." He paused, his hand instinctively resting on his holstered baton. "I'm afraid I'll have to request that you allow me to search the premises."

"I am compelled to refuse without a magistrate's warrant," Poole said. "Household privacy still holds."

The inspector took his baton tucked under his arm so he could reach into his pocket, pulling out a folded up paper and holding it out infront of Poole, the butters face suddenly going white. "Compelled to search, sir."

Alarm bells rang in Henry's head as he listened to the conversation at the door. The gravity of the situation hit him like a ton of bricks. He silently motioned to Alice, beckoning her to get up from the floor. She met his gaze, her eyes wide with fear and confusion, but she understood the urgency in his eyes. With a firm grip on her hand, Henry led her down the back hall, their footsteps muffled by the carpet. He guided her swiftly through the garden, the dew-covered grass leaving cool stains on her shoes. Finally, they reached the door to his lab, and he opened it, pulling her quickly inside before closing it behind them. The room was dimly lit, with various cabinets and equipment filling the area. His grip on her hand tightened as he turned to face her, his expression a mix of concern and determination.

He paused for a moment, his mind racing. "Stay here. Don't make a sound," he whispered, his voice urgent but soft. "I'll deal with the situation. Just stay hidden and don't come out until I come to get you, understood?"

She grabs his hand in protest, "No," she says almost immediately, tears pricking her eyes filled with fear and refusal. She shook her head stubbornly, silently conveying that she didn't want to be left alone, as she coked out the word, "Please."

He met her gaze, his heart panging at the sight of her fear and desperation. He couldn't leave her alone, not in this state. He took a deep breath, his expression shifting to something more composed. "Alright, alright." He spoke softly, his voice filled with understanding and concern. "We'll stay here together."

He led her over to a small closet in the corner of the room. He hurriedly pushed aside various equipment, creating just enough space for them both to hide. "Get in," he whispered, gesturing for her to crawl into the cramped space. "And make sure you stay quiet, no matter what you hear."

He joined her in the cramped space, pulling the closet door shut behind them. The cramped quarters forced them to sit extremely close together, with nearly every part of their bodies touching. He wrapped an arm around her waist as they squished together, her head ending up against his chest. He could feel her trembling form, her body tensed with fear and anxiety, and he had to resist the urge to pull her closer. He felt her tears on his shirt, and he had to swallow the lump in his throat. He could feel her trembling begin to subside as they both sat there in the cramped space. She seemed oddly calm, as if she had done something like this before. He found himself wondering, not for the first time, about the horrors that she had endured in that asylum. But for now, all he could do was hold her close and try to comfort her.

The sudden sound of the door opening snapped them out of the silence. Henry's senses went into overdrive as he pressed closer to her and held his breath, listening intently. Poole's voice echoed through the lab, the sound of him trying to deter the constable from his search. Henry's heart was racing, his body tense with anticipation, his arm still wrapped around her waist.

The voices of Poole and the Chief Constable echoed through the room, the sound of their footsteps growing closer to the closet. Henry's heart was pounding in his chest as he held her closer, his mind racing with panicked thoughts. He knew that if they were discovered, things would not end well for him or her. He tensed even more, holding his breath as the footsteps drew closer. He could hear the sound of the constable searching through the lab, his footsteps coming closer and closer to the closet. Henry's mind raced as he tried to think of a way out. He knew they couldn't stay hidden forever, and he could feel his heart beating faster and faster as the minutes ticked by. He just hoped that the closet would be one place they wouldn't search.

On the other side of the door, Chief Constable Hargreaves and Poole engaged in a tense exchange. Henry could hear the annoyance and determination in Hargreaves' voice as he insisted on the necessity of a search. "I understand your concern for Dr. Jekyll's privacy, Mister Poole, but I can assure you, this is a matter of great importance." He went on, his tone growing more insistent. "A lunatic has escaped from the asylum, and we believe she may have sought refuge in a residence near her last sighting. I need your permission to search the premises."

Poole remained firm in his denial, trying to maintain a sense of composure despite the growing pressure. "I'm afraid that is not possible, Chief Constable. Dr. Jekyll is in an important meeting and cannot be disturbed. And I cannot allow you to search the premises without a warrant."

Hargreaves let out an exasperated sigh, clearly not satisfied with Poole's response. "I don't have time to wait for a warrant, Mr. Poole. Every minute counts in these cases. I need to search the premises immediately."

Poole stood his ground, his voice calm but unyielding. "I'm sorry, Chief Constable, but I cannot permit a search of the premises without legal authorization. Dr. Jekyll values his privacy, and I am bound by my duty to protect it."

Exasperated, Hargreaves sighed, recognizing that he wasn't getting anywhere with Poole's staunch resistance. "Very well, Mr. Poole. But I want you to understand the gravity of the situation. If you encounter the escaped lunatic or come across any sign of her, I expect you to notify me immediately." He paused, his tone becoming sterner. "And I'll be keeping a close eye on this property until further notice. Good day, Mr. Poole."

He takes a last glance at Poole, his eyes narrowing as he leaves the residence. Poole's shoulders slumped as he closed the front door, exhaling a sigh of relief. He locked the door and walked back to the lab, aware of the fact that hiding the escaped 'lunatic' was highly illegal. But he respected his employer and did not want to let any harm come to him or his guests. He opened the door to the lab and walked over to the closet.

As the door to the closet swung open, they were met with a wave of relief, but also a pang of fear. Henry and Alice emerged from the cramped space, their bodies still pressed close together from the long few minutes that they had spent hidden away. They inhaled deeply, taking in the fresh air as their hearts pounded in their chests from the close call. Henry and Alice emerged from the cramped space, emerging from the darkened closet into the lab. Henry's heart was still racing as he slowly released his grip on her waist. He looked at Poole, grateful for his loyalty and discretion, but the fear still lingered in his eyes. "Thank you, Poole," Henry said, his voice quiet and tense.

Poole gave him a nod, understanding the gravity of the situation. "I tried to stall him as much as possible, sir, but his search was very thorough," he said, his tone laced with a hint of worry.

Henry nodded, still tense and on edge. "I know, Poole. You did as much as you could. Thank you." He turned his gaze to Alice, checking on her, seeing her trembling slightly. His concern for her had not lessened, even though they were out of immediate danger.

***

That night, everyone in the house slept peacefully, not a single disturbance to be seen nor heard. In Alice's Room, the wallpaper was lined with brass silhouetted outlines of orchids on a livid colored backdrop, giving the space an elegant yet whimsical feel. The walls seemed to shimmer softly in the moonlight, creating an ethereal ambiance that wrapped around the room like a gentle embrace. Her bed, warm and cozy, lay in the middle of the room along the far wall, adorned with cushions in varying shades of blue and cream that invited a feeling of comfort. A thick, plush quilt completed the setup. Across the room, the closet stood like a silent guardian of secrets, its dark wood finish contrasting beautifully with the brass accents on the wallpaper. The dresser, with its polished surface gleaming faintly in the dim light, was adorned with a delicate glass vase atop it, filled with dried lilies, its soft fragrance mingling with the cool night air, adding a touch of serenity to the space. Thin lace baby blue curtains draped in front of the window, wafting gently with the slightest stir of an evening breeze. The moonlight seeped in through the fabric, casting a silvery glow that danced across the room, illuminating the delicate patterns in a soft light.

Alice bolted upright in bed, her heart racing like a trapped bird within her chest. The thin sheets clung to her clammy skin, and the scent of dampness and something rancid filled the dark air around her. She blinked into the shadows, the dim light of the moon casting ghostly fingers through the tattered curtains. Panic clawed at her throat as familiar dread flooded her senses—she was back in the asylum, that dreadful structure of stone and silence standing oppressive and unyielding. The walls of her room seemed to breathe, expanding and contracting as if caught in a rhythm of dark memories. She could feel the weight of the night pressing upon her, making it hard to draw breath.

A whisper floated through the air, soft and sibilant, like winds weaving through a long-forgotten hall. "Alice... Alice..." It called her name, each syllable a chilling caress that sent shivers running down her spine.

Suddenly, a morass of darkness slithered into view from beneath the bed, a writhing mass like a black leech made of living ink. It pulsed and quivered, glistening in the moonlight, growing larger with every heartbeat. Fear jolted through her body; it slithered like a serpent, each undulation pulsating with grotesque glee, as if savoring the hunt. "No!" Alice gasped, scrambling back against the headboard, her pulse drumming in her ears like thunder. She glanced down to find the monstrous thing inching closer, tendrils reaching out with a mind of their own, searching for the warmth of her skin. It coiled and twisted, a dark promise of entrapment that both horrified and mesmerized. With a sudden surge of desperation, she leaped from the bed, feeling the rough chill of the floor against her feet. The room surrounding her shifted into jagged shapes, the furniture warped into sinister silhouettes looming like sentinels of despair. She stumbled toward the door, but the monster was quicker. A black tendril lashed out, wrapping around her ankle with a grip like iron, pulling her back into its dark embrace. "No, no, no!" she screamed, her voice cracking against the weight of her terror. The air thickened around her, saturated with the cloying scent of decay and the unearthly, muffled whispers of the souls trapped in that cursed place. Each breath tasted of fear, of memories she desperately wished to forget: the scream of another patient, the coldness of the padded room, the lingering shadows at the end of the hall. The creature writhed, its inky form expanding, tendrils sprouting like sickly flowers, dancing with delight as Alice struggled. They twisted tighter around her, constricting her breathing, suffocating her sanity. She could feel it—an insidious pull, drawing her toward the darkness within its belly. Suddenly, the window rattled violently, the curtains billowing outward as if something sinister beyond them sought to enter. A gust of wind came rushing into the room, punctuated by distant cries, echoes of torment that clawed at her heart. In that fleeting moment, clarity pierced through the dream.

Alice jolted awake, her breathing ragged and panicked, her body drenched in sweat. She blinked rapidly, taking in the dimly lit room, desperately trying to shake off the lingering nightmare. The scent of dampness and something rancid still clung to her nostrils, and her heart thumped so hard she feared it would burst from her chest. Every sound, every flicker of shadow, made her flinch, as if the monsters from her dreams were still lurking in the corners of her room. With each passing moment, reality slowly returned.

Henry sat in the living room, a book opens in his lap, though he was staring into space, lost in thought. The silence of the night was thick, broken only by soft drips from a faucet in the kitchen that Poole had forgotten to turn off. Suddenly, he heard a soft, distressed mumbling from down the hall from Alice's room. Henry's eyebrows knitting together with concern. He marked his place in his book and put it aside, rising from his armchair and crossing the living room. He stood outside of Alice's doorway, the murmur becoming more distinct, though he couldn't make out the words. He hesitated at the door, debating whether to knock and wake her, or to let her be. But the worry won out, and he eventually gently knocked on the door, his voice soft and hesitant. "Alice? Is everything alright?"

Alice's heart was still pounding, every nerve in her body screaming out in panic. The images from her nightmare played over and over in her mind, like a gruesome film stuck on repeat. She was so lost in her own world that she didn't even register Henry calling to her outside the door. She continued murmuring incoherently, rocking back and forth slightly, her eyes fixated on a spot on the floor.

After a few seconds of hesitation, he slowly opened the door and entered the room. Henry's heart lurched as he saw Alice rocking back and forth, clearly distressed. But she didn't answer his question, lost in her own world. He approached her carefully, not wanting to startle her. Then, he knelt down beside her, his voice quieter, more soothing. "Hey, it's alright. You're okay. You're safe, I promise."

Her breathing became shallow, and she raised her hand to her head, clutching at her hair, shaking her head, shutting her eyes.

Henry's concern only increased as he saw her clutch at her head, shaking her head as if trying to drive away some unseen force. He reached out, hesitantly at first, then more firmly, he placed his hand on hers, gently trying to untangle her fingers from her hair.

"Alice, you need to listen to me. You're here, safe, in my house. You're not in the asylum." He continued to speak softly to her, his voice a gentle but firm grounding point. He gently pried her fingers away from her hair, still keeping his hand on hers, as he tried to soothe her with his words. "Just breathe, okay? Slowly, in... and out. In... and out. Can you do that for me?"

It took a moment but she started taking deep breaths; a few of them were a bit shaky, but she just tried to focus on his soothing voice.

Henry could see the panic in her eyes begin to subside. He gave her hand a reassuring squeeze and continued to speak in that same soft, soothing tone. "That's it, just keep breathing. Nice and slow. You're doing well." Henry understood that she needed a distraction, something to anchor her to the present and chase away the nightmares. He nodded, squeezing her hand one more time before getting up. "Okay, I'll be right back. Just focus on your breathing, alright?" He patted her shoulder reassuringly, then headed out of the room, disappearing into the darkness of the hall. Henry then made his way down the hall to his study. It was a small room lined with wooden bookshelves on three walls, a fire burning softly in the stone fireplace. He quickly found the book he was looking for. Treasure Island, one of his favorites. The leather-bound volume was well-worn, a testament to how many times he'd read it. He grabbed the book and headed back to Alice's room. When he returned to Alice's room, he found her a bit more composed, still breathing slowly and deeply. He gave her a reassuring smile and took his place beside her again, the book clutched in his hands. He shifted a little to get more comfortable, holding her hand still. He held up the book in his other hand, showing her the cover. "I brought something for you. A story. I think it might help take your mind off things. It did for me... Do you trust me?"

Alice sat, focusing on her breathing and steadying herself as she listened to Henry's words. His reassurance comforted her; her mind still a bit foggy from the intense nightmare. When he showed her the book, her eyes lit up. Her eyes met his, and she nodded, "I trust you." She shifted, scooting over to make room for him. She pulled the covers over her legs and patted the now-empty space next to her.

Henry smiled warmly, her acceptance and trust filling him with a gentle joy. He settled into the empty space beside her, careful not to disturb her too much. They both shifted to get comfortable under the covers, his body creating a steady presence next to hers. "Here we go then," he said quietly, opening the book to the first page. He began reading aloud, the soft glow from the nearby oil lamp providing the only light in the darkened room. The words of Treasure Island, familiar

40

and soothing, filled the air, the rhythmic tone of his voice an anchor in the calm night. He continued to read, the words of the story filling the room with a steady, comforting rhythm. Henry could feel Alice relax beside him, her breath becoming more even and less panicked. He stole a glance at her every now and then, checking her expressions to ease his own concerns. She was quiet, her attention still on the words he was reading. The room was enveloped in an almost intimate tranquility, the only sounds being his voice and her slow breaths.

***

The next morning, the sun streamed in through the window in the parlor, bathing the room in a warm, golden light. Henry stood in the doorway, watching Alice sitting by the window, her fingers gently tracing the outline of a photograph in her hands. The soft glow of the morning sun kissed her features, making her look almost ethereal. He watched her for a moment, noticing the soft melancholy in her eyes as she stared at the photograph.

Poole approached Henry, holding out the watch. "Sir, I finished cleaning your grandfather's old pocket watch. It's looking quite dapper now, if I do say so myself." Poole's eyes drifted to Alice, who was still sitting by the window, her gaze fixated on the photograph in her hands. He gave a subtle, almost concerned glance. "How is she faring?"

Henry tore his gaze away from Alice, his eyes focusing on the pocket watch in Poole's hand. He took the watch, running his thumb over the polished surface. "She's doing better. I think," he sighed, his voice softer than normal. He turned back to look at Alice, his gaze lingering on her for a moment before turning back to Poole. "She had another nightmare last night. But she seems calmer now."

Poole nodded, his eyes flickering back to Alice. "Perhaps she'd like some fresh air? Being cooped up here all day can't be good for her."

Henry sighed, his gaze lingering on her figure by the window. He knew Poole had a point. "I know. But it's just not safe yet. The constable was here yesterday. If he finds her here…" He trailed off, the potential danger hanging heavy in the air.

Poole nodded, his expression thoughtful. "If you don't mind my saying so, sir, one person can only do so much. Perhaps it would be wise to… engage some assistance."

Henry considered Poole's words, his thoughts lingering on the idea of getting more help. But something held him back, a nagging feeling of worry. "I appreciate your concern, Poole. I do." He paused, his eyes shifting back to Alice, her figure still illuminated by the morning sunlight. "But... I just... I don't know if it's wise to involve anyone else just yet. The danger of it all, the implications of someone finding out..." He trailed off, his worry palpable. "It's not just the risk. It's... it's everything. It's her safety, my reputation, the risk to my career." He ran a hand through his hair, his frustration growing. "What if they don't understand? What if they can't keep the secret?"

Poole nodded, understanding the gravity of Henry's worry. "I understand, sir. It's a risk." He glanced back at Alice, a sympathetic look in his eyes. "But sometimes, the burden is just too heavy to carry alone. And having someone you trust, someone you can count on, can make a world of difference." He paused, the silence in the room nearly suffocating. "I'm not saying it'll be easy. Or that there won't be any risk. But it could be worth it, especially for her."

Henry let out a heavy sigh, his shoulders slumping. He knew Poole was right. But the risk... it felt so heavy, so real. "I know you're right. But what if... what if they don't understand? What if they react badly? Or worse..."

Poole gave him a reassuring squeeze on the shoulder. "Trust me, sir. Those men have known you since childhood. If there's anyone who will understand your situation and be willing to help, it's them." He looked at Henry, his gaze unwavering. "They'll support you. I know it."

Henry let out a long sigh, looking down at the floor. He knew Poole was right. He knew that his friends would do anything for him. "Alright." He said, finally meeting Poole's gaze. "I'll tell them. But they have to swear to secrecy." He paused, a hint of determination in his voice. "No one can know. Not a soul."

Chapter 04

Three Best Friends.

December 7th~ Alice carefully balanced herself on the edge of the kitchen counter, determined to reach the pot perched on the top shelf. Mr. Poole, the elderly butler, watched from the corner of his eye, gasping in concern. "Miss Alice, please be careful," he pleaded, worry etched on his face. "We don't want you to fall and hurt yourself."

Henry, leaning against the doorframe, couldn't help but chuckle at the sight. "I never thought I'd see the day when an elegant lady would be climbing on the counters," he teased.

Alice rolled her eyes, shooting him a playful glare. "Well, Henry, you really should get out more!" she retorted playfully, her smirk breaking into a triumphant grin as she finally reached the pot. But as she was about to climb down, something caught her eye. A recipe book lay open on the counter. Curiosity piqued, she flipped through the pages, reading aloud, "Precision and patience? Sounds boring. I prefer throwing everything together and seeing what happens."

Mr. Poole shook his head, an amused yet serious glint in his eye. "No, no, no. We are doing this properly." He took over, guiding Alice through the intricate steps of the recipe. Despite her initial resistance, she found herself intrigued by the methodical approach he showed her. Just then, a knock echoed from the door, and Mr. Poole excused himself to tackle the visitors.

"Harry, there better be a good reason for your urgency, we know we missed your birthday on the 9th, but we couldn't pass up La Musée d'Orsay, but you should refrain from being upset with us, we did ask if you wanted to join," said a voice from the doorway, tinged with curiosity as two men entered the parlor.

"I agree," said the second man, "Couldn't you have better prepared us?"

Henry rolled his eyes playfully and took Alice's hand, leading her toward the newcomers. As Henry guided Alice into the parlor, the two newcomers, Gabriel Utterson and Doctor Hastie Lanyon.

Henry first met Hastie and Gabriel when he was 11, shortly after he moved from Scotland. He was initially drawn to their charisma and their seemingly carefree lifestyle in grammar schools. The three boys quickly became inseparable, often sneaking out and exploring the city together. They found a hidden shack where they would introduce Henry to wine from Utterson's uncle's winery, and they'd drink and smoke, away from the watchful eyes of adults. Henry's parents, particularly his mother, Catherine Jekyll, loved Hastie Lanyon and considered him a perfect friend for their son. Despite their different social backgrounds, Catherine saw Hastie as a positive influence on Henry, and his presence in their home was always welcomed and celebrated. Hastie and Utterson played a significant role in helping Henry fit into the London social scene. They showed him the ropes, guiding him through social norms and helping him navigate the complexities of London society. They introduced him to new people and experiences, expanding his worldview and allowing him to see past the boundaries of his own sheltered upbringing.

They turned to face them as they walked in, and their eyes widened in surprise at the unexpected presence of Alice. Gabriel Utterson, tall and lean, was known for his rugged demeanor, rarely gracing a smile on his stern face. His stoic expression remained unchanged even as he caught sight of their unexpected guest, nearly losing his grip on the handle of his large bag.

On the other hand, Dr. Hastie Lanyon was quite the opposite, He was a friendly and boisterous character, with rosy-tinted cheeks and a hearty laugh that echoed whenever he spoke. His bright eyes sparkled with curiosity as he watched Alice, his expression betraying his surprise at her presence.

"Henry, this is certainly not what we were expecting," Utterson said, his voice laced with intrigue. "Mind enlightening us about our company?"

Henry couldn't hide a smirk at their reaction. "Gentlemen, allow me to introduce you to Alice Lumsley. She's a dear friend who has been staying with me for the past few months. Alice, these are my good friends, Gabriel John Utterson and Hastie Lanyon."

Alice raised an eyebrow as they entered the room, noticing how Henry had called her his 'dear friend', and she smiled at that. She carefully observed the two men, taking in their appearances and demeanors. "Pleasure to meet you both." She said, her voice smooth and even.

Both Utterson and Lanyon's eyebrows shot up, clearly not expecting to be introduced to a young lady by their friend. Utterson almost dropped his bag. Utterson, ever the stoic, was the first to compose himself, inclining his head in a polite greeting. "Miss Lumsley," he said, his voice steady, "a pleasure."

Lanyon, on the other hand, was visibly surprised, his eyes darting back and forth between Henry and Alice. He cleared his throat, trying to hide his shock. "Miss Lumsley," he said, his voice tinged with disbelief. "I've got to say, I didn't expect..." He trailed off, his gaze flickering towards Henry. "Is this true? You've managed to find a..." He paused, searching for the right word, before settling on, "Companion, have you? How on earth did you manage that? How come we've never been introduced?"

Alice's smile faltered briefly as her eyes darted to Henry for reassurance.

Sensing her discomfort, Henry interjected smoothly, "Alice has had a tough past, and I've been helping her heal and rebuild her life. I wanted her to feel comfortable before introducing her to anyone else. She's been through a lot, and I'm just helping her get back on her feet."

Utterson nodded slowly, his gaze softening slightly. He understood Henry's protective nature, and he could see the pain behind Alice's eyes.

Lanyon chuckled. "That's quite commendable of you, Henry," he said, his tone slightly skeptical. "But don't you think you should've informed us sooner?"

Henry chuckled sheepishly, running a hand through his hair. "You're right, I suppose I have been a bit preoccupied lately. But I assure you, Alice is a wonderful woman. Infact, she has helped prepare supper, and I'm not sure about you, but I'm famished."

Henry's response seemed to ease the tension in the room, if only a bit. Utterson's gaze shifted back to Alice, studying her carefully while Lanyon's skepticism was still apparent. But the mention of supper seemed to pique their interest. "I must say, the thought of a home-cooked meal does sound delightful. Lead the way, Henry." Utterson said, a small smile on his face.

He led them into the dining room, the smell of lamb, potatoes, and corn, filled the air. Henry whispered in her ear as he pushed her chair in for her. "Ignore their questions. They're a bit nosy but mostly harmless."

Alice forced another smile, trying to maintain her calm facade in front of the two men. She was still struggling to trust and open up, especially in a room full of strangers.

Lanyon cleared his throat, the first to speak up as they began to eat. "So, Alice, how did you and Henry meet?"

Alice's smile froze for a moment, feeling uneasy as the attention was shifted back to her. She had been trying so hard not to let things get under her skin, but they were starting to find chinks in her armor.

Seeing her uneasiness, Henry gently squeezed her hand under the table, hoping to calm her down. Then, he cleared his throat and answered for her. "Ah, yes. We met quite randomly, actually. She was looking for a place to stay, and if luck would have it, she ended up here. That was about six months ago now."

Utterson nodded in understanding, seemingly satisfied with Henry's answer. Lanyon, however, continued to observe Alice closely, his perceptive nature picking up on her unease. He could tell that there was more to the story than what Henry had told.

As they continued to eat, a silence fell over the table momentarily. Utterson decided to break it. "That reminds me, I brought you a gift, Jekyll." Utterson grabbed his bag, that was on his side and placed it in front of him.

Henry's face lit up at the sight of the bag, "Oh, Gabriel, you shouldn't have." Henry opened the bag and withdrew a cane, long, sleek, and sturdy. The cane was well-made, the handle smooth and polished, a silver head capping it off. As Henry held the cane in his hand, and his expression faltered momentarily, his fingers gripping it tightly, forcing a grateful smile. "Utterson, you really shouldn't have. It's, uh, it's quite something," he said, his voice betraying a bit of discomfort. He quickly placed the cane down, distancing it from himself as if it were a poisonous snake.

Meanwhile, Lanyon took a sip of his whiskey, not quite realizing the effect the cane had on his friend. Alice, however, noticed the change in Henry's demeanor and the tension that filled the room. She looked at him, a silent question in her eyes.

Utterson, on the other hand, seemed oblivious to Henry's reaction. He smiled, seemingly pleased with the gift he had given. "It's a remarkable piece. It reminded me of your father's, and seeing as you look so much like your father, I thought it would suit you well. You were always staring at it so longingly."

Henry's chest lurched at the mention of his father. A dark cloud of resentment and anger loomed over his mind, and his jaw clenched involuntarily. He swallowed hard, trying to push the memories away.

Lanyon, sensing the tension, finally noticed the cane and Henry's distressed demeanor. He raised an eyebrow, confused. "Did I miss something?" He asked, glancing from Henry to Utterson and then the cane.

Henry closed his eyes for a moment, composing himself. "No, nothing," he said, his tone betraying nothing. He forced a smile, trying to mask the storm of feelings that was churning inside him. "It's just a gift from Utterson, nothing to worry about."

Alice, on the other hand, was observing the scene closely. She could sense the undercurrents of tension, the subtle flicker of pain in Henry's eyes. She shot a subtle glance at Utterson, her gaze sharp.

Henry responded with a polite smile, "It's truly beautiful, Gabriel, and your thoughtfulness is much appreciated," he said, keeping his voice steady. "I'll make sure to put it to good use."

After the meal concluded, Utterson and Lanyon readied themselves to depart. Utterson bid farewell first, shaking Henry's hand firmly before heading out the door. Lanyon, still somewhat more suspicious, lingered for a moment and shared a few hushed words with his friend.

As soon as they were gone, Alice breathed a sigh of relief, the tension in her shoulders ebbing.

Henry noticed the late hour and suppressed a yawn, running a hand through his hair. He glanced at the clock, realizing they've been talking for a while. "Looks like it's getting quite late," he said, looking at Alice with a mix of exhaustion and contentment. "You must be tired."

Alice managed a smile, grateful for the end of the evening's events. Her eyes flicked to Henry, noting the tired expression on his face, a contrast from the composed demeanor he'd been holding up during their guests' presence. "Yes, quite tired," she replied quietly, her voice betraying a hint of exhaustion. She rose from her seat, smoothing down her skirt. As she began to collect the few dishes that were still on the table. She wanted to ask him about it, to know what had triggered such a response, but she decided to hold her tongue. But as she looked back at Henry, leaning over the sink, rinsing off his plate, she walked over and hugged him from behind.

Henry was caught off guard by Alice's sudden embrace, but he didn't push her away. Instead, he let his shoulders slacken, leaning into her hug. The comforting weight of her pressed against his back was soothing, the tension in his body slowly ebbing away. He could feel her warmth seep into him, chasing away the chill of the evening. He let out a soft sigh, his hands still dripping with dish-soap, turning around to face her, his arms moving to wrap around her waist, pulling her close. "Thank you, Alice," he said, his voice a low whisper.

***

January 3rd 1885~ The three men sat around the fireplace in Dr. Jekyll's study, sipping on brandy and conversing, as Jekyll attempted to butter them up. It was a usual gathering for the three old friends, but tonight, Dr. Jekyll had a confession to make. "My dear friends," he began, setting his glass down on the table. "I must confess something to you. You see, the young woman who has been living with me for the past month, Alice... she comes from a rough situation."

Lanyon raised an eyebrow, intrigued by Jekyll's words. Utterson leaned in, his curiosity piqued as well. "What do you mean, Jekyll?" Utterson asked.

"I mean that Alice... she... is an escaped lunatic from the asylum," Jekyll replied, his tone serious. "She has suffered greatly at the hands of the doctors there. But I believe she is not beyond help. I have taken her in and have been working with her to help her heal from her traumatic experiences."

Lanyon and Utterson exchanged concerned glances before turning their attention back to Jekyll. "Good heavens, Jekyll have you gone mad!" Lanyon exclaimed. "Bringing an escaped lunatic into your home? What if she is dangerous?"

"I must agree with Lanyon, Jekyll," Utterson added. "It is quite risky to have someone like that living with you. What if she causes harm to you or to others? Can you trust her?"

"Look, I understand your concerns, but Alice is not dangerous. Yes, she has escaped from the asylum, but only because she feared for her safety and well-being." Jekyll's voice was steady and firm. "She has been through a lot, but with my help, she is slowly healing and adjusting to her new life. I can vouch for her character. She is not a threat to me and those around her." Jekyll reached for his brandy glass and took a sip, "Please trust me on this, my friends."

Lanyon raised an eyebrow, still skeptical. "But Jekyll, why bring her into your home? Surely there must have been other options besides bringing an escapee into your home. It seems quite reckless."

"I understand your concerns," Jekyll continued, choosing his words carefully. "But as a doctor and a good man, I couldn't leave her to wander the streets alone. I believe that kindness and care can bring more healing than any asylum could ever provide. Plus, as a medical doctor, my home is well-suited for the purpose. Please, my friends," he begged, "trust me, and give Alice a chance. She deserves to be treated with dignity and respect, like any other person."

Utterson leaned back in his seat, a thoughtful expression on his face. "If I may share my perspective, Jekyll, I believe trust is earned, especially in a situation like this," Utterson said firmly. "I don't mean to be distrusting, but I can't help but have reservations about allowing an escaped lunatic into your home. It puts us, as your friends and associates, at risk."

Lanyon nodded in agreement with Utterson's words. "I concur with Gabriel. It is understandable to want to help someone in need, but we must also consider the safety of ourselves and the community."

Jekyll sighed, understanding Utterson and Lanyon's concerns. They had been his closest friends for years, and he valued their opinions. "I understand your worries," he said softly. "But I can assure you that Alice poses no threat to any of us. I have been working with her closely and with great care. She is a young woman who has been sorely mistreated by the asylum, and she deserves our compassion and healing. I promise you, I will not put any of us in harm's way." He leaned in closer, looking at them with earnest eyes. "Please, give me your trust."

Utterson glanced at Lanyon, and they shared a brief look of understanding before turning back to Jekyll. "Very well, Jekyll," Utterson said finally. "We will trust your judgement on this matter. But," he added, holding up a finger, "we will have to keep a watchful eye on her. The safety of ourselves and the community comes first."

Lanyon nodded in agreement, his eyes narrowing as he sipped his drink. "I hope you know what you're doing, Hanry."

Jekyll felt a wave of gratitude wash over him. Despite their concerns, his friends had ultimately trusted him. "Thank you, my dear friends," he said sincerely. "Your trust means everything to me, and I promise to be careful. As I've said, I have been working closely with her, and she has been making great progress." He smiled, trying to reassure them. "Let's not ruin such a wonderful evening with this matter. Let's have another round!" He poured another glass of brandy on them. "Cheers, gentlemen."

Utterson smiled reluctantly. He took his glass from Jekyll's hand. "To trust," he muttered before taking a drink.

Lanyon, on the other hand, looked more tense but nodded in agreement and took his glass. "To hope," he said with a hint of irony in his tone.

As they resumed their conversation, the atmosphere in the study became a bit more strained. Utterson and Lanyon couldn't completely shake off their doubts and concerns about Alice's presence in Jekyll's home, but they chose to remain silent for the moment. The unease faded into the background as the hours slipped away, their conversation becoming more animated and boisterous.

As the night wore on, the three men continued their conversation, the air of tension gradually dissipating as they became lost in the flow of discussion. The topics ranged from their latest research projects to witty anecdotes and playful banter. However, Jekyll couldn't help but feel a tinge of unease knowing that his friends' doubts lingered in the air, despite their efforts to keep up the conversation. He took a deep breath and focused on the present moment, trying to push away those thoughts for another time.

Chapter 05

A Puzzling Conundrum Of A Fancy

April 15th~ As time flew, their bond grew stronger. They spent their days laughing, sharing stories, and exploring new hobbies together, and Henry made it a priority to take her around England as much as he could. And as the sun set, they would sit by the fireplace, enjoying each other's company and the warmth it provided. Alice found herself more and more drawn to Henry's company with each passing day. His understanding and patience had begun to touch her heart in unexpected ways. The moments they shared became more precious, and she found herself longing for his presence even when he was absent.

One night, Alice was sweeping the floor as Poole washed the dishes. She peeked into Jekyll's study and saw he had fallen asleep.

Poole observed Alice's glance at Jekyll, his eyebrows furrowed in suspicion. He continued washing the dishes, but his eyes never left her.

She set the broom against the wall and picked up a soft blanket from the sofa. Quietly, she entered his study, a tender smile danced across her lips as she gently draped the blanket over his sleeping form, her heart swelling with affection. Her hands lingered on his shoulders for a moment longer than necessary. She moved the book from his lap, placing it neatly on the desk. She reached out again and carefully slid his glasses off his face, setting them on top of the book. A pang of affection stirred within her chest. His face looked almost boyish and vulnerable when he slept, and the sight of him made her heart feel strangely tight. A soft smile graced her lips as she gently brushed his hair from his forehead, her touch tender and affectionate. The silence of the room seemed to amplify her own heartbeat as she leaned down, her lips hovering above his head. She planted a feather-light kiss on the top of his head, her breath warm against his skin. As she stepped back, a sense of contentment washed over her. With one last lingering glance at his sleeping form, she quietly stepped out of the room, "Sleep well," she whispered, her voice filled with tenderness, closing the door behind her.

Poole's eyes widened in surprise. He almost dropped the dish he was holding. "Bloody hell…" Poole muttered under his breath, trying to process what he had witnessed. His brain was racing, trying to understand what this meant. It was obvious she was growing fond of Jekyll, that much was clear. But how deep did her feelings run? Poole set the dish in the soapy water, his gaze locked on that door, his mind racing. He turned off the water, drying his hands on a towel without breaking his gaze from the closed door, he walked out from the kitchen, moving across the living room towards her. He stood silently behind her for a moment, watching as she cleaned. His brow furrowed deeper as his concern grew. He took a step towards her and spoke softly, not wanting to startle her. "Alice? May I have a word with you, please?"

Alice stopped sweeping, and turned around, "Of course, Poole. Is something wrong?"

He took a step closer, his hands clasped behind his back. "I have seen things that trouble me immensely," he said carefully, his voice low enough that their conversation wouldn't reach Jekyll's ears. "And I believe we must talk about it."

She feigned nonchalance, continuing to sweep as though nothing was wrong. But inside, her mind was racing with nervousness. "Troubled you? What have you seen?" She asked, her voice a touch too high-pitched.

Poole saw right through her facade. The slight tremble in her voice, her higher tone, and the way her gaze avoided the study door didn't escape his notice. "Don't play coy with me, Alice. You know exactly what

I've seen," he said, his tone stern, yet tinged with concern. "I've seen you in the study with Henry. Your...affections towards him have grown to a dangerous degree." Poole let out a deep sigh, his expression turning more serious. He stepped closer to her, his eyes fixed on hers. "Alice, I want you to listen to me very carefully. Your growing affection for him is... it's dangerous. It could very well mean disaster for you, for him, and for all of us." He took another step, his gaze never leaving hers as he spoke firmly. "You cannot let your heart lead you into this. I must make you promise me, right here and right now, that you won't give into these feelings for him."

She swallowed hard at his words, her heart sinking. Her grip on the broom handles tightened, her knuckles turning white. "P-Poole, it's not like that. I... I care for him, yes, but it's not what you think. I-I'm just grateful he's shown me kindness and-" She cut herself off, her voice betraying her. She knew her words did not sound believable even to herself.

Poole's expression softened as he saw the pain in her eyes, a pang of sympathy tugging at his heart. Yet, his loyalty to Henry trumped everything. He had to protect him, no matter the cost. "Please, Alice, for both our sakes, you must put an end to this. You can't continue like this. This... affection of yours, it's dangerous. It will only bring pain and heartache – to you, to him, to everyone involved."

She closed her eyes for a moment, taking a deep breath, gathering her thoughts before speaking again. "I... I don't want to hurt him. I never meant to... but it's more complicated than it looks." She couldn't bring herself to admit out loud the true depth of her feelings. It was too much, too confusing, and frankly, too scary. She looked up at Poole, her eyes filled with a mix of confusion and helplessness.

Poole saw the turmoil in her eyes, the struggle within her heart. Part of him wanted to soften, to comfort her and tell her everything would be alright. But he knew better. "No, it isn't," he said, his tone a mix of firmness yet uncertain. "It's simple. You have feelings for a man you can never have. And, it's as clear as day you're only going to make this situation more difficult for him then it needs to be." He felt a pang of guilt, knowing that he had to protect Henry, but also his compassion for Alice. He understood her feelings were real, and that only made this situation more complicated. "Alice," he began, his voice gentle yet firm, "I know you don't want to hurt him, and I believe you that you never meant for this to happen. But sometimes, our hearts have a will of their own, and we find ourselves in situations we never intended. But you have to understand that this can't continue. It's not just about love and hurt. It's about safety, about our livelihoods, about everything we've worked so hard to maintain. Henry and I... we have built a life here, a life that needs to remain stable and safe. We can't let emotions, as powerful as they may be, threaten all of that."

She met his eyes, a mix of resignation and anguish in her eyes. She knew Poole's argument was firm, but the thought of losing the connection they shared, it was unbearably painful. "A-Alright. I understand." She replied, her voice barely above a whisper. Her hand gripped the broom tighter, her knuckles turning white. She looked away, unable to maintain eye contact with him any longer. The weight of their conversation hung heavily in the air.May 30th~ Alice found herself struggling to stay true to her promise. Every waking moment was a battle, fighting her own heart. The way his laughter made her heart flutter, the gentleness in his eyes when he looked at her, the sound of his name on her lips. She tried to push the thoughts away, to bury them deep within her mind. But they would always surface, creeping up like an unstoppable tide. The more she tried, the harder she fell.

Alice stepped into the laboratory, balancing a tray of tea in her hands. Her heart raced as she looked around. She caught sight of Henry, immersed in whatever experiment he was working on, his brow furrowed in concentration. She took a deep breath, trying to steady her nerves before walking over to him. She set the tray down gently onto the edge of the table, the clinking of the cups echoing softly in the room. She perched herself on the edge of the table, her fingers fidgeting with the hem of her skirt as she watched him.

Henry lifted his gaze from the beaker he was examining and noticed Alice by his side. He pushed his glasses up the bridge of his nose and smiled softly at her, the corners of his eyes crinkling. His gaze flickered between her and the tray. "Tea? You really didn't have to bring me tea, you know." He said, reaching for a cup and taking a sip. The warmth of the liquid spread through his veins, slightly alleviating the tension in his shoulders, "but I appreciate it."

Alice smiled, her nervousness subsiding momentarily at the sight of his smile. "You're welcome, Henry. Figured you could use a bit of a break," she replied, the sound of the raindrops creating a soothing background music. She watched him fondly, her eyes following his careful movements as he examined his work. "Henry, what are you working on anyway?"

Henry glanced down at the papers scattered across his table. They were covered in notes, diagrams and equations over the years."I'm creating a serum. I've been working on a chemical formula. It's supposed to alter the... properties of one's very mind. If I get it right, I believe it can become the solution to a number of medical ailments. However, this version of the formula is a little unpredictable. My studies show that the human mind appears to exist in two discrete forms, as if two people reside within one body. The 'good Self' - striving for noble values and virtues, while the 'bad Self' yearns for primal instincts that bind us to this Earth. They are in a constant struggle, locked together in a cycle of repression and regret. However, if we were to free them from each other, imagine the freedom the freedom it could bring, especially for people struggling with addictions or certain mental conditions like melancholia or sociopathy, where we don't need to rely on asylums to deal with people who are deemed mad for no reason, but rather make a proper effort to help them." Henry snapped out of his rambling as he suddenly realized he had spent rather a lot of time talking about his project. A slight shade of pink tinted his cheeks as he hastily collected his notes and arranged them on the table, in an attempt to tidy up the disordered papers. A sheepish smile played on his lips as he tried to divert the conversation. "But it is rather complicated... so it might take some time until it's fully developed...." Henry chuckled, glancing over at Alice. "You probably think I'm insane, rambling on about such things." He took a sip of tea, looking out the window.

Alice chuckled lightly. "I don't think you're insane. A bit mad perhaps, but definitely not insane," she said in a lighthearted tone. She took a sip of her own tea, letting the warm liquid wash over her tongue. Her eyes glanced over the sheets of paper before shifting her focus back onto Henry. "But tell me, if this formula turns out to be what you think it is, what then?" she asked.

Henry leaned back in his chair, taking a moment to gather his thoughts. "Well," he began, running a hand through his hair again. "If it indeed has the potential to do what I believe it can, the applications could be enormous..." His gaze returned to the papers on his desk as he continued to explain. "Imagine being able to help people with addiction, dementia, praecox... or even just those struggling with inner battles..." He looked up to meet her gaze, his expression serious. "But you understand, don't you?"

Alice listened intently, seeing the passion on his face, the determination that burned within him. "I understand. I think it's brilliant," she said softly, a hint of awe in her voice. "How did you ever come up with the theory?" she inquired curiously.

Henry smiled, appreciating her genuine interest. "I started thinking about it when I was younger, but a few years back, I found my grandfather's research books, and..." He paused, considering how much he should really reveal. Then he continued. "And... Well, let's just say I've had my reasons... .In my grandfather's research on alchemy, he talked about how they'd try to purify lead into gold, the same idea of purity in a human soul. And I thought if I could isolate and control those parts, it might... help people become a better person."

She tilted her head, she could tell that he was holding something back, but she couldn't understand what it was. She spoke, her voice still soft but laced with a cautious note. "People?"

He tried to keep his tone casual as he answered, shrugging it off with a slight smile, "Yeah." He returned his gaze down to his paper, trying to focus on the formulas and equations, anything to distract from the questions he knew she wanted to ask.

She observed his gaze darting back to the papers on his desk and knew he was trying to distract himself. "Henry," she said softly, her voice breaking through the silence. She reached out and gently placed her hand atop one of his, which rested on the table. "For what it's worth, I think you're brilliant."

Henry's gaze flicked up briefly at her touch, surprised by the sudden contact. He looked up into her eyes, her sincere compliment taking him a moment to process. "Alice..." he started, his voice trailing off, caught off-guard by her support. "...Thank you. I appreciate that." He could feel his defenses slipping for a moment as her kind words washed over him. But he quickly regained his composure, gently slipping his hand out from under hers and returning his focus back to the papers in front of him.

Alice withdrew her hand, trying not to feel too disappointed by his withdrawal. She knew he was trying to keep his walls firmly in place, but she could see glimpses behind the cracks. She continued to watch him, studying his expressions closely. She knew that he was struggling with something, something he wasn't ready to share, and she respected that. But at the same time, she couldn't help but feel a pang of desire to know more about him.

With a soft smile, she got up from the edge of the table and settled herself comfortably on the chair beside him. With a casual motion, she leaned her head against his shoulder, letting out a soft sigh of contentment.

Henry's heart skipped a beat when he felt Alice's head against his shoulder. He froze for a moment, feeling the warmth and closeness of her touch. He hadn't expected her to get so close, to invade his personal space in this way. It caught him off guard, making his carefully constructed defenses falter for a brief moment. For a second, he considered pulling away, as he had done before. But the comfort of her presence and the pleasant scent of her hair made him hesitate. The unexpected closeness somehow felt nice, warm… familiar…. As the two of them sat there, Alice's head leaning against his shoulder and the rain continuing to gently patter against the windows, a sense of peace washed over Henry. The usual distractions and anxieties that plagued his mind seemed to fade into the background, replaced by a calmness he hadn't felt in a long time. The rain created a soothing ambiance, the soft rhythmic sound like a natural lullaby. The air was filled with an aura of comfort and closeness. Henry found himself relaxing more and more into the moment, letting out a soft exhale as he allowed himself to bask in the quiet intimacy between them, if only for a moment.

Chapter 06

Keep Away.

February 19th 1886~ The streets were filled with people, carriages, and the constant sound of horse hooves on cobblestone. Spring had come and gone as quickly as the trains from London reach Switzerland, and the two had become inseparable. Alice had kept her feelings for Henry a secret, knowing it was best that way.

Henry had been working on his serum in his laboratory. The testing phase was almost complete, and the tension in the air was palpable. Henry was clearly stressed about his serum. He is wearing a light-colored button-down dress shirt underneath a dark reddish-brown waistcoat. A burgundy maroon silk cravat knotted around his neck, and black pants, quite the signature look for him, really.

Alice could see the frustration on his face as she walked into his study. She stood next to him, placing her hand on his shoulder. The room was filled with the smell of burning candles, whatever ingredients he was using, and the faint sound of carriages passing by outside. There was a tense moment before Alice spoke softly, breaking the silence, "Henry, how about we take a break? You look exhausted."

He snaps out of his trance and rubs his eyes. His clothes were rumpled, as if he'd been wearing them for days, and his eyes seemed bloodshot and tired. The once neat workspace was now scattered with papers and notes, the result of sleepless nights spent working. He had paper upon paper all over his desk. He never left his room; it was as if the frustration of his work reeked in the air. His hair was a mess, and his anxiety was at an all-time high. He never liked to admit that he was overworking, let alone that when he did, his mind was all over the place. He sighs, looking at the vials of his latest experiment. He took his pen and wrote in his journal.

She tried to take his notes from him, but he pulled them away from her, looking determined.

"Alice. This could be my best work yet. I need to try one more time. Once I have succeeded, I can afford some proper rest, and I will spend all my time with you, I promise," he said with a hint of desperation in his voice.

"I'd rather never leave the threshold again than see you look like this. Stop working. Or else," she said firmly, crossing her arms.

He looks at her, a hint of humor in his eyes. "Oh, really?" He laughs in a tired way.

She smirks and continues, "Are you really wagering your entire life on this? You think I won't?".

Henry rolled his eyes, "Yes. Absolutely. You wouldn't dare!"

She takes his glasses and walks out of his study room door, dangling them in front of him.

He just stands there, a little shell-shocked. It doesn't even occur to him to get up and chase her. He just sits there for a moment, then sighs, chuckles, and finally gets up to run after her. "Hey! Give me back my glasses this instant!" he calls out as he chases after her.

"Oh no, you don't," she says with a mischievous smile, putting his glasses on her face and stealing his laboratory keys. She quickly locks the door and smiles triumphantly. He tried to pull open the door, turning to her. "Alice! You can't just steal my laboratory like this! Come on, I need to make more of this serum, I'm on the brink of discovery!"

"You're on the brink of working yourself to death. You'll get your keys back, and I promise they'll be fine. Now, off we go," she says, taking his hand and leading him past the yard, up the stairs and to his room. He follows her without protest, though he doesn't look happy at all. When they arrive at his room, he flops down onto his bed, groaning. "This is for your own good, Henry Jekyll," she says with a giggle, handing him a towel and starting to run a warm bath for him.

He sits patiently as she prepares the bath for him. His exhaustion really shows, and he has a hard time keeping his eyes open. He lets out a quiet groan before asking, "Can I really not go back to the lab?"

She shakes her head with a smile, taking his hand to lead him to the bath, "Nope. And don't think I've never swallowed a key before." She turns around so he can undress.

He sighed and started to undress, untying his cravat, taking off his vest, unbuttoning his waistcoat, and lastly, sliding off his pants and throwing them into a pile. "Okay, fine, you win. If there's one thing you're better than me at, it's being stubborn. And stealing things..." he says with a tired smile.

She giggles and responds, "I'm not stubborn, I'm a lunatic. But you, my dear friend, are the stubborn one."

He rolls his eyes playfully before sighing and stepping into the warm bath, feeling the hot water wash away the stress and tension from his body. The luxurious bathroom is filled with steam, creating a relaxing atmosphere. "Alright, Alice, you win. I'll stay in the bath for as long as you want if that means I can have my keys back. No more experiments until I'm fully rested, I promise." He yawns and leans his head back on the rim of the tub, closing his eyes for a moment before sitting up to look at Alice. "And you, my dear, deserve some rest too. What have you been up to while I was working?"

She pauses for a moment, thinking. "Mostly reading and doing chores...I must admit, I miss reading with you. Oh, and I caught Poole cheating as Lansquenet."

He raises an eyebrow. "Cheating? He's just using a legitimate strategy," he chuckles. He leans back into the tub, feeling the tension in his muscles slowly melting away. "I've missed you too, Alice. I've been so consumed with my serum that I haven't had much time for anything else. I should be grateful you've brought in my meals, otherwise I might have starved." Jekyll's voice sounds warm and gentle, his hazel eyes shining with affection.

She sits on the edge of the tub, pouring in a bit of lavender oil until the water turns a light purple color. "I won't stop trying to get you to rest."

He lets out a content sigh, feeling the lavender on his skin. He sits up again, rubbing his eyes and feeling exhausted. "I know. But trust me, I'm almost there. Just a few more tests, and then it will all be worth it. The solution to all my problems, and everyone else's." He takes a deep breath before looking at her with a tired smile.

She puts the bottle down and sighs. "Henry, it's been five days since you've had a proper rest. I'm starting to wonder if you even remember what a bed looks like."

His face softens as he looks at her, feeling her genuine concern. He nods and sighs, running his hand through his hair. "I understand, Alice. But you must believe me, I'm so close to success, and then I can rest."

She looks away for a moment, her worry evident on her face. "After tonight, you can do whatever you want with your serum. I just want you to be okay...I can't help but worry."

A look of pure relief washes over him as he hears her words, his shoulders relaxing. He smiles softly and reaches out to hold her hand, giving it a gentle squeeze for reassurance. "Thank you, Alice. I promise you, after tonight, I'll make sure to get plenty of rest. This won't happen again. I'll go straight to bed, and I won't leave for at least 3 days. And I will be okay, my dear. I promise you. This is the last few tests, and then we can finally leave all this mess behind and spend our days in London, just the two of us."

She smiles as he holds her hand, feeling content. She adored him more than words could express, knowing he was going to take it ease was a relief. "I'll hold you to that promise." She gets up and leaves him to relax in the bath.

He leans back, feeling his eyes grow heavy and his limbs feel weak. He closes his eyes, allowing himself to fully embrace the rest he so desperately needed. Henry nods and takes a deep breath, the water and lavender oil relaxing him, causing his muscles to melt away. He sighs and opens his eyes before looking for Alice. She's gone. He sighs and tries to stand, but he still feels weak from so many days of sleep deprivation. "Perhaps she's right..." He mutters under his breath before sinking back into the bathtub. He closes his eyes and tries to relax for at least a few hours.

After a while, Henry begins stirring as he finally becomes too restless to stay still any longer. He gets out of the bathtub and puts on the pajamas that were carefully laid for him. Henry on the neatly made bed in his room. . When he goes back to his room, he finds that the room was decorated in a traditional Victorian style, with rich burgundy curtains and a plush carpet. The crisp white sheets were adorned with delicate lace trimmings, and a tray with a steaming pot of tea and a plate of snickerdoodles sat on the nightstand. The sweet aroma of the cookies filled the room, mixed with the soft floral scent of the fresh flowers arranged in a vase on the dresser. Alice sat on the bed, her pajamas keeping her warm in the chilly London air. She absentmindedly twirled the key to Henry's laboratory in her hand, almost teasingly, as she lost herself in her book. Henry Jekyll was surprised to see how beautifully Alice had decorated his room, and a sense of calm washed over him as he sat down beside her on the bed.

His eyes were drawn to the key in her hand, and he couldn't help but feel a flutter of excitement at the thought of finally being able to continue his experiments. "You're going to drive me mad, you know," Henry said with a teasing grin, his heart racing at the sight of the key.

Alice simply smiled and closed her book, teasing him back. "Good, you'd make a great lunatic."

Henry chuckled and playfully nudged her. "I'm already halfway there." He said teasingly before leaning back with a sigh and pulling her close. "But I suppose I'll make do with the little lunatic I already have." He was already halfway to insanity with his work, but he couldn't help but feel grateful for the little bit of craziness that Alice brought into his life.

As he reached for the key, Alice pulled it away with a mischievous glint in her eye. "Not so fast! I will tickle you if you try that again… now go eat your cookies, drink your tea, and just enjoy a night without your work." Henry groaned but couldn't help but smile at her playfulness. He made a few more attempts to grab the key, each time being foiled by Alice's quick reflexes. Eventually, he gave up and reached for a snickerdoodle instead.

"I'm not letting you into your lab, but I will enable you to have your notes. Hopefully, looking at them with a freshened mind shall bring a new light," Alice said, handing him one of his notebooks.

Henry's face softened as he looked at her, feeling grateful for her thoughtfulness. "Thank you, Alice. But you're still an evil woman." Alice giggled and leaned her head on his shoulder. Henry leaned his head against hers, feeling content and warm in her presence. "You know, if I didn't know any better, I'd think you wanted to spend time with me, and that's why you're holding me hostage." Henry teased, his voice soft and playful as he reached for another cookie.

Alice thought for a moment before standing up. "I should probably go and let you sleep. I shouldn't be in here with you anyways."

Henry's face fell, and he quickly grabbed her hand to stop her. "Please... stay.. just for a little." He didn't know what came over him, but he didn't want her to go.

Alice smiled softly, placing the key in her pocket before sitting back on the edge of the bed. "Just for a little while."

Henry smiled gratefully and wrapped his arm around her, pulling her close, and they both stayed in bed, earthen rest of the snickerdoodles.

Chapter 07

Wonders That Flabbergast the Noggin.

The next morning, the sun shone through the curtains of the room, slowly illuminating the room and the face of Henry Jekyll. He had been sleeping well despite his exhaustion, but he still looked somewhat tired, his eyes half open. His lab journal was closed. The last page he'd written on was dated for the previous night. He fixed his glasses and sat up till he noticed a hand under his. He remained still in bed, looking over to his side. Alice had passed out last night before she left Henry's room. She was snuggled close, smiling in her dreams. It was a refreshing sight that her nightmares of the asylum were fading away. Henry looked at her for a moment as she slept, taking in the sight of her peaceful face, brushing the hair away with his fingers. He looked away with a bit of a bittersweet smile before rolling out of bed and stretching slowly. Henry then got dressed and went to the kitchen to get food before he went down to his lab to start preparing his notes from the previous day's experiment. But Henry forgot Alice was holding him hostage, so he could rest, she still has the key to his laboratory in her back pocket. He didn't want to wake up Alice, so he decided to get some work done with what he had available. He took out the notebook and went to the living room, deciding to read more into his research to make this day somewhat productive. There was something he was missing, and he had to find it out, or otherwise, the serum he had been working on for almost 3 years would have been all for nothing.

Alice woke up, realizing she had fallen asleep in Jekyll's room on his bed. She blushed immensely and got out of bed. She went down to the kitchen and noticed Henry was eating breakfast with Poole cooking. "Morning."

Henry glanced up as he sat, sipping his coffee. His eyes widened when he saw Alice, and his cheeks flushed, embarrassed as he saw her still in her pajamas, her hair messy from sleeping as she rubbed her eyes with her hand. "Morning, sleepy head," he said softly, trying to mask his embarrassment with a smile.

Poole went to go grab the newspaper, as a letter came in. The letter was sealed at every corner, handwritten and addressed to Dr. Henry Louis Jekyll. "My God. MASTER!" Poole ran back to the kitchen.

Alice had never seen Poole act like this; she and Henry were intrigued. "What is it Poole? You finally got that autograph from Sherlock?" Henry teased.

Poole's usual calm demeanor was thrown to the wayside, his eyes filled with a mix of worry and excitement. "No sir, but I think you'll be very interested in this; it's from Sir Danvers Carew."

Henry's head shot up from the letter "Of Parliament!". He immediately opens the letter. Alice watched the two men, having no idea who they were talking about, which often happens. Henry's eyes widen as he reads through the letter, and he slowly reads it a second time to make sure that he wasn't hallucinating. "I have been invited to discuss my work at Sir Danvers... My God, it's really happening." The news of his work being accepted made him so happy that he was speechless, and he looked towards Alice with a bright smile. "See, this is why I've been working so hard these past years! This is truly the opportunity of a lifetime!"

Alice pauses for a moment with her eyes widened. "So, this means-"

Henry nods enthusiastically, clearly excited. "Yes! It means I will present the results of my research to one of the most prominent and richest men in Britain. Sir Danvers has been funding experiments and projects of interest to him. If I can show him my serum, I could potentially have this used as an actual medicine. This is the kind of opportunity I've been waiting for my whole life. To present my research, my serum, to society, and prove my intelligence, this is a dream come true!"

Alice smiles, "Oh Henry, Congratulations!!" She hugs Henry tightly.

Henry can't help but embrace her tightly, holding her close with a grin on his face. When he speaks again, it's much more enthusiastic. "Thank you, I really couldn't have done it without you. You've kept me sane these past few days. It's only right that I share this good news with you. And I promise to share more soon. But first, I must get to work. There's a lot I need to do today, so if you could return my lab key, I'd be much appreciated."

She giggles, reaching into her pocket and taking the key out. "Now, I hope you learned your lesson, an t-eòlaiche cuthach agam."

'My mad scientists' .... Since when did she learn Scottish? She'd just called him her mad scientist in Scottish Gaelic, and Henry couldn't help but feel his cheeks growing hot. But he tried to brush it off and cleared his throat, trying to ignore her teasing. Henry laughs as he gently takes the key back from her. "Yes, yes. I'll get more sleep." He pauses when she giggles, his lips curling into a teasing smile as he speaks. "It's an awfully cute sound you make. You know that?".

She shook her head, trying not to blush. "Go back to your lab, will you! Jeepers."

Henry smiles again, still not trying to deny her teasing, and nods his head. "I understand, off to my lab it is then. I promise to talk to you later, okay?" Henry takes a quick sip of his morning tea before leaving the table. He gives her a hug, "Thank you, Alice, truly."

She hugs him back, and she couldn't resist a shy smile, the corners of her mouth curling up. "Of course, Henry. I'm just glad I could help.." She steps back reluctantly, her gaze lingering on him as he goes to collect his work materials. "Now, I wish you luck. I'll bring in some tea later this evening."

Henry smiles warmly as he glances at her way, his eyes sparkling when the light touches her face. "I'd appreciate that, as always." He smiles softly and gives her another small hug. He chuckles softly as he pulls away from her. He's confident that his presentation will finally be able to gain him the praise and recognition he's been striving for all this time.

February 26th~ Henry and Alice were in the laboratory, standing in front of a table Henry stood beside Alice in front of the table covered in vials, beakers, and a leather-bound journal. The table was unorganized, with each ingredient and tool in a bit of disarray, yet somehow easy for him to find. A faint smell of chemicals filled the air, and some of the vials contained colorful liquids that glimmered in the light. Henry leaned over the serum, put in 2 more drops of a red tincture into the foggy gray liquid, turning it into a bright red color. He then took a small scoop from a box of salt-like powders. He looked over at Alice, his gaze lingering on her face for a moment. He took a deep breath, collecting his thoughts before speaking. "Here goes nothing." With a hint of trepidation and excitement, he carefully added the final powder, stirred it twice clockwise and once anticlockwise to avoid bubbles, then stepped back, pulling Alice with him. As the mixture began to transform, from violet, to a dark purple, to a shimmering blood orange liquid, as smoke started to rise from the beaker, and the vapor swirled in a mesmerizing dance. "By God," he whispered, his voice filled with awe. "It worked…yes… Yes! YES, IT WORKED!"

Henry's excitement was palpable as he hugged Alice, lifting her up and spinning her around, a broad smile on his face. As Henry spun her around, the excitement in the air was palpable. He set her down gently, his hands still lingering on her waist. Henry couldn't help but smile, his eyes glinting with joy as he looked at her. Seeing her so happy made him feel a rush of emotions. "Can you believe it?" he said, breathless with excitement. "We did it! We actually did it!"

Alice's cheeks turned a shade of pink, taken aback by his excitement. Her heart raced as his hands lingered on her waist, a mix of joy and surprise at his actions. She couldn't help but smile at his words and the contagious energy in the air. "You're the one who did it!" she replied, breathless. She laughed softly, her eyes filled with wonder and amazement. "It's incredible, Henry. Truly incredible…"

He let out a sigh of relief and excitement, his grip on her waist tightening ever so slightly. He looked at her, their faces just a few inches apart now. At that moment, it felt like the world was theirs. "We did it together," he corrected her, his voice low and soft. "It wouldn't have been possible without your help. I couldn't have done it without you."

She couldn't help but let out a soft laugh of disbelief. "I was just there," she replied, feeling a flutter of nerves in her stomach. "You were the one creating it and figuring out its formula. I was just there." She trailed off, her cheeks flushed."

Henry let out a soft chuckle, his eyes never leaving hers. "You did more than just being there, Alice," he said softly. "You supported me, encouraged me, and believed in me. That means more to me than you know." He paused for a moment, his fingers tracing small patterns on her waist as he held her close. In an instant, Henry realized what he was doing and abruptly let go, an awkward moment passing between them. He quickly averted his gaze and gripped the pen tightly in his right, scribbling down the details of the experiment in his journal, trying to compose himself. The room grew quiet, filled only with the sound of his pen scratching against paper. As Henry diligently wrote in his journal, his handwriting was somewhat inconsistent, as he had been forced to learn how to write with his right hand instead of his natural left as a child. Still, despite the discomfort and slight awkward movements, his notes were carefully recorded.

Alice's eyes lingered on his right hand, noticing the uncomfortable and awkward movements he made while writing. She couldn't help but feel a pang of sympathy for him, but she didn't know what to say. Instead, she chose to focus on the serum itself. She spoke up, trying to lighten the mood. "You know, "I'm sure Sir Danvers will be thrilled with the serum."

Alice's words brought Henry back to reality. Was his serum really good enough to present to an influential man like Sir Danvers Carew? He set down his pen and rubbed his eyes, his shoulders sagging. "I sure hope so," replied Henry without lifting his gaze from the journal. No doubt that Sir Danvers will have a slew of scientists in the society pick his theory apart with a fine-tooth comb, this project he had been passionately working on for years. He hesitated for a moment, looking down at the serum that they had created, now resting innocently in its beaker.

She took a small step closer to him, trying to offer some reassurance. "You should be proud of your achievement," she said with a soft smile.

"And remember, Sir Danvers invited you. That alone shows that they're interested in your work." She paused for a moment, and her gaze remained fixed on him, trying to gauge his reaction.

Henry's heart fluttered a little as Alice stepped closer, her words of reassurance soothing him if only a little. He wanted to take comfort in her words, but he found himself unable to stop doubting himself. His face contorted in a mixture of frustration and determination. "Well, I suppose you're right. Still..." He trailed off, setting down the pen, finally looking up to meet her eyes. "I can't afford any mistakes." He ran his fingers through his hair, already trying to plan out the entire night in his head, despite it being days away. As he rose from his seat, Henry began to gather his belongings, his eyes darting toward his open pocket watch on the table. "I have to start preparing. There's so much to do..." He left the laboratory, a slight sense of urgency in his steps. Back in his room, Henry started to go over a mental checklist in his head. He opened his wardrobe and sifted through various articles of clothing, each meticulously selected for the upcoming event.

Alice followed Henry to his room, her gaze fixed on him as he opened his wardrobe. She leaned against the doorframe, watching as his fingers gently tracing over each garment, contemplating each one.

As Henry continued sorting through his wardrobe, he stopped at a brownish suit with a soft red hue, a color he rather enjoyed wearing. He ran his fingers over the soft fabric of the jacket, feeling the smoothness and admiring the craftsmanship. He then held it up against himself, examining its fit. He turned to Alice, still standing in the doorway. "What do you think?" he asked, his voice tinged with uncertainty. "Should I wear this for the presentation? Or perhaps I should go with the deep blue."

Alice tilted her head slightly, studying the suit and how it looked against his frame. It was a lovely color, she thought, and it complemented his frame. "I think it looks lovely," she replied, her voice soft. "It's classic and elegant. Plus, the color brings out your eyes. It'll be perfect for the presentation."

Henry smiled, feeling a sense of relief wash over him. "You think so?" he asked, his tone a little more confident now. He took her word seriously, knowing that her opinion meant a lot to him. He turned around, looking into the mirror, then back at her. "Well, this is it then."

He ran his fingers through his hair, making sure the stray hairs were in the right place. "I suppose I just wanted to look my best for Sir Danvers. After all, if I want to impress him, I need to look the part."

Alice smiled back, her gaze softening. "You'll definitely impress him," she said confidently. "You don't need the extravagant suit or anything flashy. You're intelligent, passionate, and capable, and that's what truly matters. And besides, you look great in anything you wear." She paused for a moment, watching him adjust his hair in the mirror. Her heart ached a little, wishing she could reach out and brush his hair back for him. "Just be yourself, Henry. That's what Sir Danvers will find impressive."

Henry's smile faded, replaced by a worried expression. Despite her reassurance, he couldn't help but feel the weight of the impending presentation on his shoulders. He continued to adjust his hair, smoothing out any stray strands. Alice's words echoed in his mind, yet he found it hard to focus on them. The pressure of the event was overwhelming, and he felt as if he had to prepare every last detail. "Yes, yes..." he said absentmindedly, his attention still elsewhere. He looked in the mirror for a few more minutes, fiddling with his hair and adjusting his shirt. "Do you think I should try a different tie?"

Alice, seeing him lost in thought, decided to take a step closer. She gently took his maroon cravat from the dresser and approached him from behind. "Let me," she said softly. Her nimble fingers deftly untied the current one and wrapped the maroon one around his neck. Her hands lingered for a moment, adjusting the knot.

Henry felt her fingertips lightly brush against his neck as she adjusted the knot. The touch was soft and delicate, sending a slight shiver down his spine. He looked at her through the reflection in the mirror, a mix of emotions clouding his features. After she finished adjusting the tie, he finally spoke. "Thank you, Alice," he murmured, his voice barely above a whisper.

As her fingers lingered, she hesitantly spoke up. "Henry-" Her voice was soft. "Promise me something, will you? Promise to tell me about it? About the presentation, what happens... What's it like?" She finished adjusting his cravat and looked up into his eyes.

Henry's thoughts were interrupted when he realized that Alice wasn't joining him in the upcoming events. He felt a pang of selfishness, realizing how unfair it was to leave her out. She had been by his side through it all, supporting him and encouraging him. And now, he was leaving her behind. He couldn't shake the feeling of unease that settled in his stomach. He looked at her, his eyes filled with a mix of guilt and longing. "Alice. I- I want you to be there. I want…" He trailed off and let out a frustrated sigh, unable to find the right words. "It won't be the same without you… I can't imagine not sharing it with you. How could I? You're my… my…well, to be frank- and literal- my closest friend."

Alice's expression softened, her heart fluttering at his words, and a small smile played on her lips. "I'd love to be there, more than anything. But…you know I can't. I'm an escaped lunatic, remember?" She let out a small chuckle, trying to deflect the weight of the situation.

He knew she was right, but the thought of going without her felt… wrong. "I know, I know," he said, his voice tinged with frustration. "But… It's been over a year. And besides, we've been out before, remember? We went to Whitby Harbor, to Regents Park… you were safe, nobody recognised you."

"I-I suppose you have a point…" She bit her lip, considering his words. "But those were different. We were just going to the park and the harbor. This gala, it's different, isn't it? A gathering of important people, and… Sir Danvers. I mean… I'm not suitable."

Henry stepped closer to her, his eyes locked on hers. "Suitable?" he said, his voice growing a bit firmer. "What do you mean, suitable? You're just as well-spoken and intelligent as any of those people. In fact, I'd say you're infinitely more interesting than any of them could ever be." He paused for a moment before adding in a slightly quieter but no less intense tone: "And what's more, I want you there."

Her resistance crumbled. She sighed, "Oh…you're impossible, Henry. You know that? Fine. I'll go. But don't you dare think I'm not cursing you in my head right now." She joked.

A small, victorious smile appeared on Henry's face, he knew he was being pushy, but it was worth it. "Oh, I wouldn't expect anything less from you, my darling Alice," he said, his tone soft and teasing. "And trust me," he added with a smirk, "I'll willingly bear the brunt of your curses if it means having you by my side that night."

March 27th~ It's the night of Henry Jekyll's presentation at the gala of Sir Danvers. Henry wears his suit and cravat, with a red rosebud in his lapel, his hair slicked back and his glasses on his face. The door is cracked open, and he's standing outside, waiting for Alice to come downstairs. Alice was asleep on top of a pile of laundry, still in a regular, simple day dress. Henry smiles as he walks in through the door and takes note of how peaceful she looks sleeping, as if she has no worries in the world.

He tries to stay silent as he goes over to the bed to gently wake her. Alice's eyes flutter open, she looks around for a moment before her eyes meet Henry's. "Oh, hello…"

He chuckles." Why hello, my dear." Henry smiles softly at her as he takes her hands. "Are you ready for tonight's gala?"

Alice slowly sits up, rubbing her eyes "Tonight's gala…. Oh, right." A small smile spreads across her face as the memories come back to her. She looks up and down at him. "You look very nice tonight, Henry."

Henry smiles warmly at her compliment, his cheeks flushing slightly at her gaze. He straightens his tie, making sure it's perfect. "Thank you, Alice. You're too kind." He takes a moment to take her in, noticing that she's not yet dressed. "Speaking of getting ready… We have time for you to dress. Come now…" He helps Alice stand up and gets her to walk towards the bathroom.

As Henry led her towards the bathroom, Alice tried to pull away, her eyebrows furrowed in confusion. "What are we doing? I'm already dressed," she protested, looking down at her simple dress. "I don't need to change."

Henry chuckled softly as Alice protested, his grip on her arm gentle but firm as he continued leading her towards the bathroom. "Darling, I mean no disrespect, but I'm afraid your current attire wouldn't be appropriate for the event tonight."

She tilts her head, shaking it. "I don't know Henry, maybe I should just- ".

Henry doesn't wait for her to complete her sentence, as he pulls her into the bathroom. Henry leaves Alice in the bathroom, instructing her to brush her hair as he makes his way into her bedroom. He quickly scans the room, realizing that her wardrobe is severely lacking in the evening gown department. However, he spots a relatively suitable dress in the back of the closet, hidden away among her regular clothes. With a satisfied sigh, he grabs the dress and a corset and returns to the bathroom, where he finds Alice busily fixing her hair in the mirror. He gently taps her on the shoulder, holding out the dress in his hands. A beautiful white dress, a dark blue lacing across the bodice, with Daffodils and Carnations stitched along the bottom fabric in a vining indigo. "I'm not leaving without making you look just as beautiful as you are on the inside, darling."

She turned her gaze to Henry, feeling a mix of flattery and frustration. Despite her initial reluctance, Alice could not deny the sheer beauty of the dress. As she looked at the intricate design and soft material, she couldn't help but feel a growing sense of excitement. She ran her fingers across the delicate fabric and looked at the stitching. "This.... It's beautiful." She turned and looked at Henry, a sly smirk on her face. "This is payback for me stealing your lab key, isn't it?"

Henry chuckled, seeing her reaction, feeling a slight sense of satisfaction that he had picked something she would like. As he leaned against the wall, he couldn't help but appreciate the way the dress hugged her curves and accentuated her features. A sly smile played on his lips. He shook his head, pretending to be innocent. "Now Alice, you know me better than that," he said, his tone playful. "I am many things, but I'm certainly not petty. I just wanted to make sure you looked your best tonight."

As Alice looked in the mirror, she began to feel a bit self-conscious and uncomfortable in the beautiful dress. Despite how stunning she looked in the lovely dress, she couldn't help but feel a sense of guilt and unease. "Seriously Henry, I'm fine. I don't need to be pampered," she protested.

"Darling..." Henry sighs, placing a hand on her shoulder. "You've spent your life hiding. This is your chance to finally be the one to get attention, to get compliments, to be admired. You deserve this chance. If not for your own happiness, then for me.... Of course, you don't need pampering. But I want to give it to you, because you deserve it. So, I ask you kindly, please allow me to pamper you, if only for one night…"

He was right; she had spent most of her life in the shadows, never being able to shine and truly be seen. And she could see the sincerity in his eyes, the genuine desire to make her feel special. She sighed, her resolve weakening as she looked in the mirror once more. "… But I'm just not… pretty enough… and they'll see that no matter what I'm in."

He pulls her close as he helps her tighten the back of the navy-blue corset gently, and fluffs out her hair. "My dear…You are extremely pretty. I've seen you at the worst of times and the best. Even at your worst, you are beautiful." Henry smiles softly and pulls a silver pendant on a chain, in the middle was a Peridot stone in the shape of a teardrop, from his pocket, and clipped it around her neck, taking her hands in his and caressing them. He turned her to face the mirror. "Now… look in the mirror. Tell me what you see, darling."

Alice looked into the mirror, her reflection staring back at her. She couldn't help but admire how different she looked; her eyes shimmered in the flickering light of the bathroom. She let out a soft sigh, feeling a mix of disbelief and admiration. "I look… like Alice…" she said, her voice barely above a whisper.

Henry smiles softly, putting his forehead against hers and looking at her in the mirror. "Yes, dear… that's the beautiful person that I see before me. The person I feel so incredibly proud to call my friend… She may not know it, but she's strong. She's the definition of perseverance, and you've earned this."

Her eyes are slightly red-rimmed as he pulls away, giving her hands a squeeze. She looks down at the floor. "… I might not say it enough, but I truly am grateful for everything you've done and sacrificed for me… thank you so much, Henry Jekyll." Alice smiles, hugging him tightly.

Henry doesn't say anything at first, enjoying the hug. It's an incredibly simple thing, but it means so much to him. He lets her hold him for a good while before pulling away, giving her hands a tight squeeze. "The pleasure is all mine. Now… let's make sure you don't get too nervous before that gala tonight. I want this night to be memorable for you." She smiles, nuzzling her forehead against his. She's so kind and gentle to him, in a way she doesn't fully comprehend. He feels something deep in him warm up whenever she acts like this, almost as if his entire body is smiling. But it's time to go. He breaks away from the hug, looking at her over again, making sure her outfit is perfect. "All set, darling? The carriage should be here to pick us up in twenty minutes." She nods, taking his hand in hers.

Chapter 08

The Carew Gala.

Henry had a habit of leaving his glasses on the stand next to the door whenever he left the house out in public. It was a routine action that he did almost unconsciously. He didn't even notice the slight look of puzzlement on Alice's face, befuddled, knowing fully that he needed them. As they left the house and climbed into the carriage, Henry smiled softly, taking her hand into his and squeezing it gently. It was lightly raining, the raindrops gently tapping against the windows of the carriage as it began to move, carrying them towards the gala. Throughout the journey, Henry remains close to her, their hands still interwoven. He watches her out of the corner of his eye, seeing how her eyes flicker around the carriage, taking in the experience. Finally, when the carriage reaches its destination, Henry helps her out of the carriage, and they walk towards the grand doors of the venue. The venue was elegant, with chandeliers glowing from the ceiling and the walls covered in rich silks. Guest chatter fills the air, and the aroma of fine cuisine wafts through it. It's obvious that this is a gathering for high society; everyone dressed in their finest outfits. Henry keeps his hand gently placed on her back as he guides her through the crowd. Henry catches sight of a few old acquaintances of his throughout the room. Some greet him with a nod and smile, while some shoot curious glances in her direction. They are all used to seeing Henry alone.

Her eyes widen as she takes it all in, trying to appear nonchalant, but the excitement is evident on her face. She is clearly overwhelmed and out of place in the sea of rich, high-society folks. She can hear whispers and feel stares as they pass, and she clings a little bit tighter to Henry. She takes a moment to collect herself before speaking, "Everyone is staring at us," she whispers, her voice barely audible over the noise of the party. "I feel like I stick out like a sore thumb here."

"Don't worry Alice, it wasn't easy my first time either, but it's just how you approach it. Just smile, and act like you understand what they're talking about, and you'll survive."

Utterson and Lanyon had come to the gala, at least Alice knew 3 people here; she didn't interact with the other guests. Since she had met the two men, they had all grown to get used to her presence in Henry's life, even Utterson had gone on walks with Alice when he had the time, and Lanyon would every so often would ask Alice all sorts of things as he was still trying to understand her better, but Lanyon was very concerned about Henry and Alice's closeness. After a while, he takes Alice to sit with him at a sideline table away from the crowd. A waiter walked by and offered them a drink, Henry took two, handling Alice a glass of champagne. Alice sips her champagne, but she's never drank before, and spits it back out with a silly, disgusted look on her face.

Henry laughs, taking her glass from her. "You don't have to drink this, but it would be a shame not to see an adorable look like that again," he teased her.

Alice finds herself giggling softly, embarrassed that she can't keep her composure and act more refined like Henry and their friends are acting. "I beg your pardon! I was not aware that I was providing such amusement!" she said, with a teasing posh accent.

He looks at her with genuine admiration and appreciation and gently grabs her hand. "No need to beg my pardon, dear, you're adorable! I'm glad you're having a good time." His eyes are sparkling with a warmth she's never seen on his face before. "You are quite a character, Alice. An absolute enigma."

She smiled, looking out at the crowd and back to Henry. "So, are you ready to convince Sir Danvers? Nervous?" She tilts her head.

Henry raises an eyebrow and shrugs his shoulders. "I'm... quite nervous, yes, I'd be lying if I claimed otherwise. But I know my research is worthwhile, and he'll be willing if I can convince him to not be afraid of my work. He is a man of reason and logic, but also one quick to judge." He reaches into his pocket and pulls out his small black notebook that has a summarized version of his notes.

As Alice scans the crowd, her eyes land on the dance floor where couples are twirling and spinning around in time with the music. Her gaze lingers, a wistful look in her eyes. "Why don't you dance?" she asks, her voice soft. "Look, you're all dolled up. You look as handsome as always. It might help loosen you up a bit, ease your nerves."

He followed her gaze, and looked back at her, shaking his head as he chuckled dryly. "No, no. Besides, I have a feeling dancing is not exactly the image Sir Danvers would want to see."

Alice tilted her head, studying his face closely. She could see the nervousness in his gaze, masked by a veneer of casual indifference. "You're being silly," she said firmly. "Who cares if it isn't the image Sir Danvers wants? You don't have to be perfect in every single way. It's alright to have a little fun and let loose once in a while, you know."

Henry's expression softened as she called him out on his excuse. She was right, of course, and he knew it. He took a deep breath and let out an exaggerated sigh, feeling the tension in his shoulders. "Fine, you win." He said, rolling his eyes. "I suppose it wouldn't hurt to have a little fun. But don't blame me if I make a fool out of myself out there," he stood up and put his hand out.

She suddenly feels a rush of butterflies in her stomach, realizing she has no idea how to dance. She's never danced before, and she hesitates for a moment. She looks up at him, her cheeks flushed. "Wait, wait... I- I don't know how to dance," she stammers.

Henry's eyebrows shot up in surprise when she confessed that she didn't know how to dance. But then a small smirk appeared on his face, and he took a step closer to her, his voice teasing. "You don't know how to dance? Well, that's simply not acceptable." He took her hand, his touch both firm and gentle. "You can't expect me to dance alone, now, can you?"

Her gaze wandered towards the crowd. He noticed a middle-aged woman standing nearby. The woman was smiling politely, but Alice could sense her eagerness to dance. Taking advantage of the moment, she blurted out, "Of course, you need a partner!" Alice twirled Henry around, giving him a push.

He stumbled forward, nearly landing straight on the women, his face turning red in embarrassment. He quickly regained his composure and muttered an apology to the woman. "I…um, I-" He took a deep breath, his cheeks still red, and shot a glare at Alice. "I- uh..I'm so sorry about that-" he managed to sputter, his cheeks flushed.

The older woman, on the other hand, was clearly thrilled to have a young man's attention, and she beamed up at him. She leaned in, "It's quite alright, luv." She gave him a kind smile. "You look like you could use some practice, young man," she purred. "I must say, I didn't expect to be dancing with such a handsome young man tonight," she patted his cheek and moved his hand in position to dance. "That's it luv, don't be shy."

He was feeling increasingly embarrassed and flustered, and he couldn't help but give Alice a pleading look over his shoulder. "I…" He cleared his throat, trying to regain some composure. "Thank you, ma'am." He turned back to her and swallowed hard, trying to focus on the dance.

The older woman continued dancing with Henry, having the time of her life. She leaned her head on his shoulder, reminiscing about her past. "Oh, this reminds me of the first dance I had with my darling Albert. It was many years ago, at a grand ball in London. We were so young and in love." She let out a wistful sigh. After the dance had ended, the older woman smiled at Henry and leaned in, planting a kiss on his cheek. She patted his cheek and said, "You're such a good boy. You dance very well, young man."

Henry was taken aback by the sudden kiss on the cheek. He tried to hide his embarrassment behind a polite smile. He took a step back, trying to regain his composure. "Thank you, ma'am," he said, rubbing the back of his neck. "You flatter me."

She chuckled softly, clearly amused by his flustered demeanor. "Oh, don't be so modest, my dear. It's been a long time since I've danced with someone so charming. You remind me of my late husband, but he had glasses."

Henry's expression softened at her words. He could sense the sadness and longing in her voice. He knew all too well the pain of losing a loved one. "I... I'm sorry for your loss," he said gently.

The older woman offered a bittersweet smile, her eyes filled with nostalgia. "Thank you, dear. He was truly the love of my life. We had so many happy memories together." She sighed, then perked up. "But you have your entire life ahead of you. I hope you find love like I had. It's the most precious thing in the world... speaking of your little friend is waiting for you," she pointed to Alice.

Henry followed the woman's gesture, and his gaze landed on Alice. A small smile crept across his face as he saw her standing there, waiting for him. Despite the embarrassment and frustration, he felt earlier, he couldn't help but feel a sense of fondness for her. He nodded at the older woman, grateful for her advice. "Thank you, ma'am. I hope you have a splendid evening." And with that, he excused himself and walked back towards Alice, his expression a mix of flustered and fond.

She raised an eyebrow jokingly, a small smirk on her face. "You're quite the ladies' man, aren't ya?"

Henry rolled his eyes but couldn't help but smile at her comment. "Oh, ha ha. You think you're so funny, don't you?" he said, trying to sound annoyed, but failing to hide a small chuckle.

Alice laughed, her smile widening. She couldn't help but find his reaction amusing, and her eyes sparkled with mischief. "I do, indeed."

"You're enjoying this a little too much, aren't you?" He shot her a playful glare as he took her hands. "But let's see how you fare, shall we?"

Alice's amusement dissolved, replaced by uncertainty. "Wha- Me? Oh, no. no, no, no. No!" She shook her head, trying to back away, but Henry's grip on her hands kept her in place. "I- I don't dance. I don't know how to dance. I-"

Henry chuckled at her protests, his grip on her hands still firm. "Now, now, don't go backing out on me now. You're the one who decided to send me over to the older woman in the first place, remember?"

She looked up at Henry, her brown eyes filled with hesitation and slight fear. "Oh no, no, no. You know I'm a terrible dancer. I have the grace of a newborn zebra. It would be a tragedy to watch me try to dance. I'd end up stepping on your toes or worse, tripping over my own feet! I'm telling you, I'll embarrass you. I have two left feet, no sense of rhythm, and a complete lack of coordination"

Henry saw the hesitation in her eyes and knew he had to be careful with his approach. He softened his grip on her hands, gently rubbing her knuckles with his thumb in a reassuring gesture. "It's alright, darling. I won't let you make a fool out of yourself. Just follow my lead, okay?" He gently lifts her arm and pulls her into the ballroom.

Her heart raced, her palms sweaty and clammy as nervousness coursed through her. She took a deep breath, lifting her gaze back up to him, her eyes wide and filled with fear. She shook her head once more. "I-I… I don't think I can do this, Henry. I've never danced before, and I-"

Henry chuckles softly. "It's ok." He says a soft and gentle expression on his face as he smiles. "Just relax. It isn't so hard, just let your body move to the music, and follow me. All I need you to do is put your arm around on my shoulder, and the other hand in mine. I'll keep a steady hand on your waist, and I'll take it from there…" he dropped her hands and stood in front of her.

She looked up at him, her eyes widening in surprise. "You want me to do what!?"

He takes a step closer, his fingers gently brushing a strand of her hair from her face. "Alice Lumsley…" He begins, his voice soft and smooth, like silk. "…May I have this dance?"

She chewed on her lip, her heart pounding against her ribcage. She stared at his hand for a moment, feeling a rush of anxiety. She looked up at him, his comforting gaze giving her a sense of reassurance. She took a deep breath and took his awaiting hand.

Henry gently pulled her towards him, his hand still holding hers, as he gently placed his other hand on her waist, pulling her body closer to him. The music continued to play, filling the room with a slow and gentle rhythm. Without saying a word, Henry started leading her into a gentle waltz. His gaze stayed locked on hers.

As they moved in sync with the music, Alice felt herself slowly relaxing. Her body seemed to move effortlessly with his, her feet following the rhythm of his lead. She kept her gaze locked on his, feeling a sense of comfort and safety in his eyes. As they danced, Alice found herself opening up to Henry, "You know… back at the asylum, they had a small ball every other month. My friends, Mazy, Artem and Hazel, loved dancing, but I could never join them. My doctor… he…, would always take me for… tests." She paused, a sad expression on her face. Her eyes lowered, a tinge of guilt crossing her features. "I… I feel guilty for escaping without them. They were the only friends I had, and I left them behind. They encouraged me to escape, but I can't help but wonder if I should have tried to bring them with me."

Henry notices her guilt-stricken expression and sighs softly. "You know it's not your fault, right?" He says softly, looking down at her. Henry's tone is so gentle and caring, like he really does understand… and he just wants to see her smile again.

"I wish it was that simple," she admitted, her voice faltering. "Some days are easier than others… but having you here truly helps." Ignoring the whirlwind of emotions she had been suppressing was no longer a viable option; the weight of it all pressed heavily on her chest. But Henry, with his unwavering support, felt like a balm for her wounded heart.

Henry smiles softly as he sees her open a little more. She was brave to make herself so vulnerable like this. As Henry guides her, he leans slightly closer. "That's because you're finally free. But it also means that you can finally begin to heal… You're stronger than you know… you'll see it someday, Alice, just as I do." He adds softly, gently holding her close to him as they begin to move to the music.

She smiles at him, and in that instant, her sadness seems to dissolve, replaced by a surge of hope, thanks to him.

He twirls her around, delighting in the way her laughter fills the air, and pulls her back into his embrace. In the midst of the swirling crowd, their connection makes them feel like the only two people in the room, and it's a feeling that warms him. They move together, light as leaves caught in a gentle breeze, spinning off into a beautiful unknown. As Alice loses herself in the dance, Henry's hand glides softly along the small of her back, guiding her with care. The grand ballroom buzzes with energy, but to them, it fades into a soothing background hum, replaced by the quiet melody of their own hearts. Wrapped in each other's presence, it's as if the world outside has fallen away, leaving only the magic of their shared connection. She absentmindedly moved her arm around his neck and started playing with the ends of his hair. Henry chuckles softly as he feels her hand caress his hair. His expression is full of love and tenderness as he stares into her eyes as he leans slightly closer, like he's being pulled to her. She can practically feel his breath on her face. As he gets closer, she can feel their hearts beat in sync with one another.

But suddenly, a group of partygoers all burst into laughter, so loud that Henry was startled a bit, looking over. The group was filled with many wealthy and prominent people in society, that's when Henry caught sight of Sir Danvers Carew.

Alice followed Henry's gaze, and her smile brightened. "That's him!?"

Henry notices her expression lightning and chuckles softly. He brings her in close so that she can still see Sir Danvers, but without him being able to see her. "Yes, it is. That's him." His voice sounded tight.

She squeezed the crook of his arm. "Don't worry, you've got this, Henry," she looked at him with sincere admiration.

Henry glanced at Alice, her encouraging words giving him a final burst of determination. He took a deep breath, straightened his jacket, and composed himself. With a nod of acknowledgment, he turned away from Alice and made his way through the crowd, his eyes locked on Sir Danvers. Henry stood patiently waiting for the opportune moment to interject. After a few moments, Danvers excused himself from the previous conversation, and Henry seized the opportunity, extending his hand confidently. "Good evening, Sir Danvers," he greeted, his voice tinged with a hint of nerves.

Danvers looked up, his eyes not recognizing the man before him. "Good evening to you too," he replied politely. "Do I know you?"

He chuckled awkwardly as he shook his head and offered a friendly smile. "No, Sir Danvers, we've never been properly introduced," he clarified. "My name is Henry Jekyll. I was a medical student at Oxford University. The one you sent the invitation to about my research."

Danvers's eyes widened in realization. "Ah, I see. You're the son of George Jekyll. I apologize, my boy. Your father and I go way back. It's been a while since I've seen him." He turned to the people around him, a smile on his face. "Yes, that's right. This young man here is the son of George Jekyll, a brilliant engineer. I remember him from years ago when he was a young boy, already demonstrating impeccable manners." The people around them murmured, impressed by the connection. Danvers placed a hand on Henry's shoulder, gesturing toward the room. "Now, tell us all about this little project you have in store for us. Take notes, ladies and gentlemen." The crowd chucked as they formed a circle around them. Danvers patted Henry on the back, "Everyone is very eager to hear."

Henry's heart pounded in his chest as the attention shifted onto him. Speaking in front of groups wasn't exactly his strong suit. He nervously fidgeted with the cuff of his jacket, his eyes quickly darting around the room. The sound of clinking glasses and chatter filled his ears, creating a cacophony of noise that he wanted to shrink away from. He swallowed hard, plastering on a forced smile. "Of-of course," he stammered. "It's… it's a …um…" he paused, his voice trailing off, his heart pounding faster and faster.

Danvers raised an eyebrow. "Come on, my boy, speak up. We're all waiting eagerly to hear about your little experiment." The people around them exchanged glances and murmurs.

Henry's face flushed slightly. He took a shaky breath, his words stumbling. "M-my most recent experiments on duality have yielded remarkable p-progress," his eyes darting around the room, his heart pounding. "My findings suggest that within each individual, a profound duality exists, a constant battle between two sides of the soul," he explained, his words now flowing more freely. "Man, contrary to popular belief, is not truly one unified being, but rather a complex amalgamation of two distinct facets, perhaps even more…. I believe I have stumbled upon an extraordinary breakthrough. The ability to isolate the purest aspects of good, while exorcising the darkest forms of evil from within a person's soul. So if each individual could be relieved of their internal struggles, and separate the good and evil within them, life would be easier for some. The good would be allowed to flourish unburdened, free from the guilt of the evil that exists in each of us. No longer would the just be plagued by the actions of the unjust, and not only with that, but the evil within could go its separate way." The crowd fell silent. He pushed forward, trying to ignore the judgmental stares directed his way. "...The serum I developed -whilst untested, of course- could... usher in a new epoch of moral clarity," he continued, his voice wavering slightly. "But... it necessitates a willing subject.... for final validation..."

Silence blanketed the room after Henry finished speaking. The weight of his revelation hung heavily in the air. People exchanged puzzled glances, their expressions ranging from confusion to shock. He felt the eyes of the crowd boring into him, their stares searing through his very being.

Sir Danvers's eyes darkened considerably, a look of incredulity mixed with disdain crossing his features. "My dear god, have you truly lost your sanity?"

Henry's mind raced, trying to come up with a response. "Sir Danvers, I haven't lost my sanity. I assure you, my research is sound. The idea is... unorthodox, but-"

Danvers chuckled in mocking disbelief, a smile plastered on his face, though it only masked a thinly veiled judgment. "Ah, young man, the audacity! Have you been reading too many Gothic novels? This sounds more like something out of a penny dreadful than real science." He leaned in, his voice filled with an air of condescension. "My dear boy, you need to realize the unruliness in human nature is mere fantasy, something that should remain locked away in the realm of fiction. Let me impart some wisdom upon you. You clearly have been reading too many fanciful tales. The idea that there's some kind of primal darkness lurking within every person, just waiting to be unleashed, it's just absurd. Every single man, like every gentleman in this very room, is a good man. Our morality, our values, they're the very core of who we are. To suggest otherwise, it's just unfathomable blasphemy."

Henry's cheeks burned with shame and frustration. The condescending tone and the belittling remarks made it clear that his idea, which he had passionately poured his heart and soul into, was being dismissed as nothing more than wishful thinking, nothing more than the musings of an imaginative young boy. He tried to push back, to defend his theory, "Sir Danvers, you must understand, it's not just my belief. This idea resonates beyond fiction and fantasy. I've gathered substantial data, conducted extensive research-"

Danvers held up a hand to silence Henry, his expression hardening with a stern look. "Enough! The notion that there is some sort of wicked force coiled deep within each and every one of us is utterly ridiculous. It suggests that we are all at the mercy of some primal, uncontrollable aspect of ourselves. We're civilized gentlemen, my boy, a higher class of people. We possess the capacity for reason and rationality. To suggest that there's some dark shadow lurking in the recesses of our souls. It's absurd!"

Henry stares, frustration etched across his face as he grapples with the man's harshness. "Sir, I... I comprehend your distress. But I assure you, the potential benefits would prove my theory, if you would only allow me the opportunity-!!"

Danvers held a hand up again, his eyes narrowing at Henry's persisting insistence. His voice was firm and commanding, his authority unyielding. "I said, enough, you audacious charlatan! Your father would be greatly disappointed."

Henry's breath hitches in his throat, despair engulfing him as his aspirations crumble before this disdainful figure. He nods slowly, repressing the torrent of emotions swirling within, "I understand... Thank you for your past assistance. I-... I apologize for wasting your time... Thank you." He resolves fully on his heel.

Sir Danvers watches as Henry slowly walks away, looking defeated. A mix of pity and disappointment crosses his face. After a moment of contemplation, he turns to the guests in the room. "Let this be a lesson to us all," he calls out, his voice authoritative. "The line between scientific progress and moral responsibility is thin. We must tread carefully, lest we fall into the depths of arrogance and delusion."

Henry pauses, glancing over his shoulder at him. In that fleeting moment, anger flashes in his eyes as his knuckles whiten, gripped with hate for the man. He inhales deeply, a deep, shaky and ragged breath, before he exhales, attempting to release the tension and quells the storm raging within. He ultimately decides to turn away and distances himself further.

Alice's heart sinks as she watches the conversation between Henry and Sir Danvers. She can tell that the conversation isn't going as well as Henry had hoped and that he was clearly very upset by the turn of events. She came out of her hiding spot, even though she didn't want to interject and cause even more damage, she could see the obvious disappointment and hurt on his face, and immediately rushed over and hugged him.

He was stunned to feel her embrace; he hadn't expected that. He was still upset and disappointed and just... Defeated. He took a shaky breath and hesitantly wrapped his arms around her "I... I'm sorry you had to see that."

She hugged him tightly; her slender arms wrapped around him almost protectively. She could feel the heaviness in his voice, and it broke her heart. "Henry... don't apologize. It's not your fault." She pulled back just enough to look up at him, her eyes searching his. "It's going to be alright..." She said softly.

He pulls her close, holding her against him. "Thank you, Alice." He says, his tone quietly. The only sound is the music playing in the distance, as he holds his head against hers and sighs deeply.

She gently caressed his back, "You know... you can figure this out. You don't need some rich snob's money; you have a good head on your shoulders and a good heart."

Henry chuckles softly as he looks down at Alice. The sweet and kind expression on her face truly gave him the warmth he needed in this moment. "It's true... I don't. I'll find a way. After all, I'm a genius, aren't I?" He said in a sarcastic tone.

But Alice just smiled and, and gave Henry a squeeze. "London's most bloody brilliant."

Henry gives her a squeeze back. The two remain like this for a little while, enjoying each other's company in silence. Neither wanting to let go of this connection of peace and gentleness, the only sound being the sounds of the music and dancing in the distance. Just being together is enough for both of them.

Eventually, they went back to the crowd, a solemn expression on Henry's face. Utterson and Lanyon noticed the look on his face and approached him. Utterson pointed over to a woman with strawberry blond hair updo, and light pink dress with white gloves. "Did you hear? Elsa van Delthy is here, didn't your parents say you'd end up- Harry, my lad! What happened? You look quite vexed." Utterson asked with concern on his face.

Henry takes a deep breath, shaking his head. "I had a rather unpleasant conversation with Sir Danvers," he replies, his tone weary and dejected. "He refused to support my experiments. He said my research was an affront to morality and nature." He couldn't help the hint of bitterness and despair in his voice.

"Henry, I've always had my doubts about the direction your research was taking. But perhaps this serves as a lesson for us both," said Lanyon, as he sipped his wine.

"Sir Danvers's words are unfair and unjust," Alice interjected, her voice firm but filled with a hint of anger. "Henry's research is groundbreaking and has the potential to benefit many. Just because it clashes with societal norms doesn't make it wrong."

Lanyon's words hit a sore spot in Henry. But it was Alice's words of protest against Lanyon that caught him off guard, his heart skipping a beat as her passion and anger defending his experiments echoed in his ears. It was a side of Alice he had never seen before; it actually made his cheeks flush with embarrassment for some odd reason.

Utterson sighed, rolling his eyes, and really not wanting to go through this argument again.

Lanyon returned his gaze towards Jekyll, his expression remaining solemn. "I understand the disappointment, Jekyll... but Sir Danvers is a man of wealth and power. He's influential, and his voice carries weight. You can't expect him to support your unscientific balderdash."

Henry huffed in frustration "I don't expect him to understand the nuances of my work!" said Henry, raising his voice slightly. "I'm not here to seek out the approval of the masses... I simply want a chance to prove my theories, that's all... "

Lanyon raised an eyebrow, his expression hardening. He took a step back, his eyes narrowing at the sudden change in Jekyll's tone. "Jekyll, control yourself," he said firmly. "There's no need for violence.

I'm simply speaking the truth. Your research is, by many, considered unorthodox. And you know that better than anyone."

Alice stepped in, "Don't you see the potential in what he's trying to do? Instead of discouraging him, you should be supporting him and helping him prove his theories!"

Utterson groaned and spoke out. "Gentleman, let's not start a spat now. We've all had a bit to drink."

Lanyon shot Utterson a side-long glance at the comment before returning his gaze to Alice, his gaze almost harsh. "And you, miss," he said, his tone slightly condescending, "should not be meddling in matters that you do not understand. You were locked up in an asylum. Please, spare me the nonsense."

Henry felt a rush of defensiveness and protectiveness towards Alice, his hand clenching into a tight fist. "Do not dare to speak to her that way," he said, his voice low and intense. "She has been through more than you can imagine, and yet she remains strong and resilient. So don't you dare treat her like some ignorant child."

Lanyon's expression shifted, the realization slowly dawning on him. He saw the protective, almost intimate way that Jekyll defended the young woman, the stern, almost dangerous tone in his voice as he spoke. It was all the confirmation that Lanyon needed.

Utterson, sensing the growing tension between Lanyon and Henry, stepped in to try and defuse the situation. "Let's not argue, lads. We're friends, after all. And we're here to celebrate our good health, not to hash out our differences." Lanyon's expression grew stern as he turned his attention to Utterson, who stood in between them. "And what do you propose, Utterson?"

Utterson held his ground, his gaze steady and calm. "I propose we forget about this for tonight and enjoy the rest of the party in peace."

Lanyon's jaw clenched. "And let this issue fester further? Are you seriously suggesting we ignore the fact that Jekyll is trying to push this outlandish research?"

Henry felt a sense of helplessness surge through him. He was so tired of everyone questioning and belittling him, his ideas, and his research. He felt a wave of anger towards Lanyon, but he fought to keep it contained. He knew that in the end, they were all right. His research was seen as unorthodox, perhaps even taboo. He knew that he had something to prove, even if no one else believed in him.

Alice stepped forward, placing a gentle hand on his arm, trying to express her support.

Henry's heart skipped. He felt his anger and tension drain away, replaced by a sense of comfort and assurance in her presence. He looked at her, his eyes meeting hers, and he saw the empathy and understanding in her eyes. It was as if she could read him like an open book. He placed his hand over hers, not wanting her to let go just yet.

***

As they say their goodnights and make their exit. As he walked towards his home, the night air crisp in his lungs, he smiled, feeling an incredible sense of hope and joy fill his soul. Henry turns to look at Alice with a soft smile, his heart starting to flutter at the sight of her in the moonlight. She took his hand, and as they walked out, she gave him a little twirl, giggling. The two walk and walk, until they finally make it back to Henry's home. When they step inside, there's a quiet, peaceful atmosphere about it. Henry walks up over to the stairs, taking her with him. He smiles softly and leans his head towards her. "It's pretty late, and Poole is asleep. I'll see you in the morning."

She gives him a tight hug "Good night, Henry."

Henry can't help but find the sight of her adorable as she hugs him so close. He smiles softly and hugs her back, wrapping his arms around her.

He is exhausted from the emotional roller coaster of tonight. He is just now starting to relax. Henry sighs softly and takes a deep breath. "Good night, Alice." The two-part ways for now, heading to their respective bedrooms.

Alice walked into the guest bedroom and immediately changed out of her dress and into a sleeping gown, her mind still racing from the events of the evening. She could barely believe all the happened in such a short amount of time. As she climbs into the big, comfortable bed, she lies on her side, staring at the ceiling, and she couldn't help but think of Henry. She thought about how his eyes shone and how warm and steady his hands were as he held her. Alice sighs softly, feeling a flutter in her chest. She closed her eyes, replaying the events of the night again and again in her mind. It all felt like a dream, a beautiful dream. She could still feel his hands on her waist as they danced. She could still smell his scent as she slowly drifted off to sleep…

Henry, now alone in his room, feels a mixture of emotions. He is frustrated and upset with himself for his inability to secure the necessary funding for his research. However, the memories of Alice's support and loyalty give him hope. He sits down on the edge of his bed, his mind racing with thoughts. He laid down and tried to fall asleep, but he stared at the ceiling, deep in thought. He couldn't take his mind away from his serum. He has the ingredients and the formula, but has no one to test it on. He lets out a deep sigh and sits up, staring ahead. He lets out another deep breath before he throws the blanket off his bed and starts pacing around the room. There must be a way to test his serum. He just needs one person... and he knows the perfect candidate... Himself. He had been experimenting on his serum for a while now, but he had never considered testing it on himself. The thought was frightening, but he had no other options. He couldn't test it on an innocent volunteer. Henry takes a deep breath, and leaves his room to head to his laboratory. Once inside, he stares at the ingredients before taking out a beaker. As started putting in his ingredients, but most importantly the red liquid, and large quantity of a particular salt. He compounded the element, the red color changed, to purple, and then the blood orange colour, and vaporized. He could hear the clocks tick with every second as he watched them boil and smoke together in the glass. He lets out another deep breath, his heart starting to beat a thousand miles an hour. Henry realizes there was nothing he could really do, except forsaking the damn thing and hope to God that it would work. Taking a deep breath, he finally picks up the beaker with his right hand and drinks the contents....

Chapter 09

Frrrrrreeeeeeeel

A wave of sensations washed over Henry almost instantaneously. Nausea rolled through, and he stumbled back, his hand instinctively reaching for the edge of the table. But he missed his grip, and with a loud crash, he hit the ground. Henry let out a strangled scream, clutching his waist with one arm and draping the other over his face, an inexplicable horror seeped into his very being, far greater than any fear he had ever felt. Henry's body convulsed, racked with pain as the bones within him shifted and morphed. His hair now stood on end, growing longer and more unruly. The soft locks frayed into a haphazard mess or a wild, frizzy mane. He writhed on the floor, his eyes squeezed shut in anguish.

Gradually, the excruciating pain that had consumed his every fiber in his being began to fade, leaving him panting on the cold lab floor. Slowly, he removed the arm from his face. His breathing became less labored as he propped himself up on one trembling elbow. He lifted a hand to his hair, running his fingers through the now longer and more unruly. It was as if a fog had lifted, and he found himself glowing with an unfamiliar vitality. His body felt lighter, almost buoyant, and a sense of exuberance replaced the earlier torment. It was as though he had shed layers of weariness and doubt. He felt reborn. This newfound state was intoxicating; a profound sense of freedom flooded his being. No longer shackled by the moral burdens that once weighed him down, he reveled in a delicious sense of liberation. The constraints of conscience felt distant, as if they had been stripped away along with his former self. In this exhilarating moment, he ran back into the house, into the bedroom, almost tripping over his own shortened feet, he quickly made his way to the mirror. What he witnessed left him breathless. Gone was the tall, gangly young man he remembered, replaced by this shorter man, with tousled hair that shimmered like rich bronze or warm cinnamon, and his skin was a striking, almost ethereal pale. His hazel eyes now tinted with gold. His once rounded and gentle profile appeared more angular and a prominent jawline, creating a sharper overall appearance. The transformation was indeed significant, leaving him both stunned and perplexed. As he continued to examine his reflection, a sense of fascination replaced his initial shock. This new being, this other self, felt familiar and yet alien at the same time. It was as though a part of him that had been suppressed for so long was now manifesting itself in the physical realm. And yet, he didn't feel repulsed by this reflection. In fact, he found something almost soothing about it. As if it was a part of himself that he had denied for far too long.

As he continued to stare at the reflection, a thought crossed his mind. He needed a name. He chewed his lip in contemplation. He tossed out names like 'Edmund' and 'Archibald,' but none seemed to fit. 'Bartholomew.' Nope, too pompous. 'Sebastian.' Too posh. 'Alfred.' Nah, too common. 'Theodore.' Too long-winded. "Harold.' Too old-fashioned. 'Quentin.' Too pretentious. 'Maxwell.' Too square. 'Edgar.' Sounds like an old geezer. 'Orland.' No way. 'Horatio.' Come on, now. 'Montgomery.' Absolutely not. 'Benedict.' Too many syllables. 'Gerald.' Blah. However, as he continued to think… uncle Edoardo has an interesting name, but… And then it clicked. Edward. And Hyde was his mother's maiden name, beside, it fit perfectly. It all fit together in a strange, almost poetic way. "Edward Hyde." It was a name steeped in familial history, and there was a certain symmetry in using it to name himself. He slowly lifted his left hand and touched the mirror. He then touched his face, feeling the texture and smoothness of his own skin. He took a step back, his eyes wide with surprise, before a smile crept onto his face. He chuckled, a mixture of shock and awe in his eyes. "Free…" he murmured; his voice almost melodic. He looked at himself in the mirror some more, his hand coming to his face again. He touched his nose, his cheeks, his hair. His eyes were glued to his reflection, a strange fascination in his gaze. Hyde's reflection stared back at him, and he couldn't help but smirk. He looked different from Jekyll… He looked powerful, dangerous…And he loved it…

He examined the rest of himself. His new form felt different, livelier than before. His muscles ached, but in a good way, like after a good workout. He rolled his shoulders and twisted his body this way and that, taking in the new sensations. He laughed, the sound reverberating in his chest. "Bloody hell," he muttered, grinning widely. He flexed his fingers, his hands curling into fists and watching the new strength thumbing in them in fascination.

Hyde's expression immediately fell when he heard the sound of the door to Alice's room opening. He stood frozen for a moment, listening intently. He hadn't considered the possibility of Alice seeing him like this. He was certain the shock of his current appearance would bring more questions than answers. Hyde quickly sprang into action. He rushed to the window and wrenched it wide open, peering through the gap. He climbed onto the windowsill, bracing himself against the frame, his palms pressed flat against the wood. He then swung one leg over the edge, his toes gripping the gutter outside, and shifted his body weight forward. His other leg followed as he pushed off from the window, balancing precariously for a moment before swinging his body down onto the drainpipe. The cool night air swept through his tousled hair, sending tingles down his spine. The moon shone brightly overhead, casting a pale glow over everything. In that moment, he felt truly alive. He inhaled deeply, savoring the feeling of the wind caressing his face. As he began the slow, tentative descent, a strange sense of contentment washed over him. The world seemed different from this perspective, the familiar streets and buildings taking on a new form. Landing on the grass with a soft thump, He darted towards the laboratory, his footsteps quick and silent. He entered the building, rushing up the stairs and towards the cabinet. He reached the door and hurried inside, moving quickly and quietly. He darted towards the cabinet, grabbing the serum from the table with shaky hands. Hyde unscrewed the cap, bringing the bottle to his lips. The cool liquid felt foreign on his tongue as he swallowed it, the taste almost bitter.

He takes a swig of the serum. A ripple of pain passes through Hyde's body as he suddenly feels a change, and then the pain of transformation hits him. His bones shifting painfully, his body expanding, and then it all stops in a moment, and he collapses onto the floor, coughing and gasping for air and feeling weak and drained. As Henry caught his breath, he forced himself to his feet with a mixture of determination. He looked down at his hands and saw that they had returned to their original state—the normal, familiar hands of Henry Jekyll. He sighed in relief, grateful for the return to his normal appearance. He still felt shaken and a little bit dizzy, the effects of the transformation lingering in his body. He took a few steps around the room, testing out his limbs and muscles, making sure everything felt back to normal. His eyes fell on the bottle of serum sitting on the desk. He picked it up and examined the clear liquid inside, a mixture of curiosity and wariness filling him. Henry couldn't help but feel a mix of disappointment and excitement at the unexpected effect of the serum. But taking Alice's words to heart, he reminded himself to celebrate the small victories. "Small victories," he murmured to himself, gripping the bottle tighter.

Chapter 10

Juxtaposition.

Almost every night since then, Henry took the serum, which became something of a phenomenon to him. Being Hyde was like the delighted drunkenness of wine, but as much as he took pleasure in this new life, he took care in keeping it as much of a secret as possible. He bought a cheap run down house in Soho where Hyde frequented most often, and told Poole that Hyde was allowed to roam his home when he wishes. As for Alice, he didn't want him near her.

*****

May 10th~ A chill breeze wafted through the streets, carrying the stench of garbage, liquor, and other...unmentionables. Hyde walked among the dark alleys, his footsteps echoed on the cobblestones. The sounds of drunks and rowdy men could be heard in the distance, and a few prostitutes stood in the shadows, offering their charms to passersby. Hyde's gaze wandered to the music hall palace on the corner, its windows illuminated by a sickly light. The place seemed to pulse with an eerie sense of decay. The music hall was a dark, seedy place. Its walls were painted a dull brown, and its cheap carpet was covered in stains and filth. The air was thick with smoke, and the stench of alcohol was ever-present. A small stage at the far end of the room hosted a mediocre band, and women danced on the edge of the stage, their faces caked with makeup and their flimsy dresses barely concealing their bodies. Patrons crowded the bar, loudly drinking and gambling, while others watched the performance with bored expressions.

Hyde made his way through the crowded room, approaching the bar with an air of confidence. With an indifferent wave, he gestured to the bartender. "Gin, neat." He said. He leaned against the counter, his gaze falling on a group of men playing cards in the corner. They seemed to be getting quite heated. Hyde took a swig of his cheap gin, noticing one of the men at the card table, a small, weasel-faced man who seemed to be very agitated. Hyde's gaze lingered on him for a moment before he pushed himself off the bar and made his way towards the table.

As Hyde approached the table, the weasel man looked up at him with a sneer. "Whadda ya want, ya bleedin' bastard? Can't ya see we're in the middle of a game here?" He said in a gruff voice.

Hyde smirked and grabbed a chair from the neighboring table, pulling it up to the edge of the table and plopping down on it. He leaned forward, his eyes glinting with mischief. "Now now, is there any way to talk to a fellow player? I just came to join in the fun." He said, his voice dripping with mockery. He picked up the deck of cards, shuffling them effortlessly between his pale fingers. He glanced at the small man, his eyes narrowing. "Let's raise the stakes a bit, eh?"

Hyde reached into his pocket and pulled out a wad of crumpled banknotes. He slammed them down on the table with a smirk. "I'll raise you gentlemen…20 pounds," he said casually, his eyes flickering around the table. The men looked at Hyde in shock, their eyes fixed on the pile of money.

The small man spoke up. "You… You're jokin' right? Where'd ya get so much bleedin' money?"

Hyde huffed a laugh, "Let's just say it fell into my lap. Lucky me, eh?" He picked up the cards and started to deal, while men at the table exchanged glances.

The game continued, the tension growing with every hand. Hyde's sharp eyes flicked across the table, taking in every expression, every gesture. The small man became increasingly agitated. He made a rookie mistake, and Hyde seized the opportunity. With a smirk, he slammed his hand down, his cards revealing a perfect royal flush. The men at the table froze, their mouths hanging open in shock.

The small man's face twisted into a snarl. "You… You cheated, you bastard! There's no way you could've gotten so lucky!" Hyde simply chuckled, the sound cold and cruel. He picked up the pile of money, his hand gripping it tightly as he stood up from the table. "Luck has nothing to do with it, my dear boy," he said softly. "I just know how to play my cards right."

The men at the table let out a low growl, their eyes burning with murderous intent. They made a motion to stand up, but a quick look from Hyde that made them in their tracks. "I wouldn't if I were you," he said, his voice edged with pure menace. "I'd rather not have my fun interrupted this evening." The men slowly sat back down, their gazes flicking between Hyde and the pile of money. Hyde chuckled, a dangerous glint in his eyes. "That's what I thought. Now, if you'll excuse me, I have better things to do than play with amateurs." With a sly grin, he spun on his heel and walked away from the table, the wad of money clutched tightly in his hand. As he walked away, he noticed the eyes of the patrons following him as he moved, their gazes filled with curiosity and unease. He revelled in the attention, his lips curled up in a knowing smirk. He made his way towards the exit, his footsteps echoing on the creaky floorboards.

He was suddenly stopped by a group of women. They were dressed in gaudy outfits, their faces caked with heavy makeup. One of them, a redhead with a low-cut dress, sidled up to him. "Leaving so soon, love?" She purred, batting her eyelashes coquettishly. The woman moved closer, draping her arm around Hyde's shoulder. Her eyes glimmered with a mix of attraction and desperation. "We were hoping you'd stay a bit longer, handsome. There's plenty of fun to be had here."

Hyde smirked, his gaze flickering over the woman. He could practically smell the cheap perfume assaulting his nostrils. He was tempted, of course. It was easy to give in to his impulses, to indulge in the fleeting pleasure of the moment. But he felt a tug inside of him, and he knew it was Jekyll. It was never a real agreement on what he could and couldn't do when in control, but Jekyll always tried to stop him from having his fun when it came to women. Could he not be selfish for once? They were all over him. He seethed internally before he leaned closer to the woman, his lips barely brushing against her ear. His voice was a low purr, tinged with mockery. "You're a pretty little thing, I'll give you that. But I'm afraid not tonight." He reluctantly pushed her away.

As he walked away from the woman, Hyde finally made his way out of the music hall and back to the townhouse, his thoughts turned to

Jekyll. He could feel the other man's lingering gratitude. He couldn't help but roll his eyes as he muttered under his breath. "You owe me for that, Jekyll."

***

July 15th~ Hyde stumbled back to Jekyll's place after a long night in Soho. He was still quite tipsy, as he swayed and stumbled along the street. He had a dark tan worn top hat. A cetacean blue Inverness cape, a muddy brown jabot. And a black and white plaid waist coat, with a frilly long sleeved shirt underneath and long brown pants. When he finally reached the building, he tried the door, only to realize he had left the key within the lab. "Oh, bollocks…" He mumbled under his breath. Hyde leaned against the cold wall of the building, his mind racing as he tried to come up with a solution. The thought of knocking on the front door and interacting with Jekyll's butler seemed less than desirable. Hyde rolled his eyes, letting out a frustrated sigh as he reluctantly pushed himself off from the wall and trudged his way towards the front door.

Alice was inside sweeping, when she heard the knock, wondering who it could be. She tilted her head, waiting to hear another knock, just in case. When she did hear it, albeit louder, she stood the broom against the wall, and opened the door "Hello?"

Hyde raised an eyebrow at the sight of Alice, a smirk tugging at the corner of his lips. He leaned against the door frame, his gaze wandering over her form. "Well, well, well. Who do we have here…?" He drawled, his voice dripping with a hint of sarcasm and a hint of curiosity. "Alice, is it?" He let out a small chuckle as he took in her appearance. "You're a lot different from what I remember from Jekyll. Anyways, love," He greeted her, his voice smooth and slurred. "I seem to have locked myself out. Any chance you can let me in?"

She tilted her head, holding onto the door a bit tighter. "I'm sorry, who are you again?"

Hyde chuckled, his smirk never leaving his face. He took a step closer, his eyes tracing up and down her figure. "I'm a friend of Doctor Jekyll's. Just had a bit too much to drink and locked myself out. Names Edward Hyde, by the way."

She recognised the name, and put her hand out to shake, "How do you do?"

Hyde's smirk widened, and he took her hand in his. He brought her hand up to his lips, placing a gentle kiss on the knuckles. "Pleasure to finally meet you, Alice," He drawled, his eyes locked on hers. "You know, silly little Jekyll really set the bar low." He walked past her, entering the Foyer.

She was taken aback, closing the door behind her as he walked into the foyer, her expression still a bit uneasy. "So... you are friends with Jekyll then?"

"Oh, yes. Yes, we're quite close friends, you could say. He's a bit of a bore, though. Always so prissy and proper.", he went to the kitchen, ripping off a piece of bread Poole had made himself, looking at her with a sly smile. "You know, I expected more. He described you as the most beautiful creature he's ever laid eyes on. Said your curls were as soft as a cloud and your green eyes could mesmerize a man for hours." His eyes traveled down her body, taking in her appearance. "I can now see that was all a big exaggeration." He smirked again, biting into the bread.

She folded her arms over her chest, she was a bit stunned by the man, but she knew that if Henry told him about her, then he must trust him.. for some reason. "Henry talks of me often then. Does he?" she didn't believe a word of it, even though she wanted to, he was just getting to her. "Well, I remember him saying something to Poole the other day about his new little assistant, quite literally." She retorted back, though Hyde wasn't much shorter.

Alice's response caught Hyde off guard, his smirk faltering. He clenched his jaw. "Assistant, assistant..." He scoffed, the corners of his lips curling up in a snarl. "I'm no assistant. I'm no one's damn servant. Jekyll should be grateful for me. He's a weak, spineless coward who wouldn't have the courage to stand up for himself if it smacked him in the face. I'm the stronger one, the one who's not afraid to take what he wants."

The smirk wiped off her face as he inched closer to her. There was something in his eyes that she couldn't quite place that made her question if her words were a little too harsh. She shook the feeling off, her arms were still tightly crossed across her chest, and her chin was lifted in defiance. "I hope that you lock yourself out again, and you end up freezing." She called over her shoulder.

He took another bite of his bread, chewing thoughtfully as she left. "You know, that was not quite what I expected," he said after a pause, his voice casual. "I guess Henry has a thing for feisty women, or a breathing thing in general, after all."

***

July 31st~ Hyde leaned against the wall, watching as Henry stood in front of a full-length mirror, adjusting his tie with meticulous attention.

Henry was dressed in formal attire, a suit tailored to perfection, every detail carefully considered. He ran a hand through his hair, trying to tame his wild curls, and couldn't shake the feeling that something was off.

Hyde smirked. He couldn't help but find amusement in his efforts to look just right. Hyde pushed himself off the wall and sauntered over to Henry, eyeing him with a mix of curiosity and skepticism. "What's the special occasion? You look like you're dressing for a funeral."

"Might as well be," Henry muttered. "I'm seeing my parents today," he explained, his tone a mix of worry.

Hyde's smirk vanished instantly, replaced by a sneer of disdain. "Your...parents? Are you crazy?" He frowned at Henry's appearance, shaking his head in disapproval. "Why are you all dressed up for them, anyway? It's not like they're worth the effort..."

Henry let out an exasperated sigh, finally giving up on the tie and letting it hang loosely around his neck. He turned to face Hyde, his expression a mix of annoyance and exasperation. "I have to see them, Edward. It's been 3 years since I left, and they've been pestering me about coming back home." He ran a hand through his messy hair, exasperated. "And I can't exactly show up looking like a mess, can I? They'd never let me hear the end of it."

Hyde chuckled, his gaze fixed on Henry. "Oh, they'd have more to worry about than your appearance, my dear friend. They'd be utterly scandalized by your 'wild London life' with Alice." He put emphasis on the last word. "Just imagine the horror on their faces when they realize their prim and proper son is now living in sin with his mistress. They never did get over your dismissal of Elsa Van Dethy." He let out another chuckle.

Henry felt a pang of guilt and defensiveness rise in him, conflicted emotions that he had been trying to suppress. "It's not their business what I do in my personal life, Edward. And for the record, I'm not 'living in sin' with Alice. We're friends, that's all," he stated firmly.

Hyde scoffed, "Oh, come now, Henry. We both know it's more than just 'friendship' between you two. I've seen the way you two look at each other when you think no one's watching. It's quite obvious. But if you say it's all chaste and innocent, who am I to doubt you, besides well, literally being you?" He said sarcastically.

Henry clenched his jaw, unable to defend himself against Hyde's words. Perhaps there was something there he was blind to. But the thought of his parents discovering their relationship filled him with fear; just them knowing she was living with him would be a disaster. "It's complicated, Edward. You wouldn't understand. And it's not like I can just come clean to my parents about it. They would never approve."

Hyde raised an eyebrow, feigning surprise. "Oh, I see. So, you're keeping secrets from dear old Mummy and Daddy, eh? How intriguing. But I suppose it makes sense. They'd never understand your 'complicated' love life with Alice. They're too stiff for that kind of thing. Lest we know why you're an only child."

Henry gave him a sharp glare, his frustration growing. "Stop it, Edward. This is not something for you to mock. And my parents don't need to know a thing," he retorted, his voice tinged with defensiveness.

Hyde shrugged his shoulders, sitting down on the bed and crossed his legs, looking at Henry with his signature playful smirk. "Then that settles it. We're not going."

Henry turned around to face Hyde, utterly exasperated. His tone was firm, verging on a growl. "Edward, I don't have time for your games. I am seeing my parents, and that is final, understand?" He shot Edward a stern glance, as if challenging him to continue this argument.

Henry grabbed a flask containing the serum and put it in his coat pocket. He knew he might need it, just in case, especially after this nightmare of a trip. On the way there, Henry practically dragged Hyde with him. He was determined to visit his parents, even if it meant dealing with Hyde's constant bickering. The walk from Henry's house in Leicester Square to Finsbury Park was a relatively long one. Throughout the journey, Henry was tense and anxious, his mind on the upcoming encounter with his parents. Occasionally, he cast a sidelong glance at Hyde, who was walking beside him with a mix of annoyance and boredom on his face. "You know we're walking to our own execution rather than a family reunion."

Henry shot Hyde a sharp glance, his expression becoming more agitated. "Don't exaggerate, Edward. It's not going to be that bad. They're just my parents." He tried to convince himself more than Hyde, but the growing knot in his stomach betrayed his true feelings.

After about an hour of walking, Henry and Hyde finally arrive at his parents' house, a familiar sight that brings both dread and nostalgia to Henry's mind. The house is a well-maintained two-story Victorian building, with its mud colored brick facade and white trim exuding an air of quiet prosperity. The small front garden, framed by a meticulously maintained hedge, is filled with an array of autumn flowers that add a touch of color to the muted surroundings. There are several windows on the first floor, one of them belonging to Henry's old bedroom. As they approach the front olive green door, Henry takes a deep breath, steeling himself for the upcoming encounter. He can practically feel Hyde's mocking presence beside him, but he tries to ignore it and focus solely on the task at hand. He reaches out and knocks on the door, feeling his heart beating loudly in his chest. After a few moments, the sound of footsteps approaching can be heard from inside the house.

The door swings open to reveal a familiar figure. It's Henry's mother, Catherine, who stands before them with a mix of surprise and curiosity on her face. Catherine, a woman in her mid-40s with graying copper hair, blinks a few times before a warm smile spreads across her face. She recognizes her son instantly and quickly embraces him. "Henry! Oh, my darling boy," she exclaims, her voice filled with affection. "It's so good to see you."

Henry tensed up slightly, feeling awkward. He expected a cold welcome or a casual greeting. "Hello, Mother," he replies, his voice a little hoarse. "It's good to see you too."

Catherine pulls back from the embrace, her gaze sweeping over him with a critical eye. "Oh, look at you. You've grown more handsome since I last saw you. Although your hair is a bit of a mess," she remarks, reaching up to try and smooth out his unruly curls.

Hyde leans against the wall, rolling his eyes and exclaiming in his head. "Oh, how touching. Mommy dearest is concerned. Must have missed her little show dog."

Henry, still caught up in the moment, tries to ignore Hyde's snarky commentary. "Sorry about my appearance, Mother," he says apologetically, glancing at his disheveled hair. "I didn't really have time to fix it before coming over."

Catherine chuckles softly and pats his cheek affectionately. "Oh, don't worry about that, we can have the mess fixed while you stay," she assures him. "And who knows, it might give you a reason to stay longer, me and your father have a party to attend, and we do miss taking you." She steps back from the door, gesturing for them to come inside. "Well, come on in. Your father has been eagerly waiting for your arrival."

Henry follows his mother inside the house, a mix of apprehension and nostalgia filling his mind. Hyde trails behind, his gaze wandering over the familiar surroundings and occasionally making sarcastic comments in his head. The entrance hall is just as Henry remembers it, with its high ceiling and a sweeping staircase leading to the upper floor. The walls are adorned with a few paintings and family photographs that capture moments from his parents' lives. Henry pasted a picture of Elsa, and grimaced walking past it a bit faster, while Hyde knocked the photo face down. The sound of his father's voice can be heard from the living room. There, sitting in an armchair sipping tea with a newspaper in his hand, is Henry's father, George Jekyll. He looks up from the newspaper as they enter and stands up to greet them. George, a man in his early 50s, has a rugged appearance with graying temples and a sharp-featured face. "Henry, my boy! It's been too long."

When George approaches Henry and claps him on the back, it causes Henry to tighten his shoulder blades, and his eyes slip shut for a beat longer than a natural blink.. Hyde, standing off to the side, observes the interaction with a critical eye, his disgust for George deepens.

George doesn't seem to notice anything amiss, however, and continues with his greeting. "You look tired, son. Have you been working too hard lately?"

Henry composes himself quickly, plastering a polite smile on his face. "Yes, Father, the work has been rather demanding lately," he replies, his voice steady. "Lots of research and experiments to oversee."

Catherine, blissfully ignorant of Hyde's presence, gives her son a knowing look. "Come now, Henry. You must be starving after your journey. Let's have a seat in the living room and enjoy some tea." George, with his arm still around Henry, leads them both towards the living room. Hyde, reluctantly following behind, his gaze scanning the room with barely concealed boredom and disdain. Henry takes a seat on the armchair opposite his parents, and Hyde settles on the countertop behind Henry.

George launches into a detailed account of his work as of late, something about a new bridge design.

Henry listens halfheartedly, politely interjecting with occasional questions to keep the conversation going, and the spotlight off himself. Meanwhile, Hyde, still perched on the table behind Henry, sulks as he listens to the mundane chatter.

A plate of cranberry Jammy dodgers sat in the middle of the table, a recipe from his mother that he had struggled to swallow as a child. Just from the smell of cranberry, he had always despised them. Henry reaches for a cranberry Jammy dodger, when suddenly Hyde snatched his hand with a surprising grip, preventing him from taking the biscuit. Henry froze, taken aback by the sudden action. He glanced down at his hand, now held firmly in Hyde's grasp, before looking up at his parents. With a mix of confusion and curiosity, tried to protest silently, his eyes pleading with Hyde to let go. "What…what are you doing?" he thought, wondering how Hyde had managed to physically touch him.

Hyde's grip on Henry's hand tightened as he leaned closer to Henry's ear. His voice was a low, insistent hiss. "Don't even think about eating that abomination. There's no way I'm letting you put that in our mouth." Henry's eyes widened in surprise. He tried to twist his hand free, but Hyde's grasp was like an iron vice.

His mother and father, witnessing the little dispute, exchanged a puzzled glance. "Is something the matter, dear?" his mother spoke up.

Henry tried to act as if nothing was amiss, and chuckled awkwardly. "Oh, it's nothing, really. Just having one of these.. delicious cookies." As he tried to bring the cookie towards his mouth, Hyde suddenly flung Henry's arm backwards, causing the cookie to fly out of his hand and land somewhere behind him with an audible thump.

For a split second, the room fell into an awkward silence. Henry's parents stared at him, their faces filled with confusion.

Henry's eyes darted nervously between them, desperately trying to come up with an explanation. "Actually, I'm not that hungry right now. I think I'll just have some tea instead."

Henry's mother, Catherine, glanced at her son with a quizzical expression. "Are you sure, Henry? You've barely eaten anything since you arrived. You must be famished."

George, her husband, chimed in. "Yes, son. It's not like you to turn down one of your mother's famous cranberry Jammy dodgers. They're your favorite, are they not?"

Hyde snorted, his grip on Henry's wrist finally loosening. "Favorite? More like his worst nightmare. Who on earth likes cranberries!?"

Henry tensed at Hyde's words. He took a deep, steadying breath, trying to maintain his composure. "I just had a heavy lunch earlier," he replied hastily. "I'm still quite full of that."

His father chuckled, shaking his head with an amused expression. "Ah, the insatiable appetite of youth. I remember eating more than a bear when I was your age."

His mother's lips curled up in a playful smile. "Indeed, dear. But you also had a much more active lifestyle back then. Our little Henry here spends most of his time cooped up in his laboratory, doing lord knows what."

Henry forced out a strained chuckle, not finding much humor in their lighthearted remarks. He gently pried his wrist out of Hyde's grasp, still conscious of appearing normal to his parents. "I'll just have some tea," he said, his voice sharp with suppressed irritation. "That should quell my appetite well enough." He took the cup closest to him and took a sip, as Hyde huffed and sat on the arm of Henry's chair.

Cathrine, observant in her own way, picked up on his strained tone. She frowned slightly. "Are you certain, dear?. You look a bit pale."

George was preoccupied with his own thoughts, "Come now, Catherine. He's an adult, not a child. If he says he isn't hungry, we should respect that."

Hyde suddenly jumped up. "When have they ever respected him?" Hyde snapped. "They've never respected him. Never respected us!"

Henry jumped in his seat and accidentally spilled his tea on himself. "Hyde!" he hissed through clenched teeth, wincing from the hot liquid seeping into his waistcoat and under shirt.

George gave a puzzled expression as he watched the scene unfold. His mother was equally taken aback, a look of concern etched on her face as she noticed the spilled tea. "Why, Henry, are you alright, dear?" she asked, awkwardly.

Henry's face flushed with a mixture of frustration and embarrassment as he tried to control the situation. He quickly tried to downplay Hyde's outburst. "I'm fine, just clumsy, that's all," he muttered, using a napkin to dab at his tea-soaked clothes.

Cathrine stepped closer to him, her hand reaching out to touch his forehead. "You're sure you're not running a fever, dear? You're looking quite flushed."

Henry evaded her touch, trying to dismiss her worries. "It's nothing, Mother. Really, I'm fine. Just a bit tired, that's all."

His father's eyes narrowed. "You look more than tired, son. You look like hell. I can't believe you let yourself go. If you keep going like this, you'll never give us grandchildren. You already look like a tired old man. Imagine how you'd look after a night with a crying infant keeping you up all night."

Henry could feel his face turn a deeper shade of crimson at his father's comment. The situation was starting to take an increasingly embarrassing turn.

Hyde burst into a stifled laugh, his eyes gleaming with amusement. "Oh, Father, you really are hilarious. Implying that our dear Henry has even had the pleasure of bedding a woman, let alone kiss one. That's a laugh."

Henry clenched his teeth, as felt a surge of anger and embarrassment wash over him, and before he could stop himself, he lashed out mentally at Hyde. "Shut your mouth! You blathering insufferable idiot!"

Henry's parents exchanged a look of surprise and disbelief, their mouths agape at his sudden outburst. "Henry, what on earth is the matter with you?" his mother exclaimed.

George spoke loudly, "Son, we raised you better than to use such profanity in our presence. We do not condone cursing in this household."

Henry, thoroughly embarrassed and desperate to escape the situation. "I'm so sorry, I... I'm just really tired," he stuttered, struggling to keep his voice steady. "I think I should probably go home and rest. I didn't mean to lash out like that."

His parents looked at him in confusion and concern, not quite understanding the extent of his behavior. "Are you sure, dear?" Cathrine asked, placing a hand on his shoulder. "You can stay the night if you'd like."

Hyde pushed hard against Henry, his voice booming with determination. "Like hell I am!" He exclaimed, his words laced with venomous defiance. "Who the hell would want to spend another single minute in this stuffy, suffocating, and utterly insufferable household?"

Henry couldn't control the involuntary twitch. He turned to his parents, forcing a polite yet firm smile. "It's alright, Mother. I think it's best if I head home now. I need some time to myself."

George furrowed his brows, obviously not convinced. "But it's getting late, son. Why don't you stay the night, like your mother suggested?"

NO!" He gave Henry a final push and the door shut behind him.

George shook his head. "I swear, that alchemy gibberish of his is messing with his head. He hasn't been the same since he started with all those elixirs and concoctions. And did you see the way he looked? Like a stray dog."

***

Henry walked away from his parents' home with his head down and his hands in his pockets. The cool night air did little to soothe his troubled thoughts. Hyde's words and actions echoed in his head, a constant source of irritation. Once he was out of earshot of other pedestrians, he allowed himself to unleash his frustration. "Damn it, Hyde!" he exclaimed, his voice a hoarse whisper. "Can you not behave like a lunatic for one minute?"

Hyde responded with a scoff. "Oh, so now you're ungrateful, are you? I saved your ass in there! You should be thanking me. That's two favors you owe me now."

Henry gritted his teeth. "Save me? Save me how? By making an even bigger fool of myself in front of my parents? Congratulations, you succeeded splendidly!"

Hyde huffed, his voice tinged with disdain. "Parents, schmarents. Who cares about those two? They're just a pair of meddlesome, overbearing idiots. All they do is nag, bunch of uptight prunes, if you ask me."

Henry sighed, resigning himself to the conversation. "Fine," he muttered, his voice flat. "You want me to thank you? Here it is, then." Henry pulls a vial of the serum from his pockets.

Hyde grins, his eyes glinting with mischief as he catches sight of the serum in Henry's hand. "Going to dose me, are you? Oh, how exciting. You just can't help yourself, can you?" He leans closer.

He uncorks the vial, staring at the vibrant liquid within. He brings the vial to his lips and downing it in one gulp. The potion's effect is immediate. Henry's face contorts as he swallows the bitter, viscous liquid. It burns as it slides down his throat, a taste akin to death and damnation. The transformation is swift, almost violent. His body contorts and shudders, and within moments, he is no longer Henry. Henry's consciousness retreated to the back of their shared mind, "There, happy?" he responded, his words tinged with bitterness and resignation. "Now you can strut home like the arrogant jackass you are."

Hyde, now in control of his body, grinned wickedly. He stretched his limbs, taking a moment to look at himself, savoring the transformation. "Oh, very happy, Henry," he said, his voice dripping with sarcasm. "But walking? No, no, no. We don't walk. We take a cab. I demand a more refined mode of transportation."

Henry's voice, though mentally confined, refused to concede. "Absolutely not. We are walking. This isn't a game. You've caused enough chaos for one night."

With a stubborn expression on his face, Hyde reluctantly began walking down the street, grumbling under his breath. "You're such a killjoy. So what, you want me to act as stuck up as George? Fine."

As Hyde walks down the street, the city lights casting a dim glow on the surrounding area, Henry's consciousness remains within his own mind, frustrated and irritated. Henry observed Hyde's cocky strut, the way he carried himself with an arrogant confidence

Henry gritted his teeth. "You're acting like a petulant child," he muttered internally, his irritation growing with every step.

Hyde, on the other hand, seemed undeterred by Henry's annoyance. He continued to swagger down the street, his steps purposeful and confident. As Hyde turned the corner, the unexpected collision with the young girl caught him off guard. He stumbled briefly, the confident gait momentarily interrupted. He looked down at her with a mixture of annoyance and surprise. "Watch where you're going. Can't you see I'm-" Hyde's footsteps halted the moment he realized that the girl's parents were nowhere to be seen in the darkness of London. The sight of her wandering the streets alone stirred a mix of alarm and unease within the twisted recesses of Hyde's mind, though he concealed this concern beneath a callous exterior. Teaching her parents a lesson about neglect, Hyde trampled calmly over the child's body. She screamed in fear, her shrill cries piercing through the night air. "Oops, my bad," he said, his tone devoid of remorse. "Shouldn't have been wandering the streets in the dark. Be sure to tell your parents, 'Play stupid games, win stupid prizes'." He chuckled darkly, his eyes glinting with an ominous golden light.

Henry's disgust was palpable in their shared mind as they watched Hyde. He couldn't believe the callousness of his alter ego. "Oh my god! Are you insane?" he exclaimed angrily. "We need to help her!"

Hyde shrugged, his expression unapologetic. "Relax, Henry. She is fine, just a little frightened."

Hyde's heartless display in the alleyway, trampling the little girl, didn't go unnoticed for long. Enfield (as Jekyll recognized, having met him one summer when he and his cousin Utterson came from France with wine, the first bottle Henry had ever had) quickly intervened, firmly grabbing Hyde by the lapels and forcefully pulling him back. A small crowd had formed around the scene, their anger and disdain towards Hyde visible in their sharp words and accusatory stares. The young girl continued to cry out pitifully in fear as a few women tried to pounce on Hyde, while Enfield and Dr. Sawbones were cursing him into blackmail. Meanwhile, Hyde remained eerily quiet, his eyes fixed on the crowd, but he was trembling slightly.

Henry desperately sought a way to defuse the situation before it escalated. He projected his thoughts directly towards Hyde, urging him to try to resolve the matter without causing further chaos. "Hyde, listen to me," Henry's voice reverberated in his mind. "We need to avoid a scene here. Please, try to remain composed and offer to compensate the child's family a generous sum."

Hyde took a deep breath, his demeanor transforming from his usual arrogant attitude to something more calculated and cunning. Stepping forward, he addressed the growing crowd with feigned humility. "Ladies and gentlemen," Hyde began, his voice carrying a hint of false regret. "I apologize for any distress I may have caused. I understand your anger and disappointment, but I assure you, it was an honest mistake. I will, of course, take responsibility for my actions," Hyde continued, his tone slightly condescending. "I will generously compensate the child's family for any suffering I may have caused."

The crowd murmured among themselves, some of their anger beginning to subside. A few nodded in agreement, satisfied with Hyde's proposed solution. Nevertheless, there were still a few suspicious eyes.

Despite the growing support, Henry couldn't help but feel a pang of guilt, both for his alter ego's actions and for the young girl's suffering.

Hyde swiftly excused himself from the scene. He produced a peculiar key from his pocket, the metallic object glinting in the dim streetlights. With a quick motion, he unlocked the door behind him, the rusty hinges creaking loudly. The small gathering of people watched in curious silence as Hyde vanished through the door, disappearing from their sight. The door slammed shut behind him with an echoing thud, leaving the crowd speculating about the mysterious place beyond.

Alice had been tossing and turning all night. When she finally tried closing her eyes, she heard the footsteps of Hyde, one that was hard to forget. She poked her head out into the hall, she saw the figure of Hyde. She moved ever so slightly, a dog wouldn't hear here, hoping to find out what he was up to. She saw the man take out a checkbook from Jekyll's drawer and a pen. But when he wrote on the check, the pay was about ninety pounds... and the name was 'Dr. Henry Louis Jekyll' in his handwriting? He grabbed a small bag and filled it with ten more pounds, and walked out towards the child's mother, the woman who was holding her daughter, a look of surprise on her face as she witnessed the money being offered. Hyde extended both the sack of gold and the bank note towards her. "For your troubles, I presume," he said coolly.

Alice watched with curiosity, her gaze fixed on Hyde's actions. She couldn't help but wonder why Hyde was using Henry's money. Her mind raced with questions, wondering what Henry would think of this.

Poole came up behind Alice and whispers, "Anything on him yet?"

Alice jumps from the sudden presence of Poole, but quickly regains her composure. She shakes her head, replying in hushed tones. "No, not yet. He's acting...differently... Poole, how did Henry meet Hyde?"

Poole surged, "Jekyll said he's an old friend, but I've never seen him before."

Alice didn't like this. Poole had known Henry since before he was born, and when they moved from Scotland, there was no way Henry had a secret friend, and Poole himself didn't know. But she thought of how Henry had taken her in and hid her from his friends for the first few months. Maybe this was the same? Maybe.

As Hyde returned to Jekyll's residence and spotted Poole and Alice in the hall, a mix of annoyance and defiance flared within him. He couldn't stand the butler's prying eyes, always keeping tabs on his every move. Turning towards Poole, Hyde's voice was sharp and commanding. "Oi, mate," he hissed, his gaze fixed on the butler. "Keep your bloody nose out of me damn business. I don't need you following me around like a damn shadow. And if you knew what was best for you, you would take the girl with you, or have you forgotten Jekyll placed me in charge?"

This made her stomach turn. She'd never heard someone talk to Poole like this. It is true, he is the butler, but he was proud to bear the burden of that title. Henry has always treated him with respect, as have his previous visitors. Nobody has ever seen fit to criticize him as boldly as Hyde.

Poole stood in Hyde's way, "This is not your house, you are a guest, not an owner, no matter what Jekyll says."

Hyde pushed past Alice and Poole, his gaze locking with her for a moment. He grabbed two Champagne bottles and walked towards Jekyll's laboratory.

Alice couldn't help but be puzzled by his odd behavior, the way he seemed to both acknowledge and dismiss her presence. She knew that Hyde was a complex character, but this mixture of familiarity and distance puzzled her. What was going on inside that twisted mind of his?

When the door closed, Alice looked at Poole. "Well, don't we have a 'lovely guest'?".

Poole glances at Alice and nods slightly, looking back to Hyde with a furrowed brow. Once Hyde closes the door, Poole turns to Alice. "Yes, it appears that way. He is certainly not who I expected Dr. Jekyll to have invited into the house. And yet, cannot say his face is familiar to me."

She shakes her head, "I'm sorry for what he said. You're more than just the butler; that is more than certain. Poole, how about you sleep tonight? I'm sure Henry would understand." Alice smiles, tilting her head slightly.

"Very well, I shall return to my quarters. Rest well, Alice. I shall see you in the morning." And with that, Poole bows slightly and heads up the stairs. For a while, Alice stared at the study door, feeling that there had been some foul play...

Chapter 11

Muffled Words.

Henry woke up the next morning, lying on the ground with a bad hangover. He was completely exhausted and felt like he hadn't slept in days. Henry groaned a bit as he rubbed his forehead, trying to ward away the pounding headache. He didn't want to think about the things he did under the influence of Hyde, but the memories of last night just wouldn't leave him alone. He felt guilty for the pain he caused, both to himself and others. Henry sat up with a groan and stared out of the window, thinking over his actions and trying to make sense of it all. Suddenly, the door creaked open, and outside his room stood Alice. She was still in her nightgown and had brought a cup of his morning tea. She took one look at him and could see the worry and guilt on his face, but she didn't know why.

She sat at the edge of the bed beside him, hoping to cheer him out of the gloom. "Morning, sleepy head. I brought your favorite tea; of course, you can't survive the morning without it." She ruffled his hair.

Henry smiled weakly and leaned his head into her hand, rubbing his forehead with the opposite. "I am glad to see you too. Thank you, Alice, for the tea, and… for your kindness. You're right, you know. I'm quite certain that I would be quite ill if not for the morning tea." Henry sipped at the tea and let it warm up his body. It was quite bitter, but he needed the warmth and energy that it would bring him. Alice's touch was comforting. His brow furrows slightly. "You look a bit tired yourself. Didn't have the best night's sleep?".

"Not really, no. But I guess we all had an odd night," she sighed. "Are you feeling alright? You haven't been acting all yourself, and well... You've been out with Hyde a lot lately." She pries.

Henry's expression changed from a weak smile to a hint of guilt as he set the cup down. "Ah, yes," he said, looking away from Alice. "I have been spending a bit too much time with Hyde lately, haven't I?" He shifted uncomfortably.

Alice knew him well enough to sense that there was something more to his interactions with Hyde than he was letting on. "Henry," she said softly, her voice tinged with a mixture of worry and frustration. "I can tell there's something you're not telling me. Something about these nights out with Hyde. You've been different lately, distant even."

Henry sighed, "I-I can't tell you, Alice... You wouldn't understand. It's- complicated." He took another sip of tea, trying to appear calm, but his hands were trembling slightly, betraying his inner conflict.

She reached out, gently touching his arm in a soothing gesture, her voice soft yet firm. "Try me, Henry. I'm not a child. I can handle whatever it is you're keeping from me. We've been through so much together, haven't we? Don't shut me out now."

Their conversation was abruptly interrupted by the arrival of Poole, announcing that breakfast was ready. This brief interruption seemed to give Henry a fleeting moment to collect his thoughts and compose himself. "Thank you, Poole," he said, his voice calm and composed. He placed the empty cup of tea on a nearby table and stood up, avoiding eye contact with Alice. "Let's go and have some breakfast, shall we?" he said, forcing a small smile.

Alice didn't want to let the subject drop, but she also didn't want to cause a scene in front of Poole. So she nodded, understanding that the conversation would have to wait. "Of course, let's go have some breakfast."

As they sat down at the dining table, the room fell silent except for the soft clinking of silverware against plates. The tension between Alice and Henry was palpable, each silently contemplating the conversation that was left unfinished. Alice couldn't help but steal glances at Henry, studying his every movement, trying to gauge his reactions. She longed for him to open up, to let her in, but his demeanor remained distant and guarded. Alice couldn't bear it any longer. She set her silverware down and took a deep breath. "Henry," she began, her voice firm yet tinged with vulnerability. "I can't pretend that everything is okay when it's not. I can see that something is troubling you, and I want to help. But for me to help you, you have to start by being honest with me. I deserve that much, don't I?"

Henry looked at Alice, a mix of guilt and stubbornness in his eyes. He was torn between his desire to protect her and the overwhelming urge to keep his secrets hidden. "I'm fine, Alice," he replied, his voice betraying a hint of irritation. "There's nothing for you to worry about." He took a bite of his omelet, avoiding her gaze as he continued to eat. The silence between them was heavy, filled with unspoken words and lingering tension.

Alice clenched her jaw, frustrated by Henry's stubborn refusal to open up to her. She took a deep breath and tried a different approach. "Fine, if you won't talk to me, then at least tell me this: who is Hyde? Who is this "friend" you've been spending so much time with lately? You say he's your assistant, but I never see him in your lab, let alone with you." She poked him.

Henry's eyes flashed with a mixture of irritation. "Don't poke me like that, Alice," he snapped. "And don't worry about Hyde. He's just a friend, a bit of a libertine perhaps, but harmless enough. There's no need for you to concern yourself with him." He poked her back.

She reached across the table and gave him a firm poke in the arm.

He grabbed her wrist, holding onto it firmly.

Alice decide to poke him on his side, specifically where she knew he was ticklish.

Henry's resolve crumbled as Alice found his ticklish spot on his side. This time, he couldn't hold back his reaction, a soft but involuntary laugh escaping his lips. "Hey, stop that!" he protested, a hint of a smile on his face despite himself.

Alice couldn't help but chuckle to herself as she saw the reaction she had gotten from him. It brought her a small sense of satisfaction to see him cracking a smile, even if it was momentary. "Oh, so you do know how to smile," she teased, her tone slightly lighter now. "I was beginning to think you'd forgotten how."

After several minutes of playful shoving, Henry pushes back a little too hard, sending both of them tumbling to the floor in a heap. He quickly gets up and helps her up as they both laugh hysterically.

Poole then interrupted the two, clearing his throat. They both looked at him, Alice was blushing and still a bit giggly, but when she looked back at Henry, his smile seemed sheepish, trying to brush the incident off. "Master Jekyll, Lanyon is at the door, shall I let him in?"

Henry nodded, "Let him in."

Poole leaves, bringing Lanyon in, to enter the room, he seems to have a worried look towards his friend, as he looks at Alice, then back at Jekyll, seeing their exchanged glances. Lanyon waves Jekyll over into another room, leaving Alice and Poole in the other. Henry waited awkwardly as they stood in front of the fireplace. "I know you are in love with her Jekyll," Lanyon said, staring into the fire.

Henry's eyes widened at Lanyon's words. He swallowed, his heart thumping in his chest. How could Lanyon have known about his feelings for Alice? He tried to maintain his composure, his mind racing with thoughts. "What... what are you talking about, Lanyon?" he managed to say, trying to sound nonchalant.

Lanyon sighed, turning to look at Jekyll directly. He crossed his arms, his expression stern. "Oh please, Henry. You're not fooling anyone." He took a step closer, voice quiet. "The way you look at her, the way you two act around each other. It's all too obvious."

Henry blushed a bit, rubbing the back of his neck. "It's terribly obvious... isn't it?" he blushed furiously, his face going a scarlet red. "Ive never felt this way before." He sits down on one of the chairs next to the fireplace.

Lanyon moves to the chair across from him. "Yes... she's a unique woman..." He pauses grimacing. "However, it's her origins that concern me. Her parents gave her up because she was a freak." He leans forward. "I'm worried."

Henry's expression shifted from embarrassed to serious. He leaned forward, his hands fidgeting on his lap. "I understand your concern, old friend, but you don't know Alice the way I do."

Lanyon sighs again. He wasn't sure how to bring this topic up. "I don't know exactly how to tell you this, but... I'm worried that this.. girl.. is trying to trick you, or is just some... criminal, and is going to use you to get killed, money, or whatever. I'm worried that she's some crook using you to her own advantage."

Henry looks utterly baffled by the statement. "What!? That's absurd! Alice is the most innocent person you'll ever meet. Why would she ever use me?" He says with a look of disbelief.

Lanyon takes a deep breath. "Think about it for just one second. She just shows up at your door, and for some reason, you, being the compassionate, kind-hearted man you are, decide to take her in. She could be a criminal! How do you know she isn't? The only thing we know about Alice is what she tells us. All I'm saying is, think with logic instead of your heart."

Henry's eye began to twitch almost imperceptibly. "Lanyon, you are being absurd. You talk as if she's some masterminded psychopath! Do you even know Alice? Do you even know how kind, sweet, and caring she is? You sound crazy! She's far too innocent and kind for that kind of deception. You're just paranoid and don't trust her!"

Hydes's apparition appears right next to Lanyon, and he circles him and steals ghostly versions of his scarf and coat, trying it on. It was making Henry dizzy, seeing Hyde there, and seeing Lanyon in the same clothes next to him. "Well, he's gained a few pounds." He throws them on the floor half haphazardly, "Are you seriously going to believe him? Haiste Lanyon? Just look at him... His clothes... I bet I could handle this, no problem."

Henry scowls, "Be quiet." Hyde shrugged and disappeared.

Lanyon looks at him strangely, "Who are you talking to?"

Henry sighs, pinching the bridge of his nose. "Do not mind. I'm just... talking to myself."

Lanyon scoffs, "Talking to yourself? And you say I sound crazy... Talking to yourself. You need to go on holiday."

Henry rolls his eyes at Lanyon. "I'm perfectly fine. I'm just.. I'm a bit tired and stressed."

Lanyon crosses his arms, "I can see that much. You've been acting all kinds of strange since the gala, at least Alice isn't acting as weird as you."

Henry grows loudly. "Yes, I'm aware I've acted strange. I'm upset, Lanyon! I messed up and made a fool of myself; nobody believes I have what it takes but thinks I can do everything at once to perfection, and it's making me a bit crazy! I can't stop thinking about it, and it's making me stressed! Not to mention the incident with Hyde!"

"Who the bloody hell is Hyde?" Lanyon interjected in utter confusion.

"I- er…. never mind…" he muttered. "Forget I said anything. What do you want, Lanyon? I was having a peaceful morning before you rudely interrupted me."

Lanyon wasn't in the mood for any of Henry's shenanigans. "I wanted to check up on you. We haven't spent much time together since the gala, and I was concerned about you. Not to mention being concerned about you letting a lunatic girl stay here with you."

Henry stood up, his own temper starting to rise as well. "A lunatic girl? Her name is Alice!"

Lanyon scoffs, his hand coming up to cover his chest. "Please, Jekyll, she's quite literally the definition of insane! She's been locked up in those loony bins for years! She's obviously crazy and needs to go back to the asylum where she belongs!"

Henry hands grip the edge of the table in between them, his knuckles turning white. "Don't you dare say another word about her like that!"

Lanyon rolls his eyes, clearly annoyed with Jekyll's reaction. "Oh, calm down Henry! Don't be so dramatic. You've got to admit, you hardly know this girl, and yet you're practically head over heels for her, letting her stay in your house and practically fawning all over her! It's so unlike you to be so... smitten!" He crosses his arms.

"ENOUGH!" Henry slams his hand on the table, causing Lanyon to jump in surprise. Henry glares at him, his eyes blazing with anger. "Don't you dare insult Alice. She's not crazy, she's just been through a lot. You don't know anything about her or what she's been through! She deserves kindness and compassion, something you seem to have little of yourself. I will not have you slander her like this!"

Lanyon stares at Jekyll, dumbfounded. He's never seen his friend so protective and defensive of someone before. He crosses his arms, a skeptical look crossing his face. "Jekyll, listen to yourself. You're practically foaming at the mouth defending some random looney girl. You hardly know her, and she's living under your roof! You need to think with logic, not your emotions."

Henry's expression hardened, his eyes narrowing. He clenched his fists, trying to keep his emotions in check. "I'm tired of hearing this from you, Lanyon!"

Lanyon shook his head, sighing once more. He ran a hand through his hair, clearly frustrated. "You're starting to sound like some stubborn child. I care about you, you idiot!"

Henry bristled at Lanyon's words, his jaw clenching tightly. He sat up straighter in his chair, his eyes narrowing. "Oh, please, it's not like that with Alice, and you know it. And care about me? When? All you ever do is lecture me like some mother hen and criticize everything I do! It's no wonder I don't confide in you about things when you treat me like a child in need of supervision! You sound like my damn parents!"

Lanyon huffs . "God, I have half a mind to slap some logic into you! I'm just looking out for you, you bloody fool! Why is this so hard for you!"

Henry sighs, his shoulders slumped as he turns back towards Lanyon, and his eyes grew dark. "Emotions? Logic? Isn't it funny how you always bring up those two words whenever I do something you don't approve of? Well, I'm tired of it! I'm tired of always having to listen to your logic and reason and never being allowed to trust my own instincts! And maybe being emotional and impulsive isn't such a bad thing. Maybe I'm tired of trying to be the perfect doctor, the perfect scientist, the perfect friend. I'm tired of trying to meet your damn expectations all the damn time! I'm tired of being the logical, composed, and 'perfect' Doctor Jekyll all the damn time! …Maybe I am being irrational, maybe I am being emotional… What do you want me to say, Lanyon? That you're right? That I'm being stupid and careless by letting Alice stay with me? That I'm a fool for defending her? for actually caring about her? Is that what you want to hear? Because if it is, then fine. You were right, and I was wrong. That I should've listened to you in the goddamn first place, and I'm such a screw up…" Henry's anger started to soften, and he rubbed a hand over his face, trying to calm himself down. "I know you're just trying to look out for me, Lanyon. I'm not angry at you, I'm angry at… everything, I guess. It's just… sometimes it feels like nobody trusts me, like everyone thinks I'm incapable of making my own decisions. It's exhausting…"

Lanyon was taken aback by Jekyll's confession. He had never seen his friend so vulnerable and open about his feelings before. It was a side of Jekyll he rarely saw, and it was uncomfortable. He rubbed the back of his neck awkwardly, trying to find a way to steer the conversation away from the uncomfortable topic. Seeing a bottle of claret on the table, he picked up the bottle and poured two glasses. "Why don't we have a stiff drink? It might help us both lighten up a bit." He handed a glass to Jekyll, "Maybe it'll help loosen your tightened corset."

Henry accepted the glass and took a generous sip. The claret was rich and full-bodied, and he felt the tension slowly start to loosen in his shoulders. He took another sip, feeling the alcohol begin to soothe his frayed nerves. "Thank you," he said gruffly, "I needed this." in the back of Jekyll's mind, he felt strange, like Hyde was listening in on him again, but this time it felt different, stronger. He suppressed a shudder and poured himself another glass, hoping the claret would numb the strange feeling...

Chapter 12

You Must Suffer Me To Go My Own Dark Way.

August 16th~ It wasn't long after Alice's 20th birthday, that things were a bit calmer in the house. Jekyll has been a little more cautious about letting Hyde out into the world, even though sometimes Hyde got furious and desperate to take control.

Meanwhile, Poole could see the longing look in Alice's eyes. Her eyes often strayed towards the forbidden room in Jekyll's laboratory, where Alice was temporarily banned. He approached her as discreetly as possible, as she sat on the inner window cell, "Excuse me, Miss Lumsley," Poole whispered. "Is everything quite alright with you?"

Alice turned to Poole and smiled wearily, "I'm alright Poole. Is there something you need help with?"

Poole returned the smile, his eyes filled with a slight hint of concern. "No, no, it's not that. It's just that I've noticed you seem to be a bit distracted lately. You keep glancing towards the cabinet."

She sighed, shaking her head, "When will I ever learn…"

Poole chuckled lightly, a knowing glint in his eye. "Ah, the heart can be quite relentless, can't it? It often wants what it cannot have." Poole stepped closer, joining her by the window. "You know, Miss Lumsley, sometimes it's better to be honest with yourself. Ignoring your own heart's desires can only lead to more pain in the end."

"I know, Poole… And even if I don't want to admit it, I'm terrified of what could become of everyone and everything if I even told him, you said it yourself." she grimaces.

Poole nodded, a solemn expression on his face. "I understand, Miss Lumsley. The consequences, should things not go as desired, could be formidable. I'll admit, I wasn't found of the idea of Henry risking everything when he decided to take you in, but seeing how much you've changed him, seeing how happy he is with you around, it warmed my heart. Yes, there will be backlash to the scandal, but is it fair to keep your heart locked away in silence? To deny yourself even a chance of being happy?"

She nodded her head in thoughtful agreement. "I suppose not."

Poole laid a comforting hand on her shoulder. "Sometimes, taking a leap of faith, even if it's fraught with uncertainty, is worth the risk. Especially when it comes to matters of the heart."

Alice looks at Poole, a mixture of surprise and curiosity in her expression. She takes a deep breath, considering Poole's words. "Perhaps you're right," she replies quietly, her voice tinged with a hint of both hesitation and resolve. "Thank you, Mr. Poole."

***

That night, just as everyone was getting ready for bed, Poole had kept making subtle jabs at Alice to tell Henry.

"Goodnight, Poole," Alice said, attempting to slip past him.

But Poole gently nudged her toward Henry, his eyes sparkling with mischief as he mouthed, "Go for it, lassie."

Alice shook her head, her resolve wavering as she bit her lip in uncertainty.

Poole simply nodded, an encouraging smile on his face, and gave her another little push toward Henry and they headed up the stairs.

Before Henry walked in his room, Alice took his hand. If she was going to do what Poole said, she was going to rip it off like a Band-Aid,

"I just wanted to say.... I... I wanted to wish you a good night, Henry.... And... Sweet dreams."... Well, she inevitably faltered. Instead, she took a deep breath and gave him a kiss on the cheek.

Henry's eyes nearly popped out of his head. His mind was reeling, and he seemed both surprised and flustered, stuttering slightly. "Ah... well... good night yourself, Alice. See you in the morning," he managed, his face still red. As soon as he had gotten inside and shut the door, he leaned back against it with a bewildered expression on his face. A million thoughts ran through his head until two prominent ones made themselves known: 'She kissed me... and I liked it.' His mind filled with excitement. The memory of Alice's kiss ran in his head repeatedly. He just couldn't believe it. Even though it was just the cheek, Alice just kissed him.

Henry walked over to his bed and fell back on the mattress, but before he got the chance to shut his eyes, he could hear Hyde in his head. "So, Jekyll...," said Hyde. "Who's up for another evening of debauchery? Dare I say, I do feel something steering inside this body of ours."

At the sound of Hyde's voice, Henry groaned and buried his head in his hands. "I'm not in the mood tonight..." he said quietly. "...I've got a lot on my mind." Suddenly, he felt his head pounding.

"Obviously, you do, I can't feel it. Now go get the serum ready." Hyde said in a sharp tone.

"I said I don't want to tonight, and I mean it. Don't push me." His head was still pounding. Henry took a deep breath and tried to calm himself down.

"Oh, come on, Jekyll, I'm sure whatever you're doing is pointless and boring..., Let me fix that for you. You know you want to. All you must do is just take one small sip of the serum, and-".

"I said, no! No more of your nonsense, Hyde." Henry snapped. "I'm serious. Leave me alone right now, or else..." Henry's face was still red from the incident tonight, and he was determined not to let Hyde ruin it for him.

"Fine... have it your way." Hyde said with almost a sense of warning in his voice.

"Good. Now leave me in peace." Henry breathed in relief that he could finally relax and lay down in his bed. He was still trying to wrap his mind around everything that had happened tonight. He could barely believe that Alice had kissed him, and he was still trying to figure out what that meant. Henry tossed and turned for several minutes, unable to sleep due to the events of tonight. Eventually, he rolled over in bed and let out a yawn, closing his eyes and hoping to finally get some rest. But he couldn't stop thinking of Alice's soft lips, and in the silence of his room, he could hear Hyde's voice in his head, chuckling. Finally, exhaustion took hold, and he drifted off to a dreamless sleep.

***

That morning, Henry woke up with a bleared vision, his arm under his pillow and his forelock over his forehead as usual. He reached out for his glasses on the nightstand, but he must have turned on the right side of the bed and wasn't stimulated enough to roll over and get out of bed just yet. The room around him seemed more rundown, the windows covered in thick dark drapes that the morning light couldn't peek through. The room was lit by only a few candles on the dresser, and the sheets were thin and hardly used, but were warm. Something didn't feel right. He rubbed his eyes, and when his hand fell back down on the bed, he stared at it for a moment. He furrowed his brow in confusion, "This is not my hand," he whispered to himself, just staring at his hand. It was, lean, with defined knuckles. Not only that, but it was the hand, arm, and body of Edward Hyde, in the home of Edward Hyde. He sat up, recognizing the home in Soho, and looked down at himself. His blood rushed in his veins as he tried to figure out what had caused this. "What the hell happened last night?" He cursed to himself, still unable to remember the night before, he turned to the other side of the bed to reach for his glasses, and he looked down only to find the girl still asleep in bed next to him. Seeing her there caused Henry's mind to race with confusion and panic. 'Who the hell is she?' he thought to himself. He could make out her features in the dim light: the curve of her back, the tousled hair that spilled onto the pillow, and the steady sound of her breathing. The girl let out a soft, almost indistinct yawn, stirring slightly, the bed sheets slipped off her shoulder, revealing the bare skin of her back and a glimpse of her delicate collarbone. Henry quickly and cautiously got out of bed and grabbed his clothes, feeling embarrassed over the situation. He hurried to dress, gathering his thoughts, before remembering the etiquette of the situation. "Damn it," he muttered, reaching into his pocket and pulling out a few coins. He tossed the money onto the nightstand, hoping it would suffice as payment for the girl's services with Hyde. Henry quickly finished dressing, not daring to look at the woman in the bed, making his way out of the room, closing the door softly behind him. He stood in the hallway for a few moments, taking a deep breath to collect his thoughts and try to piece together the fractured memories of the previous night. As Henry stood in the hallway, he realized the urgency of the situation. Poole and Alice would likely be wondering where he was, and the longer he stayed in Hyde's home, the more difficult it would be to come up with a believable explanation. Without further delay, he quickly made his way out of the house, hurrying through the dimly lit streets of Soho.

***

Once he got to the back door of his laboratory, he quickly mixed and drank the serum. After the effects subsided, he took a deep breath. He was finally home in his body, he was more grateful to see the old place, more than ever. He hadn't even had his morning tea with breakfast yet, and hoped it was still warm. Alice was sitting upside-down, drawing on a notebook in the parlor room, and Poole was reading the newspaper. Henry quietly closed the door, till it made a clicking sound as it shut, causing Alice to look up. She smiled brightly and ran up to him to greet him, but this time, he stepped back. He thought that if Hyde could take over him without his control by using the serum, how long would it be till he lost control and hurt Alice?

"Henry?" she tried to move closer to him.

Henry flinched and took a step back from her as a deep sense of shame and guilt washes over him. "Err……I-I have… research…to do…" He looks at her apologetically before rushing up the stairs.

Alice could see something was wrong. "Henry, wait!" She rushed after him.

He quickly shut and locked the door behind him, not wanting anyone to come in, especially her. He leans against the closed door, breathing heavily and nearly hyperventilating. He collapsed to his knees and sighed, rubbing his face with his hands. Henry's mind racing with questions. How did this happen? What had he done to that poor woman in Soho? What if this happens again? Is he going to lose control permanently? And most importantly, how could he keep Alice safe? "… What have I done…?" He thought to himself.

Alice stood outside of his room; her mind was filled with questions as she just stood there staring at his door, perplexed, wanting nothing more than to just be there for him. Poole came upstairs, putting his hand on her shoulder, shaking his head, as he led her away back down the stairs. Alice stole one last glance back at the door before she lost sight.

***

August 23^{rd~} For a week and a half, the door stayed closed… a whole week of silence… a whole week of uncertainty, pain, and questions… Alice's worry grew with every tick of the clock, wondering what was going on behind the door. She laid trays of food out for Henry, hoping to catch a glimpse of the reason for his absence, but every time she did, Henry would steal away the tray when nobody was looking, as she'd come back unanswered questions and empty or half-empty trays outside the door…

The silence that filled the corridors of the house was deafening as Henry's self-enforced isolation continued. Each passing day felt like an eternity as he wrestled with his inner turmoil, shutting himself away from everyone. Hyde's latest transgressions had left him feeling guilt-ridden and terrified of what he might do. He buried himself in his work, desperately trying to suppress the memory of what had occurred, but his mind was plagued by images of the woman he had met in Soho, and her face was now permanently etched into his mind. Henry lay on his bed, his hands over his face as he groaned. 'God damn it!' He hissed in frustrated anger - at himself. He knew he couldn't hide away in his room forever, but he didn't want to see anyone. Especially not Alice. The memories of what he'd done as Hyde haunted him. He was ashamed and filled with remorse for the things he'd done, but most of all, he was terrified of losing control again. He let out a heavy sigh, falling back on his bed, his head in his hands. He thought about Alice, and how she must be feeling. He knew she was worried about him, but he just couldn't face her. Not now. Not after what he'd done.

Hyde chuckled as he appeared in Henry's bed chamber, finding Henry lying on his bed. He leaned against the door, watching Henry intently with a smirk on his face. "Hey, Dr. Jekyll!" he practically sang, his voice oozing with sarcasm. "Been quite a while since we've last talked, it's almost as if you're avoiding me." Hyde strolled about the room, examining Henry's surroundings with a critical eye. His boots clicked loudly on the hardwood floors, causing the quiet room to fill with noise.

Henry gritted his teeth in frustration as Hyde's voice echoed through the room, the sound breaking the silence he had been so determined to maintain. He slowly sat up, his irritation evident in the way he clenched his jaw. "Hyde," he said coldly, his eyes tracking the other man's movements across the room, "what do you want?"

Hyde slowly sauntered over to the bed, his arms folded behind his back, before he flopped down on the bed next to Henry, resting his head on one hand. "Oh, can't a guy visit his other half once in a while?" he asked teasingly. "I just missed your charming company so much."

Henry scoffed, shifting away as Hyde made himself comfortable on the bed next to him. He glared at the other man, his eyes narrowing in irritation. "Spare me the false sentiment," he retorted, his voice sharp and cold. "I know you're not here because you 'missed' me. What do you want, Hyde?"

Hyde chuckled, his smirk never leaving his face. He rolled onto his back, his arms behind his head as he stared up at the ceiling. "Now, is it really so hard to believe that I might just want to check up on you? After all, we're stuck together, aren't we?" he said. "But, if you really must know, I'm bored. Nearly 2 weeks, you've been in here, avoiding everyone. What's the big deal? Why hide yourself away like a coward?"

Henry bristled at the accusation. "I'm not hiding," he snapped defensively. "I just need some time alone. I have work to do... I can't deal with people right now." He crossed his arms, his expression growing more frustrated. "And I'm not a coward," he added, his tone almost petulant.

Hyde let out a melodramatic sigh, rolling his eyes. "Oh, please," he drawled out condescendingly. "You're literally hiding away in your room like a frightened child, avoiding everyone. Sounds pretty cowardly to me. Plus, you're a terrible liar. I can practically smell the guilt on you." He sat up on the bed, swinging his legs over the edge and facing Henry directly. "So, spill. Why the self-enforced isolation?"

Henry visibly tensed he clenched his jaw, his annoyance growing as Hyde continued to needle him. But as much as he hated to admit it, Hyde was right. "Fine," he snapped, his voice filled with irritation. "You really want to know? It's because… because of you, alright? I'm sick of dealing with the mess that you create. I'm always cleaning up after your mistakes. I need a break. Especially what you did with that woman."

Hyde smirked as Henry's words hung in the air, and he leaned in closer to Henry, a wicked glint in his eyes. "I know you have this…crush on dear Alice. But come on, Henry, where's the fun in only liking one person? That sort of restraint is so…boring." He leaned back again, a smug smile on his face.

Henry's expression hardened further, his eyes narrowing. He knew arguing with his other half was pointless, but he couldn't help himself. "Boring? Are you kidding me? That's your reasoning? You used my body to do God knows whatever with some harlot, and your defense is that it's boring to have a monogamous relationship?"

Hyde can't help but let out a bark of laughter at Henry's reaction. "Oh, come on, Henry. Don't be such a prude." He teases. "You're not even doing anything with Alice, even though you clearly want to. She's practically throwing herself at you, and yet you're too scared to make a move."

He let out a heavy sigh, running a hand through his hair. "I can't do this anymore, Hyde," he said, his voice strained. "I need a break from you. I need some time to figure things out without your constant… influence."

Hyde's smug smirk faltered for a brief moment before he regained his composure. He stood up from the bed, pacing the room. "Really? A break from me? How touching. But let's be honest here, we both know it's not just my mistakes that are causing this. You've become addicted to the power, the freedom. You may deny it, but there's a part of you that craves the release that comes with being me."

Henry glowered at Hyde as he paced, his words striking a nerve. "That's not true," he protested, his voice edged with defensiveness. "I have no desire to be free of my moral obligations." But his protest was weak, and even he knew it didn't entirely ring true. A small part of him did long for the freedom Hyde offered, a guilty secret he kept buried deep within. "I am not addicted to anything..." he insisted, his voice quieter now, lacking conviction.

Hyde's grin returned, seeing the flicker of doubt in Henry's eyes. He stopped pacing, turning to fully face Henry. "You can lie to yourself all you want, but you can't fool me. I know you better than anyone. I am you, after all. And I know that deep down, you love the rush you feel when you become me. You love letting go of your perfect facade. It's exhilarating, isn't it? Liberating... You're in denial, pretending to be the perfect gentleman when we both know damn well you want the thrill of letting loose." He took a step closer to Henry, his tone becoming more taunting. "Stop avoiding the truth and admit it. You like being me." Hyde took a step closer, his voice dropping to a sinister whisper. "But you can't deny it, can you? Sooner or later, you're going to give in. And when you do, I'll be waiting." Hyde chuckled and disappeared from infront of him.

Henry was left alone in the quiet room, his mind racing with confusion and self-doubt. He buries his face in his hands, groaning in frustration.

***

August 30th~ Alice's worry for Henry was growing by the day, and she couldn't just ignore it. As she passed by the shut door to Henry's room, which had been locked for 2 weeks now, she hesitated, her hand reaching out to the handle but then stopping halfway. She wanted to knock, to check on him, to confront him, but something held her back.

A mix of concern and respect for his privacy weighed heavy on her mind. But she couldn't shake the feeling that something bad was going on behind that door.

Poole was in the drawing room when he noticed Alice approaching down the stairs. He could tell from the worried expression on her face that she had come to talk about Henry. "Good evening, Miss Lumsley," He greeted her. "Is something troubling you?"

Alice was pacing once more, as Poole was going over a list of things at the table. "I can't take this, Poole. Something is wrong. What if Hyde did something to him?"

Poole looked up from his list, setting down his pen, "While Mr. Jekyll's actions are perplexing, I doubt it's anything catastrophic." He spoke in a reassuring tone, although his own concern for his master was evident. "Mr. Jekyll has barricaded himself in times past. Perhaps it's best to leave him be, for now."

"What did you mean? He's never done this before… Right," she stopped to face him, with one of her arms across her chest, and the other she was biting at her nails.

He sighed softly, taking a moment to gather his thoughts and to choose his words carefully. "Mr. Jekyll… has always been a very private individual," he began, "there have been times when he has isolated himself from others for days. Though," he said, pausing as though recalling something, "Never for quite this long."

His words reminded her of her past in the asylum, and it sent an unpleasant shiver through her "I've spent more time than I care to admit in a padded cell, Poole, and let me tell you, the only times anyone chooses solitude in a place like that is when they're completely without hope. Trust me, it's not a good sign. Something's definitely not right with Henry. Maybe I should try to get him to open up again?"

Poole understood the implications of her words and quickly sought to ease her fear. "Miss Lumsley, this is different. Mr. Jekyll isn't in the padded cell. This is his own way of coping, albeit rather extreme." He tried to sound reassuring as he continued, "He's just… going through some things, and he needs time alone so that he can figure them out, in his own manner."

She nodded slowly, but the crease in her forehead told Poole she didn't completely trust his words. Alice continued to chew at her nails as she thought. Suddenly, she stopped pacing, her eyes widening as an idea popped into her mind. "I have to go see him." With a determined expression, Alice began to bake. The kitchen was filled with the warmth of vanilla and the sweetness of sugar. As she mixed the ingredients and placed spoonfuls of dough onto the baking tray. As the cookies baked in the oven, their aroma filled the house, and Alice hoped that they would be the key to coaxing Henry out of hiding. Once the cookies were baked to perfection, their golden edges just turning brown, Alice took the tray out of the oven. The room filled with a warm, comforting scent. She carefully set the tray down on the counter, letting the warm cookies cool for a few moments before she started to plate them. With a steady hand, she took a deep breath, she made her way towards his room, her heart pounding in her chest. Standing in front of the door, Alice hesitated. The fear of what she might find on the other side filled her with a mix of dread and anticipation. But she knew she had to at least try, even if it might be a futile attempt. She knocked on the door gently, her knuckles making a soft tapping noise against the wood. She called out his name, "Henry?" Inside her mind, a million thoughts were racing; would he be angry? Would he respond at all? What state would she find him in? "I brought you cookies" She cringed internally at herself, feeling like it sounded stupid as she said it. But she quickly recovered and tried again. "May I come in?"

Henry at the door. He closed his eyes for a moment, taking a deep breath before responding. "Not now, Alice," he called out, his voice weary. "I'm not hungry." Even as he said the words, he could smell the aroma of freshly baked snickerdoodles wafting through the air, making his stomach rumble involuntarily.

Alice's heart sank as she heard his response. "Well.. They're still warm…" She paused, but didn't hear a word. "Fine." She set down the tray of cookies on the ground, right in front of the door. But instead of stepping back, she pressed her back firmly against the wall next to the door. She refused to give up so easily. She waited, her heartbeat hammering in her chest as she quietly held her breath.

Henry rose from his bed, his footsteps heavy as he approached the door. As he opened his door and reached down to pick up the tray, he paused, sensing something amiss. He could have sworn he heard the rustling of clothing.

Alice slowly crept her hand towards the doorknob, her fingers gripping the doorknob, hoping that Henry wouldn't hear her.

Henry's eyes narrowed, his suspicions aroused. He didn't believe for a moment that Alice had simply walked away after leaving the cookies. He could practically feel her presence on the other side of the door, trying to sneak a peek. With a smirk, he picked up the tray of cookies and stepped back from the door. He waited a moment, listening intently, before speaking. "You know I can tell you're still there, right?" he said, his voice laced with amusement. "You're not very stealthy."

As soon as he opened the door a little more, Alice sprang into action, with almost weasel-like grace, she maneuvered herself past him and into the room before he could react, shutting the door. She quickly spun around to face him, a mixture of worry, determination, and a bit of defiance etched across her features. "Henry," she said calmly. She takes a deep breath, closing the door behind them. She turned to face him, and once she started yelling, "How dare you scare us like this! Do you have any notion of the worry you've caused your friends and I? I've been worried! Hiding in room 247, not a word to be said, leaving us in the lurch! I've spent days and nights outside your door, fearing the worst, fearing you'd done something rash. I don't want to see you hurt yourself, Henry! I know you don't see how much you mean to us, but... we care about you. I care about you. Please, just talk to me. Let me-"

Without warning, Henry grabs her by the arms and pulls her close to him, hugging her tightly. The two of them are almost the same height, but still, the top of her head rests on his chest. His grip is warm, and she could feel his heart beating through his clothes. "Alice... I... am sorry. If I had known you'd been worrying so much, I would have done something about it. I...don't know what to say."

"Of course, I'm worried, you numpty!" She exclaimed, exasperated with him. "You've locked yourself away for weeks without a word. Do you have any idea how maddening it is for us? For me? I've been running myself ragged, thinking the worst, imagining all sorts of terrible things happening to you behind that blasted door! And I love you too much to just-"

"You love me...?" Henry cuts her off and says, before he can stop himself. He has a look of realization on his face that was as red as a tomato. The room was still as Jekyll took time to process what he had just heard. He couldn't believe it! Alice truly cared for him the same way he cared for her. 'She loves me too. She really does'. Suddenly, his expression brightened as a broad smile began taking shape. 'Alice loves me,' he thought excitedly, still struggling to believe that it was possible.

Alice flushed a deep shade of pink as she let go of him, her heart suddenly beating faster in her chest. "I...I... meant to say," she stumbled, trying to backtrack. "I meant to say that we're friends. I care about you... You're my best friend. But I.. I care about you."

Henry's smile continues to grow wider as he listens to Alice's flustered explanation. 'She's so adorable when she's embarrassed,' he thought fondly. He chuckled softly, his eyes still fixed on her flushed face, enjoying the sight of her trying to backtrack. "Best friends," he repeated, his tone playful. "Is that all we are, then?" He takes a step closer to her, "Or can I dare to hope for more?"

She sighed, feeling like a fool for having been caught red-handed. It was hard to keep her mouth shut sometimes, especially when it came to Henry. He was someone she felt she could be completely open with, having shared even her most embarrassing moments and darkest secrets. "I really am hopeless," she muttered, looking down at the floor. "I'm sorry, Henry... There are countless reasons why you shouldn't be with me. I'm a lunatic, a mess. I come with a whole lot of baggage. I'm damaged goods, not fit for anyone. You're brilliant and successful, you deserve someone who can keep up with you, who can match your intelligence and drive. Not me. I'll just bring you down... I can not and will not hold you back."

"Stop that..." Jekyll says, grabbing her arm.". Don't call yourself a lunatic, you are so much more than that Alice. There is nothing wrong with you. And don't talk like I'm better than you either. In fact, most of the time, I feel like I'm worse off than you, if for no other reason than just the sheer amount of stress... If a girl like you says that she loves me, then I am one of the luckiest men alive... And if you really think you're a Looney... You're my looney... My sweet, lovely looney."

She stares at him for a moment, as if he had just spoken in some foreign language. She couldn't believe what she was hearing. Her heart was pounding in her chest, as tears prick at the corners of her eyes. She had never dared to imagine that he might see something special in her, something worth loving. But here he was, telling her that she was his looney. It was everything she had ever wanted to hear, and it made her heart swell with emotion.... "I love you, Henry Jekyll... My mad scientist."

Without any prompting, a smile comes to his face, and he wraps her in an embrace. His arms wrap around her so tight... so warm... so... safe. He ran a hand through her hair and chuckled softly into her shoulder. The two fit together like puzzle pieces, like two halves of the same coin. No matter what happens, even if the whole world is against them, the two of them can hold each other. "I love you too, Alice Lumsley."

After what felt like an eternity, Henry tilted his head slightly, creating just enough space to look into Alice's eyes. The intensity of the moment made her heart race as she met his gaze, the depths of his warmth reflecting back at her. She could see the flicker of hesitation in his expression, mingled with a hope that made her breath catch in her throat. He was searching her face as if trying to read her thoughts, and in that silent exchange, her heart whispered a thousand affirmations. She could feel the fluttering in her stomach as he leaned in closer, his lips inches away. It was a delicate dance of fear and anticipation, both of them teetering on the edge of something beautiful yet overwhelming. She closed her eyes, surrendering to the moment. In a gentle, tentative gesture, Henry brushed his lips against hers, a feather-light touch that sent a spark coursing through her veins. It was a sweet, hesitant kiss that spoke volumes.

The kiss was slow and gentle at first, but then it grew stronger, both of them pouring all their emotions into it. She brings her hand up to his face, her fingers tracing across his cheek. His arms wrapped around her waist, pulling her closer as he savored the sensation of being so close to her. He had spent so long trying to push his feelings away, convincing himself it could never work, but now, with her in his arms, he knew with absolute certainty that he'd been wrong. When he pulls away, he looks into her shimmering emerald eyes, smiling and chuckles softly. "I think that's the first time either of us has had the courage to do that," He whispers softly.

Alice couldn't help but giggle, her cheeks flushed and her eyes sparkling with happiness. "Yes, it was." She leaned her head against his chest, her ear against his heart, listening to its steady rhythm. "But now that we've done it, I don't think I can go back to pretending we're just friends. I want to be with you, Henry. And I want you to be with me. No more holding back, no more hiding how we feel… For starters," she pushed his shoulder. "What were you thinking! Locking yourself in your room, what possessed you to do such a thing?"

He pauses, his expression conflicted as he tries to find the right words to explain himself. "There's something I need to tell you, Alice…" He took a deep breath, steeling himself for the conversation he was about to have. He knew that what he was about to reveal would change everything between them, and he could only hope that she would understand and forgive him. He led her over to his bed and sat down, patting the spot next to him. "Sit down, Alice," he said, a hint of trepidation in his voice. He took a moment to collect his thoughts, trying to find the right words to explain the complicated situation. "It's not easy to say. So, please, just listen to me without interruption, okay." Henry's heart was pounding in his chest as he told her the truth about Edward Hyde. It wasn't easy to admit what he had done, to reveal the darkness that lurked within him. He spoke of the incident with the child, how Hyde had taken over his body without warning. He spared no details, laying bare his fears of his worst mistakes. As he spoke, his voice trembled with the weight of his guilt and shame. But she stays silent and listens, her hands folded in her lap. Once he was finished, he sighed, covering his face, "I didn't tell you that because I feared how you'd react. I didn't want you to think I was a horrible person. I wanted to protect you from any potential danger and... him... but... well, it's obvious I haven't been successful at that, especially now." When a long moment of silence goes by and she doesn't say anything, his heart drops. 'She's probably in shock,' he thinks to himself, a little scared of what her answer will be. 'This is it. This is it. She's probably going to think I'm a freak, just like everyone else.' But he doesn't show it on his face, he simply stays sitting, fidgeting nervously. Eventually, expecting the worst, he spoke tentatively. "...say something...please..."

Instead, she let out a small chuckle, a mix of incredulity and disbelief. "Wow." She said, shaking her head. "Henry, I... wow." Her hand came up to cover a part of her face. "I know your.... But... wow... That explains a LOT."

He couldn't help but furrow his brow at her initial reaction, his stomach doing a series of somersaults. "Wait... wow? That's it? Just ... 'Wow'?"

She shakes her head to herself, a rueful smile creeping onto her face. "It explains a lot. I should have figured it out sooner." She scooted closer to him until their knees were touching. "How I could never find both of you at the same time... And the look in your eyes... I came from an asylum and not even I could have come up with that answer. I'll give it to you, I didn't expect it."

His face relaxed a little bit. She was... smiling, and it was still taking some time to process. Was... was she not afraid of him? Did she really not care that he could turn into someone evil? "...You're... not upset? Not horrified? Not... disgusted?"

She shook her head, her expression one of gentle understanding. "The things I've seen... Well, I've seen worse." She shrugged her shoulders lightly. "I don't think you're a monster, Henry. I think you're... human. But disgusted? Upset? No. Not at all. I could never be disgusted with you, Henry. Not for something like this."

For a few seconds, he was just trying to process her words. She... wasn't upset, she wasn't afraid. She didn't care that he was a monster inside. It was a strange feeling to say the least. Looking from their intertwined hands and up at her face, a small, slightly flustered smile grew onto his. "...You really don't care, do you?" He laughed softly for a second and leaned closer, resting his forehead against hers. "If I had known you would have reacted like THIS, I would have told you sooner..." Her head rested against his. He could feel her breath against his face as they were sitting so close, and a feeling of relief started to wash over him. Maybe with her on his side, he can keep Hyde under control.

"If you had only told me sooner..." she teased softly, and pressed a gentle kiss to his forehead. She thought about it for a moment pulling back to look at him, "But you do have it all figured out now, right? You're going to be ok?"

His mind briefly wandered to what the future might hold. Would he and Alice be able to be together, even with society or Mr. Hyde? He was silent for a moment, thinking about his next words carefully. "...I promise, I'm never going to take that serum again, I can control him." He reached up, his arms wrapping around her in a tight hug, pulling her against him, the words tumbling out of him in a broken whisper. "I... won't take the serum again." He repeated, but this time the words didn't sound as firm as he had wanted them to. There was a faint hint of uncertainty, a tremble in his voice that betrayed the doubt that lingered in his mind. He held her tight, as if trying to convince himself as much as he was trying to convince her. "I can control him."

Chapter 13

Murder Seance Happens!

October 18th~ After two months of rigorous self-control, in an attempt to resist any and all triggers, he avoided alcohol, any social gatherings, and any activity that might even remotely ignite Hyde. It was akin to placing a delectable piece of cake in front of a hungry child and telling him to refrain from taking a single bite. Although he attempted to keep his feelings and desires hidden, every passing day felt suffocating, and the temptation to give in became stronger and more unbearable. The internal battle raged on; the desire to take "just a little sip" slowly began to consume him. It was far worse than before he had created the serum - he knew the taste of freedom. Perhaps... perhaps if he just took a tiny bit, just a fraction, he could find control. Before he knew it, Henry had uncorked the vial and poured the serum down his throat. Instantly, a familiar tingling sensation spread through his veins as the transformation began. His body contorted, features twisting grotesquely into the visage of Mr. Edward Hyde.

Hyde took a shaky breath, reveling in the intoxicating robustness of his form. "Ah, much better," he murmured, his voice rougher and harsher, a jagged edge that spoke volumes of his newfound freedom. With a devilish smirk, Hyde stepped out into the shadowed streets of London, the flickering gaslights casting eerie patterns against the cobblestones, the night air abrisk and invigorating against his skin. As he prowled deeper into the heart of the night, a figure emerged from the mist. Sir Danvers Carew. The man's silhouette seemed almost noble, and a wild thrill shot through Hyde's spine. It was as if fate had conspired to deliver him this moment.

"Well, well, well. If it isn't Sir Danvers Carew himself," he mocked, his voice laced with venom, a predatory glint flickering in his golden eyes. "Fancy meeting you on this dark and lonely street, all alone without your entourage."

Sir Danvers turned slowly, scrutinizing Hyde with a blend of suspicion and unease rippling across his dignified features, his posture rigid despite the palpable threat brewing in the air. "And who might you be?" he demanded, his voice steady, trying to exude an air of authority.

Hyde swept his top hat from his head, bowing theatrically before the man, a grotesque parody of respect. "Edward Hyde, at your service," he replied, his voice dripping with sarcastic politeness, the air thick with irony. "And you, sir, are none other than Sir Danvers Carew, the renowned member of parliament."

"Mr. Hyde," Carew said stiffly, the way he enunciated the name suggesting a cold disdain, "what are you doing out here at such a late hour?"

"Just enjoying a leisurely stroll," Hyde said innocently, his tone mocking, as he closed the distance between them, spinning his cane around his finger. "But it seems rather reckless to be out here alone. Anyone could be lurking in the shadows, ready to pounce."

Carew stiffened, his eyes narrowing. "I can take care of myself," he insisted coolly, a stressed confidence that barely masked the tremor in his voice, as he attempted to brush past Hyde. But Hyde blocked his path with ease.

"Oh, but we have some unfinished business," Hyde revealed, the words spilling from his lips like honey laced with poison, his predatory gaze boring into Carew's. "Your refusal to fund my friend's project..."

"Who?" Carew replied, eyebrows raised, his composure slipping.

"Doctor. Henry. Louis. Jekyll," Hyde spat back, irritation bubbling beneath his deceitful facade, his features contorting with disdain as he spoke the name.

"Ah yes, that foolish project," Carew replied dryly, taking a step back, a smirk of disbelief dancing on his lips. "I stand by my decision."

Hyde's grin morphed into one of pure malevolence. "Foolish? Well, my dear Sir Danvers, I think your judgment may be a bit… flawed," he taunted. "It seems there needs to be some ramifications."

As the tension escalated, something fragile within Carew quivered, "You wouldn't dare harm a member of parliament," he protested weakly, his eyes widening with fear that betrayed the veneer of nobility he desperately clung to.

Hyde cackled coldly, a sound that sliced through the silence of the night like glass. "Your title means nothing to me. You arrogant old fool!" With calculated ease, he raised his cane high, striking Carew brutally. The sickening thud resonated through the quiet street, a macabre echo in the stillness of the night.

Carew crumpled to the ground like a discarded rag doll, clutching his abdomen, his breath escaping in sharp gasps. "Please…stop…" he managed to plead, the desperation in his voice drowning beneath the cruel laughter that poured from Hyde's lips.

"Your arrogance deserves punishment, mo mhac," Hyde sneered. With each hit, he felt a twisted sense of triumph. The sweet taste filled the air, mixing with the hot blood that spilled upon the cobblestones. Finally, when the old man lay crumpled and motionless, the realization of what he had done washed over Hyde like ice water. He had crossed a line, ending the life of a member of the British Parliament, no less, and the gravity of his actions sent waves of panic through him. With haste, he scanned the deserted street, searching for any witnesses as shadows swallowed the evidence of his crime. Realizing he was far from his lab; he felt desperation clawing at him. He needed the serum to transform back, to escape this nightmare. "Where is it?" he muttered, rifling through his pockets in a frenzy. "Damn it all," he cursed. The night air was eerily still; he had to move fast. He knew his only sanctuary was back in Jekyll's lab. He glanced back at Carew's lifeless body, the terror painted across the old man's face now haunting him. "This is a real mess," he muttered, guilt clawing at him as he took off into the London night.

***

Once back in his laboratory, Henry's heart raced painfully in his chest, each beat reverberating like a drum in his ears. He could still remember the rush of adrenaline he felt as Hyde. The memory alone was enough to send a shiver down his spine. Now, as Henry looked down at his trembling hands, he felt sick to his core. He had broken his promise to Alice, and the consequences of his actions felt like a weight pressing down on his conscience. He gripped the beaker tighter. "What have I done?" he murmured, the words catching in his throat. Sir Danvers Carew's lifeless eyes and the horror of his transformation loomed in his mind like a specter. How could he have allowed Hyde to roam free? He looked at the beaker, his image stared back from the glass beaker, reflection distorted much like his fractured soul. In a moment of anguish, he hurled it against the wall, the glass exploding into shimmering fragments. Crumbling to the floor by the fireplace, he buried his face in his arms, tears streaming down his cheeks. With every shuddering breath, the memory of what Hyde had done replayed in his mind: the violence, the anger, the irreversible decision. He clenched his fists, his knuckles turning white with the force of his self-hatred. The silence in the room was deafening, broken only by the occasional crackle from the fireplace.

***

After a few minutes, Alice silently opened the door to the laboratory... her heart sank at the very sight of her dear Henry. She walked over to him and, without a word, sat right beside him, their shoulders touching gently, offering a comforting presence. Henry's body stiffened at her touch, but then he allowed himself to lean into her embrace. He was usually so composed, so put together, but in that moment, he felt exposed and vulnerable. He buried his face in her shoulder, choking back a sob as tears streamed down his cheeks. "I'm sorry," he muttered, his voice shaking. "I'm so sorry. I took the serum, and killed Sir Danvers Carew."

Alice wrapped her arms around him in a gentle hug, gently rubbing his back, "Shh, it's alright." She whispered softly, "This isn't your fault."

He pulled his head up, his eyes were red and puffy from crying, and his cheeks were flushed. He took a deep breath, trying to compose himself. "Yes, it is," he muttered, his voice hoarse. "I don't deserve your kindness-"

"Hush, Henry," she said softly. "You do deserve this." She gently cupped his face in her hands, her thumbs brushing away his tears. "Forgive yourself," she asked. "What if I refuse your guilt? What if I reject the idea that your pain is deserved? Perhaps it's not forgiveness that you need, but acceptance. To accept that this darkness is a part of you, and that… that you are still worthy of love and acceptance, no matter what. What would you say to that, Henry?" As Alice spoke, his gaze flickered from her eyes to the ground, his mind wrestling with her words.

"Acceptance…" Henry muttered softly. "Is that what you're suggesting? Accept the darkness that lives within me? The darkness that is Hyde…" He was silent for a moment, considering her words. "I don't know if I can. How can I accept something like that? Something so monstrous, so wicked, when I'm a murderer."

She moves closer to him, sitting beside him on the floor, their shoulders touching gently, offering a comforting presence. "You are not a murderer," she said, her voice filled with conviction, meeting his gaze with unwavering certainty. "Hyde is the one who committed the crime, not you, Henry. You are not responsible for his actions. It's not your fault."

"But it is!" Henry snapped, his voice cracking with frustration and self-directed anger. He ran his fingers through his hair, pulling on it as if trying to physically extract the memories of his heinous acts. "I took the serum. I created him. Hyde is my darkness. My inner demons made flesh."

"Henry," Alice whispered, her voice filled with empathy and concern. "Do you honestly think you're the only one with darkness inside? Everyone has a monster inside themselves, some just hide it better than others." She paused, her gaze softening as she stared into his eyes. "We're all flawed. We've all done things we're not proud of."

Henry's eyes widened at the honesty in Alice's words. Her words struck a chord within him. He swallowed hard, his voice barely above a whisper as he responded, "I don't understand. How can you look at me like that, knowing what I've done? Knowing who I truly am?"

She moved, so she sat in front of him. "Every single living thing is capable of darkness, Henry… and I'm so sorry that everyone isn't willing to believe or accept it themselves... Henry, I would love to kill every doctor in the asylum for what they did and burn down the building itself. I want to carve out their organs and feed them to the rats. I want to drill holes in their skulls and let their brains rot. I want to watch them scream and beg for mercy as I rip their limbs apart, piece by piece. I want to make them feel the same agony they've inflicted on us. I want to break them. I want to reduce them to quivering wrecks, begging for their next fix of medication just to dull the pain...... But I don't... Because I don't want to turn out like them." She took his hand gently in hers. "I've suffered under their hands once, and I refuse to become like them. But that doesn't mean I'm not tempted, oh, I am tempted to. Because of them, I've lost my innocence, I have nightmares, I get panic attacks, I can't stand being in any room alone, and I'm terrified of every person I meet. Why should I show them restraint when they never showed me any?" A tear rolled down her cheek as she swallowed back her anger. She looked into his eyes, her gaze unwavering. Her grip on his hand tightened slightly. "You have no idea how much you mean to me. You saved me from the darkness. You gave me a home, a purpose, a life. And the thought of losing that... it's more terrifying than any vengeance I could ever seek."

Henry's heart skipped a beat as he listened to Alice's impassioned confession. The raw honesty in her voice, the fire in her eyes, it all floored him. He had never seen this side of her before, and it left him both shocked and strangely mesmerized. He raised his hand, gently wiping away the tear that rolled down her cheek. His touch was gentle, almost reverent. "Alice, I..." He trailed off, unsure of what to say. Here she was, confessing her own dark desires, her own demons. And she still looked at him with that same love in her eyes. He took a deep breath, trying to collect his thoughts. "I had no idea you felt that way..." he muttered softly.

"Henry," she said softly, her voice filled with urgency, "please don't misunderstand. I'm not trying to compare our experiences. I'm just trying to make you understand that we all carry darkness inside of us. You're not alone in this. But I want you to know something else. Your darkness doesn't scare me."

Henry let out a shaky exhale, his voice trembling as he spoke. "But... but how can you say that? How can you look at me, knowing what I've done... knowing what I'm capable of... and still love me?"

Alice took both of his hands in hers, holding them tightly, her grip steady and sure. "Because, I've seen the worst of you," she said firmly, gazing right into his eyes. "I've seen Hyde. And yes, he's a part of you, but he's not all of you. You're so much more than your darkness, so much more than your mistakes." She paused, her voice softening with sincere affection. "And I love all of you. Every part, even the parts you're ashamed of."

Henry looked into her eyes and saw nothing but honesty and tenderness. He swallowed hard, the lump in his throat growing larger. "You're... you're completely insane, you know that, right?" he smiled slightly.

Alice rolled her eyes affectionately. "And you're completely ridiculous," she retorted playfully, the edges of her lips curling into a smile. "And in desperate need of some self-confidence." She released one of his hands and gently flicked his forehead. "Now quit trying to push me away with self-deprecation and just accept it, for god's sake. I love you. You're stuck with me."

Henry let out an involuntary gasp at the flick on his forehead and rubbed the spot with a mock pout, though his eyes crinkled in amusement. "I'll try," he mumbled reluctantly. "But you're quite the handful, you know that?" a smile pulled at the corners of his mouth.

Alice gave his hand a gentle squeeze, "You'd better," she said firmly. "Because I'm not going anywhere. You're stuck with me." She paused for a moment, her expression growing serious. "But... there's something else we need to talk about." She paused, taking a deep breath before continuing. "Henry, what do we do about Hyde? He... he can't come out anymore, not after what he did. And suppressed like that... it's not healthy for either of you."

Henry sighed deeply, his shoulders slumping as he admitted quietly, "I know... But I don't know what else to do about him. He's... he's too unpredictable. Too dangerous to be let loose freely."

Alice nodded. "I understand," she said softly. "But... maybe we could try something different. What if we lock away the serum? And Hyde's clothes, any of his belongings... put them somewhere where you can't access them easily. That way, the temptation won't be there. And Hyde won't be able to take control without the serum."

He nodded slowly, considering her words. "It's... it's worth a try," he murmured, his voice hesitant yet hopeful. "It could work... it could help me keep control, and keep Hyde from causing any more trouble..." He paused for a moment, a look of determination crossing his face. "I'll do it. I promise," he said quietly. "I won't hide it from you anymore. If I start to feel the pull of Hyde, or if I'm struggling to contain him, I'll come to you. I won't try to deal with it on my own." He reached out and gently took her hand, his grip firm yet tender.

"Good," she said softly, her expression softening. "I trust you, Henry. And I'll be here for you whenever you need me. We'll get through this together." She paused for a moment, a small smile tugging at the corners of her mouth. "Now, why don't we go and lock away that serum before you change your mind?"

Henry gave a half-hearted chuckle, rubbing the back of his neck sheepishly. "You know me too well," he muttered, a hint of a smile on his face. "Alright, let's get this over with before I come up with some excuse to procrastinate." He stood up, still holding onto her hand. Together, they headed towards the cabinet where he kept the serum. Henry took a deep breath as they reached the cabinet, steeling himself for what he was about to do. He slowly opened the cabinet, revealing a few vials of the dreaded serum sitting innocently on the table. He paused for a moment, his eyes fixed on the vials, the weight of what he was about to do feeling heavier than ever before. "Are... are you sure about this?" he asked, his voice quiet and uncertain. "What if... what if I need it one day? What if I..." He trailed off, unable to voice his own darkest fears.

She stepped closer to him, her expression solemn and firm. "Henry," she said softly but firmly. "You don't need it. You never did. You're strong enough to handle whatever the world throws at you without it." She reached for one of Hyde's shirts, folding it up, and nudging Henry towards a chest in the corner of the room. "And as long as you have me by your side, you will never need Hyde again."

Henry listened to her words, his heart growing warmer with every word she spoke. He looked at her with a mixture of gratitude and awe, feeling humbled by her unwavering faith in him. "How are you this wonderful?" he murmured, taking the shirt from her and dropping it into the chest. He turned to the table, hesitating for a moment before reaching out and wrapping his hand around one of the vials of serum. He held the vial for a few moments, feeling the cool glass against his fingers. But then he looked at her, seeing the trust and confidence in her eyes. He knew she was right. He didn't need it. With a steeling breath, he dropped the vial into the chest, watching it land with a soft thud amongst the clothing and belongings of Hyde.

Alice smiled, giving him a kiss on the cheek. "That's the first step... Now, let's pack up the rest." She watched him as he packed Hyde's possessions away, along with the serum's ingredients and his notebook. As he closed the lid on Hyde's possessions, he felt a strange sense of finality. She stepped up behind him, wrapping her arms around his waist and resting her chin on his shoulder. "You're doing the right thing," she whispered, her voice filled with reassurance. "I know it's hard, but it's necessary. For both of you... I'm so proud of you Henry."

As he locked the chest, sealing Hyde's belongings away tightly and locking in in his chest. They put the chest in a large drawer and locked it, and when Henry gave her the key, he felt a wave of relief wash over him. It was done. Hyde was, temporarily at least, secured. He wrapped his arms around her and pulled her closer, burying his face in her hair, letting out a sigh of relief. "I... I can't believe I actually did it," he mumbled, his voice slightly muffled by her hair. "It... it feels surreal..."

She rested her head against his chest, listening to the steadying rhythm of his heartbeat. "You did it," she confirmed softly. "And I knew you could." She stepped back slightly, looking up at him with a mixture of affection and pride in her eyes.

Chapter 14

We're Both Mad Here.

October 18th of 1887~ Henry opened his eyes to find the sun's warm rays gently streaming into the room. Turning his head to the side, he couldn't help but smile widely at the sight before him. Alice was asleep beside him, her unruly curls framing her face like a halo. A tender smile spread across his lips at the sight of her. He leaned closer, pulling her into his arms and brushing soft kisses along her shoulder, his fingers tracing light, delicate patterns on her skin. "Good morning, my love," he whispered, his voice still thick with sleep.

Alice felt the familiar warmth of his affection, pretending to remain asleep. His kisses tickled her shoulder, sending delightful shivers down her spine.

Henry chuckled softly, clearly aware that she was awake despite her best efforts. With a playful glint in his eyes, he leaned in closer, taking a lock of her curly hair and brushing it against her nose.

Unable to hold back any longer, Alice let out a stifled giggle that turned into a bubbling laughter. She opened her eyes to meet his gaze, the amusement that danced between them was infectious, "Alright, alright, I give up. I'm awake!" With a grin, she turned towards him and snuggled closer. "Good morning, you cheeky thing." She pressed a gentle kiss to his knuckles, cradling his hand beneath her chin.

Henry's hazel eyes sparkled with affection as he leaned in to press a light kiss to her forehead, his fingers still playfully twirling another strand of her hair. "You mischievous little minx." His other hand moved to brush her curls back from her face, revealing more of her green eyes. "Now, how long were you planning on pretending to be asleep, hm?

Alice couldn't help but smirk, enjoying the playful interaction. She reached up to run her fingers through his messy morning hair. "Oh, I could've pretended to sleep a little longer. But as much as I'd love to stay in bed all day with you, I have plans," she says with a soft smile, placing a kiss against his neck, before sitting up in bed.

Henry's arm still lazily slung across her waist, not quite ready to let her leave the bed quite yet. "Oh, really? Plans, huh? What kind of plans could possibly be more enticing than spending all day in bed with me?" He jokingly pouted, one hand propped himself up, the other reaching out to lightly trail up her back in an affectionate manner, pulling her back into his arms. "Do these plans involve me, or am I going to be left out in the cold today?" he teased.

Alice rolled her eyes playfully, unable to resist his charming pout. "Oh, I don't know…" She feigned indifference, playing along with the banter. "Perhaps I just found something more interesting to do. But since you must know, it's our anniversary today."

He chuckled softly, his hand continued its gentle path up her back, a small smile playing on his lips as he watched her reactions. "Oh, is it now? But dear, our anniversary isn't until October."

Alice glanced over to his nightstand where his glasses sat, reaching over and plucking his glasses from the table. "Love, Today is October." She put the glasses on him. "Maybe you need these more than you thought."

Henry's eyes widened slightly as he felt Alice place his glasses on him. "October… a year already?" He exhaled, running a hand through his already tousled hair. He paused for a moment, his mind reeling slightly as he realized the date. The year anniversary of… that night. His brow furrowed for a brief moment before shaking himself from his thoughts and sitting up. "Seems like just yesterday you came into my life."

Alice rested a comforting hand on his arm, feeling the soft fabric of his nightwear. "It has been a rollercoaster of a year, hasn't it?" She said softly.

Henry turned to look at her, his gaze meeting hers, and a soft sigh escaped him as he nodded. "You could say that again," he murmured, his voice tinged with a mix of emotions. He reached out and covered her hand with his, taking a moment to collect his thoughts. "I don't know where I'd be if you didn't come into my life." He wrapped an arm around her shoulder.

Alice leaned her forehead against his. "I can't imagine my life without you by my side, not for a single day," she nuzzled her forehead against his.

Suddenly, a knock on the door broke the silence. Henry and Alice were both pulled abruptly from their moment of intimacy. Henry sighs, but there is a hint of a smile on his lips as he calls out in return, "Come in."

Poole enters the room, his expression betraying nothing but the usual dutifulness. His eyes flicker to the scene before him and clears his throat softly before speaking. "Sir, miss. Breakfast awaits downstairs, but we're running low on supplies. I took the liberty of preparing a list for today's errands."

Henry straightens himself slightly, he smiles at his butler and nods appreciatively. "Very good, Poole. We'll be down shortly. Thank you for taking the initiative with the shopping list. Please leave it on my desk, and we'll discuss it further over breakfast."

With a polite nod, Poole retreated and closed the door behind him. As he quietly slipped into the corridor, his mind drifted to thoughts of Henry and Alice. Despite the potential scandal in their relationship, he couldn't deny the positive impact she had on Jekyll. There was a noticeable change in his demeanor ever since Alice entered the picture. A subtle smile tugged at the corners of Poole's lips. In a metaphorical sense, he felt like he was entrusting Henry into Alice's care, surrendering the responsibilities that he had held for nearly 24 years.

Meanwhile, Henry turned back to Alice, a soft smile still lingering on his lips. "Well, Alice, seems like our peaceful morning has been interrupted by the realities of the day. Breakfast awaits downstairs, and

I suppose we should tend to those errands, eh?" He shifted position, stretching his arms and sitting up straighter, the sheets pooling around his waist. He glanced over at Alice, his eyes shimmering with affection, and reached out to gently tuck a lock of her unruly hair behind one ear.

Alice leaned over and gave Henry a quick, affectionate kiss. "Right," she chuckled, sliding out of bed. Stretching her arms above her head, she savored the delightful release of her muscles from the remnants of sleep. Turning to the corner of the room, where a water basin and a mirror awaited, she splashed her face with water, washing away the morning drowsiness before grabbing a small towel to dab at her skin.

Henry pushed aside the bedding, he swung his legs over the edge of the bed. Running a hand through his tousled hair in an effort to bring some order to it, he padded over to his dresser. He selected a pair of gray trousers, a crisp white linen shirt, suspenders, and a brown waistcoat, laying them out neatly on the bed. Henry glanced over at Alice, and couldn't help but marvel at how natural this scene felt, the domesticity of sharing a morning routine with her. After a few moments, realizing he may have been staring, he shook himself from his thoughts. Once he was done dressing, Henry glanced up, only to find Alice already dressed in a charming white dress with navy blue spots. The fabric was modest with short puffed sleeves and four navy buttons to the bodice and ruffles and chiffon towards the bottom. A broad smile spread across his face as he took in the sight of her, clearly smitten.

Alice spun around in a flourish, feeling the soft fabric of her dress flow around her legs. She glanced over to Henry, a delighted smile spreading across her face as she noticed his expression. She let out a soft chuckle, "Seems like you approve of the dress."

Henry chuckled warmly, reaching over to a soft, charcoal gray jacket, with his grandfather's pocket watch inside. He slipped it on and walked towards her. His arms found their way around her waist, pulling her towards him. He couldn't help but admire her, admiring the way the fabric of her dress seemed to bring out the vibrancy of her eyes. "Approve?" he mused, his hands sliding up and down the small of her back in a gentle caress. "That would be quite an understatement. You look simply ravishing. As you always do."

"Careful, Henry," Alice teased, tilting her head slightly, "You're not allowed to be charming before breakfast, especially when you look all handsome. It's a rule." She leaned in closer, her fingers tracing the collar of his shirt, her touch light and gentle. "But then again, we've always been known to break a few rules, haven't we?" She leaned in, her lips meeting him in a soft kiss.

Henry melted into the kiss, tightening his grip around her waist, holding her close. He kissed her slowly, savoring the closeness between them. When they finally parted, he rested his forehead against hers, gazing into her eyes, his voice barely above a whisper, "I love you, Alice."

Alice's heart fluttered at the sound of those three simple words. She gently traced her fingers along his jaw. "I love you, Henry," she replied softly, her voice filled with genuine tenderness. She nuzzled her nose affectionately against his, a light laugh escaping her lips. "Now come on," she pulled away from him, taking his hand. "We were promised breakfast."

***

Their day was filled with various tasks and errands, both simple and mundane. They visited the local bakery to stock up on fresh bread and pastries and made a stop at the butcher's for meat provisions. They browsed the stalls in the market, hand in hand, as they purchased fresh fruits and vegetables, and they even stopped by the florist to pick out some vibrant flowers for the home. Amidst the errands, they found moments to steal away and share quiet, affectionate moments- a quick kiss here, a lingering touch there. Their exchanges were playful and filled with warmth.

They decided to have their weekly walk through the park early. It was a beautiful day out, the sun was warm on their skin, yet there was a cold, gentle breeze that tousled their hair.

Henry enjoyed strolling through the park with Alice. It was moments like this, surrounded by nature's beauty and free from the confines of his laboratory, that he felt the most at ease. The corners of his lips curled up into an amused smile, and he reached out his free hand to gently brush a lock of hair that had fallen across her forehead.

As they walk through the park, Alice notices a small, open area next to a small pond. Excitedly, she grabs his hand, pulling him over to it, her smile wide. "Ooh! Let's sit over here, the view is just perfect." She plops down onto the soft grass, setting the bags on the other side of her, patting the spot next to her, urging him to sit beside her. The sound of the water gently lapping against the banks of the pond provides a soothing backdrop to their time together. Alice leans back on her hands, tilting her head towards the sky, her smile radiant.

Henry let his gaze linger on her for a moment, admiring her relaxed demeanor and the way the sunlight danced across her features. "You're right, this is perfect." He shifted his position, making himself more comfortable, and leaned back on his hand, still holding Alice's hand in his. He lifted their intertwined fingers to his lips and softly kissed the back of her hand.

She leaned her head against his shoulder, basking in the silence and peace that surrounded them. Henry's scent of pine and honeydew mingled pleasantly with the fragrance of the surrounding flora.

Henry turned his head slightly, nuzzling his cheek against her hair, the soft locks tickling his face. "It's getting late" he whispered, but he was in no rush to leave.

When they were getting ready to leave the park, Alice couldn't resist the playful urge within her. With a flick of her fingers, she sprayed Henry's face with a slight mist of water. She giggled as she saw the surprise on his face, the water drops shimmering on his skin.

He shook his head, trying to clear the water from his face, before turning to Alice, his eyebrows raised in mock disbelief. "You did not just do that!" he exclaimed in a playful tone, a smile tugging at his lips. He suddenly lunged forward, his long arm reaching out to grab Alice around the waist, pulling her towards him. She squeaked in surprise as she was yanked off her feet and onto his lap. He chuckled, as he wrapped his arms around her waist, preventing her from squirming free. He leaned back against the large oak tree behind him, his grip firm yet playful. His heart thudded against his ribcage, anticipating her reaction. "Got you now, my love," he murmured, a teasing smile on his face. "You asked for it, you know," he murmured, his breath warm against her ear. He began to lightly tickle her side.

Alice erupted into a fit of laughter. "Hahahaha! St-stop! You know I'm ticklish there!" She squirmed and wriggled in his lap, trying to escape his playful torment.

As the two women passed by, they couldn't help but shoot a judgmental glare in Henry and Alice's direction. They watched as Alice escaped from his grip and Henry ran after her, nearly forgetting the groceries.

The older women exchanged a look of disapproval, shaking their heads in disapproval. "I swear, these young folks have no decency anymore," one of the women muttered to the other, her voice dripping with disapproval.

"I couldn't agree more. Can't even walk through the park without bumping into someone acting like a couple of squirrels in heat," the other woman responded, rolling her eyes.

***

Henry and Alice were back home. The house was aglow with soft candlelight, the warm light flickering and dancing across the walls and furniture. The smell of freshly cooked food filled the air, making their mouths water in anticipation. Henry had finished setting the table, and he was standing in the kitchen with Alice, helping her put the last few finishing touches on their anniversary dinner. Henry stood just behind Alice, his hands on her hips as he peered over her shoulder at the pot on the stove. He gave a small, content sigh, nuzzling his face into her hair, and gently placed a kiss on her temple.

Alice's heart fluttered at the gentleness and sweetness of Henry's gesture. She leaned back into him momentarily, relishing the closeness, before returning her attention to the food. She stirred the pot and added some final seasonings, the enticing smell wafting up to greet them. "Almost done," she said, her voice soft and tinged with excitement. "Just needs a moment longer. Why don't you go sit down, love?"

Henry smiled, "Of course, dear." He placed another soft kiss on her temple before reluctantly stepping back. He walked over to the table, taking his jacket off and laying it on the back of his chair, taking a seat and observing the setting with a content smile. The food smelled absolutely delicious, and he couldn't wait to dig in and enjoy their meal together. "I must say, you've done an exceptional job in the kitchen, love," he said, his voice soft and sincere. "Everything smells absolutely divine, no offense to Poole, but then again, I'm sure he enjoys having the night off, wherever he is… It's just us tonight."

Alice finished stirring the pot and turned off the stove before taking out two plates and scooping some dinner onto them. "Thank you, Henry." she replied, walking over to the table with the plates in her hands. She carefully set down the food in front of Henry and then took a seat next to him, her eyes gleaming with excitement. "I hope you enjoy it. Oh, one more thing." Alice went to the cupboard and pulled out a bottle of Henry's favorite wine. Even though she didn't drink herself, knowing how much he appreciated a good vintage, even though she didn't understand the fuss, she wanted to make the evening special for him. "I picked up your favorite," she said, holding out the bottle for him, sitting back down. "I hope you like it."

Henry's eyes lit up with surprise. He took the bottle from her, admiring it for a moment, "You shouldn't have," he said, his voice laced with gratitude. "But thank you, I appreciate it. You really know how to spoil a man." He popped the Cork.

***

Dinner was an absolute success. By the end of the meal, both of them were feeling warm, full, and content. Henry leaned back in his chair, a feeling of contentment washing over him as he looked at Alice with a smile. Henry slowly stood up, holding out his hand towards Alice. "Dance with me," he said, a hint of playfulness in his voice.

Alice's eyes widened slightly, surprised by the sudden invitation. "Dance with you?" she repeated, a mixture of surprise and excitement in her voice. She stared at his outstretched hand for a moment, a small, coy smile forming on her lips. "Well, I guess I could humor you, love." She said nonchalantly, but really, she adored it, taking his hand.

Henry pulled her towards him, wrapping his arm around her waist and drawing her close to his body. He found himself staring down into her sparkling eyes, captivated by her beauty as they gently swayed to the soft music.

She wrapped her arm around his shoulder, letting the other hand find its place within his. The music, the soft candlelight, and the feeling of being in his embrace all combined to create a bubble of intimacy that enveloped them.

He chuckled and gave her a twirl, the soft candlelight casting a warm glow around them. "You look absolutely radiant tonight," he said, his voice low and sultry.

Alice's face tinged with a soft blush, her cheeks taking on a lovely shade of pink as he twirled her around. His compliment made her feel a bit self-conscious, and she found herself attempting to cover her face with her hands in a shy gesture. "Oh, stop it," she muttered, feeling her cheeks heat up even more.

Henry grins at this, "Aah," He teases, "Don't try to hide your face from me." He gently pulls her hands away from her face. "Oh, darling..." He chuckles softly, moving his hands to her cheek. "You look like a ripe tomato right now..."

Alice couldn't help but giggle as Henry teased. She playfully tried to push him away, "You're not helping, you know," she protested, her cheeks still flushed with a warm blush. "Stop teasing me."

Without warning, he scoops her up into his arms in one smooth movement, carrying her bridal-style, holding her tightly against his chest.

Alice instinctively clings to him, a small, involuntary squeal escaping her lips. As he begins to spin and twirl around with her, she can't help but burst into a fit of giggles. However, her laughter is abruptly interrupted as she accidentally kicks over his wine glass, the last remaining drops of the dark red liquid staining the sleeve of his coat. "Oh no! I'm sorry!" she exclaimed, looking at the red stain with worry. "Your coat!"

Henry glances at his jacket, then looks back at her. "Don't worry about it, love," he says, his tone reassuring. "It's just a jacket; it can be cleaned." He looks at the stain, then grins down at her. "Besides, having you in my arms is far more important than a jacket, don't you think?" He starts walking up the stairs towards the bedroom with her still in his arms, holding her close against his chest. As they enter the room, he gently lays her down on the bed, his eyes never leaving hers. He gazes down at her with tenderness and adoration, his thumb tracing the contour of her face. "You're so precious to me, you know that?" He kisses her deeply and slowly, his hands sliding up her arms and over her back.

She can feel her heart racing as she kisses him back, her fingers playing with his soft hair. They seem to drift away from everything around them, just him and her, the world fading away. His breathing grows softer, his kisses become gentler and sweeter, and more loving. Henry's lips travel down Alice's neck, leaving her heart beating quickly and her breathing hitched. But once he gets to her collarbone, he finds himself coming across a scar Alice has had since the asylum. His lips pause abruptly, as she instinctively tries to cover the scar, shame creeping into her features. But he gently moves her hand, his eyes filled with tender understanding. He looks at her, his eyes full of love and acceptance. "Dear, why would you cover it? It's part of who you are, and I love that part of you just as thoroughly as all the other parts. I adore you, in all your forms, in all your glory. It's not something I can ignore. It's a part of you, it's you, and it's part of why I adore you so. You need to understand that I'm not ashamed of your scars or marks, but rather happy that you have survived the experiences that you gave them."

She feels his touch, his words, and the unwavering acceptance he radiates. Her heart swallows the lump in her throat, her voice barely a whisper. "Henry... I..." She takes a deep breath, trying to find the right words to express the maelstrom of feelings within her. "...I just don't want you to see me as... broken."

Henry shakes his head, "I wish that the things you had been through hadn't happened to you, yes. But I wouldn't change who you are now." He gives her hand another squeeze, as he brings it to his chest over his heart. " I don't know what you went through, I will never understand what it's like... But I'd be a fool not to see the beautiful, amazing girl that survived." He gently traced his fingers over her collarbone, right above the scar. "I know you don't like looking at them, but your scars, my dear, are a testament to your strength. They are a part of you, a part of this journey that made you who you are... and made me fall in love with you, even more, and make me fall madly in love with you every day. And that strength has helped me in ways I never could have expected. It's not just your strength that's admirable, but also your kindness and compassion. You saw the weakness within me, and you helped me overcome it. I don't know how to ever thank you enough for that."

She nodded, her mind was suddenly flooded with dark memories, and her joyous expression faltered; her thoughts briefly drifted to the bite mark on her shoulder. She took a deep breath, pushing away the dark thoughts. She was safe now, with Henry, away from the asylum. She leaned in closer to him, her hand finding its way to his cheek, her touch tender and filled with affection. "I know I've already said it a million and a half times, but... I love you..."

Henry couldn't help but smile at her words, placing his own hand over hers, keeping it in place against his face, his eyes still locked onto hers. "And I'll never tire of hearing it," he murmured softly, his voice filled with warmth. "I love you too, Alice. With all my heart."

***

Hours later, Henry lay still in bed, he didn't want to disturb her, even as he carefully and gently moved her soft brown locks away from her eyes. He stared at her with love in his eyes, imagining a future with Alice, a life far from the madness of London. A place where they could simply be together. He imagined waking up every day together, in a small house by the sea. He saw himself sitting beside her in bed, admiring the view from their home. He wanted to be with Alice forever. Suddenly, the image of a simple ring came to his mind... And he knew just what to do...

Chapter 15

Lanyon.

January 9th~ As they finished their breakfast, Henry's mind was still wandering to the errand he had to run. He knew he had to find a way to distract Alice so he could secretly go shopping for the engagement ring. "My dear," he began, speaking casually, "I was wondering if you would be willing to do me a small favor. Utterson has asked me to drop off some papers at his office, and I'm afraid I won't have the time to do it today. Would you be willing to stop by and deliver them for me?"

Alice, who had just finished eating her breakfast, looked up at Henry with wide green eyes. She was both intrigued and excited to have something to look forward to today. "Of course, Henry," she replied with a smile. "I'd be happy to go visit Mr. Utterson. It'll be nice to get out of the house for a bit."

As Henry prepared to leave, Alice approached him and gently wrapped a soft scarf around his neck, her touch tender and affectionate. She adjusted the scarf carefully, ensuring it was snug and secure, before planting a kiss on his cheek.

A smile crept across Henry's face as he relished the warmth of her touch. When she kissed him, he felt a flutter in his heart, a reminder of how much he would miss her during his short errand run. "Thank you, love," he said quietly, his voice filled with gratitude and affection. "I'll be back soon." He gave her a quick kiss on the forehead before making his way to the door, so excited that he forgot to leave his glasses. Alice followed him out, carrying a small stack of papers meant for Utterson that had been left on the table. Just before they parted ways, Henry pulled her close and gave her another kiss, causing her to giggle. He smiled back at her, feeling the warmth of the moment, and tugged his scarf tighter around his neck as he began walking down the street, his mind swirling with thoughts about his plans.

The jewelry store was bustling with people browsing and admiring the sparkling jewels on display. There was a small crowd of customers around the engagement ring display, with couples discussing the best options for their loved ones. As Henry approached the counter, a young salesperson with a smile on his face came over to greet him. "Good morning, sir. How can I assist you today?"

Henry smiled politely, his eyes never leaving the engagement rings before him. "Good morning. I'm actually here to look at engagement rings. Do you have any recommendations, perhaps something a bit more unique?"

The salesperson perked up at the mention of engagement rings, and he immediately led him over to a different display case. "Of course, sir. We have a wide selection of unique and one-of-a-kind engagement rings. Follow me, please," he said, leading him to the counter where the rings were on display. "Each of these rings is handmade and crafted with meticulous care. Perhaps you see something you like?"

Henry surveyed the rings intently, looking at each one with careful consideration. They were all gorgeous, but he had something specific in mind. He wanted something special, something that would reflect the uniqueness of his love for Alice. His eyes landed on a beautiful ring with a simple, elegantly designed band, a cluster of small diamonds, and a single emerald at the center. He pointed to the ring. "Can I see this one, please?"

The salesperson nodded and retrieved the ring from the display case. He placed it on a velvet display pad, carefully turning it to showcase its sparkle and design. "This is indeed a beautiful ring, sir. Handcrafted with delicate stones, each one exquisitely cut and set in a simple, elegant design. It's a lovely choice."

Henry studied the ring intently, turning it slightly to examine it from different angles. The stones caught the light, sending flashes of sparkling color across the room. It was perfect. "It's beautiful," he said quietly, his voice filled with awe and appreciation. "How much is it?"

The salesperson smiled at his admiration and leaned in a bit closer. "I'm glad you like it, sir. This ring is currently priced at 50 pounds. However, if you prefer something less expensive, I could show you some other options." He pointed to a different display case with more affordable rings.

Henry shook his head, his eyes still fixed on the ring. "No, no, this is the one I want," he said firmly, his decision final. "I'd like to buy this one, please." He reached into his pocket for his wallet.

The salesman's smile widened, "Excellent, sir. This ring is a fine choice, and we can offer a complimentary engraving on the inside of the band as well. Is there a message you'd like to have engraved?"

Henry paused for a moment, thinking carefully. A small smile played at the corner of his lips as he thought of his unique relationship with Alice. The words he wanted to have engraved on the ring came to mind immediately. "Yes," he said quietly. "Could you please engrave 'My lovely looney' on the inside of the band?"

The salesperson raised an eyebrow at his request, "Of course, sir," he said, taking one of the rings from him. "We can have that engraved for you. Will you be paying in cash or cheque?"

Henry pulled out the money and placed it on the counter. "Cash, please," he said.

The salesperson took the money and smiled, then disappeared into the back room to have the ring engraved. A few minutes later, the salesperson returned with the ring, now engraved with the requested message. "Here you are, sir," he said, holding the ring out to him. "The engraving has been done just as you requested."

Henry took the ring carefully between his fingers, running his thumb over the engraved words on the inside. The words 'My lovely looney' brought a smile to his face. It was perfect. "Thank you," he said, looking up at the salesperson. "This ring is perfect."

"You're very welcome, sir. It's a beautiful ring, and I'm sure your special person will love it." He carefully placed the ring in a velvet box and placed it in a small bag, which he handed to Henry.

Henry nodded and accepted the bag, his heart swelling with anticipation as he clutched the small bag close to his chest. He thanked the salesperson again before turning and making his way out of the jewelry store, his mind already fixated on when and how to give the ring to Alice.

***

Henry made his way through the cobblestone streets, his mind preoccupied with thoughts of Alice and the ring safely tucked away in his pocket. As he passed by the entrance of Regent's Park, his pace slowed to a stop. His eyes were drawn to the park, its lush greenery and tranquil pathways beckoning him to take a few minutes to clear his mind before returning home. He took a deep breath, savoring the fresh air and the familiar scent of the park. He glanced around, noting that it was a bit quieter than usual for midmorning. Deciding to take advantage of the solitude, he found a secluded bench and sat down, overlooking the serene beauty of the park. Henry closed his eyes and let out a sigh, his mind finally quiet for a moment. As Henry held the ring box in his hand, his thoughts wandered to his parents. They had always pushed him to strive for perfection and uphold the family's reputation. Introducing Alice to them was sure to cause an uproar. He could already imagine the shocked expressions on their faces, the disapproval in their eyes, and the harsh words they would say about her. He then thought about Utterson and Lanyon, his dear friends and confidants. He knew they didn't approve of Alice, but he also knew that they would keep her secret if he asked them to, but would they if he told them about wanting to marry her? Suddenly, Henry felt a wave of dizziness wash over him. The world around him seemed to spin for a moment, and he had to clutch the edge of the bench to steady himself. Concern crept in as he tried to gain his bearings, wondering what could be causing this unexpected sensation. Henry closed his eyes and took a few deep breaths, "No, please not now." He leaned back against the bench, his hands trembling slightly as he clutched the ring box tighter, trying to keep Hyde at bay… but it was too late.

***

Hours later, Alice paced the the foyer, wondering why henry hadn't come back yet, till there was finally a knock on the door. She rushed over, but to her dismay, Lanyon was on the other side when she opened it.

Lanyon, expecting poole, looked at her with equal dismay, "I got a letter from Henry, but I'm not quite sure what to make of it. Can you take me to Poole?"

Alice took the letter and began reading with increasing bewilderment and concern. The words on the page only served to worry her more, and she couldn't help but feel a sense of dread creeping up her spine. Taking a deep breath, she folded the letter and handed it back to Dr. Lanyon. "When did you receive this letter, Doctor?"

"Half an hour ago, Alice, what is going on?" He pushed his way through.

Alice looked at the clock. "Midnight is only two hours away. We need to do as the letter says. We don't have much time."

Alice quickly hurried through the corridors, making her way to Henry's laboratory. "I'll explain everything once this is sorted. We have no time to lose." She pushed open the door to Henry's cabinet, heading directly for the drawer marked "E". She unlocked it, and carefully picked up the chest, trying to keep her shaking hands steady. Alice quickly handed over everything to Lanyon, her eyes meeting his with determination. "Keep hold of that. We need to get you back to your house quickly. There's no time to lose," she said firmly, already leading him towards the door. Once they reached the front door, Alice didn't pause for a moment, quickly throwing open the door and stepping outside. The night air was cold and crisp, the shadows of the evening just beginning to stretch out across the path. She turned to Lanyon; her gaze intense. "Go straight home and arm yourself if necessary." Alice's eyes met Lanyon's; her expression solemn. "I promise, I'll explain everything when you return. But right now, you must trust me, and you must hurry."

There was a moment of hesitation as Lanyon seemed to hesitate, but at that moment a clock tower in the distance chimed the hour – 11pm. It was a sharp reminder of the time they were against. Lanyon's expression hardened, and he nodded in acknowledgement of the urgency. Then, without another word, he turned and rushed off into the night.

***

Alice had stayed awake in the library, and finally, at 2, she heard a knock at the door. She walked out and opened the door to see Henry. Letting go of the breath she was holding. "Henry? That goodness, you're alright, what happened?" she said, looking him up and down.

Henry stumbled into the house, his body shaking and his hair disheveled. He looked exhausted and distressed and was still holding in the heartbreak of the terror on Lanyon's face. "Alice," he managed to say, his voice hoarse. "I'm so sorry..."

Alice quickly shut the door and walked over to him, taking his hat and coat and setting them off to the side. "Hush..." she said softly, wrapping her arms around him in a hug. "You have no need to apologize... I just want to know if you're alright..."

Henry let out a shaky breath and allowed himself to collapse into her embrace. All the emotions he had been holding back came flooding out, and he buried his face in her shoulder, his body trembling with suppressed sobs. "I didn't mean for any of this to happen. I didn't want to hurt anyone," he mumbled, his voice thick with tears.

Alice held him in her arms, gently caressing the back of his head as she felt his body shaking against her. She ran her fingers through his messy hair, trying to soothe him with her touch. "I know, I know," she whispered, her own voice quivering slightly, "I know you didn't mean for this to happen."

Henry melted further into her embrace, his hands clenching the fabric of her shirt as if his life depended on it. The tension in his body gradually relaxed as her soothing words and gentle touches seemed to soothe the storm within him. He took a deep, shaky breath, trying to steady himself. "I didn't know what to do."

Alice held him closer, feeling his body slowly relax under her touch. She continued to run her fingers through his hair, hoping to offer him some comfort. "It's going to be alright," she whispered, her voice full of reassurance. "It's late, let's get you to bed, and we can sort it out in the morning... ok?"

Henry nodded, his energy completely drained. He was so tired, all he wanted to do was lay down and try to forget the events of the day. "Thank you," he managed to whisper, his voice hoarse and weary. "I don't know what I would do without you…" As Alice led Henry upstairs, he felt his legs tremble with each step. The events of the day had left him feeling exhausted, both physically and emotionally. And the weight of the box in his pocket suddenly felt heavier than ever. He stumbled a bit up the steps, his body on the verge of giving out. But he forced himself to keep moving, following Alice's lead.

She smiled softly, taking his hand and leading him back upstairs. "You'll always have me."

When they finally reached the bedroom, Henry practically collapsed onto the bed, letting out a tired sigh as he sank into the soft mattress. He closed his eyes, feeling the weariness and exhaustion settling into his bones. The room was quiet, aside from the sound of the rain pattering against the window. It was a soothing sound, but it did little to ease the turmoil in his mind. He sat up slightly, looking over at Alice, who was sitting nearby, watching him with a mixture of concern and tenderness.

***

The next day, around noon, Henry put away the ingredients of the serum, he suddenly felt a wave of nausea washing over him. The room seemed to spin slightly, and he had to clutch the edge of the table to steady himself. This was the second time he had felt this dizziness in a short time, and it was starting to worry him. He paused for a moment, taking a deep breath, trying to calm his racing heart. He closed his eyes and leaned back against the table. As Henry braced himself against the table, his eyes fell upon the serum he had just been putting away. It was right there, just a few inches away. The dizziness and nausea were increasing with each passing moment, and he knew that the serum was the only thing that could make it stop. He reached out and grabbed the vial with shaky hands. With a trembling hand, Henry uncorked the vial of serum. The smell of the concoction filled his nostrils. He took a deep breath, the scent of the drug both familiar and terrifying at the same time. He brought the vial to his lips, and took a large swig. As the serum took effect, the room gradually came back into focus, and the dizziness subsided. With some relief, Henry put down the vial.

However, a few hours later, he found himself suddenly dizzy and ill once more. This time, the sickness came after a short nap, catching him off guard. Henry stumbled out of bed, his head spinning and his stomach churning. He called out for Alice, the panic evident in his voice. "ALICE!"

Chapter 16

Endless Moonlight

For days, the cycle continued, with Henry falling asleep and Hyde emerging like clockwork. Despite the exhaustion written on her face, Alice remained steadfast and determined to help him. Every time Henry woke up, she would be there, by his side, offering comfort and support. Her eyes were constantly heavy with fatigue, and her usually bubbly personality was dimmed by the constant worry and stress. Despite her exhaustion, she didn't let it show. She masked her weariness with a smile and words of reassurance, but deep down, she was struggling to keep it together.

***

She picked at her food with her fork; her appetite diminished. She looked up at him, her usual sparkling eyes now dimmed by fatigue. Despite her numbness, she couldn't let him know she was tired; she forced a small smile and spoke softly. "How are you feeling, darling?"

Henry, being observant, noticed the signs of exhaustion on Alice's face. He could see the fatigue in her eyes and the strain on her normally cheerful demeanor. The guilt weighed heavily upon him, knowing that his own predicament was causing her distress. "I feel ok. Alice…" Henry began, his voice soft and filled with genuine concern. He reached out a hand to gently touch her shoulder. "You look tired."

Alice shrugged, trying to brush off his concern. "I'm fine, really," she said, forcing a weak smile. She didn't want to worry him about her tiredness, not when he had enough on his mind already. Alice continued to pick at her food, pushing it around her plate. She was trying to eat, but her appetite seemed to have disappeared.

Henry furrowed his brow, not convinced by her response. He knew she was trying to brush it off, but he could see right through her. He leaned forward. "You're not fine, Alice. I can see it in your eyes. You're exhausted. You haven't been sleeping properly."

Alice let out a deep sigh, unable to hide it from him any longer. "Okay, maybe I am a little tired," she admitted, her voice soft. She knew there was no use in hiding it from him; she was too tired to try to act otherwise. "It's just…this whole situation, it's taking its toll on both of all," she continued, her eyes meeting his.

A pang of guilt shot through Henry's heart at her words. He knew she was sacrificing her own well-being to keep him at bay. "Alice, you can't keep doing this. You can't keep sacrificing your own needs for mine. You need rest, too. It's not fair to you."

Alice's jaw tightened slightly, her expression growing stubborn. "I don't mind, Henry," she insisted. "I want to be there for you. You're going through a lot, and I'm not going to abandon you, I don't care what Hyde's done."

Henry's face became grave as the thought of Hyde taking over crossed his mind. The idea sent shivers down his spine. "I… I understand your concern. I do. But you can't keep pushing yourself like this. It's not sustainable. He sighed deeply, his expression a mix of worry and guilt. "You can't stay up every night worrying about me. We need to find another solution, one where you don't have to sacrifice your own health for my sake."

Alice's determination started to give way to a hint of vulnerability. She knew he was right, but the need to be there for him was stronger than her exhaustion. "But who will watch out for you?" she whispered, her voice laced with worry. "If I don't stay up, if I don't keep you from turning into Hyde, then who will?"

Henry clenched his jaw. He could see the determination in her eyes and knew that she wouldn't back down. He let out a deep breath, an idea forming in his mind. A smirk tugged at the corner of his lips. He knew what he had to do. "I see. So, you won't go to bed, huh?"

Alice's stubbornness flared up at his smirk. She raised an eyebrow, a defiant glint in her tired eyes. "No, I won't," she retorted, crossing her arms over her chest. "I care about you too much to leave you alone with Hyde. I won't risk it."

Henry chuckled softly, a mixture of playfulness and determination in his eyes. He had made up his mind. He couldn't let her continue like this. With a swift movement, he stood up from the table. "Well, in that case, I guess there's only one thing left to do then." Without warning, he moved quickly, grabbing Alice gently but firmly by the waist and lifting her from her chair. He scooped her up in his arms, one arm supporting her back and the other beneath her legs, carrying her with surprising ease, even if she struggled like a fish. Henry chuckled, a hint of mischief in his eyes as he held her close. His grip was gentle but firm, ensuring that she couldn't escape his embrace. "Don't try to fight me on this, love. You're not staying up all night, regardless of how stubborn you're being." He carried her through the house, easily maneuvering around corners and down corridors. He finally reached the parlor room, where a comfortable couch was situated in front of the fireplace. With a soft ease, he gently placed her down on the couch, making sure she was settled in comfortably.

Alice felt a mix of embarrassment and stubbornness as Henry gently placed her on the couch. "I don't want to sleep, I told you!" she protested.

Henry expected her resistance. As she tried to get up, he blocked her path with a smirk on his face. "Oh no, you don't." He gently but firmly pushed her back down onto the couch. "You're not going anywhere. You're staying here." Henry took a seat beside her, his expression unyielding. He was determined not to let her win this battle. "You're going to sit here and rest, whether you like it or not," he said, his voice affectionate yet firm. "I'm not going to allow you to keep sacrificing your own well-being for my sake. It's time for you to take care of yourself, even if it means I have to force you to do it."

Alice crossed her arms, her expression becoming as stubborn as a mule. She averted her gaze from Henry, her irritation evident in the way she stubbornly pursed her lips. The room fell into a tense silence, interrupted only by the sound of the fire crackling in the fireplace. She refused to speak, her frustration manifesting in the form of silent treatment.

Henry chuckled softly at her stubborn expression, a mixture of fondness and determination in his eyes. "Oh, now you're just being cute. Crossing your arms like a little pouty kitten." He reached out, gently unfolding her arms and taking her hands in his. "But it won't work on me. I'm not budging on this, Alice. You need rest. End of discussion."

A flicker of a smile tugged at the corners of Alice's mouth, her annoyance slowly fading as she felt the warmth and gentleness of his touch. She looked at their intertwined hands, her resolve weakening. "Fine," she finally muttered, her voice still tinged with stubbornness. "But if I'm going to sleep, I'm doing it snuggled up with you."

Henry raised an eyebrow at her smirk, a playful glint in his eyes. "You think you're going to turn this situation around on me, don't you? You're clever, I'll give you that." He chuckled softly, his thumb rubbing gentle circles on her hand. "Alright then, if that's what it takes to get you to rest, I suppose I have no choice but to oblige." With a smirk, Henry shifted closer to her on the couch. He placed his arm around her shoulders, pulling her toward him and gently guiding her to rest her head against his chest. "There you go, love. Just relax. Close your eyes and let yourself unwind."

She wrapped her arms around him, feeling safe and comforted in his presence. Exhaustion washed over her, making her eyelids heavy as she snuggled closer to him. Slowly, her resistance faded, replaced by a sense of comfort and trust. "Mkay..." she whispered; her voice drowsy.

Henry let her head rest against his chest, and his heart swelled with affection. As he held her close, he took a moment to breathe in the scent of her hair, a familiar and soothing presence in his life. He could feel the weight of her exhaustion as she leaned into him, and the guilt of her sacrifices tugged at his heart. He gently stroked her hair, his hand moving in a soothing rhythm. "Alice..." He paused for a moment, gathering his thoughts and courage.

She hummed softly in response, her mind hazy with the onset of sleep. Her eyes were still closed, her body limp and relaxed, as she mumbled out a sleepy reply. "Mmm...yes, love?"

A smile tugged at the corners of Henry's lips as he heard her drowsy voice. He continued to run his fingers through her hair, the gesture almost subconscious in its tenderness. "There's something I want to ask you, something important." His voice was gentle and soft, filled with a mix of nerves and determination. He took a deep breath, his hand stilling on her hair as he gathered his thoughts. "Alice, we've been through so much together. We've been by each other's side through all the ups and downs, the struggles, the sleepless nights. You've sacrificed so much, always putting my needs before your own..." He paused, his gaze shifting to her face. He admired her features, her eyelids fluttering gently in the drowsy state she was falling into. He gently brushed a strand of hair away from her face, his touch soft and tender. "You've been there for me, supporting me, caring for me, when I didn't even know I needed it. I can never thank you enough for that." He took another deep breath, finally letting the question he had been holding onto for so long slip from his lips. "Darling... would you do me the honor of becoming my wife?"

She was so close to the realm of sleep that his words sounded like a dream. She opened her eyes slightly, a soft smile playing on her lips. Her voice was barely audible, a sleepy whisper. "Of course, darling. Of course I will."

Henry's heart swelled with a mix of emotions at her sleepy confirmation. A wave of relief washed over him, followed closely by excitement and joy. A wide grin spread across his face, and he couldn't help but laugh softly. "You're not even fully awake, and you still said yes. That either means you're crazy or you really love me."

A tired giggle escaped her lips, her eyes still heavy with sleep. She snuggled closer to him, her words slurring slightly. "Or maybe... it's both. I'm madly in love with my mad scientist."

A soft chuckle rumbled through Henry's chest as he heard her sleepy comment. He smiled down at her, his heart overflowing with tenderness. "Well, I can't argue with that. I'm the lucky mad scientist who gets to marry the most beautiful, selfless, and loving, lovely looney in all of England." He held her closer, gently stroking her hair. He could see her struggling to keep her eyes open, her fatigue quickly taking over. "You should rest now, my love."

Despite the exhaustion that tugged at her every fiber, Alice forced her eyes open just a crack and looked up at him. Her voice was soft, laced with remorse. "Sweetheart," she whispered, her words slightly slurred from sleep. "I'm sorry this wasn't more romantic. You deserve better than this sleepy proposal. I just… I never thought you'd ask."

Henry shushed her softly, his eyes warm with understanding. He knew she was apologizing for her sleepy state, for the less-than-perfect proposal moment. "Shhh, love. There's nothing to apologies for. This was perfect. Perfectly us." He pressed a soft kiss to her forehead, his voice gentle and reassuring. "I didn't ask you to become my wife to have some grand, dramatic moment. I asked you because I love you, and I want to spend the rest of my life with you."

Her heart swelled with a mixture of gratitude and love as she listened to his soothing words. She could feel the sincerity in his voice, the unwavering love that wrapped around her like a warm blanket. In that moment, she realized he was right. This was perfect, because it was them. A soft smile tugged at the corners of her mouth. "You're right," she whispered, her voice still laden with sleep, but filled with heartfelt conviction. "This is us. It's perfectly imperfect."

Chapter 17

Malice.

January 3rd~ KNOCK, KNOCK, KNOCK...

Lanyon stares at Alice for a few moments before he speaks. "Is... Hen- Jekyll home right now?" His expression shows he's trying to put on airs of unbothered, but Alice could tell with one glimpse that he's distressed and exhausted.

She shook her head and let him in. "I'm afraid not... Lanyon, you don't look so good... is everything alright?"

He hesitantly followed her inside and sat down on the nearest chair. ".... Honestly, I'm not exactly... in the best state at the moment."

She sat across from him, folding her arms over her chest, and sighed. "Henry didn't mean for all this, I promise. He's been beating himself up about it ever since the... incident."

He pinched the bridge of his nose as he sighed, he didn't even have it in him to raise his voice. It was clear the events in question took a physical and mental toll on him. "Oh, really? Does he have any idea of how I feel on this matter? Does he have the slightest bloody idea of how I've been suffering ever since witnessing...that?" Lanyon looked back up at Alice. "Please, you must understand that this has been a living hell for me. To have to watch and then help keep it secret and act like it never even happened. I'm tired, Alice. I'm tired and scared, and all I want to do is rest, but I can't even do that because all I can see when I close my eyes is...him."

She fidgeted with the hem of her sleeve; the tension in the room was palpable. "I get it, I do. Trust me, I do. It's been hell for me too, more so than you'd think. But he's trying, Lanyon. He's fighting every day to keep Hyde contained. You have to understand that."

Lanyon's expression hardened at Alice's words, his own pent-up frustrations starting to slip out as he stood and took a few steps forward. "And what about me, hm? Have you considered for a single second how I feel about any of this? How I'm suffering? How hard I've been struggling to keep everything in order? How much of my own sleep has been interrupted by the memory? Does Henry even know how bad I've been struggling?" He let out a tired sigh as all aggression left his tone. "...Does he even care..."

Alice stood with Lanyon, speaking in a firm tone. "Of course he cares, Lanyon. He'd be devastated to hear how much you've been struggling. He's been under so much stress trying to find a cure for this. He's putting everything on the line to fix this issue. He's trying, Lanyon. We both know he didn't want any of this to happen. And we know he hates seeing all of us suffer because of it. He's struggling just as much as we are. And don't even think for a moment that I enjoy this... I'd do anything for this to go away, to go back to normal, where things are good and no one's lives are being uprooted..."

Lanyon took a deep, shaky breath slowly sitting back down in the chair, burying his face in his hands as he spoke. "I'm just so... tired, Alice... I don't know how much longer I can keep this up... I don't want to keep going through the motions like nothing happened... But I don't see any other way."

Alice's heart squeezed in her chest. She swallowed the lump in her throat and struggled to maintain her composure. "...How long?" she asked quietly.

Lanyon raised his head and gave his best attempt at a smile. It was weak, obviously forced, and did nothing to hide the pain and exhaustion it was masking. "I'm not sure... I've been pushing my body and mind to the very limit. It's been... difficult to keep up the act. I don't know if I'll be able to hold on much longer..."

Alice took a deep breath, trying to find the right words. "Lanyon, I hope you know that Henry... he loves you like a brother. You might not believe it right now, but he does. He's been beating himself up over this entire situation. He's a mess because he's worried about you, about me, about everything, and yet still trying to make light of it." She paused, her gaze dropping to the floor for a moment before continuing. "And honestly... I wish I could've gotten to know you better. You're a good man, Lanyon... Though I don't think you like me too much." She attempted jokingly, but there was truth to it.

Lanyon let out a tired chuckle as he heard her comment. "Ah, I suppose I haven't exactly made myself particularly likable. Most of our interactions have been brief and somewhat hostile. I suppose I've been... a bit too tense recently to be friendly..." He went silent, contemplating, then spoke again, "How do you even deal with all this, Alice?... This... constant fear and stress..."

Alice shrugged slightly, a small sigh escaping her lips as she tried to articulate her thoughts. "...I'm not exactly sure, to be honest." She paused, her brow furrowing in thought. "Maybe it's because I've already dealt with a lot in the past... and being around Henry so much helps me keep it together... I must just be mad."

Lanyon chuckled at her joke, but he couldn't find it in himself to make any sarcastic or mocking reply. He was tired; he had far more serious things to keep him up at night and worry over than any banter. "I... I suppose that could be a decent enough explanation..." He fell silent, his expression showing the fatigue and tension in his body. After a few moments, he spoke again, "You really... love Henry, don't you?"

Alice's face flushed a light pink, a soft smile spreading over her lips as the memory of Henry's proposal flooded her mind. "I do," she said quietly, her eyes shining with love and joy. "I really, truly do. He means everything to me. He's my light at the end of the darkest tunnel... and I plan on sticking with him till the end."

Lanyon looked at her for a moment, his expression hard to read. He could see the love in her eyes and hear it in her voice. A pang of envy and sadness shot through him, but he forced it down. He wasn't in the right frame of mind. He leaned forward in his chair, leaning partially onto his knees as he spoke, his voice filled with exhaustion and frustration. "Have you and Henry… discussed getting married?" He wasn't sure why he was asking, but he felt like he needed to know for some reason.

She was caught off guard by the question. The conversation felt… different. There was a strange tone to his voice, and it made her pause. "Yes," she replied, her voice soft and tinged with a trace of happiness. "We have discussed it. Whenever we get the chance."

He leaned forward, his expression serious as he looked at her. "When I'm gone… can I ask you to do something for me?"

Her eyebrows raised slightly, curious about what request he was about to make. She nodded. "What is it?"

Lanyon took a deep breath, his gaze steady as he spoke. "Take care of Henry. Make sure he's okay. Make sure he doesn't… do something stupid or foolish… make sure he's happy, at least as much as possible. The man can hardly take care of himself as it is… He's… he's not like most people. He needs someone who will not only take care of him… but will also not judge him and support him. He's… fragile… inside, deep down, and he tends to let the world get to him… he needs someone strong to lean on… someone willing to help him." He paused, a hint of hesitance and guilt in his voice. "Can you do that… for me?"

Alice's expression softened as she listened to Lanyon's request. His concern for Henry was evident, and she understood what he was asking of her. "Of course, Lanyon. I'll take care of him. I promise." She spoke sincerely, her voice soft yet firm. She genuinely wanted to take care of Henry and support him in any way she could. Being able to fulfill Lanyon's request only solidified her feelings.

***

January 8th~ As they walked back from Lanyon's funeral, Henry's demeanor had darkened, his usual politeness replaced with a solemn silence. The weight of Lanyon's death, and the knowledge that it was all his fault, hung over him like a thick fog. He wanted nothing more than to be left alone, to drown in his guilt and despair in solitude. But Alice, sensing his pain, stayed by his side.

They entered the house, the silence inside feeling heavy and oppressive. Henry sank onto the couch, his shoulders hunched, his eyes distant and unfocused. He didn't speak, didn't look up as Alice approached. He just sat there, lost in his own thoughts, his mind racing with a thousand regrets and what-ifs.

Alice stood by him, unsure of what to say or do. She knew that Henry needed time to process his grief and guilt, but she also saw the pain etched on his face and wanted nothing more than to comfort him. She sat next to him, balling the ends of her sleeves into her palms.

Henry stayed silent for a moment, his gaze still fixed on the floor. Then, he spoke, his voice low and strained. "..... I should have never created that damn serum. Lanyon didn't deserve to die because of my mistakes..." He buried his face in his hands, his shoulders trembling with unshed tears.

She reached out slowly and pulled him to rest his head against her and caressed his hair, feeling his trembling, offering what little comfort she could.

Henry didn't resist as Alice pulled him against her. He shut his eyes, feeling the steady beat of her heart and the gentle rhythm of her breath. For a moment, he just sat there, letting the warmth of her body soothe him, and the sound of her heartbeat calm his racing thoughts. He wrapped his arms around her, holding on tight, as if she was the only thing keeping him grounded in this world. A mixture of guilt and regret welled up, and he let out a stifled sob. For a few moments, he just stayed like this, his head against her chest, her fingers stroking his hair. He took deep breaths, trying to steady his ragged breathing. The tears that had been prickling at the corners of his eyes finally broke free, and they ran silently down his face, soaking into the fabric of her dress.

Alice continued to hold him close, her hand never stopping in the motion of caressing his hair. Her arms encircled him in a tight grip; she couldn't help the feeling of worry that shot through her as he trembled. "Shhhh...," she whispered soothingly. "You didn't mean for that to happen," she said softly, her voice a gentle reassurance. She continued to stroke his hair, her fingers gliding through his locks in languid movements. Her other hand moved to his back, rubbing soothing circles between his shoulder blades in a bid to further comfort him.

"Lanyon didn't deserve death, that much is certain," she murmured. "But you didn't want that. Lanyon died of shock, not because of you."

Henry let out another sob, his grip on her tightening. "I created that monster," he murmured, his voice ragged. "I created Hyde, and it's my fault he killed Lanyon, intention or not... all I could feel as Hyde was fear and spite."

She moved her hand from his back to his face, gently tipping his chin up so she could look at him. "Look at me," she said quietly, her voice taking on a firm, yet gentle edge. "You created Hyde in the hope of helping people," she reiterated, her voice resolute. "You didn't design him to be a monster, and you certainly didn't intend for him to be this destructive force. His actions are not your fault, no more then. Do you understand that?" She paused, letting her words sink in before continuing. "Yes, your relationship with Lanyon was strained. He doubted your work, questioned your motives, and yes, perhaps even fueled some of your insecurities. That is true. But to say that Hyde killed him because of you, simply because you harbored feelings of jealousy and anger? That's a stretch, Henry. Your feelings towards him did not directly lead to his death. You did not command Hyde to kill - nor would you ever."

Henry's body trembled slightly as he listened to her words. His grip loosened a bit, but he still held onto her tightly. His mind was a whirlwind of emotions and thoughts. "Maybe... Maybe you're right. Maybe I didn't tell Hyde to kill Lanyon. But... he wouldn't have attacked if I had kept my damn feelings in check. Lanyon would be alive if I hadn't been so... angry with him." Henry slowly pulled away from Alice's embrace, straightening himself up. He wiped away his tears with the back of his hand, trying to regain his composure. Without a word, he got up and headed towards the drinks cart. He poured himself a glass of whiskey, taking a generous gulp.

She watched as he pulled away from her, a small pang of pain in her heart as the warmth of his body left hers. She didn't move; however, her gaze fixed on his back as he walked towards the drinks cart. When he poured himself a generous glass of whiskey and took a large gulp, she couldn't help but flinch. The sight only furthered the worry she felt for him. She didn't speak for a moment, letting the silence hang heavy between them. But the silence weighed on her, and she couldn't ignore it any longer. "Henry," she said softly, her voice careful and measured. She stood up from the couch, hesitating for a moment before moving towards him. She stopped a few feet away, watching him closely. "You know that drink isn't going to make you feel better," she continued, her gaze fixed on him.

Henry's fingers gripped the glass tightly, his knuckles turning white. He didn't turn to face her, his gaze fixed on the amber liquid in his tumbler. "I'm fine," he said, his voice slightly bitter. "Just… need to clear my head a bit." He lifted the glass to his lips and drained it in one quick gulp, wincing as the alcohol burned his throat. He poured himself another drink.

She approached him cautiously, her hand reaching up to gently take the glass from his grasp. The gesture was gentle but firm, and she held it away from him. "Henry, darling," she said softly, her voice filled with concern and love. "Please, come to bed. Let's rest."

Henry's gaze darkened as she took the glass from his hand. He turned to look at her, a mix of irritation and desperation in his eyes. But her gentle words and soft touch seemed to penetrate the walls he had put up. Henry sighed and nodded, his shoulders slumping in defeat. Even though he was in no mood to sleep, he couldn't refuse her. Not when she had that pleading look in her eyes and that soft, yet insistent tone. "Alright," he murmured, a hint of reluctance in his voice.

***

January~12th As Alice woke up in the dead of night, realizing that Henry was gone, panic immediately set in. She bolted upright in bed, her heart racing. "Henry?" she called out, her voice filled with desperation. When there was no answer, she realized that Hyde must have taken control. With a sense of urgency, she quickly got out of bed and quickly donned her cloak, feeling the weight of the important task ahead of her. As she prepared to leave the bedroom, she noticed the vile of serum on the desk and carefully picked it up, her heart pounding with a mixture of fear and determination. With a deep breath, she tucked the vile securely into her cloak. She knew she had to find Henry – or rather, Hyde – and change him back before he did anything rash. With a final glance back at the room, Alice left the safety of Henry's home and ventured into the London night. The city was quiet, but the danger was ever-present. She hurried through the narrow streets, her cloak wrapped tightly around her body to keep up the façade of a late-night wanderer. Where could he have gone? Soho, perhaps? That's where he often retreated when he took control.

She quickened her pace as she made her way towards Soho, her senses on high alert. Every shadow seemed to hold a threat, every sound made her nerves jump. She prayed that she would find Hyde soon, before he caused any more trouble. As Alice continued her way through Soho, the sound of a familiar laugh caught her attention. Her heart skipped a beat as she recognized the distinct tone of Hyde's laugh. She followed the sound, her steps quietly and purposefully, and approached the pub. The pub was called "The Black Swan" and was a dingy, cramped establishment located in the heart of Soho. Alice cautiously entered the pub, her eyes immediately scanning the room. The exterior walls were covered in peeling paint, and the windows were streaked with dirt. The sign above the door creaked in the wind, bearing the image of a black swan with a lantern in its beak. Inside, the pub was dimly lit, with only a few candles flickering to illuminate the patrons. The air was thick with smoke and the smell of stale beer and sweat. The walls were adorned with old maps, faded portraits, and dusty trophies, giving the place a worn, decrepit feel.

It didn't take long to spot him, his auburn hair and his tall, brown top hat. His face was angular and gaunt, giving an almost sinister appearance. His eyes were his most striking feature: large, almond-shaped, and a striking golden amber color. Hyde was in a booth in the very back of the pub, swirling a nearly empty glass of dark ale and cackling to himself. His hat was sitting nearby on the table, his eyes darting about the people in the pub. He had only arrived maybe 20 minutes ago, and he was already causing a disturbance. His laughs were loud and obnoxious, and he kept making snide comments to anyone that passed by him. He was clearly very drunk, his cheeks rosy and his eyes hazy. He suddenly caught sight of Alice, and his smile widened. His eyes gleamed with malicious glee.

Hyde finished off his ale with a loud 'Ahhhhh' before setting the glass down with a thud. He leaned back into the booth, his eyes locked on Alice as she approached him. He smirked, his gaze roaming over her figure. "Well, if it isn't my favorite little stray cat," he said playfully, his voice low and slightly slurred. "What are you doing here, hm? Come to keep me company?"

Alice approached Hyde cautiously and with a sense of trepidation. Her chest was pounding heavily throughout her entire body, her heart was thumping against her ribs with an intensity that made her breath grow shallow. Her gaze was fixed on Hyde, every fiber of her being consumed by a mixture of wariness, concern, and love for Henry. She took a deep breath, trying to steady herself, and sat down opposite him. "Actually, I came looking for you... or rather, I'm here for Henry. To change you back." Her hand wrapped around the small vial in her pocket. She said softly, her voice barely above a whisper.

Hyde chuckled, leaning forward, his eyes never leaving hers. "Ohohoho, is that so? You came all this way to change me back? How sweet...and brave," he said, chuckling softly. "But I have to say, little cat, I'm quite enjoying myself right now. Why would I want to go back to be dreary ol' Henry? He's so boring and uptight, always worrying about what everyone else thinks. I'm his fun side."

"No," she said firmly, her voice tinged with both urgency and determination. "That's not true, and you know it. Henry's not boring or uptight. He's kind, he's compassionate, and he's thoughtful. He cares deeply about things that matter. He doesn't need you."

Hyde leaned back into the booth, his face twisting into a malicious smirk. He chuckled softly, his voice dripping with sarcasm. "Oh, is that so? You think you know him better than I do? You think he's so benevolent, so pure? He's weak, that's what he is. He's too sensitive, too afraid of his own desires." He leaned forward again, his face inches from Alice's. "But I know what he really yearns for. I know his true nature. And deep down, he knows it too."

Alice swallowed hard as she listened to Hyde's words, her heart heavy with both fear and determination. She reached into her cloak and withdrew the small vial of the serum. With slightly trembling hands, she rested it on the table, its smooth surface glinting in the dim light. "Hyde," she said softly, her voice steady despite the tension in her body. "Please. Just take it. Don't make me fight you, I don't want more lives on the line... Please, just come home."

Hyde's smirk faded slightly as he stared at the vial on the table. The light glinting off the glass was like a mocking reminder of the reality he was avoiding. He thought about what he had done. His mind replayed the image of Lanyon's shocked and horrified expression as he realized they were the same person. Guilt and anger churned in his chest, but he pushed them down again with a scoff. He looked at Alice, her pleading eyes and desperate plea for him to return home. He placed his index finger on the vial as he stood up. "Nah, I think I'll pass thanks. I'm rather enjoying myself without the old bore in control for a change." He flicked the vial back, grabbed his top hat, and walked away.

She quickly grabbed the vial before it rolled off the table, her heart pounding in her chest. She sat there, her heart pounding in her chest, staring at the empty seat across from her with a mixture of anger and sadness. Her hands trembled as she gripped the vial tightly, her gaze following Hyde in a state of helplessness and frustration.

Hyde stumbled over to another table of people, his eyes roaming over them with a wild and almost manic look. He tried to engage them in conversation, laughing loudly and attempting to inject himself into their conversation. But they just stared at him blankly, their eyes flickering with annoyance and disgust. They clearly wanted nothing to do with his presence. One of the men even muttered something about him being a "crazy drunk." Hyde's smile faltered for a moment, his ego taking a slight blow. Hyde tried his best to engage with the other patrons of the pub, but they all seemed to give him only a passing glance. He made jokes, he teased and provoked, but they just ignored him. He didn't know why, but the dismissal seemed to sting, as though he was desperate for their attention, for their approval. He was used to people being intrigued by him… or at least, frightened by him. But here, he seemed to just be…nothing. His expression soured, his face falling from his usual gleeful smirk to a frown.

Alice remained seated at the booth, her gaze fixed on Hyde as he continued to attempt to engage with other patrons. She watched his interactions with a mixture of pity and concern. She saw how he craved attention, seeking to provoke and bait others, but they only responded with indifference. The sight of him desperately searching for validation made her heart ache. She'd never seen him like this before. She had always seen him as a cunning, arrogant man who enjoyed causing chaos and pain. But now, she saw a glimpse of a different side of him—a side that craved approval and belonging. She felt herself hesitate for a second, torn between her anger and her growing curiosity. She realized that there was more to Hyde than just the destructive force he had been displaying to her. Alice got up from her chair, her eyes fixed on Hyde as he stumbled his way through the pub. As she made her way towards him, she was suddenly distracted by a loud noise. She bumped into a man who was playing darts, causing him to miss his shot. The dart went flying and landed on the wall above the target.

The man turned around, clearly irritated by her carelessness. He shot her an angry look before shaking his head in irritation. He was bald, tall and lean with a small beard and a stained white shirt with the sleeves ripped off. He spoke in a thick Irish accent, sounding very angry as he approached her. "You. Made me. Lose. My. Shot." he backed her into a table, his voice growing increasingly agitated. He said firmly, his eyes flashing with frustration. "I'd been winning all day, and now I lost all my money 'cause of you."

Alice was taken aback by the sudden hostility from the man. Her heart raced as she was backed against the table, feeling trapped and intimidated. "I-I didn't mean to-" she started, her voice faltering with fear. "It was an accident, I'm sorry-"

But the man wouldn't listen. He was already fuming, the anger clouding his judgment. He continued to press forward, his face contorted with rage. "Sorry, ain't gonna cut it," he growled. "You owe me. Now."

"Oi!" Hyde snapped, drawing the Irishman's attention. "Might want to let go of the girl. She's with me." He stood between Alice and the man, his face now a picture of nonchalance. Despite being shorter than the Irishman, Hyde stood with a confident stance, his shoulders squared, and his head held high. "What's your name, Rory? You look like a Rory. Now, how about you get back to your game and leave her to me."

The Irishman, still visibly fuming, turned his attention to Hyde as he stood in between them. He looked Hyde up and down with a slight air of arrogance, seemingly unimpressed by the smaller man. "Who the hell are you, you little pipsqueak?" he growled, his eyes narrowing as he stepped forward slightly, trying to intimidate Hyde. "And I ain't no Rory, I'm Lorcan."

Hyde rolled his eyes, unimpressed by Lorcan's attempt to intimidate him. "Oh, sorry. I meant Lorcan. Lorcan the Obtuse, right?" he said sarcastically, a smile playing at the corners of his lips. "Sounds a bit too fancy for a guy like you. But what do I know, right? My name is literally an analogy-"

"Shut it, you little runt," Lorcan snapped, taking another step forward and towering over Hyde. His face was twisted in a snarl as he puffed up his chest, trying to look fierce and terrifying. "You ain't got any right to be talking back to me like that. What are you gonna do, punch me? I've seen stronger pigeons than you. You think you're a big shot, huh? You're nothin' but a bloody ponce. A scrawny, pathetic little pansy."

She sighed, shaking her head, "Oh, now you've done it," she muttered.

Hyde smirk, "Looks like someone's about to learn firsthand how wrong they are," he said, his hands clenched into fists. "You should know better than to mess with what's mine."   Hyde's hand moved swiftly, his dagger flashing as he swung it at Lorcan. In a split second, he had cut out one of the man's front teeth, extracting it with a sickening 'crack'. Hyde's smirk widened as Lorcan howled in pain filled the air. He chuckled darkly as the man released his grip on Alice's cloak. Hyde quickly stepped forward, his eyes cold and cruel. "You should count yourself lucky I didn't take anything else," he said, his voice dripping with menace. Without warning, Hyde lunged forward and punched Lorcan square in the jaw, causing him to stagger back, clutching at his bleeding mouth.

Lorcan clenched his bleeding mouth as he stumbled backward and fell to the floor, looking up at Hyde with a mix of pain and disbelief. He spat out a mouthful of blood, staining the floor with red as he looked at Hyde with hateful eyes. "Who the hell are you?!" he managed to spit out between clenched teeth, his face twisted in pain and anger.

Hyde chuckled. "Hyde. Edward Hyde," he said, his voice low and menacing. He looked down and picked up the man's tooth, "or, in your case, your worst toothache." he flicked the tooth at him.

Alice stood there, her heart pounding in her chest as she watched the scene unfold before her. Her eyes darted between Hyde and Lorcan, her feelings a mix of fear, surprise, and an odd sense of admiration. She couldn't believe what she was witnessing. As a woman who'd spent nearly a decade locked away in a madhouse, she wasn't unfamiliar with acts of violence. Yet something about this felt... different. "Oh my god, Hyde-"

Hyde's eyes flicked to meet hers, and for a brief moment, there was a flash of tenderness in his gaze. But it was quickly replaced by his usual sly smirk. "What? Did you want me to let him manhandle you like that?" he said, his voice light and casual.

Hyde's gaze slowly swept the area, and he noticed the room had gone eerily quiet. The entire pub had fallen into a tense silence, the only sound being the soft crackling of the fireplace. Everyone was staring at them, their faces a mix of shock and unease. Hyde's smirk faded slightly, his eyes narrowing as he felt the weight of their curious gazes on him.

One of the patrons in the pub suddenly recognized Hyde. He gasped, his eyes widening as he whispered to his friend. "Oh, God, it's him. It's Edward Hyde. That murderer who killed Sir Danvers." He sneered, his eyes narrowing in recognition. A wave of murmurs washed over the room, and some of the patrons began to edge away from him, their eyes filled with fear.

Hyde's expression hardened as he realized the commotion they had caused. He knew they had to escape, but he was aware everyone's eyes were on them. He grabbed Alice's wrist, "You know what, I think I've had enough fun for one night." The pub had descended into chaos, with patrons shouting, glass breaking, and men shouting. Hyde looked around for an exit. He spotted a door that led out into an alleyway and pulled Alice towards it. Hyde weaved through the panicked crowd, his grip on Alice's wrist firm but gentle as he made a bee-line for the door. He shoved the door open and pulled her outside. The cold night air hit them like a slap in the face as they stumbled into the alleyway. Hyde glanced down the alley, his eyes scanning for any signs of danger, his ears pricked up at the sound of footsteps approaching. He ducked into a shadowed corner, pulling Alice with him. Hyde shielded her with his body, pressing them both against the wall. His heart raced, the adrenaline of the moment quickening his breath. He listened intently, trying to gauge how many people were coming and where they were. Hyde and Alice stood silently in the shadows, their backs flat against the wall, as the footsteps of what seemed like several men raced past them. Hyde felt the tension in his body release ever so slightly. Hyde waited until the sound of the footsteps faded into the distance before he exhaled deeply. His heart was racing; he hadn't expected things to escalate this quickly. He turned to Alice, his eyes roaming over her face as he checked her over. "Are you alright?" he asked, his voice low and his expression tinged with concern.

"I-I'm fine," Alice managed to stammer, her voice barely above a whisper. "Just… a little shaken up." She took a deep breath, trying to compose herself. "God, Hyde, that was… intense."

Hyde chuckled softly, his own hands still shaking a little from the adrenaline. "Intense? That's one way to put it," he said, his voice a little shaky himself. He ran a hand through his shaggy hair, tousling it. He looked down at her with a glint of amusement in his eyes. "You handled yourself well, you know. I was expecting you to start screeching or something."

Alice couldn't help but roll her eyes at his comment, a hint of a smile tugging at her lips. "Screeching? Really? Do you think I'm some kind of damsel in distress or something?" Despite her words, there was a hint of gratitude in her eyes. She was aware that she owed him for saving her from Lorcan's grip.

Hyde shrugged nonchalantly. "I just figured you were the type to freak out in high-stress situations. Not saying you're weak or anything, God knows from the asylum. Just…not exactly cut out for bar fights." Hyde's expression darkened slightly, his gaze becoming a little more piercing as he looked at her. "Actually, it's your fault we're in this situation. If you hadn't insisted on coming to that god-forsaken pub, I wouldn't have been forced to cause a disturbance to leave early."

Alice's expression darkened as well, her shoulders tensing as she bristled at his words. "Me? My fault?! You're the one who started a fight with Lorcan! All I wanted was to talk to you and bring you back home, but instead you started throwing punches like a damn idiot!"

Hyde's smirk faltered for a second, replaced by an angry expression. "You have no right to lecture me. All I did was defend what's mine," he snapped, his irritation growing with every word. He took a step forward, closing the distance between them. "Don't forget who saved who back there. I was perfectly fine on my own, getting what I wanted without any trouble. And then you had to show up and ruin the fun."

Alice's eyes widened as she stood her ground, not backing down from his angry stare. "Excuse you, I didn't 'ruin' anything! You were causing trouble even before I arrived, nobody in there cared for you in the slightest. And what do you mean, 'what's yours?' I'm not some possession of yours for you to claim." She clenched her jaw, her voice rising in anger. "And don't you think for a second that I don't appreciate what you did. I was grateful. But that doesn't give you the right to act like a caveman and claim me as yours. This petty argument doesn't matter, because now we both are under the peelers' suspicion."

He let out a frustrated groan, running a hand through his messy locks. "Damn it, I can't believe this is happening. I just wanted a drink, some fun, and now…now I have to deal with the damn police. And I sure as hell ain't being nabbed by some stupid peeler."

Alice's expression softened slightly as she saw the frustration in Hyde's face. She reached into her pocket and pulled out the vial. "Here." She held it out to him. "This will change you back."

Hyde's gaze shifted between Alice and the vial, his eyes locked on the little glass bottle. A mixture of hesitation and resignation crossed his face, and he reached out to take the vial from her hand. He examined it closely, his fingers running lightly over the surface. Hyde's hand clenched around the vial, his knuckles turning white. A muscle ticked in his jaw as he looked at the vial. "I… I don't want to change back," he said, his voice quieter than usual.

Alice's eyes widened in surprise, her expression turning into a mix of shock and concern. "What do you mean, you don't want to change back?" She moved closer to him, her voice filled with worry. "Hyde, you have to change back. The police are looking for you, and they're going to find you eventually."

Hyde's grip on the vial tightened even further, the glass creaking under the pressure. "No, I don't have to do anything," he snapped, his voice taking on a defiant tone. "And don't act like you care about what happens to me. You only want me to change back because you want your precious fiancé back, so he's safe and sound from the sinister devil. You want me locked up, it was your idea to put all my stuff in that chest for a year."

Alice shook her head, her eyes flashing with anger and frustration. She took a step closer to him, her voice rising in volume. "You think you know everything about me, don't you? Well, you're wrong. I don't want to lock you up. I only suggested the chest because I was worried about what would happen if you kept going like this." She exhaled loudly as she struggled to maintain her composure. "And yes, I do care about you. I care about both sides of you, even the one I don't understand." She paused for a moment, staring at him with a mixture of frustration and genuine concern. "Edward," she said firmly. "You can't keep doing this. You're only hurting yourself by staying like this. You can't keep fighting against yourself like this... You were once a part of him, so that means I love you too..." Alice took a deep breath, her voice shaking slightly. "Please listen to me. I never wanted any of this. I just don't want to see you or Henry hurt. You're both hurting yourself and each other. I don't understand why you want to be this... destructive force. Is it some sort of punishment? Is this your way of punishing yourself? If you want an enemy, then take it out on me, just please... Stop hurting yourself, you're not doing yourself or Henry any favors." She took a step closer to him, her voice growing softer. "And if you won't change back for your own sake, then do it for me. Please."

Hyde's expression faltered, his grip on the vial loosening as Alice's words washed over him. He didn't know how to respond. Her words had a strange power over him, stirring up emotions he thought long forgotten. He was used to being disliked, hated even. He was used to anger and resentment. But this? This was new. No one had ever shown genuine concern for him, no one had ever treated him as something more than a nuisance. His persona wavered under her gaze. He swallowed hard, his voice barely above a whisper. "Fine." He looked down at the vial in his hand, his heart pounding in his chest. Hyde took a deep breath, his hand shaking slightly as he raised the vial to his lips. He took a deep gulp, downing the contents in one swift motion.

Chapter 18

Seek.

January 20th- As the day grew late, Alice was in the study, enjoying a quiet moment. The room was filled with soft candlelight glow of the sun, casting a warm glow that danced across the walls. The sound of the crackling fireplace added to the cozy atmosphere of the room. Henry sipped a glass of cabernet, the dark red liquid swirling gently in the glass. He glanced over at Alice, who was curled up on the couch, her legs tucked beneath her. A comfortable silence filled the room, broken only by the occasional crackle of the fire. Henry opened the window to get a fresh breeze of air, only to find Utterson and Enfield walking by. Alice could see Henry's smile brighten once he saw his friends and started conversing with the gents. Till Henry began to feel a familiar throbbing in his temples, a sure sign that Hyde was attempting to surface. He shut the window and placed a hand on his forehead, trying to massage away the pain, but the pressure only seemed to intensify. He took a deep breath, doing his best to keep his composure, but the effort of holding Hyde back grew more difficult with each passing moment.

Concern etched across her features, Alice got up, walking over to him, and gently placed her hand on Henry's arm, her touch gentle and reassuring. "Henry, are you alright? Is it Hyde again?"

Henry nodded, the pain in his head making it difficult to think straight. "Yes, yes, the cabinet, the salt, the serum," he managed to say, each word leaving his mouth with a labored breath. "I need it, please. Quickly." The pressure in his head intensified further, making it hard for him to focus on anything but the pain. He leaned on Alice for support, grateful for her strength and determination. "Hurry, please," he whispered, his voice growing tighter. "I don't know how much longer I can hold him back."

Together, they made their way to the office room of the laboratory, each step feeling like a battle of wills. The distance between them and the much-needed serum seemed to stretch on forever, Hyde's presence growing stronger with each passing moment. The night air, cold and crisp, stung their faces as they crossed the garden, leaving shadows flickering around them. Henry slumped onto a chair, his breathing labored and shallow. The room spun around him, a dizzying blur of colors and shapes. The pain in his head became an unbearable vice, constricting his thoughts and senses. He could feel Hyde slowly taking control, his own will weakening by the second. As Alice returned with the beaker of serum, he desperately reached out for it, his trembling hands grasping the glass as if it were a lifeline.

Alice took the beaker from him, looking at the empty state, and sighed, "That was close... I'm going to make more in case, I'll be right back."

Henry nodded, still reeling from the ordeal. He sat there, eyes closed, regaining his composure. The pain eased, leaving him feeling exhausted and shaken. "Thank you," he whispered, his voice hoarse. "Yes, yes, make more if you can." As Alice searched the cabinet's numerous shelves and drawers until her eyes caught sight of the crystalline salt that was nearly gone. Her heart sank a bit, knowing that they were running low on the precious substance that held Hyde at bay. Concern etched across her face, she carefully picked up the nearly empty jar, gently shaking it to confirm the almost empty state. As Henry caught his breath, regaining control after the failed attempt of Hyde's transformation, he noticed the worry and weariness etched on Alice's face. He knew all too well that they were running low on the serum. But at the moment, he tried to hide his own fear as he asked Alice, his voice as steady as he could manage, "How much left...?"

Alice turned around, meeting his gaze, her eyes briefly flickered down to the nearly empty jar clutched in her hand before returning to Henry. With a slight sigh, she responded, her voice tinged with a hint of despair. "Not much… perhaps only a month's worth at most," she stated, reluctantly, as if the words tasted bitter in her mouth.

Henry's heart sank. A month? That's all they had left? That's it? That realization hit him like a punch to the stomach. He knew they were running low, but so soon? He tried to remain outwardly calm, masking his own panic in front of Alice. He closed his eyes for a moment, composing himself before looking back up at her. "A month. Huh? That's not good. Not good at all." Henry ran a hand through his hair, feeling a wave of anxiety wash over him. The salt was the crucial ingredient, the backbone of the serum. Without it, the rest of the ingredients were useless. He took a shaky breath, his voice barely a whisper. "Without the sault… we won't be able to keep him suppressed for long."

"Not good is an understatement," Alice murmured, her voice quivering slightly. She hugged the nearly empty jar of crystalline salt to her chest, a silent plea to defy the harsh reality. "We're in real danger now," she added, her voice laced with a hint of panic. "What do we do? Can we restock?"

Henry nodded. "Yes, yes, we can. But," His voice faltered, he looked at Alice with a mixture of guilt and concern. "It's not exactly easy to acquire, you know. It's not just something we can pick up at the local apothecary." The gravity of the situation hung heavily in the air. It wasn't just the supply of the fault that concerned Henry. It was the safety of the one person he valued the most. "We can restock, but it won't be easy. I still have a list of suppliers I can reach, just a carriage ride away."

Alice's heart sank as Henry spoke. "I understand we need to restock, but I don't like the idea of you going out there on your own. It's too risky," she protested, her voice tinged with concern. "What if something happens? What if he takes over and I can't help you?"

He ran a tired hand over his face, sighing heavily. "You're right. You're right. I can't leave you alone here. But I can't just stay here, either. We need that sault, and we need it quickly…"

As the discussion unfolded, a thought occurred to Henry. Poole. If there was anyone who could help them, it would be him. He was reliable and trustworthy. "Poole," he murmured, the name rolling off his tongue. "We might not have to go out there ourselves. We could ask Poole to help."

A glimmer of hope appeared in Alice's weary eyes at the mention of Poole's name. She looked at Henry, a hint of relief on her face. "Poole..." She repeated, a hint of optimism in her voice. "That's not a bad idea. And in the meantime, we figure out how to stop Hyde."

⁎

January 26th ~ Henry and Alice returned to the laboratory, the newly acquired salt in hand. They silently made their way over to the desk where the beaker and the rest of the ingredients were waiting. The tension in the air was palpable, the weight of their situation bearing down on them. Henry glanced at Alice, his gaze filled with determination and a hint of anxiety. "Here goes nothing," he mumbled. Henry carefully measured out the correct amount of salt and began to mix it with the rest of the ingredients. The room was quiet except for the sound of the glass stirring rod as Henry mixed the concoction. Alice watched quietly, her heart beating faster as she hoped this batch would work. As the concoction turned green. "It's not quite right," Henry said, a hint of worry creeping into his voice. "It should have turned blood orange. The consistency is off. It's not even vapouring." Henry's brow furrowed as he double-checked the ingredients and the measurements, trying to figure out what went wrong. "We followed the formula... Everything should have worked perfectly..." he said, a hint of frustration in his voice. "Why isn't it turning out right?"

Alice leaned in closer, closely examining the mixture in the beaker. "I'm not sure," she said, her voice laced with worry. "We followed your notes, mixed the ingredients exactly as you instructed." She paused for a moment, her mind racing as she considered the possibilities. With a frown, she voiced her fears aloud. "Could it be...the sault? Could it be compromised in some way?"

Henry sighed, running a hand through his hair. "I don't know... this isn't supposed to happen. The formula is precise, and we didn't make any mistakes..." He ran through the whole process in his mind, searching for where they may have gone wrong. But everything he did appeared to be correct. "It could be impure. That would explain why."

Alice nodded, her gaze fixed on the beaker in front of them. "So, the salt is the issue... We need fresh, pure salt for it to work."

Henry nodded, a mix of annoyance and determination on his face. "Yes, I think we have no choice. We need pure salt for the formula to work properly. I'll send a note to Poole in the morning," he said, his voice laced with disappointment. "We'll need a new batch, and hopefully this time it'll be the correct one."

***

A week had passed, and the routine had settled into a monotonous rhythm of anxiety and urgency. Morning light streamed through the high windows of Henry Jekyll's laboratory, illuminating the chaotic array of test tubes, flasks, and half-finished experiments that cluttered the workbench. The odor of chemicals mingled with the scent of burnt rubber and scorched paper, a fitting backdrop for the tension that had enveloped both Henry and Alice. Each failed attempt to remake the serum only deepened their frustration, and with it, the weight of their anxiety grew heavier. Henry spent countless hours hunched over his workbench, scribbling notes and recalibrating his instruments. Yet, with every measurement he took and every compound he mixed, he felt the creeping despair that their time was running out.

Henry's brow furrowed in frustration as he attempted to mix ingredients in a beaker, only for the mixture to result in a noxious gas, filling the air with an acrid stench. Cursing under his breath, he pushed the beaker away, rubbing his tired eyes with one hand. Henry set down the stirring rod, frustration etched across his face. "Damn it!" he exclaimed, his voice filled with disappointment. "Damn it, damn it, damn it!" As he gave his reflection, Henry felt an unsettling wave of unease. The sight of his own face, so familiar and yet so foreign, caused a shiver of dread to run through his spine. He touched his own cheek, tracing the outline of his jaw as if making sure he was still in his own body. The sheer emotional weight of his current situation seemed to come crashing down on him all at once. With a primal cry of frustration, he swept his arm across the desk, sending vials, beakers, and notes crashing to the floor in a rain of shattered glass and scattered papers. The sound of shattering glass echoed through the room, the fragments shimmering like broken pieces of a dream. "Damn it!" he shouted, his voice quivering with a mixture of frustration and desperation. "Damn it, damn it, damn it…Damn it all to hell."

Alice flinched. Despite her best efforts to remain optimistic, the weight of their predicament was taking its toll on her as well. "It's okay…" She said, her voice trembling. She walked closer to him, carefully avoiding the broken glass on the floor. "Everything's going to be okay..."

He took a step toward her, but stopped himself, his hands clenching into fists at his sides. "No...no, it's not," he said, his voice hoarse with emotion. He ran a hand through his hair, making it stand on end in a wild tangle. "It keeps failing... every damn time... it keeps failing." He looked away from her, unable to bear the concern in her eyes. He turned back toward the table, the shattered glass and spilled contents of his experiments a painful reminder of his repeated failures. "I'm...I'm not getting any closer," he said, his voice cracking. He picked up a broken glass tube, the shattered edges glittering in his hands. "I'm no closer now than I was a week ago...a month ago..." Henry couldn't help the bitter thoughts that raced through his mind. He remembered the harsh words his parents had once spoken, their cold disapproval and disappointment, and how it had stung, even if he had never allowed himself to show it. And Lanyon... oh, Lanyon. The betrayal in his friend's eyes still haunted his memories. He wondered, in his darkest moments, if they had been right all along.

She stood next to him, her hand gently cupped his face, her fingers delicately tracing the lines of his jaw. "Hey, listen to me..." She said firmly, her voice steady and resolute. 'We'll figure this out. You've made breakthroughs before, and you'll do it again. You're Henry Jekyll, remember? You've never let anything stop you before."

"I just... I just don't understand what I'm missing," Henry said, his voice cracking slightly as he pulled away from Alice's touch, pacing the length of the lab with restless energy. "It's hopeless," he said, his voice trembling with frustration and despair. "There is no way... no way to recreate the conditions of the first experiment. Whatever salt I used for the first batch must have been tainted, so I can't remake the serum with an ingredient that doesn't exist. I don't know if Hyde was luck or a damn accident. "

"Accident or not, you created something incredible," Alice said firmly. "You've always had this drive to push boundaries, to question the impossible. Yes, it may be difficult, but that's just who you are. You don't back down from a challenge. You've done the impossible before, and you can do it again."

As Alice spoke, her words seemed to sink into Henry's soul. He wanted to believe her, to find solace in her belief in him, but the weight of his failures and the despair of their situation held him back. "But this is different," he said, the frustration clear in his voice. "I can't just will something into existence because I want it to. I'm not a sorcerer, I'm a scientist. I work within the bounds of what is possible, or at the very least, probable."

Alice reached out and took his hand, "Yes, you're a scientist, one of the best," she said softly. "But sometimes, the impossible becomes possible when we push the limits. You've already found the path once, even if it was an accident. You can do it again." She moved closer, standing directly in front of him, her eyes locked with his. "I believe in you," she said firmly. "And I'll be here by your side, no matter what."

As Henry looked down at their intertwined fingers, his gaze was drawn to the emerald ring sparkling on Alice's finger. The symbol of their commitment to each other was meant to be a promise of love and happiness, but with their dire situation, it now seemed to mock him. Henry's grip on her hand tightened, almost reflexively, as if he was holding on to a lifeline in a storm-tossed sea. He reached out, pulling Alice into his embrace, wrapping his arms around her and holding her tight. His head bowed, his forehead pressed into her shoulder. "Damn it, Alice," he said, his voice rough.

Chapter 19

Their Last Night.

1st of March~ They lay next to each other on the bed, Alice had her head resting on Henry's chest while lying in his embrace, deep in a content slumber. His hand plays with her hair while the other arm is wrapped protectively and tightly around her, keeping her close. A gentle breeze blows against the curtain, covering the mirror. But once it glides back towards the window, Henry catches a glimpse of Hyde.

Henry's gaze is fixed on Hyde, his heart rate picks up a little as a shiver runs down his spine. He glances down at Alice, who remains peacefully asleep, blissfully unaware.

Hyde's lips spread into a Cheshire cat smile as they made eye contact. He winked at Jekyll, enjoying the man's obvious distress, "Ah, Henry," he says, his tone mockingly polite. "Did you miss me?"

Henry's brow twitched, his lips pressed into a thin line. He forced himself to remain calm to not disturb Alice's peaceful state. "Of course not," he retorted with barely contained irritation. "I was doing quite well without your interruptions."

Hyde chuckled lowly. "Oh, I can see that. You just look oh so thrilled to have me around." He glanced down at Alice briefly, his eyes lingering on her peaceful form. "You're quite the attentive lover, aren't you? Never thought that would happen, knowing you and all...but I must say, your little sins this past year have been...interesting to watch. You've been quite the naughty one, haven't you, Doctor? And Alice...well, you certainly chose something unique, didn't you?" He looked back at Henry. "Funny little thing…Makes you wonder, doesn't it?"

Henry's grip on Alice tightened, his jaw clenching, and his voice grew colder. "Shut up." His tone was low and filled with underlying anger.

"Why?" He asked, feigning innocence. "It's been a while since we spoke. I will congratulate you on that. I didn't make it easy. You did well to hold me back for a whole year…technically." He added the last word with a hint of sarcasm.

An irritated grunt escaped Henry's lips. He forced himself to speak quietly, his eyes never leaving Hyde's reflection in the mirror. "That was the point," he replied through gritted teeth. "I want nothing to do with you."

Hyde's smirk faltered slightly at Henry's words, but he quickly regained his composure. He chuckled bitterly, his gaze still fixed on Henry's reflection. "You seriously think you can amputate me from your very soul? Well, clearly that didn't work out too well, now, did it? Because here I am. You thought you could just lock me away and forget about me, didn't you? Yell, newsflash, we're one, you and me. Can't escape that. And you can't kill me, I am you." He tapped his index finger on his temple tauntingly.

Henry's eyes widened, his mind racing with the realization that there was only one possible solution. "I… I know.." he admitted in a voice barely above a whisper.

Hyde's smirk faltered slightly, his expression becoming somewhat curious as he picked up on Henry's tone. "Wait, wait, wait. Hold on a second here." He took a tiny step forward. "Did you just say…you agree with me?"

Henry took a deep breath, gathering his thoughts. "Yes. Yes, I do." He replied, looking directly at Hyde, his gaze resolute. "I've come to the realization…that there is only one way to get rid of you."

Hyde's smirk faded completely, a flicker of uncertainty crossing his face. He felt a pit forming in his stomach at Henry's words and the look in his eyes. He had expected resistance, not… agreement. "What do you mean, 'only one way'…?" He asked cautiously.

Henry's expression remained resolute. "We're intertwined. I can't get rid of you…without getting rid of myself. Which is why…" He paused, the realization of what he was about to suggest hitting him with a cold shiver running down his spine. "Which is why… I have to be the one to snuff us out…"

Hyde's eyes widened in horror. "You… you're seriously suggesting that we- you… that you-. No. No, absolutely not. You can't seriously be considering that…" Panic and desperation filled his voice. "Are you out of your goddamn mind?!"

Henry's gaze didn't waver, despite the turmoil he was experiencing. "There is no way to sever our connection. But if I do this, nobody else gets hurt." As Henry tried to get out of bed, a sudden, painful squeeze in his chest forced him back down. It was as if a hand was clenched around his heart. He gasped, clutching at his chest in pain. He looked up, his eyes meeting Hyde's reflection in the mirror, "Hyde…" he managed to gasp.

Hyde held his fist over his own heart, his fingers tightened around his shirt over his heart, as if he could physically grasp his heart, tighter until the pain was simply too much to bear. "Henry, don't. Please… Please don't…"

Henry's eyes filled with desperation. "Hyde… I… I can't keep living like this," he managed to say between breaths. "I have to end it, one way or another." At the last squeeze, Henry gasped in relief when it was over. He looked up at the mirror, tears welling up in his eyes. Hyde was gone, vanished.

Alice opened her eyes, feeling disoriented as she was roused from her sleep. Concern etched her face as she saw Henry sitting up on the bed, clutching his chest in obvious distress. She quickly sat up. "Henry, what's wrong? What happened?"

Henry snapped out of his daze, the pain in his chest gradually subsiding, though his breathing still hitched. "It's nothing." He tried to steady his voice, feigning calmness. "Just a bad dream, nothing serious."

Alice's concern didn't dissipate with Henry's explanation. She studied him closely, noticing the tightness in his voice. She placed a gentle hand on his back, attempting to soothe him. "You gave me a fright, I thought he was going to take over again."

Henry shuddered, shaking his head. "No, no, it was just a nightmare. Nothing more." He turned to Alice, his voice softening. "Alice, I... I need a moment. Could I... Could I be alone for a bit?"

Alice reluctantly nodded, understanding his need for some solitude. "Alright, Henry." The worry deepened as she looked at him.

Henry felt a pang of guilt at Alice's concern, but he forced a weak smile. "Thank you, Alice. I just... need to sort some things out in my mind. I'll be fine." He leaned over and placed a brief kiss on her forehead before tossing the covers off and standing up.

Alice watched as Henry left the room, her head tilted to the side. She could easily tell something was bothering him; she could see it in his eyes. Though she was tempted to follow him, she stayed in bed, knowing he probably needed some time alone. She settled back down under the covers; her eyes still fixated on the door where Henry had left.

Henry went back to the laboratory, up into his cabinet room, as he looked around, the memories flooded back to him like a deluge. The creature's tormenting antics, the mockery in its scribbles on his books, the broken portrait of his father he was given when he first moved in. All the signs of a being that took perverse delight in destroying everything he held dear. The only thing that had kept the creature at bay was its own fear of its own consequences. If it didn't cling to life so desperately, it would have likely destroyed him long ago. Henry let out a sigh, feeling utterly defeated. He knew deep down that there was only one real solution to his problem, the one way to stop Hyde from ever hurting Alice or anyone else. He didn't want to give in to despair, to let his circumstances get the best of him. But he knew he had to face the truth. If he truly loved Alice, if he truly wanted to protect her, there was only one way to ensure her safety permanently. In the silence of the lab, Henry made his decision. He had never felt more resigned in his life. He knew he had a little over a week left till the last of the salt was gone, and he could feel the desperation of Hyde beating against him like a wave against the shore. In that moment, he understood the complex and twisted relationship he shared with Hyde—a creature born of his own dark desires and weaknesses. In the face of such a profound battle for his very soul, Henry felt the weight of his own humanity straining against the vile grasp of Hyde. It was an abomination that resided within him, feasting on his doubts and fears, yet simultaneously a reflection of the fragments of his own being he had desperately tried to suppress. He knew that, in his heart, he felt an empathy for Hyde, an acknowledgment of the wretchedness they both shared. This craving for existence, the sheer determination to live, was something familiar and terrifying. The thought made him want to weep. It felt like a cruel joke that his own characteristics could manifest as a monster wanting to destroy everything he held dear. As he stood there, his decision looming heavy in the fragile silence, Henry wrestled with the chilling truth. As he stood there, engulfed in silence, a determination formed within him. The creature's reign of terror would have to end, no matter the cost.

***

March 8th 1887~ Henry Jekyll sat in the cabinet; his pen poised over the paper. As he wrote, his voice was barely audible, a whispered confession. "I bring the life of that unhappy Henry Jekyll to an end," he wrote. Next to him, a vial of poison lay on the table. Just as he finished writing, the door to the cabinet creaked open, and Alice walked in. Henry's head immediately turned towards the door as he heard it open, and his eyes widened and panic shot through him in an instant. "Alice!" He blurted out, his heart racing. "You... you shouldn't be here!" He quickly moved to block her view of the open vial of poison on the table.

Alice took a step forward, concern evident on her face. "I... I came to tell you Poole left to see Utterson..." She glanced around the cabinet, noticing the vial on the table behind him. "...Are you working on the antidote?" It wasn't really a question, but more like a plea.

Henry's hand tightened around the pen, his knuckles turning white. He forced a smile. "Yes, yes, the antidote," he lied, his voice a little too hurried. "I was just... making some notes, checking some details. Nothing to worry about." He moved to hide the vial more.

Alice's expression darkened, seeing through Henry's facade. "Don't lie to me, Henry," she said, her tone firm. "I can tell something is wrong. You look like you've seen a ghost." She took another step closer, her concern growing. "What are you trying to hide from me? What's on the table?" She quickly snatched the paper before he could react, and she read his letter.

Henry tried to lunge towards her, but it was too late; her eyes darted across the page, reading his words. The room felt like it was closing in on him. "No, no...please, give it back. I can explain, please."

200

As Alice read, her heart sank into the depths of her stomach. Her eyes widened in horror, and a chill ran down her spine. She took a step back, "Henry..." Her voice trembled, barely above a whisper, filled with shock. "W... What is this? This... this can't be... You can't mean it, can you?"

Henry's face paled, and a look of desperation crossed his features. His heart pounded in his chest, the weight of his deception heavy on his shoulders. He tried to reach for the paper in Alice's hand, but he knew it was too late. "Alice, please, listen to me," he pleaded. "I... I was going to tell you, I swear. Please, you don't understand. I... I can't go on like this. I can't let...Let that...monst-" He caught himself before he could say the word aloud.

Alice's heart shattered at the sight, her eyes filled with a mix of anger, hurt, and deep concern. She stepped back, away from him, clutching the letter tightly in her trembling hands. "Tell me what?" she snapped, her voice cracking. "That you were planning to take your own life? How could you, Henry? How could you keep this from me, Henry. What about us?"

Henry felt like he was drowning in his own guilt. His heart ached at the pain and hurt he could see in Alice's eyes. He wanted to reach out to her, to hold her, but he felt like she was slipping further away with every word. "I... It's not that simple. I had to... to do something.... This is killing me, can't you see? I'm losing myself every day, I can't let him win, I can't become Hyde."

She looked at him, with a glimmer of understanding in her eyes. "I know you're suffering," she softly said. "But you don't have to face it alone. I'm here, Henry. I'll help you, we can find a way through this together. Please, don't give up." She closed the gap between them, her arms enclosing around him in a tight and protective embrace. Her body trembled slightly as she held him close, the tears threatening to spill from her eyes.

Henry's shoulders sagged, and he leaned into her embrace, burrowing his face into her shoulder. "I'm sorry," he muttered, his voice barely above a whisper. "I'm so sorry. I don't mean to shut you out, I just... I can't bear to let you see me losing myself."

Alice held him tighter, her own tears stinging her eyes. "Henry, you don't have to go through this alone. You have me. I'm here for you, no matter what. We'll find a way out of this together." She pulled back slightly so she could look up at him, her hands coming to rest on either side of his face. "Just promise me, Henry, that you'll never consider something like this again. Promise me."

Henry's heart felt like it was being ripped out of his chest as he looked at Alice's tear-streaked face. He couldn't bear seeing her so upset, and the weight of his actions crashed down on him. But when he looked over to the full-length mirror... He couldn't even recognize himself anymore, even though he was in his own skin. He looked at the vial of poison behind her on the table, the solution to his problem so close. In that moment, something inside of him snapped. With a sudden burst of passion, he cupped her face in his hands and kissed her. It was a desperate, needy kiss, filled with all the unspoken feelings he couldn't even begin to put into words. He pressed her against the table, blocking her view of the vial behind her as he deepened the kiss. He needed her, in that moment, more than anything else. He needed her to remind him what he was fighting for.

Alice was taken aback by Henry's sudden, intense kiss, but she immediately melts into him, returning the kiss. Her arms wrapped tightly around his waist, her heart pounding in her chest. Tears leaked onto her cheeks, her heart aching with a whirlwind of emotions. She couldn't bear the thought of losing him.

Henry reached back blindly with one hand, his fingers fumbling around for the vial of poison. He found it, gripping it tightly in his hand, hiding it behind her back. "Alice," he murmured against her lips, "Alice, I love you... I love you so much."

Alice's heart swelled at Henry's words, "I love you too, Henry," she whispered between breaths... And then she felt it. The cold, smooth glass of the vial pressed against her skin. Her eyes widened in panic, realizing what he was planning. She broke the kiss, trying to pull away. "Henry. No, please-"

Henry tightened his grip on her, holding her in place, his forehead rested against hers. "Shh, shh," he attempted to soothe her, his voice trembling. "It's okay, Alice. It's going to be okay." He slowly uncorked the vial, "It… It's okay. It's for the best. You'll… You'll be okay without me Alice, I promise."

"No, Henry, no," Alice pleaded. "Please, don't do this. We can find another way; we can fix this. There has to be a solution." She desperately tried to break free from his grip, to twist out of his hold, to take the veil away from him as tears streamed down her face, but she couldn't.

Henry tightened his grip on her. "It's the only way I can protect you…from me," he murmured, his voice quivering. And before she could protest and fight him, Henry brought the vial to his lips, the bittersweet taste of the solution hitting his tongue, as she struggled desperately against his hold. It was cold, viscous, and had an almost syrupy texture, not too dissimilar from the cough syrup he had been given as a child. As the poison spread over his tongue, he kept his eyes locked on Alice. "I'm sorry, Alice", his eyes and voice filled with sorrow, running a shaky hand through her hair. "I'm so sorry." As the poison started to take effect, Henry's grip on Alice slowly started to loosen. His knees buckled beneath him, and he slumped forward."Henry!?" Alice cried out as he suddenly went limp before her eyes. She quickly grabbed onto him tightly, her arms wrapping around his weakening body as she eased him down gently. Tears welled up in her eyes, "No, no, no, no, no… Please, please, don't leave me." She pleaded, tears streaming down her face. She cradled him in her lap, her fingers threading through his hair as she desperately tried to keep him with her.

As he slumped against Alice, the world around him became fuzzy and indistinct. He could still hear her voice, but it sounded like it was coming from a distance. Everything felt sluggish and slow, as if he was trying to move through thick honey. The edges of his vision were shrouded in black, and he knew it wouldn't be long now. "Alice…" he whispered again, his voice so soft it was barely audible. "I'm… I'm so… sorry." Henry felt a sudden, sharp pang in his gut. It was Hyde, struggling to take control. The poison should've done its job by now, but maybe Hyde's resilience was fighting against it. He desperately fought to suppress him, to keep him at bay. His hand, still clenched around the empty vial of poison, and with his last bit of strength to push Hyde away, he crushed the vial in his grip.

She quickly reached out, gently pulling his hand away from the shards of glass and intertwining her fingers with his getting blood smothered in between. "Please, Henry… Please…" She repeated, her voice cracking with pain. She pressed her forehead against his, her fingers threading through his hair. "Please... I love you..."

He reached up, his hand shaking slightly, and cupped her cheek. He brushed his thumb over her skin, feeling the tears as they fell down her cheeks. He tried to focus his gaze on her face, his lips forming the only word he could manage. "Alice..." He pulled her down, his movements feeble, and pressed his lips against hers in a last kiss. His voice was barely above a whisper. " I... I love you, Alice," he managed to say.

She gently wiped away the tears staining his cheeks, her touch tender and pained. "I love you too, Henry." Her hand gripped the back of his neck, her fingers tightening as if trying to hold him in place against her. She rested her forehead against his, her eyes closing tightly as her body shook with sobs.

Henry's body lay motionless in her arms, his essence began to transform, morphing into the all too familiar figure of Hyde, His features distorted, his hair growing longer and wilder and a more burnished copper look, his eyes a hue of gold before they closed. When the transformation was complete, it was over.... They were gone.

She felt the shift beneath her hands as his body transformed. She didn't pull away, her embrace tight and protective. Her fingers ran through his unruly hair. She gently shifted, pulling his body closer against hers, his head nestled against her chest. She couldn't help but press a soft kiss against his forehead, her heart aching with a mix of sadness and longing. "I'm here, Henry... I'm here..." Her heart ached mercilessly, her entire feeling shattered and empty. As the weight of silence enveloped them, Alice held the twisted remnants of who Henry had been, her tears falling like quiet tributes to the love they had lost, a love now forever out of reach.

<u>To Be Continued...</u>

About the Author

I am Kyli Brown. Born 2006, I live in Florida with my mom, sister, brother, and two adorable cats. Ever since I was younger, I loved the dark and mysterious side of things. While I wasn't a good writer when it came to debate or argumentative essays, I enjoyed a good book or a good movie. I wanted to be in plays since I was 10 because I love the imagination that went into it. But when I was put into my 8th-grade creative writing class, I wanted to tell the stories that played like a movie in my head and were close to my heart. I started this book when I was in the second semester of 9th grade, with a short story that turned into my own passion project. I wrote the sequel halfway through the first book and finished both by the time I graduated. What inspired me was my love for gothic literature and some of my favourite plays from musical theatre. I worked on two books prior to this, none of which I was more passionate and dedicated to than this one. As much as it was a rollercoaster of a journey, I couldn't be happier with my official first book.

breasts, in the groin, or around the armpits. This type can be particularly uncomfortable due to friction and moisture in these areas. Inverse psoriasis can often be misdiagnosed as a fungal infection, highlighting the need for proper evaluation by a healthcare professional. Lifestyle modifications, including maintaining dryness and using appropriate skincare products, can help manage symptoms effectively.

Pustular psoriasis is characterized by white pustules surrounded by red skin. It can manifest in localized forms, such as palmoplantar pustulosis, which affects the palms and soles, or as generalized pustular psoriasis, which can be severe and require immediate medical attention. Patients with this type of psoriasis may experience systemic symptoms, including fever and chills. Awareness of this condition is essential, as it can lead to serious health complications if left untreated.

Lastly, erythrodermic psoriasis is a rare and severe form that can cover the entire body with a red, peeling rash that can itch or burn intensely. This type can be life-threatening and requires urgent medical intervention. Understanding the types of psoriasis not only helps patients identify their condition but also guides them in discussing appropriate treatment options with healthcare providers. By being informed about these variations, patients can take proactive steps in managing their condition, improving their overall well-being and quality of life.

Causes and Triggers

Psoriasis is a multifaceted condition influenced by a range of causes and triggers. Understanding these factors is crucial for individuals managing this chronic skin disorder. Genetic predisposition plays a significant role, with family history often indicating a higher likelihood of developing psoriasis. Researchers have identified specific genes associated with the immune system's response, suggesting that genetics can predispose individuals to inflammatory conditions, including psoriasis. Recognizing this hereditary component can help patients understand their risk and the importance of early intervention.

Environmental triggers significantly impact the severity and frequency of psoriasis flare-ups. Common triggers include stress, which can exacerbate symptoms by influencing the immune response. Emotional and physical stress can lead to the release of inflammatory cytokines, which may worsen skin conditions. Other environmental factors include infections, particularly streptococcal throat infections, which have been linked to the onset of guttate psoriasis. Identifying and managing these triggers is essential in developing a comprehensive treatment plan.

Diet also plays a pivotal role in managing psoriasis symptoms. Certain foods can trigger inflammation and exacerbate skin conditions, while others may provide anti-inflammatory benefits. Diets rich in omega-3 fatty acids, such as those found in fatty fish, flaxseeds, and walnuts, can help reduce inflammation. Conversely, processed foods high in sugar and saturated fats may aggravate symptoms. Patients should consider keeping a food diary to identify potential dietary triggers and work with a healthcare provider to develop a balanced diet that supports skin health.

In children, the causes and triggers of psoriasis can differ from those in adults. Pediatric psoriasis may be more closely linked to environmental factors and stressors, such as bullying or academic pressure. Early diagnosis and intervention are critical for children to manage their symptoms effectively and mitigate the psychological impact of the condition. Parents should be vigilant for signs of psoriasis and seek guidance from healthcare professionals to establish supportive routines that encompass both skincare and emotional well-being.

The interconnection between psoriasis and mental health cannot be overlooked. Individuals with psoriasis often experience heightened anxiety and depression due to the visible nature of the condition and its impact on self-esteem. This mental health aspect can create a cycle where stress exacerbates psoriasis, leading to more emotional distress. Holistic approaches that incorporate mental health support and stress management techniques, such as mindfulness and therapy, can be beneficial. Emphasizing a comprehensive management plan that addresses both physical and emotional aspects will lead to a more effective approach to living well with psoriasis.

Chapter 2: Psoriasis and Diet

Foods to Include

In managing psoriasis, the foods we consume can play a significant role in alleviating symptoms and promoting overall skin health. Incorporating specific nutrient-rich foods into your diet can help reduce inflammation and support immune function, which is crucial for individuals living with psoriasis. A diet rich in antioxidants, omega-3 fatty acids, vitamins, and minerals can provide the body with the tools it needs to combat skin flare-ups and enhance overall well-being.

Fruits and vegetables are foundational to a psoriasis-friendly diet. These foods are packed with antioxidants that help fight oxidative stress and inflammation. Berries, citrus fruits, leafy greens, and cruciferous vegetables are particularly beneficial. They not only deliver essential vitamins such as vitamin C and vitamin E but also provide fiber, which can aid in digestion and overall health. Aim for a colorful plate, as a variety of fruits and vegetables can ensure a broad spectrum of nutrients that support skin health.

In addition to fruits and vegetables, healthy fats are crucial for managing psoriasis. Foods rich in omega-3 fatty acids, such as fatty fish (like salmon, mackerel, and sardines), walnuts, and flaxseeds, have been shown to reduce inflammation in the body. These fats can help maintain skin hydration and elasticity, which is particularly important for those experiencing dryness and scaling due to psoriasis. Incorporating these foods into your meals can not only enhance flavor but also provide essential nutrients that promote healing.

Whole grains and legumes should also be staples in a psoriasis-friendly diet. Foods like quinoa, brown rice, lentils, and chickpeas are excellent sources of fiber and can help regulate blood sugar levels. Maintaining stable blood sugar is vital, as spikes can lead to increased inflammation, worsening psoriasis symptoms.

Additionally, these foods provide a range of vitamins and minerals that can support overall health and help mitigate the risk of developing comorbid conditions often associated with psoriasis, such as cardiovascular disease.

Lastly, staying hydrated is an essential aspect of dietary management for psoriasis. Water is vital for maintaining skin moisture and overall bodily functions. Herbal teas and broths can also contribute to hydration while offering additional health benefits. Reducing the intake of processed foods, sugars, and alcohol is equally important, as these can trigger inflammation and exacerbate psoriasis symptoms. By focusing on a balanced diet that includes these recommended foods, individuals can take proactive steps toward better skin health and improved quality of life.

Foods to Avoid

When managing psoriasis, dietary choices play a pivotal role in overall skin health. Certain foods can exacerbate inflammation and trigger flare-ups, making it essential for patients to identify and avoid these items. Highly processed foods, such as those high in sugar and unhealthy fats, not only contribute to inflammation but can also lead to weight gain, which may worsen psoriasis symptoms. These foods often contain additives and preservatives that can disrupt gut health, further complicating the condition and leading to increased severity of symptoms.

Dairy products are another category that some psoriasis patients may need to avoid. For many individuals, dairy can cause an inflammatory response, which may manifest as a worsening of skin lesions. Milk, cheese, and yogurt can be particularly problematic for those who find they have sensitivities to lactose or casein. Additionally, the hormones present in some dairy products may also play a role in exacerbating skin conditions. Monitoring symptoms and considering the elimination of dairy can be beneficial for patients looking to manage their psoriasis more effectively.

Nightshade vegetables, including tomatoes, potatoes, eggplants, and peppers, are often cited as potential triggers for psoriasis flare-ups. While not everyone will experience negative effects from these foods, some individuals have reported increased inflammation and irritation after consumption. This may be due to the alkaloids present in nightshades, which can affect joint health and inflammatory processes in the body. Keeping a food diary to track responses to these vegetables may help patients identify any correlations with their skin condition.

Another group of foods to be cautious about includes gluten-containing grains. For some individuals, particularly those with gluten sensitivity or celiac disease, gluten can significantly impact inflammatory responses and overall skin integrity. While not all psoriasis patients will need to avoid gluten, those who notice a connection between gluten consumption and flare-ups may benefit from exploring a gluten-free diet. Whole grains such as quinoa and brown rice can serve as nutritious alternatives that provide essential nutrients without the potential downsides associated with gluten.

Finally, excessive alcohol consumption has been linked to increased psoriasis severity. Alcohol can dilate blood vessels, leading to increased redness and inflammation in the skin. It can also impair the immune system, making it more challenging for the body to manage existing psoriasis symptoms effectively. Reducing or eliminating alcohol from the diet can be a significant step toward improving skin health and overall well-being. Patients should approach dietary changes holistically, considering their individual responses and seeking guidance from healthcare professionals to develop a personalized plan that supports their management of psoriasis.

Meal Planning for Psoriasis

Meal planning is a crucial aspect for individuals suffering from psoriasis, as diet can significantly influence the severity of symptoms. A well-structured meal plan can help reduce inflammation, support skin health, and improve overall well-being. It is essential to focus on incorporating anti-inflammatory foods while avoiding those that may trigger flare-ups. A balanced diet rich in fruits, vegetables, whole grains, lean proteins, and healthy fats can be beneficial in managing psoriasis symptoms and enhancing the body's ability to heal.

Incorporating omega-3 fatty acids into your diet is particularly important for those with psoriasis. Foods such as fatty fish (like salmon and mackerel), walnuts, chia seeds, and flaxseeds are excellent sources of omega-3s, which have been shown to reduce inflammation and improve skin health. Additionally, antioxidants found in fruits and vegetables, especially berries, leafy greens, and citrus fruits, can also play a significant role in fighting oxidative stress and supporting skin repair.

When planning meals, it is advisable to minimize the intake of processed foods, refined sugars, and saturated fats, as these can exacerbate inflammation and contribute to the severity of psoriasis. Instead, focus on whole foods that nourish the body. Meal prepping can be a helpful strategy, allowing you to plan and prepare balanced meals in advance, reducing the temptation to opt for unhealthy convenience foods. Keeping a food diary can also be useful in identifying any specific food triggers that may worsen your condition.

For families with children suffering from psoriasis, meal planning can also serve as a teaching opportunity. Encouraging healthy eating habits from an early age can instill lifelong dietary practices that may help manage psoriasis and promote overall health. Involving children in meal preparation can make them more aware of their food choices and empower them to make healthier decisions. This approach not only helps manage their condition but also fosters a supportive family environment.

Lastly, considering the psychological aspects of living with psoriasis, meal planning can also serve as a form of self-care. Taking the time to prepare nutritious meals can enhance mood and create a sense of control over one's health. Engaging in mindful eating practices can further improve mental well-being, helping to alleviate the stress that often accompanies chronic skin conditions. By integrating these dietary strategies into daily life, individuals with psoriasis can create a holistic approach to managing their condition, ultimately leading to improved skin health and quality of life.

Chapter 3: Natural Remedies for Psoriasis

Herbal Treatments

Herbal treatments have gained attention in the management of psoriasis, offering a natural approach to alleviating symptoms and promoting skin health. Many patients seek alternatives to conventional therapies due to side effects or the desire for holistic methods. Various herbs possess anti-inflammatory, antioxidant, and immunomodulatory properties that can support skin healing and reduce flare-ups. Commonly explored herbs include aloe vera, turmeric, and neem, each known for its potential to soothe irritation, hydrate the skin, and fight inflammation.

Aloe vera is widely recognized for its soothing properties, making it a popular choice among psoriasis patients. This succulent plant contains compounds that can reduce skin redness and irritation while providing moisture. Applying pure aloe vera gel to affected areas can help alleviate discomfort and improve the overall appearance of the skin. In addition to topical use, aloe vera can also be consumed in juice form, which may support digestive health and enhance the body's natural healing processes.

Turmeric, with its active compound curcumin, has been studied for its anti-inflammatory effects. Incorporating turmeric into the diet or using it in topical preparations may help reduce the severity of psoriasis symptoms. Some patients find success by mixing turmeric powder with carrier oils to create a soothing paste for application on plaques. Furthermore, adding turmeric to meals not only provides flavor but also introduces beneficial antioxidants that can contribute to overall health and potentially ease psoriasis flare-ups.

Neem, another potent herb, has long been used in traditional medicine for its antimicrobial and anti-inflammatory properties. Neem oil can be applied topically to affected areas, helping to reduce itching and redness while promoting skin healing. Additionally, neem leaves can be brewed into a tea or used in baths to provide systemic benefits. This herb is particularly valuable for children with psoriasis, offering a gentler alternative to harsher medications while still providing relief from symptoms.

While herbal treatments can be beneficial, it is essential for patients to approach them with caution and to consult with healthcare providers before starting any new regimen. Individual responses to herbal remedies can vary, and some may trigger allergic reactions or interact with existing medications. Emphasizing a holistic approach that includes dietary modifications, stress management, and skincare routines can enhance the effectiveness of herbal treatments. As more individuals seek natural remedies for psoriasis, ongoing research and patient advocacy will play crucial roles in advancing understanding and accessibility of these options for all who suffer from this chronic condition.

Essential Oils

Essential oils have gained popularity as a natural remedy for various health conditions, including psoriasis. These concentrated plant extracts possess therapeutic properties that can potentially soothe the skin and alleviate some symptoms associated with this chronic condition. Among the vast array of essential oils, certain types stand out for their anti-inflammatory, antimicrobial, and skin-soothing effects, making them particularly beneficial for those suffering from psoriasis. Incorporating these oils into your daily routine can offer a holistic approach to managing your skin health, complementing other lifestyle modifications and treatments.

Tea tree oil is one of the most commonly recommended essential oils for psoriasis due to its potent anti-inflammatory and antimicrobial properties. Research suggests that tea tree oil can help reduce the redness and scaling associated with psoriasis. When diluted with a carrier oil, such as coconut or jojoba oil, tea tree oil can be applied directly to affected areas. This application not only helps manage psoriasis symptoms but also promotes overall skin health by preventing secondary infections that may arise from scratching or skin irritation.

Lavender essential oil is another excellent option for individuals with psoriasis, particularly for its calming and soothing effects. Psoriasis can often trigger stress and anxiety, which may exacerbate skin flare-ups. The aromatic properties of lavender oil can help reduce stress levels, promoting relaxation and potentially leading to fewer flare-ups. Using lavender oil in a diffuser, adding it to a warm bath, or incorporating it into a massage oil can create a soothing environment that supports mental health and overall well-being.

For children suffering from psoriasis, essential oils can offer gentle relief when used correctly. Oils like chamomile and frankincense are known for their mild nature and skin-soothing properties. These oils can be blended with carrier oils to create a safe topical treatment for young skin. It's important for parents to perform patch tests before applying any new oils to ensure there are no adverse reactions. This cautious approach allows for the incorporation of natural remedies while prioritizing the safety and comfort of children.

As the understanding of psoriasis evolves, more patients are seeking holistic approaches that integrate natural remedies with conventional treatments. Essential oils can play a significant role within this framework by providing additional support for skin health and emotional well-being. Patients are encouraged to consult with healthcare professionals knowledgeable about both conventional and alternative treatments to develop a comprehensive management plan. By embracing a combination of lifestyle modifications, dietary changes, and natural remedies like essential oils, individuals with psoriasis can work towards achieving better skin health and an improved quality of life.

Home Remedies

Home remedies can play an essential role in managing psoriasis, offering patients additional avenues to alleviate symptoms and improve overall skin health. Many individuals with psoriasis are increasingly seeking natural remedies as complementary approaches to conventional treatments. These remedies often focus on alleviating inflammation, reducing itching, and enhancing skin hydration. Simple ingredients found in most households can provide relief and support the skin's healing process, making them accessible options for many patients.

A common home remedy for psoriasis involves the use of oatmeal baths. Colloidal oatmeal can soothe inflamed skin and relieve itching, providing a calming effect that can be particularly beneficial during flare-ups. Adding oatmeal to a warm bath allows the skin to absorb beneficial properties that hydrate and protect the skin barrier. Following the bath, applying a gentle moisturizer can enhance this benefit, locking in moisture and reducing dryness associated with psoriasis. This practice is safe for both adults and children, making it a family-friendly approach.

Another effective remedy is the use of aloe vera gel, known for its soothing and anti-inflammatory properties. Applying pure aloe vera directly to affected areas can help reduce redness and scaling while promoting skin healing. Patients should opt for natural, organic aloe vera products to avoid additives that may irritate sensitive skin. Additionally, incorporating aloe vera into daily skincare routines can enhance overall skin health and resilience, providing long-term benefits for those with psoriasis.

Dietary modifications can also serve as home remedies for psoriasis. Consuming anti-inflammatory foods such as fatty fish rich in omega-3 fatty acids, leafy greens, and nuts can help manage symptoms. Conversely, patients should be mindful of foods that may trigger flare-ups, such as processed foods, sugar, and excessive dairy. Keeping a food diary can aid patients in identifying personal triggers, allowing for a tailored dietary approach that supports skin health and overall wellness. This holistic perspective on diet can empower individuals to take charge of their condition.

Finally, stress management techniques can be considered home remedies that indirectly benefit psoriasis. Practices such as yoga, meditation, and deep-breathing exercises can help reduce stress levels, which are known to exacerbate psoriasis symptoms. Engaging in these activities regularly can promote mental well-being and improve skin conditions. By integrating these lifestyle modifications into their daily routines, patients can create a supportive environment for their skin, fostering resilience against the challenges of living with psoriasis.

Chapter 4: Psoriasis in Children

Recognizing Symptoms

Recognizing the symptoms of psoriasis is crucial for effective management and treatment. Psoriasis manifests in various forms, with the most common being plaque psoriasis. Patients often notice raised, red patches of skin covered with thick, silvery scales. These plaques can appear anywhere on the body but are commonly found on the elbows, knees, scalp, and lower back. The severity and extent of these patches can vary significantly among individuals, making awareness of early signs essential for timely intervention.

In addition to the visible plaques, psoriasis may also present with other symptoms that are important to monitor. Patients often report itching, burning, or soreness in affected areas. This discomfort can lead to scratching, which may exacerbate the condition and increase the risk of infection. Moreover, some individuals experience nail changes, such as pitting, ridges, or separation from the nail bed. Recognizing these additional symptoms can help patients better communicate with their healthcare providers, leading to more personalized treatment plans.

Psoriasis can also affect overall well-being, making it essential to recognize mental health symptoms associated with the condition. Many patients experience feelings of embarrassment, anxiety, or depression due to their skin appearance and the chronic nature of the disease. This connection between psoriasis and mental health is increasingly acknowledged, and recognizing these emotional symptoms is a vital part of comprehensive care. Patients should seek support and consider incorporating mental health resources into their management strategies.

Another aspect to consider in recognizing symptoms is the potential for comorbid conditions. Psoriasis is associated with a higher risk of various health issues, including psoriatic arthritis, cardiovascular diseases, and metabolic syndrome. Patients should be vigilant for signs of joint pain or stiffness, particularly after periods of inactivity, as these may indicate the onset of psoriatic arthritis. Early recognition of such symptoms can lead to prompt evaluation and treatment, potentially preventing further complications.

Finally, understanding how lifestyle factors influence symptoms is essential. Diet, stress management, and skincare routines can all impact the severity of psoriasis. Patients should pay attention to their bodies and identify any triggers that worsen their condition. Keeping a symptom diary can be a helpful tool for recognizing patterns and making informed decisions about natural remedies or dietary adjustments. By being proactive in recognizing symptoms, patients can take significant steps toward managing their psoriasis more effectively and improving their overall quality of life.

Treatment Options for Kids

When it comes to treating psoriasis in children, it is essential to approach the condition with care and consideration, recognizing the unique needs of younger patients. Treatment options can vary widely, from topical therapies to systemic medications, and it is crucial to consult a pediatric dermatologist to develop a tailored plan. Topical treatments such as corticosteroids, vitamin D analogs, and calcineurin inhibitors are commonly prescribed for mild to moderate psoriasis in children. These treatments can help reduce inflammation, scaling, and discomfort while being gentle enough for sensitive skin.

In addition to topical therapies, phototherapy can be an effective treatment option for children with moderate to severe psoriasis. This method involves exposing the skin to controlled doses of natural sunlight or artificial ultraviolet light, helping to slow down the rapid skin cell turnover that characterizes the condition. Phototherapy can be particularly beneficial for children who may not respond well to topical treatments alone. However, it is essential to monitor the child closely to minimize the risk of skin damage and to ensure the treatment remains effective.

Systemic treatments, which work throughout the body, are typically reserved for more severe cases of psoriasis or when topical treatments are insufficient. These may include oral medications such as methotrexate or biologics that target specific parts of the immune system. While systemic treatments can provide significant relief, they require careful monitoring for potential side effects. Pediatric dermatologists will weigh the benefits against the risks, taking into account the child's overall health, age, and any comorbid conditions.

Natural remedies can also play a role in managing psoriasis in children, particularly as complementary therapies to conventional treatments. Parents may explore options such as oatmeal baths, which can soothe itching and inflammation, or the incorporation of omega-3 fatty acids found in fish oil, which might help reduce inflammation. Diet modifications, such as increasing fruits and vegetables while reducing processed foods, can also support overall health and potentially lessen psoriasis flare-ups. However, it is essential to approach these remedies with caution and consult with healthcare providers to ensure they are safe and effective for children.

Mental health considerations are equally vital in treating pediatric psoriasis. Living with a chronic skin condition can lead to feelings of anxiety or low self-esteem in children. Support from family, counseling, and support groups can help children cope with the emotional aspects of psoriasis. Open communication about their condition and involving them in treatment decisions can empower children and improve their overall outlook. By combining medical treatments with holistic approaches, families can create a comprehensive management plan that addresses both the physical and emotional needs of children with psoriasis.

Supporting Mental Health in Children

Supporting mental health in children dealing with psoriasis is crucial for their overall well-being and quality of life. Psoriasis, a chronic skin condition, can significantly impact a child's self-esteem and social interactions. The visible nature of psoriasis may lead to feelings of embarrassment or isolation, making it essential to address the psychological aspects of living with this condition. Parents and caregivers play a vital role in creating a supportive environment that fosters resilience and emotional well-being in children.

Encouraging open communication is one of the most effective ways to support a child's mental health. Children should feel safe discussing their feelings and experiences related to their psoriasis. Parents can initiate conversations by asking open-ended questions about their child's day, friendships, and any challenges they may face. This dialogue can help children articulate their emotions and understand that their feelings are valid. Acknowledging the difficulties they face can help diminish feelings of isolation and promote a sense of belonging.

Incorporating lifestyle modifications that promote mental wellness can also be beneficial. Regular physical activity is not only vital for overall health but can also serve as an outlet for stress and anxiety. Engaging in fun activities such as sports, dance, or family walks can improve mood and foster social connections. Additionally, a balanced diet rich in nutrients can have a positive impact on both skin health and mental well-being. Parents should consider integrating foods that are known to support skin health, like omega-3 fatty acids and antioxidants, into their children's meals while emphasizing the importance of hydration and proper nutrition.

Support groups and therapy can provide children with valuable tools to cope with the emotional challenges of psoriasis. Connecting with peers who share similar experiences can help children feel less alone and more understood. Schools and community organizations may offer resources for support groups specifically tailored for children with chronic conditions. Professional therapy, whether individual or family-based, can help children develop coping strategies and address any anxiety or depression related to their condition. These interventions can equip children with the skills they need to manage their mental health effectively.

Finally, fostering a positive self-image is essential in supporting mental health for children with psoriasis. Parents can encourage their children to focus on their strengths and interests outside of their skin condition. Celebrating achievements, no matter how small, can help build confidence and resilience. Additionally, educating both the child and their peers about psoriasis can reduce stigma and promote empathy. By creating an environment that emphasizes acceptance and understanding, we can help children with psoriasis navigate their journey with greater confidence and improved mental health.

Chapter 5: Mental Health and Psoriasis

The Psychological Impact of Psoriasis

Psoriasis is not just a skin condition; it often profoundly affects the psychological well-being of those who suffer from it. The visible nature of psoriasis, characterized by red, flaky patches on the skin, can lead to feelings of embarrassment and self-consciousness. Many individuals with psoriasis report experiencing anxiety and depression, which can stem from societal stigma and the constant battle with flare-ups. This psychological burden can significantly impact daily life, making social interactions and professional engagements more challenging. Understanding the psychological impact of psoriasis is crucial for developing effective coping strategies and support systems.

The relationship between psoriasis and mental health is increasingly recognized in medical research. Studies have shown that individuals with psoriasis are at a higher risk of developing anxiety disorders and depressive symptoms compared to the general population. The chronic nature of psoriasis, coupled with its unpredictable flare-ups, can create a cycle of stress and emotional distress. Patients may feel trapped in a condition that is often misunderstood by others, leading to feelings of isolation. Recognizing these mental health challenges is essential for both patients and their healthcare providers to foster a more holistic approach to treatment.

Social implications are also significant for those living with psoriasis. Patients often report avoiding social situations or engaging in activities such as swimming or wearing certain clothing due to fear of judgment or ridicule. This avoidance can lead to a decrease in quality of life, as social connections and community engagement are vital for emotional health. Furthermore, children with psoriasis face unique challenges, including bullying and exclusion, which can have lasting effects on their self-esteem and emotional development. Awareness and education about the psychological aspects of psoriasis are critical in mitigating these social impacts.

Addressing the psychological impact of psoriasis requires a multifaceted approach. Therapy options, including cognitive-behavioral therapy (CBT) and support groups, can provide patients with the tools to manage their emotional responses to the condition. Additionally, incorporating lifestyle modifications such as stress-reduction techniques, regular exercise, and mindfulness practices can help improve overall mental health. These strategies not only enhance the management of psoriasis but also empower patients to take an active role in their health and well-being.

Finally, advocacy and awareness play a significant role in changing the narrative surrounding psoriasis. By promoting understanding of the psychological implications of the condition, we can encourage more compassionate responses from society. Patients are encouraged to share their experiences and seek support from organizations dedicated to psoriasis awareness. Such initiatives not only help in reducing stigma but also foster a sense of community among those affected. As we move forward, it is essential to prioritize both the physical and psychological aspects of psoriasis to ensure comprehensive care and support for all individuals living with this condition.

Coping Strategies

Coping with psoriasis involves a multifaceted approach that integrates various strategies to manage the condition effectively. Individuals living with psoriasis often face both physical and emotional challenges, making it essential to adopt coping strategies that address the entirety of the experience. While conventional treatments are crucial, incorporating lifestyle modifications, dietary adjustments, and natural remedies can significantly enhance overall well-being and skin health. This subchapter will explore various coping strategies to help individuals navigate the complexities of living with psoriasis.

Diet plays a pivotal role in managing psoriasis symptoms. Research has shown that certain foods can exacerbate inflammation, while others can reduce it. A diet rich in omega-3 fatty acids, found in fish like salmon and in flaxseeds, can help to lower inflammatory responses in the body. Additionally, incorporating fruits and vegetables high in antioxidants can support skin health and immune function. Patients should consider keeping a food diary to track which foods may trigger flare-ups and consult with a nutritionist to develop a personalized diet plan. Awareness of dietary influences can empower individuals to make informed choices that positively impact their skin condition.

Natural remedies can also provide relief for psoriasis symptoms. Many individuals find that topical applications, such as aloe vera and coconut oil, can soothe irritated skin and reduce dryness. Herbal supplements like turmeric and evening primrose oil are known for their anti-inflammatory properties and may support overall skin health. Additionally, regular baths with Epsom salt or oatmeal can help to alleviate itching and discomfort. While these remedies can be helpful, it is essential to discuss any new treatments with a healthcare provider to ensure they complement existing treatment plans.

Mental health is an often overlooked aspect of coping with psoriasis. The visibility of the condition can lead to feelings of embarrassment, anxiety, and depression. Engaging in mindfulness practices, such as meditation and yoga, can help to reduce stress and promote a sense of well-being. Support groups, whether in-person or online, can provide a vital space for sharing experiences and coping strategies with others who understand the unique challenges of living with psoriasis. Seeking professional counseling or therapy can also be beneficial for those struggling with the emotional impact of the condition, allowing for a more holistic approach to management.

Finally, advocating for oneself is a crucial coping strategy that can lead to better management of psoriasis. Staying informed about advances in treatments and participating in discussions about skin care routines can empower patients to take control of their health. Regular communication with healthcare providers about symptoms, concerns, and treatment efficacy is vital for achieving optimal results. By being proactive about their condition and engaging in advocacy, individuals can foster a more supportive environment, not only for themselves but also for others affected by psoriasis. Adopting these coping strategies can lead to a more fulfilling life, despite the challenges posed by psoriasis.

When to Seek Professional Help

When managing psoriasis, recognizing when to seek professional help can significantly impact your quality of life. While many patients explore lifestyle modifications and natural remedies, there are instances where professional intervention becomes essential. If you notice a sudden worsening of symptoms, such as increased redness, scaling, or discomfort, it is crucial to consult a healthcare provider. These changes could indicate a flare-up or a potential secondary infection that requires immediate attention. Early intervention can help prevent further complications and restore your skin's health more quickly.

Additionally, if you find that your psoriasis is affecting your mental health, it is vital to reach out for professional help. Psoriasis can lead to feelings of embarrassment, anxiety, or depression, particularly if it affects visible areas of the body. Mental health professionals can provide support and coping strategies, while a dermatologist can work with you to optimize your treatment plan. Addressing both the physical and emotional aspects of psoriasis ensures a more holistic approach to your overall well-being.

For those with children who have been diagnosed with psoriasis, seeking professional guidance becomes even more critical. Pediatric psoriasis can differ significantly from adult cases, often requiring specialized knowledge and treatment methods. A pediatric dermatologist can help tailor an effective treatment plan that considers the child's age, skin type, and specific needs. Moreover, involving a mental health professional can help children cope with the emotional challenges that come with living with a chronic condition, fostering resilience and self-esteem.

If you are exploring dietary modifications or natural remedies as part of your psoriasis management, consulting with a registered dietitian or nutritionist can be beneficial. They can help you identify foods that may trigger flare-ups while recommending a balanced diet that supports skin health. This professional advice can help ensure that your dietary changes do not inadvertently lead to nutrient deficiencies, which could worsen your condition. Collaborating with healthcare professionals can provide a comprehensive understanding of how diet interacts with psoriasis and overall health.

Lastly, if you are currently using topical treatments or over-the-counter products without seeing improvement, it may be time to seek professional help. Dermatologists are equipped to prescribe advanced treatments, such as biologics or phototherapy, that may offer better results for your condition. Regular follow-ups with a healthcare provider allow for ongoing assessment and adjustment of your treatment plan, ensuring that you stay on the path toward effective management of your psoriasis. Taking these steps can lead to improved skin health and overall quality of life.

Chapter 6: Advances in Psoriasis Treatments

Topical Treatments

Topical treatments play a crucial role in the management of psoriasis, offering patients a first line of defense against the discomfort and visibility associated with this chronic skin condition. These treatments are designed to be applied directly to the skin, targeting the affected areas to reduce inflammation, scale formation, and itching. Common topical treatments include corticosteroids, vitamin D analogs, retinoids, and calcineurin inhibitors. Each of these has its unique mechanism of action, and understanding them can help patients make informed choices about their skincare routines.

Corticosteroids are often the most frequently prescribed topical treatments for psoriasis due to their anti-inflammatory properties. They work by suppressing the immune response that leads to skin cell overproduction, a hallmark of psoriasis. While effective for many patients, it is essential to use corticosteroids judiciously to avoid potential side effects such as skin thinning or tachyphylaxis, where the skin becomes less responsive to the treatment over time. Patients should follow their healthcare provider's guidance on the appropriate strength and duration of use to maximize benefits while minimizing risks.

Vitamin D analogs, such as calcipotriene, are another valuable option in the treatment arsenal for psoriasis. These agents help slow down skin cell growth and promote the differentiation of skin cells. When used in combination with corticosteroids, vitamin D analogs can enhance the effectiveness of treatment, providing better control of psoriatic plaques. Patients may also incorporate these treatments into their holistic management approach, combining them with dietary modifications and lifestyle changes to further improve skin health.

For those exploring natural remedies, topical treatments that include ingredients like aloe vera, tea tree oil, or oatmeal can offer soothing effects. These natural options may not replace conventional treatments but can complement them, particularly for patients concerned about the long-term use of pharmaceuticals. Patients should consult with their healthcare providers to ensure that any natural treatments do not interfere with their prescribed therapies and that they are suitable for their specific skin type and psoriatic condition.

In addition to conventional and natural topical treatments, it is essential for patients to adopt a comprehensive approach to managing psoriasis. This includes being aware of comorbid conditions such as obesity, diabetes, and depression, which can exacerbate the severity of psoriasis. Engaging in lifestyle modifications, such as maintaining a balanced diet rich in anti-inflammatory foods, practicing stress management techniques, and cultivating a supportive social environment, can significantly improve overall well-being and enhance the effectiveness of topical treatments. By integrating these elements, patients can foster a proactive approach to living well with psoriasis.

Systemic Therapies

Systemic therapies represent an essential category of treatment for individuals suffering from psoriasis, particularly in cases where the condition is moderate to severe or has not responded adequately to topical treatments. These therapies work throughout the body to reduce inflammation and slow down the rapid skin cell growth characteristic of psoriasis. Common systemic treatments include biologics, which are medications derived from living organisms, and traditional systemic agents like methotrexate and cyclosporine. Each of these therapies has unique mechanisms of action and potential side effects, making it crucial for patients to engage in thorough discussions with their healthcare providers to determine the best course of action.

Biologics have emerged as a groundbreaking advancement in the treatment of psoriasis, specifically designed to target specific components of the immune system that contribute to the disease. These medications can significantly improve skin clearance and reduce the frequency of flare-ups. The introduction of biologics has changed the landscape of psoriasis management, offering hope to patients who previously had limited options. However, because these treatments can affect immune function, patients must also consider potential risks and monitor for infections or other complications closely.

In addition to biologics, traditional systemic agents like methotrexate continue to play a vital role in psoriasis treatment. Methotrexate, an immunosuppressant, can effectively reduce inflammation and slow cell turnover, providing relief for many patients. It is essential for patients to comply with regular blood tests while on this medication, as it can affect liver function and blood cell counts. Other systemic therapies, such as cyclosporine, are also available and may be considered depending on individual patient needs and medical histories. Patients should be informed about these options and engage in shared decision-making with their healthcare providers.

Diet and lifestyle modifications can complement systemic therapies, enhancing their effectiveness and improving overall well-being. Research suggests that certain dietary choices may help manage psoriasis symptoms. Anti-inflammatory diets rich in omega-3 fatty acids, fruits, vegetables, and whole grains can support skin health and potentially reduce flare-ups. Additionally, maintaining a healthy weight is vital since obesity is associated with increased severity of psoriasis and higher healthcare costs. Patients should consider working with a nutritionist to develop a tailored eating plan that supports their treatment goals.

Lastly, it is crucial to address the psychological aspects of living with psoriasis. The visible nature of the disease can lead to feelings of embarrassment, anxiety, and depression. Patients are encouraged to seek mental health support, whether through counseling, support groups, or mindfulness practices. A holistic approach to psoriasis management that includes both systemic therapies and attention to mental health can empower patients to take control of their condition. In doing so, they can improve not only their skin health but also their overall quality of life, fostering a more positive outlook during their treatment journey.

Biologics and Their Impact

Biologics have emerged as a groundbreaking advancement in the treatment of psoriasis, offering new hope to patients who have struggled with chronic skin conditions. These medications are derived from living organisms and target specific parts of the immune system that contribute to the inflammation and rapid skin cell turnover characteristic of psoriasis. Unlike traditional systemic treatments, which can affect the entire immune system, biologics focus on specific pathways, leading to more effective and targeted relief from symptoms. This precision can significantly improve the quality of life for those living with psoriasis.

One of the most significant impacts of biologics is their ability to bring about rapid and lasting improvement in skin clearance. Many patients experience substantial reductions in psoriatic plaques within weeks of starting treatment. This rapid response can be life-changing, particularly for individuals whose psoriasis has hindered their daily activities, self-esteem, and mental health. As biologics continue to evolve, they offer promise not only for adults but also for children with psoriasis, expanding treatment options for younger patients who may be particularly vulnerable to the psychosocial effects of their condition.

In addition to their efficacy, biologics have been associated with a favorable safety profile compared to some traditional psoriasis treatments. While all medications carry potential risks and side effects, biologics are often better tolerated and have a lower incidence of serious adverse effects. This aspect is especially important for patients considering long-term treatment strategies. Patients should engage in open discussions with their healthcare providers to weigh the benefits of biologics against any potential risks, ensuring a personalized approach to management that aligns with their unique health needs.

Diet and lifestyle modifications continue to play a crucial role in managing psoriasis, even when patients are undergoing biologic therapy. Many individuals find that a holistic approach, which includes dietary adjustments, stress management, and appropriate skincare routines, can enhance the effectiveness of biologics. For instance, certain anti-inflammatory diets rich in omega-3 fatty acids, antioxidants, and whole foods can potentially complement the therapeutic effects of biologics. Additionally, maintaining a regular skincare regimen that includes moisturizing and avoiding irritants can help protect the skin and support overall treatment goals.

Awareness and advocacy around psoriasis are also essential in the context of biologics and their impact. As the landscape of psoriasis treatment evolves, educating patients about available options empowers them to make informed choices. Organizations focused on psoriasis awareness can help disseminate valuable information regarding new treatments, including biologics, while advocating for access to these therapies. By fostering a supportive community and promoting understanding, patients can better navigate their treatment journeys and inspire others to seek effective management strategies for psoriasis.

Chapter 7: Lifestyle Modifications for Better Skin

Daily Routines and Skin Care

Daily routines play a crucial role in managing psoriasis, as they can directly impact skin health and overall well-being. Establishing a consistent skin care routine tailored to your specific needs can help reduce flare-ups and improve the appearance of the skin. For individuals with psoriasis, it is essential to select products that are gentle, hydrating, and free from irritants. This includes choosing cleansers that do not contain sulfates or harsh chemicals, as these can exacerbate dryness and irritation. Opting for fragrance-free options can also minimize the risk of an adverse reaction, providing a more soothing experience for sensitive skin.

Incorporating moisturizing into your daily routine is vital for individuals with psoriasis. Moisturizers help to hydrate the skin, lock in moisture, and provide a protective barrier against environmental factors that may trigger flare-ups. Look for products containing ingredients like ceramides, hyaluronic acid, and glycerin, which are known for their hydrating properties. Applying moisturizer immediately after bathing, when the skin is still damp, can enhance absorption and effectiveness. Establishing a regular moisturizing schedule, ideally two to three times a day, can greatly improve skin texture and resilience.

Diet also plays an influential role in daily routines for those managing psoriasis. A balanced diet rich in anti-inflammatory foods can help support skin health. Incorporating omega-3 fatty acids found in fish like salmon, walnuts, and flaxseed may help reduce inflammation associated with psoriasis. Additionally, fruits and vegetables high in antioxidants can aid in skin repair and overall health. Staying hydrated by drinking plenty of water throughout the day is another simple yet effective way to support skin vitality. Eliminating trigger foods, such as processed sugars and excessive alcohol, can also contribute to overall skin improvement.

Mental health is an often-overlooked aspect of daily routines in psoriasis management. Stress can be a significant trigger for flare-ups, making it essential to incorporate stress-reduction techniques into your day. Practices such as mindfulness, meditation, and gentle yoga can help lower stress levels and promote a sense of well-being. Taking time for self-care, whether through hobbies, relaxation, or spending time in nature, can create a positive impact on mental health and skin condition. Remember, addressing the psychological aspects of living with psoriasis is just as important as physical care.

Finally, staying informed about advances in psoriasis treatments and skincare products can enhance your daily routine. Regularly consulting with healthcare providers can help you keep up-to-date with the latest therapies and holistic approaches that may benefit your condition. Joining support groups or online communities can provide valuable insights and shared experiences that can guide your routine. By combining effective skincare practices with a healthy lifestyle and mental health support, individuals with psoriasis can significantly improve their quality of life and skin health.

Stress Management Techniques

Stress management is crucial for individuals suffering from psoriasis, as stress can exacerbate symptoms and trigger flare-ups. Implementing effective stress management techniques can lead to improved skin health and overall well-being. Various methods, including mindfulness practices, physical activity, and social support, can help mitigate stress and its impact on psoriasis.

Mindfulness practices, such as meditation and yoga, have shown significant benefits for individuals with psoriasis. Engaging in mindfulness can enhance emotional regulation, reduce anxiety, and promote relaxation. Regular meditation sessions, even for a few minutes a day, can help calm the mind and reduce stress levels, which may lead to fewer flare-ups. Yoga combines physical movement with mindfulness, offering a dual benefit of stress relief and physical exercise, both of which are vital for managing psoriasis.

Physical activity is another powerful tool for stress management. Exercise has been proven to release endorphins, the body's natural mood lifters, which can help reduce feelings of stress and anxiety. Incorporating regular exercise into your routine—whether through walking, cycling, or swimming—can improve both mental and physical health. For those with psoriasis, low-impact activities are often recommended to avoid aggravating the skin, making swimming in a chlorinated pool or gentle stretching exercises ideal choices.

Social support plays a significant role in managing stress effectively. Connecting with family, friends, or support groups can provide emotional comfort and practical advice. Sharing experiences with others who understand the challenges of living with psoriasis can foster a sense of community and belonging. Consider participating in local support groups or online forums where individuals with psoriasis gather to share their journeys and coping strategies.

Finally, adopting a holistic approach to stress management can yield substantial benefits for those with psoriasis. This may include integrating natural remedies, such as herbal supplements and dietary modifications that support skin health. Additionally, ensuring adequate sleep, practicing time management, and setting realistic goals can help reduce stress. By embracing these techniques, individuals with psoriasis can create a tailored stress management plan that promotes skin health and enhances their overall quality of life.

Exercise and Physical Activity

Exercise and physical activity play a crucial role in managing psoriasis, contributing not only to physical health but also to mental well-being. Engaging in regular exercise can help reduce inflammation and improve skin health, both of which are beneficial for individuals with psoriasis. Activities such as walking, swimming, and cycling promote blood circulation and enhance oxygen delivery to the skin, which can aid in healing and rejuvenation. Furthermore, low-impact exercises are often recommended as they minimize the risk of injury while providing significant benefits.

In addition to physical benefits, exercise has a profound impact on mental health. Many patients with psoriasis experience anxiety, depression, or stress, which can exacerbate their symptoms. Exercise releases endorphins, often referred to as "feel-good" hormones, which can elevate mood and reduce stress levels. Establishing a regular exercise routine can help individuals better cope with the emotional challenges associated with living with psoriasis. Group activities, such as yoga or dance classes, can also foster a sense of community and support among participants, further enhancing mental well-being.

Incorporating exercise into a daily routine doesn't require a gym membership or expensive equipment. Simple activities like walking or stretching can be effective and accessible. Setting realistic goals can help maintain motivation; for instance, starting with just 10 minutes a day and gradually increasing the duration and intensity. It is essential for patients to listen to their bodies and choose activities that they enjoy, as this can make it easier to stick with a routine. Engaging in family-oriented activities can also encourage children with psoriasis to stay active, fostering healthy habits from a young age.

Nutrition plays a pivotal role in both psoriasis and exercise. A balanced diet rich in antioxidants, omega-3 fatty acids, and anti-inflammatory foods can enhance the benefits of physical activity. Foods such as fatty fish, leafy greens, nuts, and berries can support skin health and improve recovery after exercise. Staying hydrated is also vital, as it helps maintain skin moisture and elasticity. Patients should consider combining their dietary choices with their exercise routine to optimize overall health and skin condition.

Lastly, it is crucial for individuals with psoriasis to consult with healthcare professionals before starting any new exercise program. This is particularly important for those with comorbid conditions that may affect their ability to exercise safely. A tailored exercise plan can ensure that patients reap the benefits of physical activity while minimizing potential risks. By making exercise a regular part of their lives, individuals with psoriasis can improve not only their skin health but also their overall quality of life, paving the way for a more positive and empowered approach to managing their condition.

Chapter 8: Psoriasis and Comorbid Conditions

Understanding Comorbidities

Understanding comorbidities is essential for individuals living with psoriasis, as the condition often occurs alongside various other health issues that can complicate treatment and management strategies. Comorbidities refer to the presence of one or more additional diseases or conditions that occur simultaneously with a primary condition, in this case, psoriasis. These can include cardiovascular diseases, diabetes, obesity, and mental health disorders such as depression and anxiety. Recognizing these associations can help patients and healthcare providers adopt a more comprehensive approach to treatment, ultimately improving overall health and quality of life.

Research has shown that psoriasis is not just a skin condition; it is a systemic inflammatory disease that may increase the risk of developing other serious health issues. For example, individuals with psoriasis have a higher tendency to develop metabolic syndrome, which encompasses a range of conditions including hypertension, high cholesterol, and insulin resistance. This interconnection highlights the importance of regular health screenings and lifestyle modifications aimed at reducing the risk of these comorbidities. Patients should be encouraged to discuss their full health picture with their healthcare providers to ensure all aspects of their well-being are being monitored.

Another critical area of focus is the mental health of individuals with psoriasis. The visible nature of the skin condition can lead to psychological distress, affecting self-esteem and leading to social isolation. Studies indicate a strong link between psoriasis and mood disorders, with many patients reporting feelings of anxiety and depression. Addressing mental health is as vital as managing physical symptoms, and a holistic approach that includes counseling, support groups, and stress-reduction techniques can provide significant benefits. Patients should not hesitate to seek mental health support as part of their overall treatment plan.

Diet and lifestyle choices also play a significant role in managing psoriasis and its comorbidities. Certain dietary patterns, such as those rich in anti-inflammatory foods, can help mitigate the severity of psoriasis and reduce the risk of associated conditions like cardiovascular disease. Implementing a balanced diet that includes fruits, vegetables, whole grains, and healthy fats can be beneficial. Additionally, maintaining a healthy weight through regular exercise can help alleviate the symptoms of psoriasis and decrease the likelihood of developing other health issues.

In summary, understanding comorbidities is crucial for effective management of psoriasis. By acknowledging the potential for additional health conditions and their impact on overall well-being, patients can take proactive steps in their treatment. This includes regular consultations with healthcare providers, prioritizing mental health care, making informed dietary choices, and adopting a healthy lifestyle. Through a comprehensive approach, individuals can work toward not just better skin, but an improved quality of life overall.

Managing Joint Pain and Psoriatic Arthritis

Managing joint pain is a significant aspect of living well with psoriatic arthritis, a condition that often accompanies psoriasis. Patients frequently experience inflammation and discomfort in their joints, which can impact daily activities and overall quality of life. Understanding the relationship between psoriasis and joint pain is crucial, as effective management strategies can help alleviate symptoms and improve mobility. Recognizing the signs of psoriatic arthritis early can lead to timely interventions, reducing the risk of long-term joint damage and enhancing one's ability to maintain an active lifestyle.

Diet plays a vital role in managing joint pain associated with psoriatic arthritis. Certain foods can help reduce inflammation and promote overall health. Incorporating anti-inflammatory foods such as fatty fish rich in omega-3 fatty acids, leafy greens, nuts, and whole grains can be beneficial. Conversely, it may be advantageous to limit processed foods, sugars, and excessive alcohol consumption, which can exacerbate inflammation. Patients should consider working with a healthcare professional to develop a personalized diet plan that addresses their specific needs and preferences while also supporting skin health.

Natural remedies can provide additional support for managing joint pain. Herbal supplements such as turmeric, ginger, and boswellia have been shown to possess anti-inflammatory properties and may complement conventional treatments. Physical therapy and regular exercise are also key components of a holistic approach to managing psoriatic arthritis. Low-impact exercises, such as swimming and yoga, can help enhance flexibility, strengthen muscles around the joints, and reduce stiffness, all of which contribute to improved joint function and decreased pain.

Mental health is another critical factor in managing joint pain and psoriatic arthritis. Chronic pain can lead to feelings of frustration, anxiety, and depression, creating a cycle that can worsen symptoms. Patients should prioritize mental well-being by engaging in stress-reducing activities such as mindfulness, meditation, or connecting with support groups. Seeking professional mental health support can also provide strategies to cope with the psychological impact of living with both psoriasis and psoriatic arthritis, promoting a more balanced and fulfilling life.

Advancements in psoriasis treatments continue to evolve, offering new hope for individuals dealing with joint pain. Biologic therapies specifically targeting inflammation associated with psoriatic arthritis have shown promising results in reducing both skin and joint symptoms. Patients are encouraged to stay informed about new treatments and discuss options with their healthcare providers. Combining medical interventions with lifestyle modifications, dietary changes, and natural remedies creates a comprehensive management plan that addresses both skin and joint health, empowering patients to live well with psoriasis.

Cardiovascular Health and Psoriasis

Cardiovascular health is a critical aspect of overall well-being, particularly for individuals with psoriasis. Research has shown that psoriasis is associated with an increased risk of cardiovascular diseases, including heart attacks and strokes. This connection is believed to stem from the systemic inflammation that characterizes psoriasis, which can lead to the development of atherosclerosis—a condition where arteries become narrowed and hardened due to plaque buildup. Understanding this link is crucial for patients suffering from psoriasis, as it emphasizes the importance of monitoring cardiovascular health alongside managing skin symptoms.

To promote cardiovascular health, individuals with psoriasis should consider incorporating heart-healthy lifestyle modifications. Regular physical activity is paramount; engaging in moderate aerobic exercise for at least 150 minutes per week can improve cardiovascular fitness and reduce inflammation. Additionally, maintaining a healthy weight through a balanced diet rich in fruits, vegetables, whole grains, and lean proteins can support both skin health and heart health. Specific dietary choices, such as incorporating omega-3 fatty acids found in fish and flaxseeds, can also help reduce inflammation, further benefiting those with psoriasis.

Moreover, it is essential for psoriasis patients to manage other comorbid conditions that may exacerbate cardiovascular risks. Conditions such as hypertension, diabetes, and high cholesterol are often more prevalent in individuals with psoriasis. Regular check-ups with healthcare providers can help track these conditions and implement necessary interventions. Adopting a proactive approach to managing these comorbidities not only enhances skin health but also significantly lowers the risk of developing serious cardiovascular complications.

Mental health also plays a vital role in the relationship between psoriasis and cardiovascular health. The stress and emotional challenges associated with living with a chronic skin condition can lead to elevated blood pressure and other heart-related issues. Engaging in stress-reducing activities such as mindfulness, yoga, or meditation can be beneficial for both mental well-being and cardiovascular health. Additionally, seeking support from mental health professionals or support groups can provide valuable coping strategies for managing the psychological impact of psoriasis.

In conclusion, the interplay between cardiovascular health and psoriasis underscores the importance of a holistic approach to treatment. Patients should prioritize lifestyle modifications that enhance both skin and heart health, recognizing that managing one aspect can positively influence the other. By adopting heart-healthy habits, managing comorbid conditions, and addressing mental health, individuals with psoriasis can significantly improve their overall quality of life while mitigating risks associated with cardiovascular disease.

Chapter 9: Holistic Approaches to Psoriasis Management

Integrative Medicine

Integrative medicine represents a holistic approach to health that combines conventional medical treatments with complementary therapies, acknowledging the importance of treating the whole person rather than just the symptoms of a condition. For patients suffering from psoriasis, this approach can be particularly beneficial, as it not only addresses the physical aspects of the condition but also considers emotional and lifestyle factors. Integrative medicine emphasizes collaboration between healthcare providers and patients, encouraging individuals to take an active role in their own health management.

Incorporating natural remedies can be a valuable part of an integrative approach to psoriasis. Various studies suggest that certain dietary modifications, such as increasing omega-3 fatty acids found in fish and flaxseed, may help reduce inflammation associated with psoriasis flare-ups. Additionally, herbal remedies like aloe vera and turmeric have shown promise in soothing skin irritation and promoting healing. Patients should consult their healthcare providers before starting any new supplements or remedies to ensure they are safe and effective in conjunction with their existing treatments.

Diet is a crucial component of integrative medicine, particularly for those managing psoriasis. A diet rich in anti-inflammatory foods can help mitigate symptoms and improve overall skin health. Fresh fruits, vegetables, whole grains, and healthy fats should be emphasized, while processed foods, sugar, and alcohol may need to be limited to decrease the likelihood of flare-ups. For parents of children with psoriasis, understanding and implementing these dietary changes can be vital in managing their child's condition and promoting a healthier lifestyle from a young age.

Mental health is another essential aspect of integrative medicine, as psoriasis can significantly impact emotional well-being. The visibility of skin lesions can lead to feelings of embarrassment, anxiety, or depression, which in turn may exacerbate physical symptoms. Integrative practices such as mindfulness, yoga, and cognitive-behavioral therapy can provide psychological support and coping strategies. Fostering a network of support, whether through counseling or support groups, can empower patients to navigate their condition with greater resilience and understanding.

Finally, as advances in psoriasis treatments continue to emerge, integrative medicine encourages patients to remain informed about all available options. New therapies, including biologics and systemic medications, can be effectively combined with lifestyle modifications to enhance overall treatment outcomes. Emphasizing a personalized approach that incorporates skincare routines, stress management techniques, and consistent communication with healthcare providers allows individuals to develop a comprehensive management plan tailored to their unique needs. By embracing integrative medicine, patients can achieve a more balanced and empowered path to living well with psoriasis.

Mindfulness and Meditation

Mindfulness and meditation have emerged as valuable practices for individuals managing psoriasis, offering a holistic approach to skin health that extends beyond topical treatments. Psoriasis is not just a physical condition; it is often accompanied by psychological stress, anxiety, and depression. Mindfulness, the practice of being fully present and engaged in the moment, can help reduce stress levels, which may, in turn, alleviate psoriasis flare-ups. By incorporating mindfulness practices into daily routines, patients can cultivate a more positive mental state and enhance their overall well-being.

Meditation, a key component of mindfulness, involves focused attention and deep relaxation techniques that can promote emotional resilience. For psoriasis patients, meditation can provide a sanctuary from the daily challenges posed by skin flare-ups and self-image concerns. Regular meditation sessions can help individuals develop a greater awareness of their thoughts and feelings, enabling them to handle stressors more effectively. This emotional regulation is crucial, as high stress levels are known triggers for psoriasis exacerbation.

In addition to its psychological benefits, mindfulness has been linked to physiological changes that may benefit skin health. Research indicates that practices like mindfulness meditation can lower inflammation in the body, which is particularly relevant for psoriasis patients, given that the condition is characterized by an inflammatory response. By reducing systemic inflammation, mindfulness practices might help create a more favorable environment for skin healing and can complement other treatment modalities, including diet and skincare routines.

Incorporating mindfulness and meditation into daily life does not require significant time commitments or specialized training. Simple practices such as focused breathing, guided imagery, or even mindful walking can be integrated seamlessly into everyday activities. For parents of children with psoriasis, modeling these mindfulness techniques can also impart essential coping skills to younger family members, fostering a family environment that prioritizes mental health and resilience against the psychosocial challenges of living with a chronic skin condition.

Ultimately, mindfulness and meditation serve as essential tools in a comprehensive psoriasis management plan. By addressing the interplay between mental health and skin conditions, these practices can empower patients to take charge of their well-being. As awareness of the psychosocial aspects of psoriasis continues to grow, integrating mindfulness into treatment strategies may not only enhance the quality of life for patients but also contribute to better skin health outcomes over time.

Acupuncture and Alternative Therapies

Acupuncture, a traditional Chinese medicine practice, has gained recognition as a complementary therapy for managing various health conditions, including psoriasis. This technique involves the insertion of thin needles into specific points on the body to stimulate the nervous system and promote healing. For patients suffering from psoriasis, acupuncture may help alleviate symptoms by reducing inflammation, improving circulation, and enhancing the overall balance of the body's systems. Research suggests that acupuncture can positively influence immune function, which is crucial for individuals with psoriasis, as this condition is characterized by an overactive immune response leading to skin flare-ups.

In addition to acupuncture, patients may consider other alternative therapies that can support their psoriasis management. Techniques such as herbal medicine, yoga, and meditation can play a significant role in promoting mental well-being and reducing stress, which is a common trigger for psoriasis flare-ups. Incorporating these practices into a daily routine may enhance the overall quality of life for individuals with psoriasis, especially when combined with conventional treatments. The holistic approach encourages patients to explore these alternatives as part of a comprehensive strategy that addresses both the physical and emotional aspects of their condition.

Diet also plays a crucial role in managing psoriasis symptoms, and some patients have reported improvement by adopting anti-inflammatory diets rich in omega-3 fatty acids, fruits, and vegetables. Integrating acupuncture with dietary modifications can create a synergistic effect, further reducing inflammation and promoting skin health. Patients are encouraged to work with healthcare providers to develop a personalized dietary plan that complements their acupuncture treatments. This collaborative approach can help individuals identify potential food triggers while enhancing their overall skin condition.

For families with children who have psoriasis, alternative therapies can offer additional support. Acupuncture can be adapted for children, and many practitioners specialize in treating younger patients. This gentle approach, combined with educational resources for parents, can empower families to manage psoriasis more effectively. Furthermore, engaging children in holistic practices like mindfulness and gentle exercise can foster resilience and help them cope with the emotional challenges posed by the condition. Parents should work closely with pediatric dermatologists to explore suitable alternative therapies for their children.

Lastly, mental health considerations are paramount in the management of psoriasis. The visible nature of the condition can lead to feelings of self-consciousness and anxiety. Acupuncture, along with mindfulness practices, can provide a platform for emotional healing by reducing stress and promoting relaxation. Additionally, patients are encouraged to engage in psoriasis awareness and advocacy, as sharing experiences can foster a sense of community and support. By integrating acupuncture and other alternative therapies into their treatment plans, individuals can take proactive steps towards achieving better skin health and overall well-being.

Chapter 10: Psoriasis Awareness and Advocacy

The Importance of Awareness

Awareness plays a crucial role in managing psoriasis, a condition that affects millions of people worldwide. Understanding the nature of psoriasis, its triggers, and its impact on both physical and mental health can empower patients to make informed decisions about their treatment and lifestyle. Increased awareness not only aids individuals in recognizing symptoms early but also fosters a proactive approach to managing flare-ups and seeking appropriate care. This knowledge can significantly enhance the quality of life for those living with psoriasis, enabling them to navigate their daily challenges with greater confidence.

One of the key aspects of psoriasis awareness is recognizing the importance of triggers. Stress, certain foods, and environmental factors can exacerbate symptoms, highlighting the need for patients to be vigilant about what affects their skin. Keeping a symptom diary can help individuals track patterns and identify specific triggers. By being aware of these influences, patients can make necessary lifestyle modifications, such as adopting a diet rich in anti-inflammatory foods or developing stress-reducing routines, which can contribute to better skin health.

Awareness also encompasses the mental health challenges associated with psoriasis. Many patients experience feelings of shame, anxiety, or depression due to the visible nature of their condition. Understanding that these feelings are common can help individuals seek support and develop coping strategies. Engaging in open conversations about mental health with healthcare providers, support groups, or friends can foster a sense of community and reduce feelings of isolation. Recognizing the link between mental well-being and skin health can lead to a more holistic approach to treatment, incorporating both dermatological and psychological care.

In addition to personal awareness, advocating for broader psoriasis awareness is essential for fostering understanding and support in society. Many people are unfamiliar with the condition, leading to misconceptions and stigma. By participating in awareness campaigns, individuals can help educate others about psoriasis, its effects, and the importance of compassion for those affected. Advocacy not only benefits patients by promoting better understanding and acceptance but also encourages research and development of new treatments, ultimately improving outcomes for the entire psoriasis community.

Finally, maintaining awareness of advancements in psoriasis treatments is vital. The field of dermatology is constantly evolving, with new therapies and natural remedies emerging that can significantly enhance the management of psoriasis. Staying informed about these developments allows patients to discuss options with their healthcare providers and make choices that align with their values and lifestyles. By prioritizing awareness, individuals with psoriasis can take charge of their health, embrace lifestyle modifications, and advocate for themselves and others, leading to improved skin health and overall well-being.

How to Get Involved

Getting involved in the psoriasis community can significantly enhance your journey towards managing the condition. Whether you are newly diagnosed or have been living with psoriasis for years, connecting with others who share similar experiences can provide support and valuable insights. Starting by joining local or online support groups can be a beneficial first step. These groups often provide a platform for sharing personal stories, discussing challenges, and exploring various coping strategies. Engaging with others who understand the emotional and physical toll of psoriasis can foster a sense of belonging and reduce feelings of isolation.

Education plays a pivotal role in managing psoriasis effectively. By becoming an advocate for yourself, you can seek out reputable resources that provide information on the latest research, treatment options, and lifestyle modifications. Websites dedicated to psoriasis, as well as educational forums, can keep you informed about advancements in treatments and natural remedies. Additionally, attending workshops or seminars hosted by dermatology clinics or health organizations can further enhance your understanding of psoriasis and the myriad of ways to manage it.

If you are interested in promoting awareness about psoriasis, consider participating in community events or campaigns. Many organizations host walks, runs, or informational booths that aim to educate the public about the condition. Volunteer opportunities can also exist within these organizations, allowing you to contribute directly to the cause. By sharing your story and experiences, you can help dispel myths about psoriasis and advocate for greater understanding and support for those affected by the condition.

For parents of children with psoriasis, getting involved can be particularly impactful. Engaging with pediatric dermatology clinics or support networks specifically designed for families can provide much-needed resources and camaraderie. These networks often facilitate discussions about managing psoriasis in children, addressing both the physical and psychological aspects. Participating in family-oriented events can also help children feel less alone in their experience, fostering a supportive environment for their journey.

Lastly, consider exploring holistic approaches to psoriasis management. Engaging with professionals who specialize in integrative health can provide alternative perspectives on lifestyle modifications, diet, and mental well-being. By adopting a holistic approach, you can learn how various factors—such as stress management, nutrition, and skincare routines—interact with psoriasis. This comprehensive understanding can empower you to take proactive steps in your self-care journey, improving not only your skin health but also your overall quality of life.

Resources for Patients

Patients living with psoriasis often face a myriad of challenges that extend beyond skin symptoms, affecting both physical and mental well-being. To navigate these complexities, a variety of resources are available to assist individuals in managing their condition effectively. Healthcare providers, including dermatologists and rheumatologists, are essential for diagnosis and treatment planning. These professionals can guide patients toward appropriate medical therapies and monitor disease progression. Regular consultations can also help in adjusting treatment plans based on the patient's response and any emerging symptoms.

In addition to professional support, patients can benefit from a wealth of online resources. Reputable websites, such as the National Psoriasis Foundation and the American Academy of Dermatology, offer comprehensive information about psoriasis, including the latest research, treatment options, and lifestyle tips. These platforms also host forums and support groups where patients can connect with others facing similar challenges, sharing personal experiences and coping strategies. This sense of community can be crucial for emotional support, particularly for those who may feel isolated due to their condition.

Diet plays a significant role in managing psoriasis symptoms, and numerous resources are available to help patients tailor their eating habits for better skin health. Nutritionists specializing in dermatological conditions can provide personalized dietary advice that focuses on anti-inflammatory foods, which may alleviate flare-ups. Cookbooks and meal-planning guides designed for psoriasis patients can also be useful, offering recipes that integrate nutrient-rich ingredients while avoiding known triggers. Engaging in a balanced diet can support overall health and contribute to improved skin conditions.

For those with psoriasis in children, specialized resources are vital for parents seeking to understand and manage their child's unique needs. Pediatric dermatologists can provide targeted treatment options, while organizations focused on childhood psoriasis can offer guidance and support designed specifically for families. Educational materials that explain psoriasis in a child-friendly manner can help parents communicate effectively with their children about the condition, fostering a supportive environment at home and in social settings.

Mental health is an often-overlooked aspect of living with psoriasis, and various resources can aid patients in addressing the psychological impact of their condition. Support groups, both in-person and online, can provide a safe space for individuals to express their feelings and share coping mechanisms. Mental health professionals who understand the intersection of skin conditions and emotional well-being can also offer therapeutic strategies tailored to the patient's situation. By utilizing these resources, patients can work towards a holistic approach to managing their psoriasis, enhancing both their skin health and overall quality of life.

Chapter 11: Skincare Products and Routines for Psoriasis

Choosing the Right Products

Choosing the right products is a critical aspect of managing psoriasis effectively. With a myriad of options available on the market, patients need to navigate through various skincare products, dietary supplements, and treatments tailored to their specific needs. It is essential to consider the ingredients, potential allergens, and the unique characteristics of psoriasis when selecting products. Individuals should look for items that are free from irritants, synthetic fragrances, and harsh chemicals that can exacerbate skin conditions. Reading labels and choosing formulations with natural, soothing ingredients can significantly enhance skin health and reduce flare-ups.

When it comes to skincare, moisturizing is a cornerstone of psoriasis management. Products that contain emollients and humectants can help retain moisture in the skin, providing relief from dryness and itching. Ingredients such as aloe vera, shea butter, and coconut oil are known for their hydrating properties and can be beneficial for those with psoriasis. Additionally, using gentle, non-irritating cleansers instead of traditional soaps can prevent further skin irritation and maintain the skin barrier. Patients should experiment with different products to find what works best for their skin type while being mindful of any reactions.

Dietary choices also play a crucial role in managing psoriasis. Patients should consider incorporating anti-inflammatory foods into their diets, such as fatty fish rich in omega-3 fatty acids, fruits, vegetables, whole grains, and nuts. Supplements like fish oil or turmeric may also support skin health and reduce inflammation. Conversely, it is advisable to limit or avoid processed foods, sugar, and excessive alcohol, as these can trigger flare-ups. Consulting with a healthcare provider or a nutritionist can help patients create a personalized dietary plan that aligns with their lifestyle and psoriasis management goals.

For parents of children with psoriasis, selecting appropriate products can be particularly challenging. Children's skin is more sensitive, and many products may not be suitable for their delicate skin. It is essential to choose pediatric formulations designed specifically for younger skin, often labeled as hypoallergenic or dermatologist-tested. Involving children in the process can also help them understand their condition better and encourage them to participate in their skincare routine, fostering a sense of control and responsibility.

Lastly, mental health is an important consideration in the management of psoriasis. The emotional toll of living with a visible skin condition can lead to anxiety and depression. When selecting products or treatments, patients should prioritize those that not only address physical symptoms but also support mental well-being. Engaging in holistic approaches, such as mindfulness practices, yoga, or therapy, can complement skincare routines and provide a more comprehensive strategy for living well with psoriasis. By choosing the right products and adopting a well-rounded lifestyle, patients can take significant strides toward managing their condition effectively.

Daily Skin Care Regimens

Establishing a daily skin care regimen is crucial for individuals suffering from psoriasis. This skin condition often leads to dry, itchy, and inflamed patches, making regular care essential to manage symptoms and enhance skin health. A well-rounded regimen should start with gentle cleansing. Opt for a fragrance-free, hydrating cleanser that does not strip the skin of its natural oils. It is advisable to avoid harsh soaps or scrubs, which can exacerbate irritation and inflammation. Instead, consider using a creamy or oil-based cleanser that can help soothe the skin while effectively removing dirt and impurities.

Moisturizing is another critical component of a daily skin care routine for those with psoriasis. A rich, emollient moisturizer should be applied immediately after cleansing while the skin is still damp. This practice locks in moisture and helps create a barrier against environmental irritants. Look for products containing natural ingredients like shea butter, coconut oil, or aloe vera, which can provide additional hydration and support skin healing. Regular application of moisturizer can prevent excessive dryness and scaling, which are common issues for psoriasis patients.

Incorporating topical treatments into your daily regimen can significantly improve skin condition. Over-the-counter options like hydrocortisone creams or salicylic acid can help reduce inflammation and promote cell turnover. For those interested in natural remedies, products containing tea tree oil, turmeric, or witch hazel may provide relief. It is essential to apply these treatments as directed and consult with a healthcare provider to ensure they complement your overall psoriasis management plan. Consistency in applying these treatments can lead to noticeable improvements over time.

Sun exposure can also play a beneficial role in managing psoriasis, but it must be approached with caution. Short, controlled periods of sun exposure can help reduce the severity of flare-ups; however, excessive exposure can lead to sunburn and worsen skin conditions. Consider applying a broad-spectrum sunscreen during outdoor activities to protect unaffected areas of the skin. Additionally, certain dietary adjustments, such as increasing omega-3 fatty acids and antioxidants, can synergize with your skin care routine, enhancing overall skin health and potentially reducing flare-ups.

Lastly, it is essential to remember that mental health plays a significant role in managing psoriasis. Stress can trigger flare-ups, so incorporating relaxation techniques such as mindfulness, meditation, or yoga into your daily routine can have a positive impact on both skin and emotional well-being. Engaging in a holistic approach that includes proper skin care, dietary considerations, and stress management will not only help improve your skin condition but also contribute to a better quality of life. By adhering to a comprehensive daily skin care regimen, patients can take an active role in managing their psoriasis effectively.

Sun Protection and Psoriasis

Sun exposure can have a complex relationship with psoriasis management. While moderate sun exposure can provide therapeutic benefits, excessive exposure can trigger flare-ups or worsen existing lesions. For individuals with psoriasis, understanding the nuances of sun protection is essential. Sunlight is a natural source of ultraviolet light, which can help reduce the symptoms of psoriasis in some patients. However, it is crucial to balance this benefit with the risk of skin damage. Patients should aim for controlled, limited sun exposure to harness these benefits while protecting their skin from harmful effects.

The use of sunscreen is vital for those managing psoriasis. Selecting a broad-spectrum sunscreen with an appropriate SPF can help shield the skin from both UVA and UVB rays. Many patients may find that certain formulas irritate their skin, so opting for mineral-based sunscreens containing zinc oxide or titanium dioxide can provide effective protection with less irritation. Regular application, particularly after swimming or sweating, is essential to maintain protection throughout the day. It is also advisable to conduct patch tests with any new sunscreen to ensure it does not exacerbate psoriasis symptoms.

In addition to sunscreen, protective clothing can serve as an effective barrier against harmful sun rays. Lightweight, long-sleeved shirts, wide-brimmed hats, and UV-blocking sunglasses can help minimize direct sun exposure. For those who engage in outdoor activities, wearing protective clothing can reduce the risk of sunburn and subsequent flare-ups. Furthermore, seeking shade during peak sun hours, typically between 10 a.m. and 4 p.m., can also help mitigate risks while still allowing for some beneficial sun exposure.

For children with psoriasis, sun protection becomes even more critical. Their skin is often more sensitive, and improper sun exposure can lead to severe reactions. Parents should prioritize finding suitable, gentle sunscreen products and emphasize the importance of sun safety practices. Educating children about the necessity of sun protection can empower them to take an active role in their skincare routine, fostering a sense of responsibility and self-care from a young age.

Finally, maintaining a balanced diet and a healthy lifestyle can complement sun protection efforts. Foods rich in antioxidants, omega-3 fatty acids, and vitamins can enhance skin health and resilience. Staying hydrated and managing stress through relaxation techniques can further support overall well-being. By integrating sun protection strategies with holistic lifestyle modifications, patients can create a comprehensive approach to managing psoriasis while enjoying the benefits of sunlight safely.

Chapter 12: Building a Support System

Finding Support Groups

Finding support groups can be a transformative step for individuals living with psoriasis. Connecting with others who share similar experiences can provide emotional support, practical advice, and a sense of community that is often lacking when dealing with chronic conditions. Support groups can be found in various formats, including in-person meetings, online forums, and social media groups. Each format offers unique benefits, catering to different preferences and lifestyles.

When searching for a support group, consider local organizations, hospitals, or community health centers that may host meetings specifically for psoriasis patients. These groups often provide a safe space to discuss the challenges of living with psoriasis, including the impact on mental health and social interactions. Additionally, local dermatology clinics may have information on support groups or may even facilitate their own, allowing patients to network with others facing similar struggles.

Online support groups have gained popularity, especially for those who may not have access to local resources or prefer the anonymity of the internet. Websites dedicated to psoriasis often have forums where individuals can share their experiences, ask questions, and offer tips on managing the condition. Social media platforms also host numerous groups that focus on psoriasis awareness, natural remedies, and lifestyle modifications. These online communities can be invaluable for exchanging information about diet changes, skincare products, and holistic approaches to management.

It's important to evaluate the credibility of any support group you consider joining. Look for groups moderated by healthcare professionals or reputable organizations, as these can ensure that the information shared is accurate and safe. Engaging with members who are informed about the latest advances in psoriasis treatments can also provide insights into new therapies and management strategies. This knowledge can empower you to take a more active role in your treatment and lifestyle choices.

Finally, don't underestimate the power of sharing your story. Participating in a support group allows you to express your feelings and experiences, which can be cathartic. It's also an opportunity to advocate for psoriasis awareness and educate others about the condition. By sharing your journey, you not only contribute to your healing but also help others feel less isolated in their struggles. Finding a support group tailored to your needs can significantly enhance your quality of life and promote a sense of belonging within the psoriasis community.

Communicating with Family and Friends

Effective communication with family and friends is essential for individuals living with psoriasis, as it plays a crucial role in fostering understanding and support. Many patients find that sharing their experiences and challenges associated with the condition can significantly alleviate feelings of isolation. Open dialogues can help loved ones grasp the physical and emotional aspects of psoriasis, enabling them to provide better support and encouragement. Discussing specific triggers, such as stress or dietary factors, can also lead to a more supportive home environment.

When communicating about psoriasis, it is beneficial to educate family and friends about the nature of the condition. Providing information about its causes, symptoms, and potential treatments can demystify the disease and help reduce stigma. Explaining that psoriasis is not contagious is particularly important, as misconceptions can lead to unwarranted fears or avoidance. By sharing knowledge, patients can empower their loved ones to be more empathetic and proactive in their support.

Patients should also express their needs and preferences regarding assistance and understanding. For instance, discussing which situations or comments can be particularly triggering or uncomfortable can help family and friends navigate their interactions more sensitively. It is vital to communicate any adjustments needed in social settings, such as avoiding certain activities that may exacerbate skin irritation or stress levels. By articulating these preferences, patients can foster a more accommodating atmosphere.

Encouraging family and friends to participate in healthy lifestyle modifications can create a more holistic approach to managing psoriasis. Engaging loved ones in dietary changes, exercise routines, or stress-reduction techniques can make these adjustments feel less isolating. It also allows for shared experiences that can strengthen relationships while promoting overall well-being. By working together on these lifestyle changes, patients and their support systems can cultivate an environment that prioritizes health and wellness.

Lastly, seeking support from family and friends can significantly enhance mental health and resilience. Joining support groups or attending educational seminars together can provide additional resources and community connections. Family members can also play a pivotal role in advocacy efforts, raising awareness about psoriasis and its impact on daily life. By fostering a network of understanding and support, patients can navigate their journey with psoriasis more effectively, ensuring that they do not face it alone.

Professional Support Resources

Professional support resources are essential for anyone navigating the complexities of living with psoriasis. Patients can benefit from a variety of professionals who specialize in skin conditions, including dermatologists, nutritionists, and mental health counselors. Dermatologists play a critical role in diagnosing and managing psoriasis, as they stay updated on the latest treatment advancements and can tailor therapies to meet individual needs. Regular consultations with these specialists ensure that patients receive the most effective treatment options available, including biologics and topical therapies.

In addition to dermatological care, nutritionists can provide valuable insights into the dietary modifications that may alleviate psoriasis symptoms. Research suggests that certain foods can trigger or exacerbate flare-ups, while others may promote skin health. Professionals trained in dietary and nutritional science can help patients create personalized meal plans that incorporate anti-inflammatory foods, such as fatty fish, fruits, and vegetables, while minimizing processed foods and potential allergens. This approach not only addresses the skin condition but also contributes to overall well-being.

Mental health support is another critical aspect of managing psoriasis, especially for those who experience stress or anxiety related to their condition. Psychologists and counselors who specialize in chronic illnesses can offer strategies for coping with the emotional toll of psoriasis. They can assist patients in developing resilience and coping mechanisms that can improve their quality of life. Support groups, whether in-person or online, also provide a platform for sharing experiences and strategies, fostering a sense of community that can be incredibly beneficial for mental health.

For families dealing with psoriasis, particularly in children, pediatric dermatologists are invaluable resources. These specialists have the expertise to address the unique challenges of managing psoriasis in younger patients. They can provide guidance on both medical treatments and lifestyle modifications that are appropriate for children. Additionally, parent support groups can offer insights and shared experiences, helping families to navigate the emotional and practical aspects of caring for a child with psoriasis.

Lastly, advocacy organizations play a significant role in raising awareness and providing educational resources about psoriasis. These organizations offer access to the latest research, connect patients with healthcare professionals, and promote public understanding of the condition. They often host events and campaigns that encourage dialogue about psoriasis, which can reduce stigma and improve support for those affected. By tapping into these professional support resources, patients can enhance their management of psoriasis, embrace holistic approaches, and ultimately lead a healthier, more fulfilling life.

9 798340 144003